Mafia Witch

The Connected Coven, Volume 1

Caterina Gregori

Published by Caterina Gregori, 2024.

MAFIA WITCH

First edition. July 15, 2024.

ISBN: 979-8224085644

Written by Caterina Gregori.

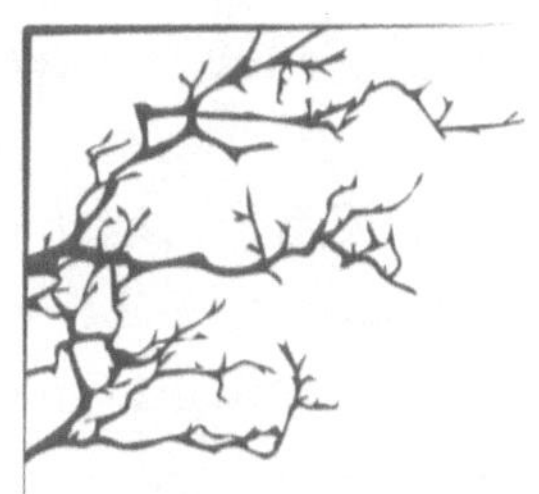

Chapter 1

"Never let anyone do a favor for you," Bea's father always said, and she always listened to her daddy.

Of course, what he actually said was: "Don't let nobody do you no favors, Bea. Because then, you owe them a favor back, you see? And you don't get to choose what kind of favor. They could ask you for something you're not willing to do, but you gotta do it, you know? Because they did you the favor in the first place."

"But," he added, "If you do somebody a favor, then they owe you. They gotta repay you somehow. You keep track of that and you make damn sure you call in every single one of those favors."

Those words rang in her mind now as she raided the storage room in the back of her father's social club, looking for the first aid kit she knew had to be back here. One of the little kids outside had fallen and scraped her knee, and Bea, like the damn goody-two-shoes she was, offered to get a bandage. How did she keep getting herself into these situations?

She didn't even know the kid. The girl was probably a fourth cousin, or maybe her grandparents had grown up in Italy with Bea's grandparents. That would make her a paisan, which meant they were as connected as if they were family because their origins were the same tiny town on the side of a mountain on the Mediterranean. And family was everything.

The thought made her ache for Italy—for the constant scent of the sea breeze on the air, the sense of history that was baked into the very earth, the nutty taste of the coffee that no one on this continent could replicate. *Soon.* Another few months and the entire family would be there for their yearly vacation.

Today should soothe some of that homesickness. Every May, the paisans returned to their home church here in Newark to celebrate the feast of Saint Michael and the Madonna della Fontana, the patron saints of their town in Italy. On the street outside Our Lady of Mt. Carmel, which was only three buildings down from the social club, a carnival of delights was set up, filled with food stands, carnival games, and booths selling statues of saints. Of course, none of it was open yet.

They had to sit through the mass first, and following that the procession around the neighborhood.

Crowds of people milled about outside, waiting for the church bells to ring and summon them inside. Bea had found herself lost in the chaos, so when the little girl had fallen right in front of her, it seemed a perfect opportunity to get a moment of quiet to herself. And help the poor kid, of course. She wasn't heartless.

She also didn't expect a thing in return, unlike what Daddy had taught her.

"I know it's here." The room wasn't even that big, about the size of a small walk-in closet. There were shelves set into each of the walls, and Bea fit inside, but there wouldn't be room for a second person. She closed the door to access the shelves behind it, and *ah ha*, there it was, on the very top shelf, of course. At 5'2," she'd have to climb up to get it.

Bea pushed the door further out of the way, almost completely shutting it, before putting her foot on the first shelf. It creaked ominously, and she winced. She'd have to do this fast. Bea pushed off her back foot, jumping high enough to grab the white box off the top shelf, before she tumbled down against the shelves opposite, the box clattering to the floor next to her.

"Ah, fuck," she said as the box opened on the bounce and the bandages flew all over the floor. Then she covered her mouth. She could hear her mother already: "ladies don't use foul language."

God, she'd only been back home for a week and she was already worried about what Mom would think. She'd had four years to shake bad habits while away at college, but damn, how they came back fast.

Bea had stuffed the bandages back in the kit when she heard the voices. She stilled, knowing she wasn't supposed to be back here. The front room of the social club—sure, everyone hung out there, either playing cards or getting drinks from the bar. But the back room? This was where her father did his business.

The business she had to pretend she knew nothing about. The thing they didn't talk about, but everyone knew. She couldn't get caught back here.

If she stayed hidden in the closet, nobody would see her. She'd have to take her chances and hope nobody needed any supplies. Bea had a view from the crack left when she almost shut the door and, curious although she damn well knew better, she slid closer to the gap and peeked out. What did Daddy do exactly? For the first time, she was going to get a bird's-eye view of how the Family business actually functioned.

From here she had a clear view of her father entering, flanked by two of his bodyguards. The men rotated, so Bea didn't always know their names. Behind them came her Uncle Guido along with another familiar face, one of her father's men named Giovanni, although everyone called him Lucky. The two of them dragged a man into the room.

He kept pleading even now as her father took a seat at the folding table set up in the center of the room. "Please. I swear. I know nothing about it."

Her father laughed, and it wasn't the jovial laugh she typically heard on a Sunday when either she or her brother said something funny. No, this had a darker edge to it. Bea never got to see the mob boss version of her dad, and if she hadn't been a total idiot, she wouldn't be seeing it now.

"Come on, Vito. Do I look stupid to you?"

"No, sir, I never said that..." Vito sputtered.

"You think I don't have my own people in the FBI? How do you think I got here, huh, Vito? Do you think I sat on my ass while you did all the work?"

Vito didn't seem to have an answer for that.

Bea pressed closer to the gap to get a better view. Odds were she'd never be this close to the Family business again.

"I have a family," Vito said.

Dad sighed. "Ah, Vito. You shouldn't have showed your face here. You make me work on a Sunday..."

"I believe I'll take it from here." Bea gasped at the sound of her grandmother's voice as the old woman entered the room.

"See that, Vito? You've upset my mother."

Bea didn't know why all the blood drained from Vito's face. It was just her nonna—a tiny woman an inch or so shorter than Bea, dressed all in black, with silvery salt and pepper hair, holding a black leather purse. Yet somehow everyone in the room seemed slightly frightened of her.

Nonna zipped open her purse and fiddled with the contents inside. Bea had often been the recipient of items hidden there—usually a piece of peppermint candy from Italy. Nonna knew Bea didn't like the licorice that her brother and cousins preferred. But obviously she wouldn't be offering anyone here candy.

"We don't take betrayal lightly," Nonna said.

"Please, Donna DiLorenzo, I am innocent." Vito got to his knees, like they were in church, and he went down to pray. He had used the old-fashioned Donna which meant "Lady" instead of the proper Signora, like Nonna was a noble or something.

"You can't lie to me," she snapped. "You pledged your loyalty when you were made, Vito. I have your blood."

He shook his head. "Please. I have a family. They would have put me in jail."

"And you should have done the time," Dad put in. "What, you think you're too fancy for prison?"

"We will not be disrespected like this." Nonna finally found what she'd been looking for in her purse. She pulled out a golden cigarette lighter. It gleamed in the fluorescent lighting, looking almost unworldly. "Occhio per occhio."

Pressure built in Bea's forehead, the kind of headache that started before a storm. But outside it was sunny and clear, with no rain in the forecast. Bea wrinkled her nose at the sudden acrid scent in the air. Somehow, she knew both were related, that something horrible was about to happen.

Nonna flicked the lighter, and as it sprung to life, Vito screamed. He grasped at his face as he went down, and the room filled with the scent of fire and burning flesh. It took Bea a moment to realize exactly what she was witnessing.

Oh god, his eyes. She scampered back away from the gap in the door until her back hit the set of shelving behind her. Bea stilled, hoping no one had heard the sound she'd just made in her eagerness to get away from whatever the hell was going on out there. She covered her mouth, holding in the bile that threatened at the back of her throat.

After a few minutes, she could hear chairs scraping against the floor, the sounds of people moving, and a low hum of voices, which Bea determinedly ignored. She'd already seen and heard too much. The only saving grace was that no one knew she was back here.

"You can come out now, Beatrice. I know you're there."

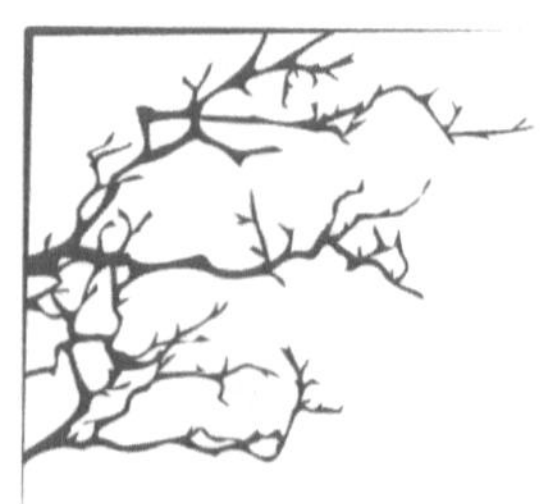

Chapter 2

Well. It appeared she hadn't been as quiet as she'd thought. Someone knew she was back here. Bea got to her feet, her hands shaking as she opened the closet door. The only person left in the room was her grandmother, who'd taken a seat in one of the folding chairs set up back here. Dad and the others had disappeared, and Bea didn't want to know what they'd done with poor Vito.

"Come. Sit." Nonna pointed to a chair next to her.

Bea had never disobeyed her grandmother in her life. A lump settled in her throat at the realization that there might have been huge consequences if she had. Still. Bea had never been one to keep her mouth shut. "What the hell was that?"

How could her grandmother burn out a man's eyes with only the flicker of a lighter and some, what, magic words?

She expected Nonna to be angry, to lecture her for using foul language in front of her elders. But Nonna only chuckled, as if amused by Bea's dismay. "If you'd come to me on your twenty-first birthday, this would not be such a shock now."

Bea sat in the chair, remembering what they said about curiosity and cats, and, *well, call me a cat then.* "What are you talking about?"

Nonna sighed. "You know about this thing of ours?"

This thing. Never name it, no. Call it anything but what it was. Don't say mafia. Pretend her dad had a normal job running a restaurant supply business. Sure, Bea knew exactly what her grandmother was talking about - the hushed whispers when they were in church, the way they had to move to a house with a security system and two guys that followed her dad around all the time.

At college, it had been easy to pretend to be normal. Bea didn't have to wonder about Dad and her brother Mike coming in late at night, or watch her mother try to get bloodstains out of a white shirt. She could focus on her studies, her art, her friends, who had no idea what really went on in Bea's home.

Although Bea realized that she didn't really *know*. She'd never seen someone get beat up—never mind watch them get their eyes burned out. It had been easy to ignore where her family's money came from. Until today.

"Yeah," Bea swallowed. "I know."

Nonna nodded, probably relieved she didn't have to explain that part. "Our family is very well known. Very powerful. And there's a good reason for that."

"Because you can do that." Bea held out her hand and mimed flicking a lighter. "Whoosh!"

There hadn't been enough time to freak out or, more importantly, process what she'd witnessed. Bea put her hand over her racing heart, trying to stop it from being so damn loud. This was her grandmother—the woman who taught her to bake bread and how to count the stitches as she crocheted. And yet...

"Yes, whoosh." Nonna sighed. "Although the spell for that had been put into place a long time ago, when Vito was made and pledged his loyalty to the family. He swore on his eyes, and so lost them when he tried to betray us."

Bea blinked and let the words settle a bit, but no matter how she thought about it, nothing made sense. This morning she'd woken up and everything was normal. Now Nonna had turned her world upside down by acting like casting spells was normal. Burning people's eyes out for betraying them was normal. A hysterical giggle bubbled up in her throat, but Bea quashed it. She didn't really want to laugh. She didn't want Nonna to think she wasn't taking this seriously.

"I don't understand." Magic was something the new age kids at school talked about. Not something she'd ever considered real, but Bea couldn't ignore the evidence of her own eyes.

"I am a Strega." Nonna held herself still, with her shoulders thrown back like a freakin' queen. Bea knew the word meant witch, but the way Nonna said it sounded different, like it meant more. "And you are as well."

"Wait, wait, what, no." Bea would know if she could do stuff like that, wouldn't she? But she would never want to. She shuddered at the thought of being on the other side of that lighter. Her stomach twisted, and she leaned forward, desperate to avoid throwing up. "I can't do that."

Nonna sighed, some of the stiffness gone from her shoulders. She looked less like the powerful woman Vito had been afraid of and more like Bea's grandmother. She reached out and took Bea's hand in hers, squeezing her fingers gently. "Because you haven't been trained. I asked your parents to send you to me on your twenty-first birthday. But they told me you had other plans."

Bea had gone out with her college friends that night last fall, enjoying being able to legally drink at a bar for the first time. Her cheeks heated with embarrassment, but she couldn't recall her parents ever telling her to go see her grandmother. "They never told me."

"Your mother never wanted you to be part of the family business. I suppose that had something to do with it."

Bea bristled at that. Why not? Didn't Mom think she could handle it? Once again, Mom kept treating her like a child, but Bea was an adult. She should have been told.

But would she have believed without seeing something like this with her own eyes? Bea didn't know. "Wouldn't I have known somehow if I can do magic?"

"Your full powers would not have manifested until your 21st birthday. Tell me, have you felt anything different since then?"

Since her birthday, had anything changed? Bea frowned, trying to think. She'd always been sensitive to places, staying away from areas that made her feel funny. That sense had seemed to extend to people recently. She'd stopped her roommate from going out with a guy one night, saying the guy gave her a bad feeling. "I think so. I can kinda tell if someone has bad intentions."

Nonna nodded. "You always had good instincts. We must speak more, but not here. Come to my house during the procession while everyone else is walking. Then I can explain better."

Bea sputtered. "You can't just leave it like that. What if I accidentally set someone on fire?"

Nonna let out a laugh. "You can't accidentally do anything. You don't know how to craft a spell and you haven't yet been awakened. I promise, carissima, I won't let anything bad happen to you. You're my heir."

She'd used the old nickname for Bea. They'd always had a special bond since Bea had been named for her. "What about Connie?" she blurted, realizing she'd have to go back out into the crowd and explain to her cousin what had happened here.

"She's only twenty, but yes, she has the potential as well. Let me worry about Connie." Nonna narrowed her eyes and Bea wondered if she was having the same trouble with Connie's parents. "Now go to Mass. I'll see you later."

Bea recognized the dismissal and stood and was halfway out of the room before she remembered the bandage. She raced back to the closet, grabbed one off the floor, and darted back out the door.

Something dogged her, a feeling of premonition deep in her gut that told her this was only the beginning.

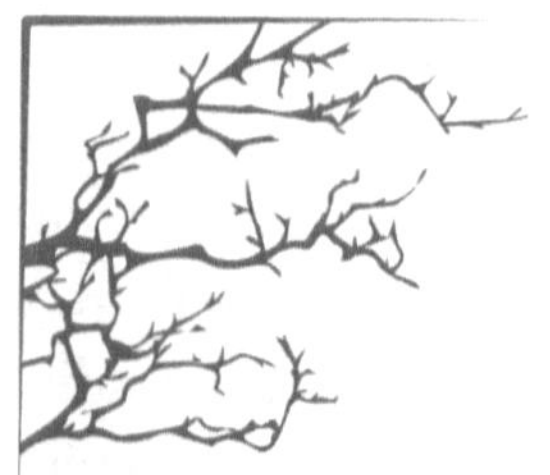

Chapter 3

Bea shielded her eyes from the sun as she stepped out onto the sidewalk outside the social club. Leaving the dim interior into this bright sunny day had her blinking away tears. Would she even be able to find the little girl in this crowd? More people had arrived since she'd got in looking for bandages, most of the faces familiar since Bea had grown up attending Mass and other family events with everyone here.

Eventually she found the little girl exactly where Bea had left her, seated on one of the folding chairs set up around one of the food stands, her mother pressing a napkin against her knee. The girl wore a poofy white dress, most likely her communion dress, which was a fairly common occurrence during this feast. Most kids had made their communion early in May, and this was a good way to get a second use out of it.

"I'm so sorry." Bea kneeled in front of the girl and pressed the bandage to her knee. They certainly didn't want to get blood on that beautiful dress. "I couldn't find where they hid the first aid kit."

The girl giggled in response.

"I'm glad you found something." The mother said, helping the girl up. "Now no more running in your nice clothes!"

Bea grinned as the duo melted back into the crowd. She'd been that little girl, once upon a time, making a mess out of her nice clothes instead of sitting quietly like a lady should. How many times had her own mom had to lecture her like that?

Her smile faded at the thought of Mom and her family. Because the Bea who'd gone into the social club looking for a bandage had come out a very different person. She couldn't ignore the act of violence she'd witnessed. If she closed her eyes, she'd hear Vito screaming in pain, the sound echoing in her mind again and again. She shuddered, suddenly cold despite the warm sun.

Daddy and Nonna seemed to think he deserved it, that it was a righteous punishment for something he'd done. He'd broken a promise, and Bea knew how serious that was. You didn't go back on your word. That was a truth she'd known forever. But she'd never witnessed the consequences before. She'd never really understood what it meant for Daddy to be the Boss.

And then to be confronted with the wonder of magic at the same time! She wanted to know more, especially about her own potential. But she couldn't separate it from the terrible thing Nonna had used magic for. She had to trust Nonna would explain everything later. Bea itched to know, now, and wasn't looking forward to having to sit through Mass before being able to sneak away.

"Bea! There you are!" Connie's voice cut through the crowd.

Her cousin had found her. Bea turned to meet her, desperate to talk about what had happened. They were only a year apart and had grown up together as close as sisters. Probably closer, since Bea had known some sisters in her time who had not gotten along at all.

They even looked like sisters, both with the same dark hair and eyes, although Connie's fell in controlled curls, while Bea felt calling her frizzy locks waves generous. Connie also had the advantage of height, having a good four inches on Bea, but her sweet cousin never bragged about it. Even though they resembled each other, they had very different senses of style.

Today Connie wore a cream-colored sundress and strappy sandals, which gave her an additional two inches. She'd probably regret those shoes when they started the walk around the city. No, Bea was perfectly satisfied with her sensible black ballet flats. She wore a brightly patterned tunic top over black leggings, which made her stand out from not only her cousin, but most of the people in the crowd as well.

"Connie, I have to talk to you..." Bea reached for her cousin's arm, ready to link arms with her and find a secluded place to chat, like they'd been doing since they were kids.

But before Bea could finish, she realized Connie wasn't alone. Bea's brother Mike and his fiancé, Lucy, followed behind her.

There went any chance Bea had of sharing her secret with Connie. Normally Mike would hang out with their cousin Junior and his best friend Dominick. But now he had a fiancé to show around. Bea forced a smile on her face as Lucy came up to give her a kiss on the cheek, the standard Italian-American greeting. Bea didn't quite dislike Lucy. Frankly, she was impressed that her brother had found someone who agreed to marry him.

Bea might still be bitter about him tearing up her One Direction poster when she was fifteen. On the other hand, he would not stop talking about the time she threw up on him on a car trip to Atlantic City. They had a typical brother/sister relationship.

Lucy wore a bright yellow sundress and had her blond hair swept up in a half-bun, held up by little clips with sunflowers on them. The same color palette would make Bea look sallow and sick, but Lucy glowed. She grasped Bea's hand and would not let go. "I'm so happy to be part of your family on such a special day!"

Lucy had lost her parents in a car accident five years ago, and never stopped talking about being an orphan and being so grateful to be part of their family now. Bea met Connie's eyes and bit her lip to keep from laughing at the sight of her cousin rolling her eyes at Lucy's words.

God, Bea might be a bitch, but she found it so damn annoying, especially since Lucy would not shut up about it. Or the wedding.

"Can you believe we'll see all these people again in only a month?" Case in point. Lucy and Mike were going to tie the knot in June.

Mike, thankfully, came to the rescue, pulling his fiancé away from Bea and sliding his arm around her. "It's going to be amazing, babe."

She cooed at him, and Bea made sure not to meet Connie's eyes. No way would she be able to hold in her laughter after that. Mike and Lucy were cute together, and she guessed she was happy for them. Bea could not put her finger on it, but something bothered her about Lucy. Before she'd chalked it up to not having anything in common with her.

After today? What if she had some sixth sense about Lucy?

"I can't wait." Lucy grinned. "Oh, Mike, we need to talk to the florist again. I saw an arrangement on Pinterest that I think would look better."

With four weeks to go? Maybe Lucy was just a Bridezilla. Bea laughed at herself. Not everything was a magical conspiracy.

"Sure, hon. Whatever."

Mike, in Bea's entire life, had never been so mellow. They were good together, Bea had to admit that. It must be nice, having someone in your life who got you. Bea wouldn't mind having a partner like that. Some day. When she figured out what she was going to do with her art degree and got herself a career or something.

But that wouldn't happen if Nonna made Bea her heir. She couldn't move to New York and be a museum curator if she had to hang around here and do...whatever it was Nonna did to keep Daddy's men in line. Bea's belly clenched at the thought and bile rose in the back of her throat again. No, she would get through today without throwing up.

"You okay?" Connie said in a low voice as one of the paisans came up to Mike and Lucy and chatted about the food that would be at the wedding.

"Sure." Not like she could discuss it here in this crowd. Maybe afterward, once they could disappear into the feast, playing carnival games and eating zeppole. Bea couldn't help but be aware of the people surrounding them now, the crowd moving slowly down the block toward the church. Mass would begin soon.

"Beatrice, Connie! It's so good to see you!" A woman in a red dress and big hair came up to them and greeted them both with a kiss and a handshake.

Bea recognized her and knew there was something important she should remember about her but for the life of her could not think of what it was. "Hello, *come sta...*" Bea murmured.

"I heard you graduated college," she said.

At least Bea didn't mind talking about her degree. She honestly wished more people would ask about it. "Yes, I got my bachelor's in Art History."

"Right, right. You know my son Nick just finished, too. He was at Columbia. Here, let me get him. You too should talk. He's single, you know?" She turned and shouted into the crowd.

Nick. *SHIT, Nick.* Bea had gone to her senior prom with him. Both of their families had been delighted about it. There had been snide comments, especially from Mike, about arranged marriages. Bea had ignored it at the time, because she was going away to school and probably wouldn't see Nick again. It wasn't like he was a bad dude, but she'd known him since they were like five and didn't have those kinds of feelings for him. She hadn't seen him or his parents in five years. No wonder Bea hadn't recognized her.

"Run, I'll cover for you." Connie moved into her space.

"Thank you," Bea muttered. She turned and ducked into the crowd, using it as cover as she sped up her pace into a run. The last thing she needed was an awkward conversation with Nick. But if they caught up to her before mass then that's what would happen. Where could she hide?

"Excuse me." She dodged some strangers standing in front of the green iron gates that led to the courtyard in front of the church, then darted up the lawn that ran along the right side of the building. Behind the church would be the tiny shrine to the Madonna that her father had built. It was a replica of the one in Italy, on a much smaller scale. While some people came here to pay respects before regular Mass on Sundays, it should be safe now, with everyone about to enter the church.

She looked behind her to make sure Nick wasn't chasing after her, and as she turned the corner, ran smack into someone broad and hard. They both stumbled and hands attempted to catch Bea as she rolled onto the concrete path.

"Shit." Bea took a second to catch her breath, the wind knocked out of her. Luckily, she hadn't put any holes in her leggings. Mom would have a field day with that one, like she was a little kid again, ruining her good clothes.

"Are you all right?" A deep masculine voice asked.

That voice nearly made her shiver in response, so delightfully rich. She looked up at the stranger she'd run into and gaped. She didn't recognize him, not even with a lagging sense of familiarity if he'd been a paisan she'd met before. Because Bea would have remembered him. He was super hot, with dark hair in messy waves that should look unkempt, but only made him look roguishly handsome. He had pale gray-green eyes, a jawline that should be in a movie, and perfectly plump, kissable lips.

Of course, she'd end up in a big mess on the ground in front of him. Bea felt her cheeks heat, and she blurted in embarrassment, "I'm fine. Why weren't you watching where you were going?"

"Hey, you bumped into me." He held out a hand, presumably to help her up.

She always did this. God, she was such an idiot. Bea ran a hand through her hair, probably making it worse. "I'm sorry. You would not believe the day I'm having."

"It sounds like it."

Bea ignored his hand and got to her feet on her own, discreetly dusting off the dirt from her butt. Well, she hoped she was doing it discreetly.

Who was this guy? It was rare to see someone completely new at the festival. Unable to meet his steady gaze, she turned to look at the shrine. It was a little stucco house, with a metal gate to protect the tiny statue of the virgin Mary inside. Outside, a fountain bubbled, sending water into a collection of river rocks.

One of the rocks called to Bea, like so many had before. She had a vast collection of rocks at home that she'd picked up at various places. Sometimes her dad would bring her a rock, although the ones he gave her never felt the same. Maybe she finally knew why. Bea scooped the rock out of the fountain.

When she turned around, the guy was still there. Maybe she was interrupting his prayer time. Her cheeks burned, and she clutched the rock tightly. "Are you here to pray to the Madonna?" She gestured to the statue. "I've seen the real one in Italy. She's much larger in person."

Before he could respond, the church bells started to ring and Bea jumped. Shit. She was late for Mass.

SPECIAL AGENT DAVID McKenna was prepared to lie. He had the words "My name is Dante," on his lips, ready to introduce himself as the cover they'd been carefully preparing for months. He'd practiced until he no longer responded to "David," thinking of himself only as his character, Dante Milano.

It had been a stroke of luck that he'd run into one of his targets like this. David had taken an Uber which dropped him off at the block behind the church which led to the nearly full parking lot. Cars were not allowed in the front or side streets, which had been shut down for the festival. He'd made his way through the lot to this shrine set up like a private little garden behind the main building of the church.

And then she'd literally run into him. Beatrice DiLorenzo.

David had memorized her face, and that of every member of the DiLorenzo family. But the surveillance images didn't paint a complete picture. First, she was a lot shorter than he expected, coming only to the middle of his chest, which became obvious when she crashed into it. Second, no photo had done those eyes justice—liquid brown, with specks of gold and so intense, as she glared at him from the ground. When she refused his hand and walked away from him, he took a moment to appreciate her curves, as she was round in all the right places.

Something must have happened for her to retreat here. This was it, his in. David couldn't have planned it better. The words were on his lips.

And then the church bells rang.

"Shit!" She handed him the rock she'd plucked from the fountain before she turned and ran up the side entrance to the church.

"Wait!" David called, hoping she'd turn back. "What am I supposed to do with this?"

The rock was cold and slightly slimy. David went to put it back, but something had him placing it in his pocket instead. It would be an excellent conversation piece for when he approached Beatrice again later.

Because he would. David had a job to do.

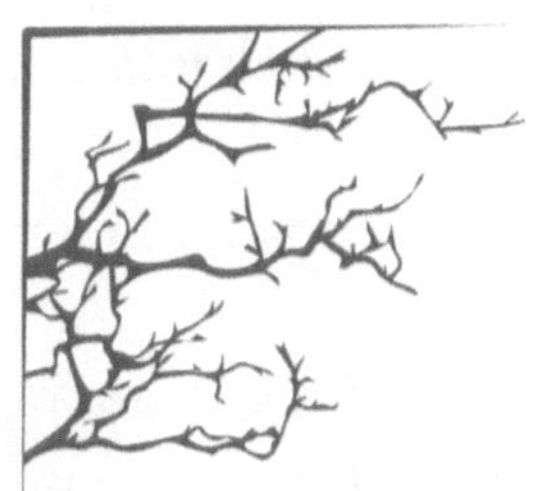

Chapter 4

Eight months ago, David had been carrying a box of files through the bullpen, filled with desks of busy agents working on cases. David had finished up following a trail of money laundering through a series of twenty different businesses. It hadn't been easy, but he'd done it. One thing he'd always been good at was following the money.

"McKenna." Agent Janet Carter stopped him before he'd made it to his destination. "With me."

"Can I drop these off at evidence first?" He gestured to his box.

"Afterward. Come on." She led him to the office of the special agent in charge, Tomas Garcia.

David started to sweat. He'd finished his two years on probation last week, yet somehow, he still worried they were pulling him behind closed doors in order to fire him. Every day he woke up, came into the office with disbelief that this was his life now, that he'd done it, become an FBI agent. Some days, he waited for it all to come crashing down on him.

Carter had him enter the office first, and then shut the door behind her. David stiffened, knowing that wasn't good. His fingers tightened on the box and he was grateful for the handhold.

"Agent McKenna, put that box down and have a seat," Garcia said from his desk.

David had been here before. He was familiar with the way Garcia kept his office, neat, sparse, and filled with file drawers. Garcia believed in paper trails, even in the digital day and age. "Yes, sir." He set the box on the floor next to him before lowering himself into one of the uncomfortable chairs in front of the desk.

"Agent Carter has a proposition for you." Garcia nodded in her direction.

Instead of sitting down next to David, she paced the length of the room, her arms gesturing as she spoke. "First, I want to give you a bit of background. For the past five years, I've been trying to crack the DiLorenzo Family. We haven't been able to get a single informant."

At one point, that wouldn't have been so unusual. Old time mafia families had a strict code of omerta—silence. They didn't snitch. But a lot of that generation had died or ended up in prison. The new blood didn't have the same honor that the mafia prided itself on.

"What's weirder is that we can't get any wire taps on them either. I think they are running EMPs or something. Nothing we plant sticks. We get digital garbage instead of recordings." Carter stopped pacing for a moment.

"You want me to find a money trail on them?" David asked. That's what he did.

He'd been recruited after college before completing his CPA. Accounting had been his sure thing, the career that would keep him financially independent and away from his family. When the FBI came knocking, David had taken the offer, another step on his plan to escape his past.

"Not exactly." She pulled a manila folder from Garcia's desk and flipped it open. Inside there was a photocopied wedding invitation and photos of two dark-haired young women. "The biggest event of the year is the wedding of the son of the DiLorenzo boss. It's going to be filled with all the powerful mafia bosses from the tristate area. We need an in."

David frowned. He still didn't know where she was going with this. "I don't see how I can help with that?"

"You did some acting in college, right, McKenna?"

It had to be in his file. Every damn detail about his life had been given up before they'd even let him into Quantico. The fact his big brother was in the slammer hadn't been a problem, as long as David had disclosed it. The FBI didn't like secrets unless they were the ones keeping them.

"Yeah." He tried not to show how much it bothered him that she brought it up.

Because being up on stage had been the one thing that had been solely his. He was good at math, sure, but it wasn't a passion. It meant a steady job. But auditioning and getting the chance to become someone else for a few nights? That had been freakin' magic.

He'd still be doing it, too. Community theater was a thing. But David had given himself to the Bureau and had little time for anything else, never mind rehearsals and performances. He missed it, but he'd made his choices.

Why was she mentioning his acting past now? He couldn't imagine how a supporting role in *Death of a Salesman* was relevant.

"I want you to go undercover, McKenna. Deep undercover. The kind of thing where you pretend to be someone else. You don't go home to your family." She finally sat down in the chair next to him, her tiny eyes narrowed on him.

Man, he would not want to be a suspect on the other end of that gaze. She had freaky eyes.

"At this wedding?"

She swallowed and exchanged a look with Garcia. "The wedding is the endgame, yeah. But I want you to use one of the DiLorenzo daughters as an in. They are both young and single. And you are an attractive young man."

David grinned at the compliment. "Oh, is that why you pick me?"

"I'm being realistic. You're our best shot at getting someone inside the family."

"Don't make the decision lightly," Garcia cut in. "You know enough about the mob to know that messing with one of their women means a death sentence."

Carter rolled her eyes. "Come on, Garcia. It's dangerous, no matter what. That's the thing about undercover missions." She turned to David. "You can turn it down. You're used to working with informants. This is an entirely different thing."

David frowned as he thought about it. "Let me make sure I have this straight. You want me to try to, what, date one of these girls?" He tapped the photos on the desk.

"If it leads to that. But remember, this isn't a long-term thing. Your goal is an invitation to that wedding."

"You need me to be a plus one." It made him uncomfortable. David never considered himself a ladies' man, and he hated the idea of leading one of these girls on. It seemed unethical. He couldn't imagine dating someone, kissing them, holding hands, or even sleeping with them for the job.

"Possibly." As if reading his mind, Carter went on. "Remember, these are bad guys, McKenna. The DiLorenzos have their fingers in money laundering all down the garden state. We're talking about money from drugs, human trafficking, theft. We shut that down? We send all their suppliers into a tailspin, which makes it easier to scoop them up, too."

Her eyes were on fire. This case meant something to her. It didn't have to be personal, per se. David knew a few agents who were super passionate about their job—putting bad guys away. It had been harder for him to feel the same. Following illegal money transfers didn't have the same wow factor.

But if he did this, he'd actually be in the thick of it, out in the field, face to face with bad guys. It sounded fun, actually. He'd have to craft the perfect character and embody it, at least for the next eight months until the wedding. Finally, something to challenge him, and he'd be putting the bad guys away? There was no question what his answer would be. He'd worry about hurting a girl's feelings later.

"I'm in."

That had been the beginning of a crash course in the DiLorenzo family, and in the particular interests of the two daughters - Beatrice and Connie. They had been much easier to put under surveillance while away at the same college. It had been a matter of getting college security to hand over their footage and data.

They'd set up David with an apartment and a new identity—Dante Milano—including credit cards and a cell phone. He lived there for two months before the official start of the operation, dubbed Operation Inferno by Janet Carter. Janet apparently had a sense of humor. She was the case agent, and the one person he reported to until it was over. That was meant to cut down on any leaks. The Mob had ears everywhere.

They'd picked the annual church festival because it seemed the best way for him to accidentally bump into one of the girls and make first contact. Buy her a cotton candy, maybe win a carnival game or two to impress her, classic. But Dante hadn't even made it to the festival part before running into Beatrice.

Well, he couldn't just stand here contemplating this rock in his pocket. He needed to follow her. Discreetly. Dante looped around the building until he reached the trio of large doors that led into the vestibule of the church. Music played so loudly from the organ that it could be heard from the street. Dante crept inside.

He'd been to church plenty of times. His mom liked to drag him along with her as she desperately prayed for his brother to straighten up and for Dad to stop cheating on her. Praying hadn't seemed to help, but keeping him with her had instilled a pretty good sense of Catholic guilt in him.

This church was a relic from the past. Hundreds of rows of dark wooden pews faced the traditional altar up at the front, although instead of a crucifix hung behind it, there stood a giant marble statue of the Virgin Mary. There were two alcoves to either side and even from the back of the church, Dante could see they were filled to the brim with statues of saints, with lit candles flickering in front of them.

On instinct, he dipped his fingers in the font of holy water near the entrance, blessed himself, and genuflected before taking a seat in the last pew. It took a moment of scanning, but he eventually spotted Beatrice, sitting with the rest of the DiLorenzo family all the way up at the front. She had turned to whisper into the ear of the girl sitting next to her and he got a clear view of her face. He'd recognize her from a mile away—those wide eyes, that slightly hooked nose, those full lips.

It took him a moment to realize the mass was in Italian. They'd given him a crash course on the language, but that didn't cover religious words. Lucky that Mass was the same no matter in what language, and he managed to sit, kneel, and stand at the right times to make sure he didn't stick out.

All the while, he kept an eye on Beatrice. It was only because of this that he noticed when she split off from the rest of the family.

A group of men in suits had wheeled two wooden carts up to the front near the altar. Music played while they lifted the two statues of the saints, and the crowd started to whisper and disperse. Beatrice left the pew, but while the rest of her family proceeded out the front, she ducked toward the back, probably the side entrance she'd used earlier when she ran from him.

Dante got up and followed.

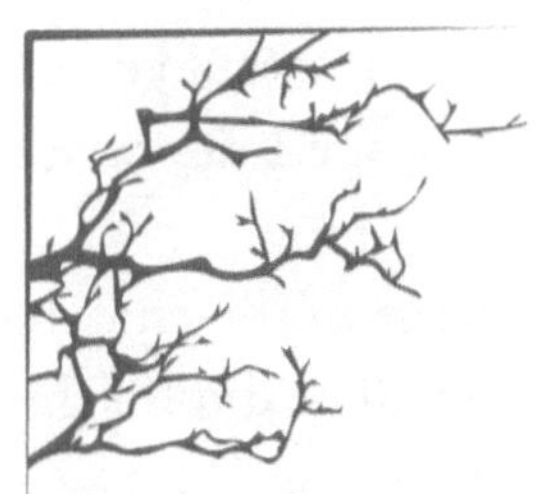

Chapter 5

Bea had been coming to this church since, well, since before she could remember. She'd been baptized in that old octagon shaped font in the center of the pews. Her parents and her aunt and uncle were both married in front of this very altar. Her brother had even been an altar boy before being kicked out, and because of him she knew the back ways in and out of the building, and the door the priests used to get in the area behind the altar where they changed into their vestments.

"Cover for me," she whispered to Connie before making her escape.

"Does this involve a guy?" Connie murmured back.

For a moment Bea flashed back to the hottie she'd run into behind the church. God, she wished this involved him. Instead, she was off to learn about magic. How could Bea explain that? "I'll tell you later." If Nonna allowed.

That was the thing. Who else knew about the magic in her family? Her dad clearly knew–and apparently relied on it. None of the men in that room had looked shocked when Nonna pulled her trick. Did that mean they knew about Bea's potential as well?

If she wanted answers, she needed to talk to her grandmother.

Bea slipped out the side of the church. All the attention would focus on the front courtyard, where the carts carrying the statues of the saints would assemble, along with the marching band that would play music as the faithful processed around the city—hence why they called it the procession. There were lots of stops along the way, with tiny stands set up with water and cookies in front of individual houses. The parade would pause, and the house's owner would come out and add their money to the garland of bills around the saint's neck. All proceeds went to the church, of course.

Bea stopped in her tracks. Not everything went to the church. Her dad often talked about receiving his 'cut' after all he did for the parish. She swallowed. Right. Chalk that up to another thing she never really thought about before.

Nonna would be home preparing her own string of money garland for the statue. Even if Dad took his cut, they were still giving back to the church. Bea needed to have faith in her family. Nonna would explain everything.

She started her walk again, this time speeding up to a near run, ignoring the glances she got from the vendors preparing to open up their stands. Her grandmother's house was only three blocks away, but Bea wanted to maximize the time they would have together before they had to rejoin the family.

The houses along her walk were all two or three-story family homes, some with tiny yards, but most without, standing up against each other like dominos. Sometimes the sidewalks were smooth, but more often than not the concrete was uneven and cracked, with tiny shoots of weeds poking through. As a kid, she always looked for the perfect sidewalks to draw with chalk. She'd loved that these few blocks always felt like a small town to her. There had been plenty of kids to play with on long evenings in the summer, playing tag in the streets.

Her grandmother's house was more than familiar—at one time Bea and her family had lived here, in the apartment above the one her Nonna still lived in. They moved out to the suburbs when Bea turned fourteen. At the time, she didn't understand why, but now she knew it had something to do with her father's promotion in the organization.

Nonna's house stood out from the rest of the houses on the block, including the one that leaned against it, because it was built entirely of red brick. There were two apartments on the second floor, and two sets of windows visible from the street. Instead of a second apartment on the first floor, there was a set of green barn doors that opened to the "garage" that was really a tunnel through the house, leading to the back garden which her Nonna planted every year.

"They used to keep horses here," Nonna had told her once, to explain the garage with a much higher ceiling than one would expect. "During the depression, the man who built this house bought all the property from the houses behind us, which is why we have a garden and they don't."

Bea had loved their little garden as a child. Four fig trees ringed the edge, carefully tended to by her father—they needed to be wrapped in canvas every winter or else they'd die. A single peach tree stood in the center, only producing fruit when it damn well felt like it. The rest of the earth was dedicated to growing tomatoes, cucumbers, and peppers. In the back, her grandmother had fenced in a small patch and that was where she grew her herbs.

As usual, Bea bypassed the front entrance and made for the smaller door cut into the two large barn doors that led to the garage. It had been left unlocked, but that didn't matter because Bea had a key. Inside there were two sets of stairs—the taller one led to the second floor where her Uncle Guido still lived. The shorter set to the right led to her grandmother's apartment.

She stopped again before climbing them, one hand curling around the railing, taking solace in the wood's solidness. Once she learned the truth, there would be no going back. Part of her wanted to run back to the church, to hide behind her mother's wishes and deny having seen anything to do with witchcraft.

The other part of her breathed "magic" in her ear. Magic—real magic—existed. Sure, she'd only seen it used to maim and hurt, but there had to be more to it than that. Could she have healed that little girl's scrape with a few magic words and a snap of her fingers? Bea didn't know, and unless she listened to her Nonna now, she never would know.

She climbed the three steps and opened the storm door. Before she knocked, Nonna opened the interior door with a smile. "Ah, *Carissima.* Come in, come in."

Bea entered directly into the kitchen. When she was a kid, this room had black-and-white checkered floors and an old farmhouse sink. A few years ago, her dad modernized it and surprised Nonna with a renovation. It now looked a little too modern, with its hexagon tile floors and matching backsplash. What hadn't changed was the giant wooden table in the center of the room. On it sat a plate of cookies—homemade pignoli—and two cups of steaming espresso.

"Sit down. *Mangia.*" She gestured to the food. Bea sat.

For a moment it felt like any other time Bea had come here to spend time with her grandmother. She'd be fed sweets and coffee and listen to Nonna's stories or end up helping her with baking or some other tasks. But today was not like every other day.

"You said you'd explain," Bea blurted.

Nonna took a sip of her espresso. "Yes. I should have told you long ago..." she trailed off, but Bea didn't want to talk about the past. She just wanted the truth now, and it seemed her grandmother finally wanted to tell her. "The women in our family have been Strega for generations. I learned how to use my gift from my mother and she from her mother and so on. But I had no daughters of my own to pass on the gift to. I believed myself to be cursed."

Nonna had three sons. Bea's father, Michael, the oldest, and her uncles Tony and Guido. Bea and Connie were the only girls out of a sea of male cousins. "How do you know I even inherited this?"

"Here. Take my hand. I'm going to open your eyes."

Bea had no idea what Nonna was talking about. It never occurred to her to do anything but obey, so she reached out with one hand. Her heart pounded loudly against her chest, despite the fact that she trusted her grandmother. Nonna would never do anything to hurt her. Still, Bea had seen for herself the terrible things magic could do. But she wanted to understand, to fill this empty cave of uncertainty. It tore at her, the fear and the need to know.

Nonna took Bea's hand and squeezed her palm tightly.

Bea waited, not knowing what to expect. She looked up at Nonna, who was now surrounded by a glittery purple haze.

Bea snatched her hand back. "What the hell is that?"

Nonna smiled, looking like a cat that caught a mouse. "That is your first taste of magic. Witches will give off a unique aura. We all sparkle. Of course, powerful Strega know how to shield and hide them."

Bea opened and closed her hand, as if she could see the light rising from her palm. "And do I glow like that?"

"*Carissima*, you have glowed since you were a child." Nonna shook her head. "I always knew you'd come into your powers one day. Most Strega don't awaken fully until they turn twenty-one."

That ignited the sense of curiosity that had been simmering in her belly since the church. This was her birthright, something Bea had been born into, and yet she knew nothing about it. Bea curled her hand into a fist and leaned forward. "Tell me more."

Nonna took another long sip of espresso. She met Bea's gaze, her eyes, so like Bea's own in shape and color, narrowed. "Before we go any further, you need to commit to the path of the Strega. I cannot tell you secrets until you promise to keep them."

Bea sucked in a breath. Something itched inside her, an urgency that told her she had to make this decision now. There would not be time later. She shook her head, trying to clear her mind, but the feeling persisted. It beat like a pulse behind her heart. She didn't want to disappoint her grandmother, but more importantly, Bea wanted this. She wanted something beyond the mundanity of life, to be more than just a mobster's daughter.

But what would they expect in return?

She cleared her throat. "What would you want from me?"

Nonna nodded approvingly, as if Bea had asked the right question. "You would be my heir. I have protected this family from long before we set foot in this country. My touch is on every one of you." She leaned forward and tugged on the chain around Bea's neck, revealing the necklace Bea had worn as long as she could remember.

Bea pulled out the round gold charm that hung on the end. She'd always thought it a religious icon, but only now did she pay attention to the symbols etched on the back. "Wait. Everyone has a necklace like this." She meant her cousins, although the ones the men wore had a charm of a golden horn, the symbol to prevent the evil eye.

"Of course. This charm will keep you from getting sick and protect you from most harm. There are similar simboli carved in our homes, the club, even the church. My power keeps them active."

So, magic could be used for good. Bea saw nothing wrong with this, or protecting her family. "You'd teach me to do this?"

"It would be essential."

Bea swallowed. "What about that other thing?" She made a gesture with her hands, trying to encompass everything that had happened only a few hours ago. Bea could not see herself burning out a man's eyes.

"There is a responsibility to our power, to use it wisely."

Bea ducked her head to hide her smile at Nonna accidentally quoting Spider-Man.

Luckily, Nonna didn't notice and continued, "When a man is made in our family, he not only swears loyalty to the family, he pledges something in return for our protection. Vito pledged his eyes. He would not have been harmed, except that he tried to betray us. You must understand."

Family was the most important thing. Bea knew this. She'd grown up understanding that the only people she could count on were her own family. Consequently, she knew she had to do anything for the family in return. Until this point, that had meant things like standing in eighty-degree heat during Connie's high school graduation, or helping in the kitchen during Christmas Eve dinner. No one had really tested her commitment to her family before.

Until now.

This wasn't Nonna telling her to do something like she would a child. This was her asking Bea as an adult. If she made this choice, Bea would have to use these abilities to serve the family. She straightened her shoulders, feeling the responsibility of it settle on her.

Nonna wasn't asking for a favor. She was asking Bea to prepare to be the matriarch of the family. And Bea liked the thought.

Even so, she didn't know if she could do what Nonna had done today. "If nobody gets out of line, I wouldn't have to punish them."

"You should be prepared to," Nonna said. "You must do anything to protect the Family."

Bea swallowed. She trusted her grandmother would never lead her astray. "All right. I'll keep the secrets."

Nonna smiled, looking absolutely delighted. "Good. Come, come." She stood and made for the back room beyond the kitchen.

"Wait, what about Connie? Can I tell her about any of this?"

Nonna shook her head. "I will tell her all she needs to know in August."

On her twenty-first birthday. Bea didn't like keeping secrets from her cousin, but it was only for a few more months.

Bea shoved one last cookie in her mouth—these were her favorite—and followed. As far as she knew, this back room was her grandmother's sewing room. She had an industrial grade machine back here, along with skeins of yarn and a vast collection of knitting needles and crochet hooks.

Nonna opened the door, and it looked exactly as Bea remembered it—the sewing machine in the corner, a comfortable loveseat along one wall, and a shelving unit filled with all the supplies one would need to make a blanket. On one shelf sat a small statue of a saint she didn't recognize, with a candle and lighter next to it. Nonna scooped this up and placed the statue on a small tray table she pulled out from the wall.

"Give me your hand." Nonna lit the candle with a match, and the flame came to life with a sharp hiss.

Bea eyed the candle warily, but did so, only for her grandmother to stab one of Bea's fingers with a sewing needle. "Ow!" Bea yiped at the sudden sharp pain. Nonna held her hand over the fire, a single drop of blood falling on the flame.

Nonna murmured in Italian, the words nonsense. A wave of dizziness hit Bea, and she swayed in place. A haze covered everything. She blinked in an attempt to focus. Something burned in her chest, an inferno angry at being kept back for so long. Pressure settled in her forehead and she wanted to curl up on the ground and weep from the pain of it.

Before she could fall over or faint, the pressure, the fire, all of it disappeared. Bea opened her eyes with a snap and pulled back her hand. Her blood thrummed in her body and everything seemed in super sharp focus. The world brightened around her and she found herself caught up in tiny details, like the wave of silver in Nonna's hair.

"You've been awakened." Nonna nodded approvingly. She blew out the candle, and put it, along with the statue, back on the shelf. "Look."

Nonna pulled out her sewing basket—made of dark wood, it had several compartments depending on which way the handle was pulled. Inside, Nonna kept thread, buttons, needles, spare parts for her machine. That was normal. Bea had played with this dozens of times as a child. But when Nonna reached the bottom compartment, she tapped something on the side, and the bottom dropped open to reveal an old notebook.

"You will inherit this one day. A lifetime of my spells." Nonna presented it to Bea, flipping through the old crinkly pages to reveal tiny handwriting. "All of my secrets."

"Whoa. That's a lot." Bea touched the book and felt a spark, a jolt of energy travel up her hand. She snatched her hand back and held it to her chest in shock. "What was that?"

"This is a dangerous time for you. Before you are trained, your power is untamed, raw. We will need to practice every day to teach you to put down protection so you do not accidentally harm yourself."

"And I thought I was done with studying when I took my last final," Bea quipped.

Nonna responded with a sharp look, one that made Bea feel five years old again and caught with her hand in the rising dough. So much for being treated like an adult. "Your words have power now. Do not use them lightly."

Bea nodded. She was taking this seriously, but she couldn't help the flutter of excitement in her chest. What else should she sense? Could she see other people's auras now too?

"Be careful what you say. Don't wish for something you don't mean." Nonna frowned. "Your senses have been opened. Don't be surprised if you see or smell what you haven't before. Most important, trust your instincts. You will find you know more than you think."

"Like auras?" Did only witches have them? What did the color mean? Bea had so many questions.

"Nonna! Are you here?" A voice echoed from the other side of the apartment.

Bea froze. That was her brother. Had they already run out of time? If he were here, then the procession was nearly at their front door.

Nonna quickly put the book away, tucking the sewing basket back in its place. "Coming!" She called, and then whispered to Bea, "Tomorrow. You come to me tomorrow."

"Tomorrow," Bea agreed.

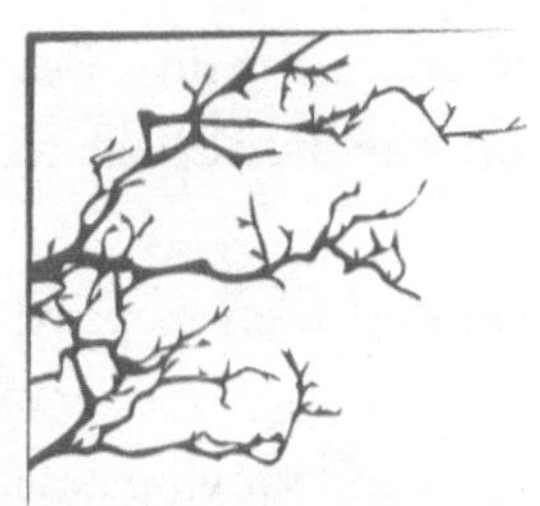

Chapter 6

Bea's skin still tingled with electricity as she made her way into the kitchen. The smile on her face faded when she saw Mike and Lucy standing there, waiting. Of course, Mike had Lucy with him. They were attached at the hip.

She wrinkled her nose as the scent of something not quite right hit her. Maybe the milk Nonna left out on the table was going bad. It seemed after her awakening that all of her senses were dialed up to eleven. Bea clenched her fists, hoping it would die down soon. She couldn't go through her day with everything this bright and intense.

Lucy's eye widened at the sight of her. "Bea? I didn't know you were here."

Bea didn't see an aura around either of them. Would she have to be in physical contact with someone to see it? Not that she wanted to go around touching people to see their auras. That would be weird. Her fingers twitched at the thought and she wanted to bounce on her toes, anything to get rid of this excess energy.

"Nonna had made my favorite cookies. You know I can't resist." She plastered a smile on her face and gave Lucy some of her own medicine back. Bea could be aggressively kind, too.

Mike reached out for the table and scooped up a cookie for himself, which he then shoved in his mouth, whole. God, he might be getting married soon, but he was still as gross as he was as a teenager.

"Is the procession here already?" Nonna emerged from the back room. She stopped to put a hand on Bea's shoulder as she passed her.

35

Almost immediately, the roiling wave of energy inside Bea calmed. Her shoulders sagged in relief. Oh good, she didn't have to vibrate like a charging battery all the time.

"Just a block away. We ran ahead to let you know." Lucy stepped forward and held out her hand.

Nonna took it and squeezed it before letting go and moving past Lucy to the living room. "We are in time, then."

The garland made of dollar bills attached to a length of ribbon had been laid over the couch, which was covered, as always, with a white bedsheet. When the statues stopped in front of the house, Nonna would be waiting on their front stoop. The altar boys would assist her to the cart, where they would set up a step stool for her to drape the money over the neck of the Madonna. It was a show of power, Bea realized. The entire parade of people waited while Nonna did this thing and showed off how much money they were donating to the church.

"I'll carry it for you, Nonna." Mike scooped up the garland.

Nonna picked up her black leather purse and tucked it under her arm. The sight of it had Bea swallowing hard, remembering the last time Nonna had gone sorting through her purse. What else did she have in there if her spell book was safely tucked away at home?

"This is so much fun." Lucy looped her arm around Bea's.

Bea had done the same thing with Connie a dozen times. Lucy must have gotten the idea from seeing them with their arms entwined, heads together and giggling to themselves. But Lucy and Bea did not have that kind of relationship, no matter how much Lucy kept trying.

Something cold prickled along Bea's elbow, where their skin met. She narrowed her eyes, trying to get a look at Lucy's aura like when she touched Nonna's hand before. But nothing happened. Or Lucy didn't glow, whatever that meant. Another thing to ask Nonna about tomorrow.

"It'll be more fun once we get to the church." No matter how old she got, Bea still enjoyed the carnival games. And nothing tasted as good as the zeppole made fresh from the street vendors slinging the dough into boiling vats of oil, before dusting them with enough powder sugar to fund a small nation. Her mouth watered just thinking about it.

Once outside, they could hear the loud horns of the band as the procession approached. The priest and his altar boys led the way. The cart carrying the saints halted to a stop in front of their house. Nonna waved to the crowd as Mike walked in front of her, carrying the money.

Bea slipped from Lucy's grip. She didn't want to spend the next three blocks with her talking about the wedding. Bad enough Bea had to wear a yellow bridesmaid's dress on the actual day. She didn't want to talk about it now. Bea backed away, keeping her eye on Lucy, who joined Mike and Nonna at the statues where they were being blessed by the priest.

A weight lifted off of her shoulders, as she no longer had to perform for Lucy. Bea dropped into the crowd, looking out for Connie and her other cousins. The band continued to play, the horns sharp and loud to her ears. Thankfully, Nonna had dampened her senses. Bea didn't want to know what that would sound like in her heightened state.

Her foot somehow found a pothole in the street and Bea stumbled backward. Solid hands caught her. "Easy."

No, it couldn't be. That voice, she recognized. But the odds of running into him again, well, those were actually pretty good. It wasn't that big of a crowd. Bea got her balance back and turned to meet the guy's eyes. "You."

"Me." He grinned at her, looking no less handsome than he'd had behind the church.

Bea immediately flushed hot all over. God, she'd embarrassed herself not once, but twice? And he had to be cute, too. It couldn't have been a paisan she had no interest in. "Well. Um. Thank you for catching me. Again."

"My pleasure." He held out his hand, just as the procession starting moving again. "Dante."

"Oh, we're doing the name thing." Bea shook his hand, still not quite focused on him.

A zap went all up her arm, like lightning, shocking her so hard it made her teeth hurt. The guy was covered by a pale blue glow, like soft fluffy clouds all around him. It was beautiful.

But what did it mean? Purple sparkles signified a witch, apparently, but she needed some kind of guide if people were going to show up all being different colors. Trust your instincts, Nonna had said, so Bea tried. She felt nothing bad from him, but there was something not quite ... truthful about his words. Maybe Dante was a nickname and not his full name. Or maybe not telling her his full name made it not true. She had no idea. So far, magic was frustrating.

"And your name?" he prodded.

She didn't quite know what to make of him. Bea never ended up flirting at the Feast. This was a time for Family and faith, not meeting cute guys. "Bea. It's short for Beatrice, but nobody calls me that except my parents."

Bea took her hand back and shook it out, a sensation pins and needles retreating down her fingers as the feeling returned. Nobody told her magic would hurt. Did the reaction mean she should stay away from Dante, or was that the natural consequence of seeing his aura?

"It's a pretty name."

At least he sucked at the flirting thing, too. Seriously, he couldn't come up with anything better than that? "Do you make a habit of being in strategic locations to scoop up swooning girls?"

He barked out a laugh, almost as if she'd surprised it out of him. "I believe you were the one who ran into me. Twice."

"It must be destiny," Bea teased. Wait, was destiny even a thing? Should she be looking for signs and portents about the future? If Connie were here, she'd yell at Bea for missing the opportunity right in front of her because she was distracted about magic. Nonna was going to explain everything later. Bea could concentrate on flirting with the cute guy. She cleared her throat, hoping he hadn't picked up on her daydreaming. "Um. I've never seen you around before. Are you new to the church?"

"I didn't come for the church." He winced. "That sounds bad. I only moved up here pretty recently, so I don't know the neighborhood well. Someone had hung flyers in my building about the festival, so I thought I'd check it out."

"We don't live in Newark anymore. A lot of the people I know are leaving for the suburbs." Although they still came back for the church.

The procession turned the corner of the block, and they continued to walk amidst the crowd. Bea still hadn't seen any members of her family. Maybe they were up by the band. Somehow, she and Dante had ended up at the back of the pack.

"I need to be close to the train for work, and it was affordable."

"Hmm?" she turned back to him. "Oh, what do you do?"

DANTE WAS LOSING HER, he could tell. *God, I'm even boring myself.* None of the hours of training could prepare him for the actual moment of trying to talk up a pretty young woman. There was the added pressure, of course, of this being part of the job. He somehow had to capture her interest and soon, since it looked like they were coming around back to the church. This had to be done before Bea escaped to her family.

He straightened his shoulders, and then let them drop into a relaxed pose. Remember the character. Dante Milano. Recent college grad. Came to the city to look for opportunities. Lover of theater and art. All the things Bea took part in at college herself.

Of course, he couldn't simply say to her, "Hey, girl, I heard you like art. I like art too." Although, honestly, it would be easier if he could.

Dante never claimed to be a ladies' man. Hell, his last girlfriend had asked him out. Women didn't work like numbers. He couldn't put them in columns and get the right answer. Why did Janet think he could do this again? Being relatively good looking meant nothing if he couldn't be suave.

Suave and sincere when every word out of his mouth was a lie. Easy peasy.

"Ok, promise you won't laugh?"

That got her attention. Bea stopped scanning the crowd and looked directly at him, a smile on her lips. "Are you going to admit to secretly being a clown?"

That surprised a laugh out of him. "What? No. Why would you even think that?"

"You were the one who told me not to laugh." Her lips twitched and he could tell she was holding back giggles.

Good. Dante ducked his head and tried to look shy. "I just graduated, so I'm freelancing until I can get my dream job. I want to do theater design on Broadway."

"Why would I laugh at that? That's amazing."

"Because all I do right now is design ads and newsletters. It's really pretty boring." Dante risked looking back up to see the reaction on her face.

They'd had been careful with his background, using enough truth that Dante could talk knowledgeably about some topics, even though he'd have to fudge others. His "art" degree was in something boring, yet still relevant. His own theater experience would help round out this character he was trying to inhabit. It was so much easier when he already had the script.

"Yeah, but you have a pretty big dream. Why set design?" Bea had her attention totally on him now, not easy when the band continued to play really loudly at the front of the parade.

Perfect. "I did some theater at college. Fell in love, but it was too late to change my major." He pulled his phone out of his pocket and flipped to the FBI curated Instagram that showed off his fake life—carefully backdated, of course. "Here's our last production before I graduated. We did *A Midsummer Night's Dream*."

"Oh, I love that play." Bea took the phone from him and swiped through the photos.

There were a few real ones in there of Dante in costume. Many of the set piece closeups were not. They had an artist at the Bureau who did work like this. Leo created filler posts, including the supposed artwork Dante had created. While he could wield a paintbrush—Dante did in fact do some set painting, everyone pitched in—he didn't have the fine art skills to put on display.

"I was cast as Theseus." He didn't have to fake the distaste in his voice. "I auditioned for Puck."

"Puck is the best role," Bea agreed. She handed him back his phone.

"What about you? What's your dream job?"

"Me?" She looked surprised at the question. Bea turned away, staring off in the distance, giving Dante the opportunity to study the shape of her face, the wistful look that appeared in her eyes. "Anything where I get to talk about art, I guess. Like a docent at a museum. Can you imagine working at the Met? Giving tours and just getting to gush about all the fantastic stuff they had?"

As she spoke, the wistful look disappeared and her face lit up. Dante found himself caught up in her joy. "Well, why can't you? Have you applied?"

She turned back to him and let out a little laugh. "I haven't even thought about it before now."

"Maybe you should consider it. You looked so passionate when you were talking about it."

Her cheeks went red. Had he mis-stepped? Dante was only speaking the truth. He needed to save this, somehow.

"So, uh, are you going to explain what this was about?" Dante pulled the rock out that she'd given him earlier. It was a solid smooth white stone, about a quarter of the size of his palm.

Bea laughed and took the rock from him. She brushed her fingers over it and her eyes went wide for a moment. "I like to pick up pretty rocks and stones. I have a collection I use in my art sometimes. When the church bells went off, I didn't know what to do with it and you were standing right there, so..." Bea ducked her head, her cheeks still pink.

She handed it back. "You keep it. It's meant to be yours now."

Dante curled his fingers around the rock, now warm from her touch. His picture of Bea DiLorenzo was changing. It was one thing to see facts about her written in a file, but by speaking to her, she'd become a real person. Someone who loved art and collected pretty stones she found.

The band switched to another song, one that vaguely sounded familiar. It had been in the training packet. "Are...are they playing the Italian national anthem?"

"Yeah, they're almost at the church. It's always the last song. I only know two words."

He was running out of time. Once they got back to the church, he'd lose her to her family and the festival. Dante needed to seize this opportunity. "Hey, so I really enjoyed our conversation. Maybe we can continue it? On the phone?"

Oh, man, now he sounded like an idiot. If Janet were here, she'd be laughing her ass off at him. Dante ran a hand through his hair in frustration. "That's my awkward way of asking if I could get your number."

Bea frowned at him. "I just met you."

He cast around for an idea, any idea. The parade had turned back on the street in front of the church, where the venders had opened up. The carnival games already had kids standing in front of them, ready to throw their money away. That gave him an idea.

"How about if I win you a prize, you give me your number?"

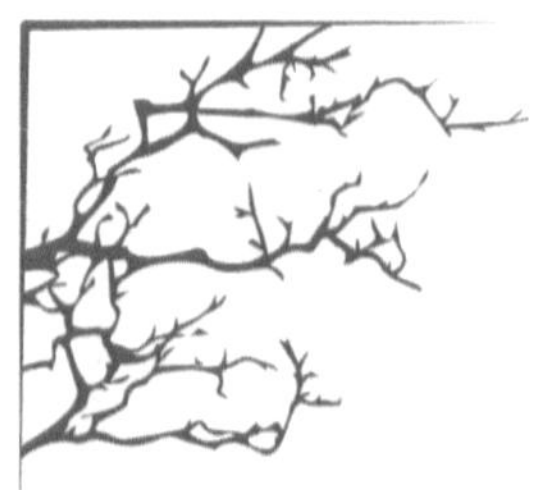

Chapter 7

Bea didn't know what to make of this guy. If someone had plucked her greatest fantasy out of her head—hot guy who loved the arts and thought she was cute—and brought them to life, then he would look a bit like this Dante. He seemed a little too good to be true.

Could this be from her magic? She'd been wishing for a partner of her own only a few hours ago after seeing Mike and Lucy be all lovey dovey with each other. Nonna had told her to be careful about what she said, but did that include secret thoughts? And besides, that had been before Nonna awakened her magic.

Still. Bea couldn't quite believe it.

She really wanted to go with him and let him try—and most likely fail—to win her one of the carnival prizes. They would laugh about it, and maybe he'd offer to buy her a zeppole to make up for it. Bea would give him her phone number and they'd set up a date. It would be too perfect.

The church bells rung, reminding her of why she couldn't do that. Bea had responsibilities. She needed to be at mass with her family, not fooling around with a stranger. But that didn't mean she couldn't take advantage of this opportunity.

"Thank you, but I really have to go." She hoped he could tell she wasn't happy about it. "My family is waiting for me."

Dante nodded, but couldn't hide the disappointment on his face. "Maybe we can meet up afterward?"

Then she'd have to answer questions, like who was this guy she was hanging out with? Bea really didn't want to have to deal with that.

"How about I DM you on Instagram?" Bea pulled out her phone and tapped the app. She'd noted his username from when he handed her his phone before and he was easy to find and follow. "I'm BeaFree63." That was her art account.

If this turned out sour, she could always block him afterward.

The band had moved off to the sidewalk, and the crowd started filing into the church. The statues were being lifted from their carts to be carried back into the building. Bea had run out of time. "Crap, gotta go."

She took off at a jog, not looking back to see Dante. The crowd closed in behind her anyway, so there would be nothing to see.

Once inside the church, darkness enveloped her, a stark contrast to the bright sunshine outside. It took her a moment for her eyes to adjust, which was why she didn't see her mother bearing down on her at first.

"Beatrice, where have you been?" Mom grabbed her by the wrist and pulled her into the alcove of the narthex.

Bea only glimpsed her aura for a second. There wasn't much to see, only a muddled bit of dulled burgundy and pink. No sparkles. She pulled her wrist back and rubbed at it, a faint sense of pins and needles receding quickly. "I went to help Nonna with the garland. I couldn't find anyone in the procession."

Mom eyed her with suspicion, like Bea was five years old again and getting her good Sunday dress all muddy. They didn't look like mother and daughter. Mom had light brown hair and pale eyes, and Bea took after her dad's side of the family completely with her own darker features.

"You shouldn't go off on your own like that. Your place is here with your family. What will people think?" Mom shook her head.

And that was the million-dollar question—what the hell will people think? Mom was always asking that, and Bea wanted to respond, "what people? And who cares what they think?" but she never had the courage to say anything. Bea knew the drill. Their family, such as it was, had a reputation to uphold. They needed to be seen in the front of that church.

"I know, Mom. I'm here now. Come on, we don't want to be late." Bea did what she always did, deflect and get out of the way. She had too much going on right now to worry about disappointing her mother. That was a daily occurrence, after all.

Mom narrowed her eyes, as if she knew Bea was hiding something. Probably didn't think it was magic. Actually, Mom was more likely to suspect Bea had been off talking to strange young men, and that happened to be true, so Bea didn't really blame her. She nodded and accompanied Bea back into the church, heading up the side to their customary pew at the front.

"Where have you been?" Connie asked as Bea slid into the pew next to her.

"Long story," Bea whispered back.

They wouldn't be here long. Once the statues were returned to their places of honor, Father Stefano would give the final blessing, and everyone would race out to take part in the feast. As a kid, she'd always been impatient to get to the good part of the feast. They'd spent the week before going to mass every single night, praying the novena. Attending for the entire series showed commitment, and you were supposed to get whatever you had prayed for by the end. Back then she'd asked for silly things—to pass her math test, for Billy to kiss her after the dance.

She didn't know what to ask for now. Father Stefano droned on when he should have been bringing this to a close, and Bea fidgeted in her seat. She looked over her shoulder to the pew behind where her father sat. The first few rows were taken up by men in suits, all big guys who looked like they were ready for a fight. Now she knew what that meant, and the thought made her throat go dry.

For a brief moment as she walked the procession, she'd let go of all of that. It had been so nice to talk to someone who shared her interests. He didn't dismiss her dreams in favor of some other topic of supposedly more importance, like a wedding or who was having a baby, or what paisan had pissed off another.

If she continued on this path that Nonna had set before her, then Bea could never pursue her dreams, no matter how amorphous they were. She'd be committed to the family, protecting their mafia interests when she didn't know exactly what that involved. Bea never wanted to hurt her family. No, that wasn't what bothered her about the whole thing.

She shouldn't let one stupid conversation put her out of sorts like this. Dante was just a cute guy who wanted her phone number. But he was the first person who ever told her to follow her dreams, and not keep doing what she was told.

Bea swallowed as she stood for the final blessing. Her grandmother sat on the other side of the pew, wedged between Lucy and Michael. She looked over at Bea and gave a slow nod.

No. No, Bea couldn't do this. She couldn't be her grandmother's heir.

At first, it had sounded like a good idea. Protecting the family. Learning magic. Bea's heart raced in her chest as the priest told them all to "go in peace." There wouldn't be any peace for Bea if she did what her grandmother wanted.

Because at this moment, as they filed out of the church, she knew one thing. She could not be who her grandmother wanted her to be. Bea could not contribute to this thing. She'd fooled herself into thinking she wouldn't have to burn a man's eyes out, but never acknowledged the fact that it could be something worse. Vita had pledged his eyes, apparently, but what had the other soldiers promised in exchange? An ear? Their lungs?

Why hadn't she asked?

If she did what her grandmother wanted, there would be no going back. She'd be tied to the family forever. Hell, her parents would expect her to marry in the Family like a good girl. Any boyfriend from outside would be rejected and, worse, possibly killed if Bea didn't break it off with him. She stiffened, thinking she'd be forced to marry someone like Nick, her prom date, and never get the chance to explore a relationship with someone like Dante.

"Do you want to get something to eat first?" Connie asked.

"I've been craving zeppole," Bea answered. Look at her, being able to have a conversation despite completely freaking out in her own mind.

"That's not dinner."

Bea laughed. "Now you're starting to sound like my mom. We are here to eat greasy food and win goldfish by throwing ping-pong balls at them."

Connie put her hand over her mouth as she giggled. "Oh god, remember that one year? We won five, and they all died by the next morning."

"And you wouldn't stop crying? What were we? Six or seven?" Bea grinned as they emerged from the church. Outside, the band played something with a nice beat, and an impromptu dance floor broke out in the middle of the street. It would be a long night of celebration ahead.

And the mob would take their cut of tonight's profits.

Bea's belly twisted, and the desire to eat something sugary and bad for her faded. How could she have a good time tonight knowing what was to come? Bea couldn't. She wanted to seize control of her own life and not forever be known as the mob boss's daughter. If that meant giving up magic, then so be it.

Tomorrow, when she went to visit Nonna, she'd tell her she'd changed her mind. She couldn't be the person Nonna wanted her to be.

Decision made, she looped arms with Connie and led her into the midst of the feast. She didn't have to worry about it tonight. Now she would spend time with her cousins and celebrate with the rest of the family.

"How about we try to win a few goldfish?"

"You're on." Connie said.

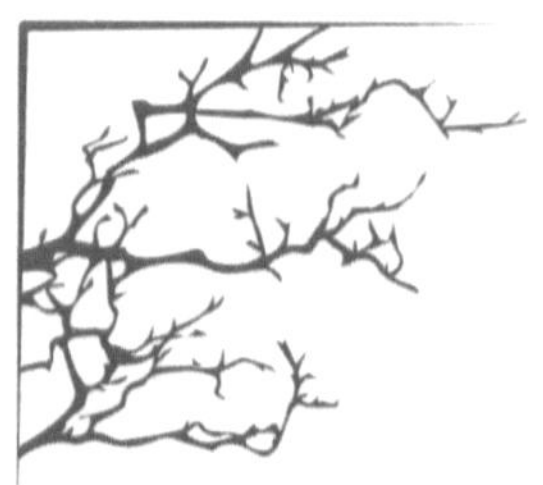

Chapter 8

Dante stayed at the festival for a few hours after Bea left him at the church. He kept looking for opportunities to interact with her again. However, she was never alone. Even if her cousin Connie left her side for a moment, there were a few of DiLorenzo's men standing behind her. He realized how lucky he'd been to catch her during the parade.

He spent the time playing carnival games and eating far too much fried food. All the while he tested his memory, identifying the DiLorenzo family members he recognized and making note of those he didn't. It seemed like mobsters mostly staffed the booths, except for the food stands. Two police cars parked at the end of the block to keep the traffic out, but Dante saw the officers eating and laughing with the crowd. It was assumed the DiLorenzos had cops on the take, being paid to look the other way.

Traitors. They were supposed to be on the side of good, not taking money from the mob. It disgusted him. Dante finished the last of his cheesesteak and tossed the wrapper in the trash. He couldn't do any more here tonight. Time to head home and report in.

He walked back to his apartment building, which was a good ten blocks away from the church and DiLorenzo territory—far enough away to give him some space from the job, yet close enough that he could be around when needed.

Should he have said something different to Bea? He kept reviewing the interaction over and over again, poking at his responses. She'd smiled and laughed at his jokes. She'd teased him back. Those were all good things. But were they enough? He held on to that Instagram DM with hope. If she completely hated him, she'd have disappeared into the crowd without saying anything.

Dante stepped out of the elevator and onto his floor. Before he got far, the door to the apartment next to his opened. His neighbor stepped out with her dog, a golden retriever mix poking his head out. The dog let out an excited bark at the sight of Dante.

"Hey Dante. I just baked some cookies. Would you like to take some? I can't eat them all by myself."

"I never say no to food." Dante patted his belly before following her inside the apartment. He stopped to pet the dog when he entered, chuckling as Rocky did a spin in response.

That's when Agent Janet Carter dropped all pretenses of being a friendly next-door neighbor. She might still look the part with her mom jeans and apron, but her smile faded and her expression was all business. Inside this apartment, she acted as his handler, though she told him to call him by her first name to keep it simple. No chances of him slipping up and calling her agent when he shouldn't.

She'd actually baked cookies - Dante's favorite, chocolate chip, cooling on a rack on her kitchen counter. Janet's cookies were hit or miss. The last time he ended up feeding the failed sugar cookie experience to Rocky underneath the table.

"How'd it go?" she asked as he swiped a cookie and shoved it in his mouth.

Dante took his time chewing, putting his thoughts together. The cookies were actually decent this time, buttery and filled with melted chocolate. Janet had a reputation at the Bureau—a good one. She'd put a lot of mobsters away, mostly going undercover in innocuous positions, like barmaid or waitress or secretary. Janet always said people didn't watch their mouths around the help. She had the arrest record to prove her methods worked. Dante could learn a lot from her.

"I made contact with Beatrice DiLorenzo," he reported, wiping chocolate off of his chin. Janet handed him a napkin with a wry smile. "Thank you. I couldn't get her phone number, but she followed the fake Instagram account and sent me a DM."

Janet laughed. "Loosen up, kid. Don't be so formal. This isn't an official report."

Dante frowned. It was hard for him to treat Janet with anything but respect. But she was right. He couldn't act this stiff around her. What if one of their neighbors saw?

"Instagram, huh? You kids and your social media these days." Janet went over to the cookies and started pulling them off the tray and into a Tupperware container.

It was still so weird to watch her do house wife stuff like that. He'd asked around about her after he'd taken the case and most agents agreed: "she'll keep you alive, but don't fuck with her." He got the sense that she frightened a lot of the junior agents. But right now, all he could see was the cover. And that's what made her so damn good at this job.

He still hadn't decided if he liked her or not.

"Leo did a good job on those fake social media profiles." They'd had a second profile set up if he'd made contact with Connie first, that one filled with pictures of the beach and Dante's fake family. The art had been more for Bea's benefit and he got lucky making contact with her first.

Rocky sat next to Dante and wagged his tail, staring up at him with wide brown eyes. "No cookies for you," Dante said. "These have chocolate in them."

Janet rolled her eyes and went to the cabinet, where she collected a dog biscuit. Rocky immediately left Dante's side for hers. Traitor.

"What are your next steps?" Janet gave Rocky the treat and ruffled his ears. As far as Dante knew, Rocky was really her dog, and not part of the cover. Just as well, since Rocky was super friendly and would make a terrible police dog.

"Um. Message her?" Dante hadn't thought that far ahead. He hadn't even been sure he'd be able to make contact today.

"Do it tonight," Janet urged. "Try to get her to meet you for coffee or something. You have to ride the momentum before she forgets about you."

"Got it." Dante didn't want to think about himself being forgettable, but it made sense. Bea was surrounded by mob guys all the time. They weren't subtle. He'd be competing with them.

"The best undercover agents are good at improvising, but that doesn't mean you don't prepare. She gives you an opening, you jump on it. She says she loves Japanese food; you tell her you know of a great place and we'll find one for you." Janet leaned against the kitchen counter and crossed her arms. Despite her outfit, the pose and expression on her face was all FBI agent.

"Got it." They'd gone over this in training, but it never hurt for one last refresher beforehand. Dante couldn't afford to slip up.

Janet sighed. "I got a report right before you got in. Our potential informant was found dumped in the hospital parking lot with his eyes burned out." She shook her head. "How do you even do that?"

Dante shivered. They'd been trying to get someone on the inside to turn. It would have been good backup for Dante, and more witness testimony was always ideal. "How'd they make him?"

Janet shrugged. "He probably did what all mob guys do. Got too cocky, and they caught him out. You gotta remember these guys like to brag. They're arrogant and think they are untouchable."

She reached for the Tupperware container, now filled with cookies, and handed it to him. Dante would gain twenty pounds by the time this operation was over. "I tell you this so you remember to watch your back."

"I got it," he said with more confidence than he felt. Dante kneeled to pet the dog as Rocky had returned from his biscuit chomping. Dante had always loved dogs, but they could never afford one growing up. "Remember, I can always be your dog walker if you need me. You know. For the cover."

She snorted and opened the front door for him. "Stay safe, kid."

Dante gave her a nod before heading back to his apartment. The Bureau had furnished it for him—keeping it simple with a mix of Ikea and thrifted pieces. He'd insisted on a comfortable couch and big screen TV, in case he wanted to invite his target over for Netflix and chill.

Bea. No longer an unnamed target, he now had a name and face that only sort of resembled her photos. When Bea smiled and laughed, there was life there that no picture could capture.

Dante put his cookies away in the tiny attached kitchen. He wouldn't be cooking any gourmet meals in here, not that he cooked. Take out and Door Dash were his best friends.

He took out his phone and found Bea's Instagram. *Hey do you want to meet me for coffee tomorrow morning?* he sent via DM.

To his surprise, a few seconds later, the alert appeared on his phone with a response. She hadn't immediately blocked him. That was a good sign.

Sure. What time? Where?

Luckily, he'd scoped the area around his apartment and knew a good little bakery that would be the perfect place to meet. *9:30? At Texiera's on Ferry street?* He also sent his phone number for good measure. *Call me if plans change.*

See you then.

Dante plopped onto his couch with a smile. Yes! He could do this. It was only a matter of time. He'd get his in and take the DiLorenzos down.

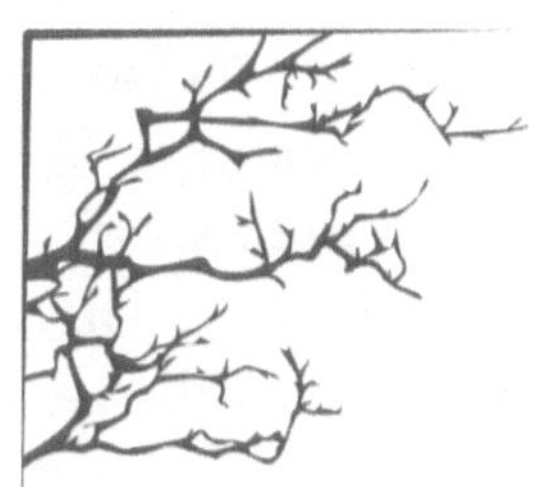

Chapter 9

Bea woke to a foul taste in her mouth and sunlight streaming in through her window. She sat up gagging, at first disoriented. She'd only been waking up in this room for a few days now, after months at her dorm, and she hadn't gotten used to being back in her childhood bedroom, not yet. There should be another bed across the room, with her roommate Stephanie teasing her about her famed inability to wake up at a decent time.

The time. She'd agreed to meet Dante for coffee this morning. Why had she done that? She knew Nonna was expecting her.

Because it gave her an out, some place to be when she broke the news to Nonna, that she didn't want to be her heir. That yesterday she thought she could do it, but now, after really thinking about it, Bea knew she couldn't. God, why had she even said yes?

Bea plopped her head back on her pillow, tempted to pull the covers over her head and forget everything. She couldn't say no to her Nonna yesterday. What made her think she could go over there today and take it all back?

Maybe she was freaking out over nothing. Yesterday had been a lot, and then Bea went and made things more complicated by meeting a cute guy she'd love to have coffee with. She had awful timing, starting with hiding in that storage room at exactly the wrong moment.

No matter what, she couldn't lie here in bed stewing over everything. Eventually Nonna would call or Dante would message her and ask where she was, and Bea would have to face the day, anyway. She threw the covers off and got out of bed, promptly bumping into one of the moving boxes she'd left half unpacked on the floor next to her bed. God, her entire room was a mess. She had boxes strewn all over the place, some filled with clothes, others textbooks, and still more with art projects. Most of those she'd have to cart to the basement where she kept her art supplies, a collection she'd been amassing since she was a kid.

She'd been avoiding it because she didn't want her mother to see her cart more stuff in there and make more noises about cleaning it out since hadn't she outgrown that by now? Mom never understood how she could lose herself in her work, even if Bea wasn't especially good at it. There was a reason she'd majored in art history and not fine arts, after all.

Her rock collection she kept in her room, carefully placed in a large clear plastic box she stored under her bed. The less clutter mom could see, the less flack she'd get.

Bea flexed her hand, wondering what she would sense now if she touched her beloved stones. She'd picked them up because she knew they were special. Maybe that was something Nonna could explain.

Nonna probably wouldn't explain anything if Bea showed up and said, "Sorry, Nonna, I can't be your heir. I need to go meet a guy for coffee."

No. She had to be committed. She had to tell Nonna that she couldn't hurt someone, even to protect the family. Bea didn't have that in her. She'd been foolish yesterday to think she could. As she stood, her necklace slipped out of her pajama top and Bea took hold of the charm around her neck, like she had dozens of times before.

"Ow!" Bea stuck her finger in her mouth. The metal was ice cold and yet somehow burned her hand. Did that mean something? Bea had ever had that happen before.

But she'd never been awakened to magic before. "What are you trying to tell me?" she said to the charm. Not to tell her grandmother no? This was her protective charm; did it mean she was in danger somehow? Maybe she should reconsider meeting Dante for coffee.

If she didn't start moving, she'd be late. She stepped through her maze of boxes and went to her closet to make a quick decision about clothes. Luckily, most of her summer stuff stayed home, so she didn't have to go digging to find something to wear. She stopped as she opened the closet door and sniffed. It smelled like... lilies?

What the hell did she have that smelled like lilies? None of her lotions or shampoos smelled like flowers. Bea was more of a neutral scent type girl. She liked vanilla and coconut. Connie was always trying some weird perfume concoction. Maybe she wore something last night that rubbed off on Bea's dirty clothes, which sat in a pile on the floor near her closet. That had to be it.

Fifteen minutes later, she was skipping down the stairs to grab her keys and head out.

"Where are you going?" Mom's voice caused Bea to miss the last step. Her mother sat at the kitchen island, the lights out, a cup of coffee in front of her.

Her mother's presence caught her off-guard. Bea had gotten used to not having to tell her mother every place she was going to be and what time she'd be home. "What?"

"Where are you going?" Mom repeated. As if Bea hadn't heard.

Mom had her light brown hair swept up in a fashionable scarf, which meant she would be off to the salon soon. She dressed down for that, wearing a white button-down blouse over tan capris. If Bea wore light colored pants, they'd end up stained in five minutes. Her mother was always so ladylike and well-kept, and Bea wasn't.

Case in point—her own outfit consisted of jeans and a t-shirt with the logo of her favorite coffee shop. She'd twisted her hair into a knot at the back of her head and threw on some lip balm instead of any makeup. Either Dante liked her as she was, or he wasn't worth her time.

"I'm going to Newark to see Nonna."

That wasn't unusual. Bea spent a lot of time with her grandmother when they lived in the same house and visited often. She left out the part about meeting up with Dante after. Daddy got overprotective when she mentioned guys, and she didn't want her mother to tell him.

"You were just there yesterday. Don't you have better things to do? Like maybe clear out those boxes?"

"I'll get to it, eventually. What's the point of unpacking if I'm going to end up packing again for August?" Bea rolled her eyes. Why did every conversation with her mother reduce her to a ten-year-old?

"You could throw a few things out. Start by clearing out some space in the spare room."

"You mean my studio?" Bea snapped back.

Mom raised an eyebrow as she slowly sipped her coffee. She didn't even have to respond to make Bea feel bad.

"I'll get to it later." Bea sighed and turned to go.

"Remember this afternoon we're going over the plans for the shower!" Mom called as Bea made it to the front door.

Bea clenched her jaw to keep from rolling her eyes. Right. Lucy's bridal shower. Technically, the bridal party was throwing it, but Mom and Daddy were paying for it because Lucy was an orphan without a mom of her own to organize things. God, she couldn't wait until this whole wedding thing was over.

"I'll be back by then, mom," she said. "I have some cool idea for the decorations!"

That seemed to stun her mother into silence and Bea could make her escape. She got out her car keys and hit the fob to open her door. When she slid into the seat, she smelled lilies again, so strong it made her cough. What the hell?

Bea rolled down her windows and headed for the highway.

Traffic was terrible. She'd run into Monday morning rush hour—something that she, as an unemployed ex-college student—forgot existed. At this rate, she'd be very late to meet Dante. Forty-five minutes later, she pulled into Nonna's driveway—after flipping off the guy tailgating her down the street.

She debated leaving the car there and heading off to meet Dante. She could talk to Nonna later. Maybe by then she'd figure out what to say to her. But when Bea locked the car door, something coiled in her belly, a strange sensation like the pins and needles she kept getting every time she'd used her magic. It told her to go inside, a compulsion so strong it pulled her toward the door. She couldn't have resisted if she wanted to.

Listen to your instincts, Nonna had said. Something weird had been going on with her all morning. Bea couldn't explain it. Maybe it had something to do with whatever Nonna had done by using Bea's blood yesterday. Her magic really wanted to be used, or something.

Bea opened the little door set into the garage and the smell of lilies hit her so hard she nearly fell over with the force of it. She stilled, one foot inside the garage, the other outside, her heart racing. There was no car in the garage—Uncle Guido must be out somewhere. She could hear nothing in here, not even the cars outside. The silence made her skin crawl.

A feeling of dread settled over her like a cloak the closer she got to her grandmother's back door. That churning in her belly came back, along with the bitter taste in her mouth. Bea went up the little porch and opened the storm door. The main door swung open behind it, but her grandmother wasn't on the other side.

There was an empty espresso cup on the kitchen table, the pot still on the stove, yet Bea couldn't smell the coffee. Her nose was thick with the scent of flowers. "Nonna!" she called, despite the prickling at the back of her neck.

She stepped inside, closing the door behind her. "Nonna! Are you in here?" Where else would she be? The garden, maybe, but...Bea saw a shadow in the corner of her eye. She turned to face it, and into the living room.

Nonna sat slumped on the couch. That was wrong. Nonna never sat on that couch. She always sat in the recliner that faced the TV, her knitting on her lap as she shouted at Italian broadcast TV.

"Nonna?" Bea entered the room, but Nonna didn't move. She went to her grandmother's side and touched her arm gently. Her skin was cold to the touch.

Nonna fell over, her head twisting at an unnatural angle.

Bea screamed. She jerked her hand back from Nonna. From the body. She stumbled backwards, tripping on the coffee table, which sent her tumbling to the carpet. The shock of it should have hurt, but she could only focus on getting away. Her chest tightened, and she couldn't get enough air.

No, no, this couldn't be happening. She had to still be home in bed, having a horrible nightmare.

Nonna couldn't be dead. She'd been fine yesterday. She'd been using magic, making men fear her with a flick of a lighter. They'd been having espresso and cookies right over there. Nonna had walked to the end of the procession, and spent time at the feast, eating zeppole and dancing the tarantella.

"Oh my god," Bea whispered, covering her mouth with her hands.

Her phone buzzed in her pocket, bringing her back to reality. She pulled it out with shaking hands. There was a DM from Dante.

He'd given her his number last night. She opened the message and hit the number, desperate to hear his voice—anyone's voice—right now. Anything to feel not so desperately alone.

"Hey," he answered on the first ring.

"Dante," she tried to croak out through her dry mouth. "It's Bea."

"Listen, I know I was a bit forward asking for a date so soon…"

A sob choked her throat when she tried to respond. Bea couldn't speak, couldn't put words to the reality she didn't want to accept.

"Bea, are you okay?" Dante's voice went sharp.

"No," she whispered. "I stopped at my grandmother's house, and," Bea gulped. "I think she's dead."

"Bea, I want you to listen to me," Dante's voice brought her back and Bea sunk into it, falling into his instructions. "I want you to go to the front door and text me the address. I will be there as soon as I can. All right?"

"Yes. Thank you." Bea ended the call and stared at the phone for a moment before she remembered she was supposed to do something. Right. Text him the address.

The book. The thought came unbidden. Right. Her grandmother's spell book. She needed to find that. It would help explain what the hell was happening to her. Bea typed the address on the phone as she made for the back of the apartment. The door to the backroom was open, which wasn't unusual, but…something felt off about the inside. The smell of lilies was gone, but in its place was nothing at all.

No, not nothing. Something she couldn't put her finger on.

She could tell that someone had been in here. The sewing box hadn't been placed back quite right. Nonna had been so careful with it yesterday. There was no way she'd leave it half in the middle of the room like this. Bea opened the lid, pressing the button that revealed the hidden panel. It slid open, but the compartment beneath it was empty.

Someone had killed her grandmother and stolen her spell book, and Bea had no idea what to do now.

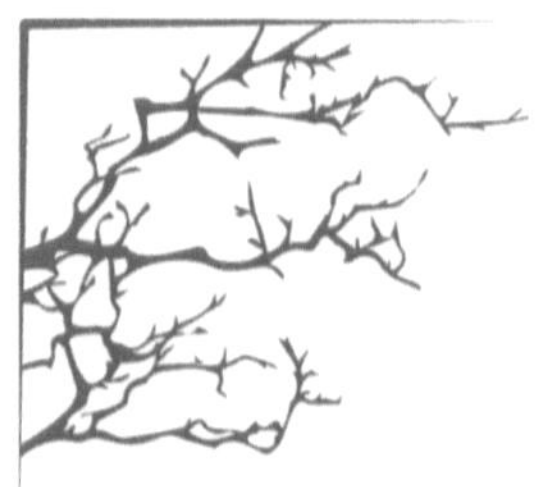

Chapter 10

Dante sprinted down the street before Bea texted the address to her grandmother's house. He already knew where to go, because he'd followed her there yesterday. It was how he'd been able to slip into the crowd of people at just the right time to "run into" Bea.

His phone had been programmed with a panic sequence that went right to the FBI, but this wasn't that kind of situation. Dante needed to call the police like a normal person. He had tapped out 911 on the phone's keyboard before he stopped. If he delayed calling the authorities until he was right there, it would give him a few extra minutes to comfort Bea, to weasel his way further into her affections. It was an excellent strategy.

Even if it made his stomach clench at the thought.

Dante had a job to do. Janet had told him to improvise, to use the situations to his advantage. And that was damn well what he was going to do.

When Dante arrived at the address, Bea stood outside, her arms across her chest like she was hugging herself. She looked so small and alone. Her hair had fallen out of the ponytail it had been swept back in, and her t-shirt had come untucked.

He swallowed and steeled himself as he approached. "Hey."

"Hey," she said back, looking up at him with red-rimmed eyes. "She...she's this way." Bea turned and led the way inside.

Dante followed, being sure to memorize everything he could about this side entrance to the house. There weren't any security cameras here, which was odd considering what he knew about the house in the suburbs where Bea lived with her family. That McMansion was locked up better than Fort Knox, complete with security that patrolled the property at night.

"I can't, I can't go back in there." Bea stopped in the doorway, like something had frozen her in place.

"I got this, okay? You wait out here." Dante stepped inside, taking stock of the kitchen, which had a half-eaten breakfast still on the table. It smelled faintly of coffee. He turned to his right, seeing the body out of the corner of his eye. He recognized the woman from yesterday, although seeing her now, crumpled on the couch was very different from the matriarch who'd led her family into the church.

It took only a moment to verify that there wasn't any pulse. Her skin was cold, meaning she'd been dead for some time. Perhaps long before Bea had come here. The coroner would determine that. Dante sighed and made the call.

When he came out of the house, he found Bea pacing. She looked over at him, hope in her eyes. "I'm sorry," he said. "I called the authorities. They should be here soon."

"Oh God." Bea crumpled, sitting down hard on the front steps that led to her grandmother's apartment. "She's really gone?"

Dante took a seat beside her and put his hand on her shoulder, squeezing lightly to give what comfort he could. "I'm sorry," he said again, words failing him.

Now was not the time for the suave character he'd created to impress Bea. Dante could only be himself and he knew exactly how she had to be feeling right now. "I know what you're going through. My grandmother died in the hospital when I was ten. I never got the chance to say goodbye to her."

Bea sniffed and shook her head. "She was fine yesterday. Healthy as a horse."

He nodded. "It happens like that, sometimes. I know it was really sudden when my grandma..." Dante bit off the words, not wanting to dwell on it now. This wasn't about him.

She looked over at him, and it became very obvious she was trying not to cry. Tears filled her eyes, and she blinked them back. "Were you close with your grandmother?"

He closed his eyes for a moment, falling back into the memory of childhood. Truth be told, Dante hadn't thought about his grandmother in a very long time. She'd been one of the few family members he'd actually liked. It had been so long, but now he could only recall the scent of the Irish soda bread she baked, and the way she smiled when he brought her a treasure, usually something he'd scrawled on a piece of construction paper.

"Maybe I would have been, if she'd lived longer." The raw honesty filled his throat, making the words come out thick with grief. Maybe things would have gone differently in his life if she'd lived. Perhaps his mother would have had a lifeline to go to, and maybe would have left his father earlier. Maybe his older brother wouldn't have turned to stealing cars to support his drug habit. Lots and lots of maybes.

Bea placed her hand on top of his and squeezed gently. "I'm sorry for your loss."

"You shouldn't be comforting me!" He let out a strangled laugh. "This is the worst first date ever."

She snorted in response, covering her mouth with her hand. Then the tears came, large fat drops that poured down her cheeks until Bea covered her face entirely as she shook with the force of her grief.

Dante put his arm around her and let her cry into his shoulder, stroking her back. He should be happy. This was what he wanted, to get closer to her. Bea felt comfortable enough to sob in his arms. Definitely a win for his mission.

But it made him feel like shit, knowing this was all a game.

"Sorry, I think I got snot on you." Bea sniffed and pulled away, her cheeks bright red.

"My shirt will accept the sacrifice," he tried to joke. "The coroner should be here soon. Do you have anyone you need to call?"

She smacked her forehead and got to her feet. "My dad."

He waited there, sitting on the steps, while Bea paced and made her phone call. He knew he should have been trying to listen in and get more intel, but at the moment, Dante wanted to give her a moment of privacy. It would be the last moment she'd have for a while.

By the time Bea got off the phone, they could hear the sirens. Dante finally stood. He held out his hand. "Let's go greet them."

She nodded and took his hand, entangling their fingers together. "Thank you. I couldn't have done this by myself."

Dante led her out to the front of the house, in time to meet the police car and ambulance that pulled up. He took the lead with the responding officer, knowing Bea was far too fragile at the moment to deal with any of this. After showing the paramedics where to bring the stretcher, he left them to their work and went back outside to check on Bea.

Only to find her sobbing in the arms of her father. A black SUV parked diagonally across the street, blocking the road. Dante stopped in his tracks. Was he ready for this? The whole point of him getting to know Bea was getting in with her family. It was happening faster than he had anticipated.

Bea's father—the "Don," Michael DiLorenzo, looked up to meet Dante's eyes as he approached.

He resembled his daughter, having the same dark curly hair and brown eyes, along with that proud nose, all on a much more masculine face. DiLorenzo was broad in his shoulders and round in the middle, towering over Bea, but still shorter than Dante. The soft look on his face faded the moment Dante arrived, and the scowl that replaced it turned those features menacing. Dante nearly took a step back in response to that glare. No wonder mobsters quaked in fear at the sight of this man.

"Bea, who is this guy?"

Bea wiped her eyes and straightened her shoulders. "Daddy, this is Dante. We were supposed to go out for coffee this morning. I met him at the feast yesterday."

Dante stiffened. Here he stood, an undercover FBI agent, before the most notorious mob boss in the state. His only safety was because DiLorenzo didn't know that. Yet now Dante was in a different kind of danger, that of dating a mobster's daughter.

"Hello, sir." Dante had to remember the role, that of someone who should have no clue who DiLorenzo really was. He was just a guy, standing in front of the father of the girl he wanted to get to know better, even though it was far too soon to meet the parents.

"He called the police for me. If it wasn't for him, I wouldn't know what I would have done." Bea swallowed, her voice catching again, although this time it seemed she had control of her tears.

DiLorenzo came forward. "Dante, was it? What's your family name, son?"

They'd had to be careful here, when they chose his cover. Janet had wanted to give him an Italian last name, since he was more likely to be accepted into the fold that way. However, if they chose a name of someone already connected to the DiLorenzo's, they'd know right away he was not part of that family.

"Milano," Dante said. He pretended to look confused why DiLorenzo would care.

DiLorenzo held out his hand and introduced himself. Dante returned the handshake, his fingers creaking from the pressure. DiLorenzo had one hell of a grip. "Thank you for being there for my little girl."

"Of course." Dante nodded.

"I'll give you the business later, but I have a few things to take care of." DiLorenzo gestured to Bea. "Stay here, for now. I have to talk to the people."

"The business?" Dante whispered to Bea as her father walked over to the police officers and started chatting away. They apparently knew each other on a first name basis.

"He'll grill you about your parents. What you do for a living. All that." Bea rolled her eyes, and for a moment she looked like herself, not the grief-stricken shell she'd been since he had arrived at her grandmother's house. "He's just being strong for me. Daddy and Nonna were very close."

This would have implications for the mob. If DiLorenzo was compromised after the death of his mother, that might mean other mob bosses might move in to seize territory. But looking at the man right now, as he chatted with police officers like they were family, he didn't look affected at all.

Until they brought the stretcher out, the body completely covered by a white sheet. Dante swallowed, still seeing the form of the collapsed old woman on the couch. DiLorenzo turned white, stopping the paramedics to put his hand over the body. He said one word, "Momma."

Dante turned away, feeling like shit. This was a private family moment, not something he should intrude on.

But he still had a job to do. He swallowed down his regrets and turned back to Bea. "Listen, I know this was a shitty morning, but now that I have your number, maybe could I call you later?"

Seize opportunities. That's what Janet told him. Dante had to remember these were criminals. DiLorenzo had been responsible for the murder of hundreds of people. It didn't matter that he grieved the loss of his mother. The law didn't take time off for grief.

Bea bit her lip as she stared at him. For a moment, it seemed like she was looking through him, seeing something he couldn't see. Then she nodded. "I'd like that. Maybe text first?"

"Of course," he agreed. Things would get messy now—a viewing and then a funeral. Finding time to fit in another date might be difficult. That didn't mean Dante couldn't give his respects at the viewing. He'd have to text Bea for the information later. It would give him another excuse to talk to her.

There were still four weeks to the wedding of Bea's brother. Would they cancel it after this? That would put a wrinkle in his plans.

"You can text me, too. If you need me." He tried to put a bit of shyness in his voice. Like he still liked her, but didn't want to intrude at the moment.

To his relief, that got a smile out of her. "Thank you, really."

Cars pulled up, even coming up the wrong way on the one-way street. More members of the Family. Dante needed to take this opportunity to escape. He hadn't established himself enough yet to be introduced to anyone else.

"I'll text you." He promised Bea before leaving.

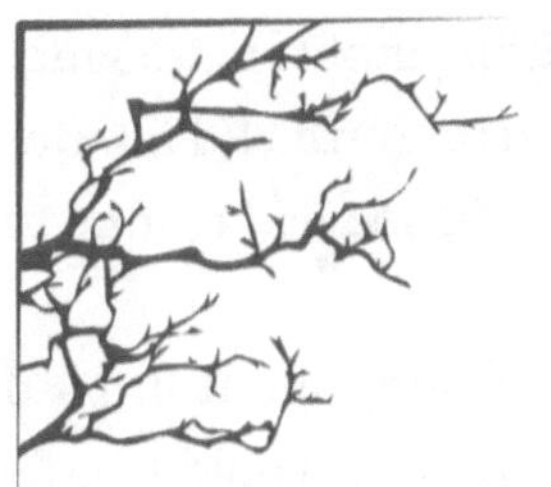

Chapter 11

The pencil scraped a line down the length of the paper, too crisp and perfect for what Bea wanted to achieve. Somehow, she needed to replicate the glint in her grandmother's eyes—the way they sparkled when she laughed. But Bea was only a passing artist, not a fantastic one. And her nonna could not be captured so easily on the page. The woman had been far too full of life for that.

Had been. Past tense.

Bea threw the pencil across her bedroom. It hit one box and landed somewhere with a clatter.

She dropped to her knees, a choking sob clogging her throat. The tears she'd been holding back all afternoon finally came, rolling down her cheeks in huge drops that seemed never ending. *I was going to tell her no.* She had gone there with every intention of telling Nonna that she couldn't be her heir, that she didn't have the stomach to do what needed to be done to protect the family.

But now? Knowing that someone had killed her nonna? Fury burned in her belly and Bea would do whatever it took to find the killer and make them pay.

If only she knew how. Bea trusted the instincts that Nonna blessed her with, the gut feeling that told her Nonna's death hadn't been natural. Even without that, Bea knew Nonna would never have let anyone else have that spell book. It had been destined for Bea, and no one else had the right.

Without that book and without Nonna to guide her, Bea did not know what to do next. How was she going to find Nonna's killer? The answer had to be with magic. Bea could feel the power thrumming inside her, like an overly filled mason jar of tomato sauce that would spill everywhere if someone tried to screw the lid on. But Bea had no way to pour the power out of her, and she had no one to ask.

She hadn't even had the chance to talk to Daddy about it. He'd put her in her car and told her to drive home. That he would handle dealing with the police and the EMTs and...the body. Bea's place was home with Mom to great the parade of family members who would visit to offer condolences once they heard the news.

Bea got to her feet and wiped her eyes. She'd been hiding in her room since she made it back here. One of Daddy's men had followed her car the entire way back. Bea had waved once she'd pulled into the driveway, but it was only once she'd gone inside that the car had pulled away. Daddy would always make sure she was safe.

But he couldn't protect Nonna from whoever had hurt her, which meant magic had to be involved somehow. Bea remembered the smell of lilies that had dogged her all morning. That scent had been a warning, one she'd been too inexperienced to understand.

She took a seat in front of her desk, putting her sketchbook back where it belonged. She tapped the keys on her laptop, waking it up. For a moment, she considered searching the web with her questions. But the answers wouldn't be found on Google. If anything, there could be some dark web subreddit or a witch discord that she needed to be invited to.

Then again, if other witches were like Nonna, they might not be on the internet at all.

"What the hell am I going to do?" Bea buried her face in her hands, fighting back tears yet again.

A soft knock on the door broke into her freak out session. "Bea? It's me." Connie's voice came from the other side.

A wave of relief flowed through her. Of course, she could rely on her cousin for help. Why hadn't she thought of that sooner? Bea got up and threw her bedroom door open. "Get in here."

Connie blinked owlishly at her. Her eyes were red rimmed, and Bea felt a pang of guilt. She was about to burden Connie with the reality of magic and Nonna's death, and she hadn't even considered Connie's own grief.

Bea shut and locked the door behind Connie. When she turned around, her cousin caught her up in a surprise hug. "Oh, Bea. I'm so sorry that you had to be the one to find her."

The body had been so cold. Bea shook herself, holding on to Connie for warmth. No, that body hadn't been her nonna. Her nonna's bright spirit, that sparkly purple aura, that was gone, moved on to wherever.

"Who told you?" Bea pulled away from Connie. She hadn't even had the chance to tell her cousin herself.

"My mom. Everyone is talking about it downstairs."

Bea shuddered. All the more reason to stay up here where it was safe. "Listen, I have something to tell you." She sat on her still unmade bed while Connie took the computer chair.

"It's okay if you need to talk about it," Connie said encouragingly.

She was so sweet. But right now, Bea didn't need sweet. She needed someone to conspire with, another person to help her figure out how to avenge their nonna. "Just listen, okay?" Bea put her hands through her hair, knowing she was turning it into a tangled nest, but unable to help herself.

"Yesterday, do you remember when I disappeared?"

"When you met that cute guy that everyone is also talking about?" Connie asked, a slight smile on her face. "The one who came to your rescue today?"

"You know, for a family that relies on secrets, everyone has a big mouth," Bea mumbled. How many people had seen Dante at her grandmother's that morning? She'd contemplated texting him, but even though he'd been so nice earlier, he was still some guy. It wasn't like she could spill all of her family's secrets to a stranger.

Bea tried to get back on track. "No, earlier, when I went into the club to get a band-aid. I saw...something." She tried to find the words to explain what she saw - her father and his bodyguards and poor Vito. The more she spoke, the wider Connie's eyes got.

"And then Nonna told me about being the family Strega," Bea kept talking, the words coming faster because if she didn't get them out now, when she had a captive audience, Bea knew they wouldn't have another chance.

Connie stopped her, coming to kneel in front of Bea and taking her hands in hers. "Bea, listen, I know you've had quite a shock today..."

Bea blinked. "What?"

"I mean, I'm sure it wasn't easy seeing your dad doing that. There's a reason they keep the family business at the club, you know? But your mind has experienced a trauma. Of course, it's going to look for an explanation for what doesn't make sense. And it doesn't make sense that Nonna died after we just spent the day with her."

For a moment Bea couldn't understand what the hell was going on. It never occurred to her that her cousin, her best friend, wouldn't believe her. Of course, Connie would understand. Of course, she'd help Bea figure this out. The alternative simply wasn't possible.

Only now, it seemed it was.

"I'm not imagining anything," Bea protested. "I saw Nonna do magic. She awakened my powers. I knew something was wrong before I found her."

Connie nodded, the look on her face sympathetic. "Look, there's probably a reasonable explanation for what you saw..."

If only Bea could show her. If she herself could do something, anything. Bea squeezed Connie's hands tightly, willing her to see the same aura around Bea that she'd seen around their grandmother.

Connie frowned, blinking her eyes rapidly. Her shoulders went stiff and her mouth opened into a little O, but no sound came out. Ah ha, so maybe she did see something.

"Beatrice! Connie!" Aunt Julia's voice came from the hallway as she rapped on the door. "Come downstairs. The DiStasi's are here."

Connie pulled away from Bea, shaking her hands as if they burned. "Coming, mama!"

I got you, Bea grinned, knowing that Connie had to have seen something. Her smile faded as she followed her cousin downstairs. Too bad that was the only thing in her bag of tricks. Not that she wanted to go out burning anyone's eyeballs out for proof.

Downstairs in the living room, her mother held court from her favorite white leather chair, the one Bea was never allowed to sit in. On the glass coffee table sat a bottle of Sambuca and several shot glasses filled with the clear liquor. Signora DiStasi and her two daughters sat on the couch across from Mom, wearing sympathetic looks on their faces. Bea didn't know them well, but that would be the norm for the next few days—those with obligations to the DiLorenzos would come to show their faces, in order to give the proper respect.

This was just the beginning. There would be more at the viewing and funeral. Bea swallowed hard at the thought. It didn't feel real.

She said hello like a dutiful daughter and sat next to Connie on the couch. Her mother thanked the DiStasis for their gift—apparently a tray of baked ziti in the fridge, and the small talk continued for another hour before the family got up to leave.

Bea sighed in relief when the door closed behind them. Bea let her shoulders relax and dropped the polite smile she'd kept on her face the entire visit. Mom and Aunt Julia talked about who to expect next. Bea couldn't sit here for that, so she made herself useful and collected the used shot glasses on the table. They were sticky and smelled overly sweet from the licorice liquor.

Bea had never liked licorice, and now she questioned every scent, considering if it was a message or if it were only the drops of liquor spilled onto the table.

"I got it," she told Connie when her cousin offered to help. Bea needed the moment to collect her thoughts.

But it was not to be. When she got to the kitchen with the dirty glasses, she met her brother coming in through the garage. Mike wore nice slacks and a white button-down shirt, but the shirt had the top three buttons undone and the sleeves rolled up to his elbows. He always chafed at the suit Dad made him wear when they were working, complaining that it was old-fashioned.

Mike bypassed her without a glance, heading straight for the sink, where he began washing his hands. He looked flushed and sweaty, his dark hair mussed and out of place.

"Where have you been?" Bea put the glasses down on the island, now unable to put them in the sink like she planned. Mike hadn't been with Daddy at Nonna's house, and he hadn't been home when she got back.

Mike finished at the sink, wiping his hands on the dishtowel next to the drying rack. He used it to wipe his forehead as he turned to face her. "Out working. Somebody has to keep the wheels turning while Dad is occupied."

She felt a chill go down her spine. Bea leaned into the feeling, wondering if this was one of those same instincts that her grandmother had warned her about, the knowing that had led her to her grandmother's deathbed. But nothing followed the chill, no weird scents or anything like that.

Maybe it was only her now realizing that when her brother said working, he meant doing whatever they did. Her mind went back to

Vito, kneeling on the floor of the club's backroom and Bea shook her head to get rid of the vision. "Isn't this a good day of all days to take off?" she snapped. "Our nonna died."

Mike opened the fridge and emerged with a can of beer. "Come on, Bea. She was in her eighties. Old people die all the time."

His words hit her with the force of their wrongness. Bea actually had to take a step back from him. "How can you say that?" Tears threatened again and Bea blinked them away as best she could. The last thing she wanted was to look weak in front of her brother. He'd never let her live it down.

Mike never could stand weakness.

He shrugged and opened his beer. "Look, I'm sorry that you had to be the one to find her..."

Bea threw up her hands. "Does the entire state know about that?"

"You told Mom. That's equal to getting out a megaphone in front of the church." Mike shrugged. He set his beer on the island before he turned back to the fridge and opened it again. "We got anything to eat? I'm starving."

"The DiStasis brought ziti." Bea's own stomach twisted in knots. She wasn't sure she'd be able to eat a thing ever again, and it was well past dinnertime.

Mike eagerly started removing containers of food from the fridge, and Bea couldn't be around him any longer. She ducked out of the kitchen, but couldn't get back upstairs without passing her mom, Aunt Julia, and Connie. Bea didn't want to talk to any of them.

Connie's betrayal still stung, along with Mike's callous dismissal of Nonna's death. Was Bea the only one who understood the implications? Her grandmother had been protecting them all with her magic. She'd expected Bea to take over, and of course, Bea had no damn clue what to do.

She slipped out the back door to the deck overlooking the backyard. The fresh evening air helped clear her thoughts, especially with the biting wind. Bea shivered and then dropped into one of the lawn chairs.

Her phone dug into her side. Bea pulled it from her pocket and impulsively sent a text to Dante.

You busy?

She watched the three dots as she waited for his words to appear.

Not too busy to text, he sent back. *How are you doing?*

Honestly, not great. She deleted the words at least once before finally hitting send.

Anything I can do to help?

She smiled. A stranger was far better at comforting her than any of her family members. Of course, Dante didn't know her, didn't know about Bea's internal turmoil. It was nice to have someone outside of the family drama who thought she was simply grieving her grandmother, not despairing over failing her family.

Glad to have someone to talk to, she responded. *Today was bad, but the rest of the week is going to be worse. Funerals suck.*

He sent a series of sad looking emojis that made her grin. Then, after some typing, the words finally appeared. *I can come to pay my respects. And hold your hand if you need it.*

Those tears finally showed up again. Bea drew her knees up and propped her head on her arms. God, it hurt so much. She'd been telling herself it was all about the witchcraft and the family business, but really, Bea ached for her grandmother. She'd never bake bread in Nonna's kitchen again. Never watch her patiently explain a new crochet stitch. Never taste her homemade cooking or spend Christmas Eve helping her Nonna cook the feast that would serve the entire family.

I'll let you know, she finally told Dante before putting her phone away.

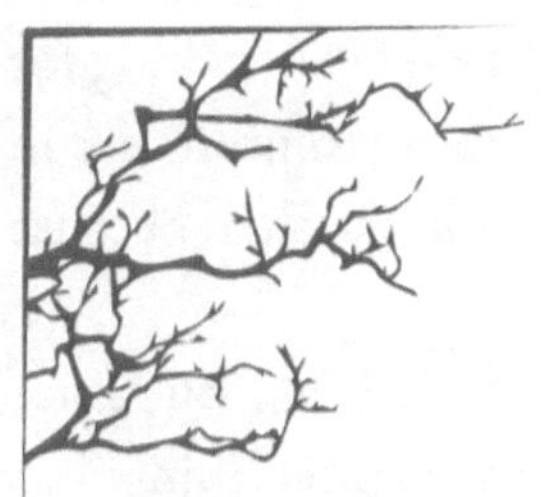

Chapter 12

On the day of her grandmother's viewing, five days after Bea had found the body, she woke up without her protection charm. She didn't notice at first, not until she showered and missed the gold chain around her neck. After a moment of panic, fearing it had gone down the drain, she retraced her steps and found it on her bed, under the pillow. The chain had broken, and the charm itself had snapped in two.

"Shit, shit, shit, this is really bad." Bea dropped onto the edge of the bed, cradling the last of her Nonna's protection in her hands. Did Nonna's death mean her spells all died with her?

Nonna had made charms like this for all of them—her cousins and uncles. Did they all break, too? She reached for her phone to text Connie, but then stopped before she could even get the words typed out.

Connie didn't believe in magic. She thought Bea was delusional. A random text about her necklace breaking would not help the situation. Bea would ask her in person when she saw her cousin later, when she couldn't leave her on read and avoid the question.

It wasn't like Bea could offer a solution. She didn't know a damn thing about creating magical protection charms. None of her "good instincts" could pass for actual knowledge.

Still, she couldn't sit around and pretend nothing was wrong. Bea put the shattered necklace in her jewelry box. Her neck felt naked without the chain that had been against her skin since she was an infant.

Damn it. Bea wiped at her eyes. Great, she was crying again.

And she still had no clue what to do next. She'd been waiting for a sign—a dream or another warning smell, anything to point her in the right direction. Apparently, magic didn't work like that, because right now she had nothing.

If only she'd been able to talk to Daddy about it all. But since Nonna's death, he'd been out of the house, managing "things" as Mom put it. That was her way of saying more than just organizing the funeral—he had business to attend to, Family business.

But if the protection charms Nonna had made for her own blood family had failed, what did that mean for whatever spells she had crafted for the business? The best-case scenario would be if it negated the spells. *God, imagine if they all started going off?* Dozens of men going down, grasping their burning eyes, like Vito.

Bea swallowed. No. That couldn't happen. She had to talk to Daddy. He'd be at the viewing. She'd be able to steal him away there. Bea hoped the churning sensation in her stomach didn't mean something horrible was going to happen today, too.

THE FUNERAL HOME WAS in Newark, a few blocks from her grandmother's house. Bea drove her mother, although every mile she wished she'd let Mom take her own car. She had enough to worry about without Mom's constant criticism. Then again, at least it distracted Bea from worrying.

The complaining had started the moment her mother came down the stairs and took a long look at Bea. "You're wearing that?"

Bea wore dress slacks and an oversized cardigan, all of which were black. The perfect outfit for a viewing. Sure, it wasn't her mother's pencil skirt and blazer, but Bea would look awful in that. "What's wrong with it?"

"Nothing, nothing," Mom muttered as she moved past her. "You could be so pretty if you made an effort."

"It's a viewing. Who am I looking pretty for?" Bea snapped back.

The conversation continued in the car, for the entire half hour drive to Newark. "You never know who you're going to meet. Didn't they make a movie about that? Four funerals and a marriage?"

"Four Weddings and a Funeral," Bea corrected, gripping the steering wheel tightly. "And I don't care what anyone thinks about my clothes."

"People are going to judge you no matter what you wear. Why make it easy for them?"

The point was that Bea shouldn't care about strangers' opinions. But that seemed to be a concept Mom couldn't understand, no matter how many times Bea voiced it. Despite the distracting conversation, her heart raced the moment she pulled into the lot behind the funeral home.

She'd been here a few times before, enough to know the drill. An attendant moved aside the chain that blocked the driveway from the members of the public and let Bea pull her car in. The building itself was tall and covered in white stone with stained glass windows that looked out of place beside all the other businesses on Pacific Street.

Mom led the way to the front entrance. Before opening the door, she turned to Bea and held up one hand. "Remember, everyone will be looking at you."

She had to mean more than a simple 'behave yourself.' Bea swallowed, a pit developing in her belly. Everyone knew she'd found Nonna's body. There would be whispers. People noticing Bea who had never paid her any attention before. And all Bea could think about was if that sour feeling in her stomach meant something horrible was about to happen.

She followed Mom inside, hoping to stick close. But then the funeral director—a tall, imposing man in a silver suit—came up to them. "Signora DiLorenzo, if we could speak privately for a moment? We need to go over the arrangements."

"Of course." Mom gave Bea one last look before disappearing with the man into the office, just to the right of the entrance, leaving Bea alone in the lobby.

She walked silently on the green and floral carpet, moving to the wooden table set up against one wall with the guest book and the tiny prayer cards with her grandmother's picture on one side. Bea picked one up, running her fingers over the plastic. She did not know where they'd gotten this photo from. The photo appeared to be professionally taken, with a blurred blue background. Her grandmother smiled at the camera, the light in her eyes so alive. She had crossed her hands in front of her, reminding Bea of her own pose in her graduation photo.

"Bea!" Connie hissed, her head ducking out from a doorway down the hallway.

She hadn't spoken to her cousin since Connie had decided Bea was crazy and magic didn't exist. But damn, she needed her right now, no matter if Connie didn't believe yet. Bea would eventually convince her. She had to.

Bea slipped the card into her back pocket. "Coming!"

The scent of flowers struck her before even making it to the room. It stopped her in her tracks for a moment. The last time a scent had hit her this strong, it had been the warning about her grandmother's death. Bea shook her head. They were at a funeral home. Of all places, other than a florist's shop, flowers would be normal here.

But that meant she wouldn't be able to tell if another smell tried to warn her of something.

Once she got inside, nearly knocking over the wooden placard with Nonna's name on it, Bea understood the cloying scent. Floral arrangements covered both walls, leading up the row of chairs to the coffin at the front of the room. She was thankful for the explosion of color—red and white and pink roses and wreaths made into a variety of shapes. It kept her from looking at the body.

"You okay?" Connie took her aside before Bea could take more than a few steps inside. Her cousin wore a black knee length dress with a delicate crocheted black shawl over her shoulders. She'd pulled her hair back into a tight bun, which aged her to where she looked older than Bea.

Bea's belly twisted, like she'd eaten something bad that settled like a stone inside her. She had to swallow a few times before she could speak. "Oh, hell no."

The last thing she wanted to do was go up to the coffin, kneel at the hassock set up there, and stare at her dead grandmother's face and pretend to pray. At viewings, she usually bypassed that step, immediately going to the family to offer her condolences. But in this case, she was the family that was due to be consoled by strangers. She'd have to spend the two hours sitting up in the chairs right in front. There was no avoiding looking at her dead grandmother.

"It's going to be okay," Connie said, and Bea allowed herself to believe it would be. "Sit with me."

Bea took the out and followed her cousin back up to the front, where her Aunt Julia and Connie's brothers were already sitting. They sat in the row right behind them, still technically where they belonged, but not in the first row. She stared at her hands, unwilling to look up at first.

They were piping in some kind of music through the sound system. After a moment of listening to the instrumental song, she turned to Connie and asked, "Is this a cover of 'My Heart Will Go On?'"

Connie tilted her head to one side, listening for a moment. "Oh my God, I think it is."

"A little bit inappropriate?" Bea couldn't help the giggle that escaped her. Connie joined in, and Aunt Julia turned around to give both of them a warning look. Despite that, it felt good to be giggling with her cousin again. No matter what, she had Connie beside her.

Bea sat back, her gaze finally going to the coffin above. They'd picked out a good one, all dark polished wood with red velvet cushions. The body nestled inside didn't resemble her Nonna at all. It was almost a relief that it did not. Her hair was all wrong, and they'd used too much makeup. Because of that, Bea could bear sitting there a little while longer.

And she had to, because the guests had filtered in. There were those she knew, paisans from the feast only a few days before. There were men who clearly were in the same business as her father. They wore dark suits, and traveled in packs, only speaking to her father and uncles before making their respects in front of the coffin and taking seats in one of the many rows behind her.

The room was chilly, the air conditioner blowing in above her. Bea shivered even in her sweater. She stood as mourners approached them, this time a group of three women she didn't know, all dressed in black. They were old, yes, with silver hair and stooped over postures. But something about their faces seemed almost ageless. They could be anywhere from sixty to ninety.

"So sorry," one of them murmured to her Aunt Julia, before coming around and approaching Bea and Connie. "Beatrice, you look so much like your grandmother." Like Nonna, she spoke with an Italian lilt to her voice.

"Um, thanks?" Bea frowned. She stood up to shake the woman's hand and gasped at the jolt that went down her arm. For a moment, a very brief moment, she saw the telltale purple aura of a witch. Then it disappeared, like someone had shut off a switch. From the smile the woman gave Bea, it looked like she knew exactly what she'd done.

Nonna said powerful witches could hide their auras. She never mentioned being about to turn it on and off. What did this woman see when she touched Bea?

"Does this mean you are the one we should do business with?" The woman raised her eyebrow.

Her words made Bea's heart stutter. She opened her mouth, but couldn't think of a response. She should say yes, pretend she knew what she was doing. But Bea couldn't speak.

"Enough, Giuseppina." One of the other women came over. "I'm sure it will be obvious enough once the funeral is over."

None of them spoke to Connie. They shuffled off as a group and made for the exit.

"That was weird," Connie whispered.

Yes, it was, but especially to Connie, because she didn't believe. These women had come to check out Bea, to see if she had inherited her grandmother's magic and had taken over her role as the family Strega. Had one of them been the one to steal the spell book? If they were witches, why would they need it? God, she wished she could share her fears with Connie. Not being able to share this with her made Bea feel alone, isolated, in a way she never had before when surrounded by family.

She couldn't let them leave. Bea had to talk to them, to get some answers. "I need water," she told Connie before she stood and made her way through the crowd. It seemed like everyone got in her way to block her, stopping her for a few words of condolences before she could catch up with the three witches.

She got held up by Mike and his fiancée, who were still standing in the entranceway. Lucy was wailing into a handkerchief—an actual cloth handkerchief and not a tissue like a normal person. She was moaning about how the wedding was only weeks away and Nonna wouldn't be there to see it. And how unfair it was.

Always about herself and that damn wedding. Bea clenched her fingers into fists and forced herself through the milling groups of people and out the door. She couldn't stand it for another damn moment. There were too many people filling it with voices and tears and it swelled her head like she had a sinus cold.

Once in the lobby, she took a deep breath and glanced around. The crowd had spilled out here, making it hard to find the women she was looking for. Out of the corner of her eye, Bea saw them dart down the hallway toward the back entrance of the funeral home. Time to get some answers.

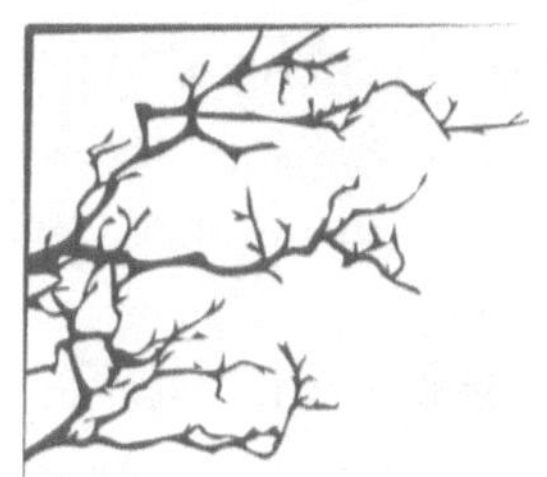

Chapter 13

Bea moved against the crowd, murmuring excuse me and thank you to the people in her way. She finally broke through, darting down the narrow passageway that led to the back emergency exit. But it was empty. She'd missed her chance.

Should she run out into the parking lot? The women were so far ahead of her that she couldn't possibly catch up. Could they have used magic to block her way to keep her from following? Was that even possible?

She leaned against the wall and tried to take a deep breath. "Nonna," she whispered. "What do you want me to do?"

The back door swinging open interrupted her moment of quiet. Bea straightened in shock, expecting it to be the witches returning. Apparently, her prayer to Nonna hadn't worked, unless Nonna wanted her to speak with Father Stefano from the church. He walked in dressed in his typical black cassock, looking like a priest from an old-time movie.

He smiled at the sight of her. "Beatrice. How are you managing in this time of grief, my child?" He reached over to touch her arm, squeezing it a bit too hard.

Bea winced and tried to pull out of his grip. She'd forgotten how handsy he could be, since she'd been going to church on campus instead of here at home. Normally she would have dodged that arm grasp. She opened her mouth to tell him she was fine, when something stopped her—a scent, growing strong now, that had no reason to be there—garlic. Not the sweet scent of cooking garlic, but the kind that happened when garlic burned, turned black and ruined

85

an entire pot of sauce. It was thick and sour, and clung to her skin like it would never come off.

And as if the scent had unlocked a door inside her, she remembered...

They had been in Nonna's kitchen. The floor was still black and white checkerboard, so she was a child at the time. Nonna hummed as she cooked, the kitchen her domain as she danced between table, counter, and stove. Bea handed over each ingredient when asked.

She had to stand on a chair to stir the gravy, the wooden spoon heavy in her tiny hands as she dragged it around the pot to her Nonna's specifications.

"You must feel the sauce." Nonna added a handful of fresh parsley leaves to the mixture. "That is why I can't teach you the recipe. It must become part of you."

Bea had nodded very seriously, as if she understood. But perhaps with the logic of a child, it made far more sense than if she'd learned as an adult seeking a recipe.

"Herbs are very special." Nonna hesitated for a moment. Then she helped Bea off the chair and led her over to her spice rack, an impressive wooden structure that took up nearly a half of her counter space. All the tiny glass jars were labeled with Nonna's careful tiny handwriting, a cursive that Bea still could barely read.

"When it's time, you will remember," Nonna said softly. Then she named each herb, and its property, before asking Bea to repeat it.

She had, her tiny lips forming words she didn't understand.

Burned garlic for guilt. Sour for regret.

That was what she scented around the priest now, although from the pleasant smile on his face, one could never know the miasma of darkness swirling around him. His hand was still on Bea's forearm, and she got a flash of a dark and slimy aura, and somehow, she knew, she just knew.

"How could you?" she snapped at him. "They were children."

His smile froze in place. "I'm afraid I don't know what you are talking about."

Anger filled her belly, a righteous indignation that there was nothing she could do. Bea had this knowledge, given to her by her grandmother's gifts, and this asshole would walk away as he had his entire life with no consequences. She wanted to take, to hurt, and she snapped out the first words that fell out of her lips.

"You stole their voices. I'll take yours." Pressure formed in her forehead, and the surrounding air grew heavy, as if time itself had stopped.

Warmth flooded her chest, and for a moment, she felt some of that sizzling power inside her do more than swirl around aimlessly. Instead of bubbling over, it had a release, like a steam valve, and a place to go—the guilty man standing in front of her.

Father Stefano blinked and shook his head. He seemed dazed.

"Father, thank you for coming." Dad had somehow found them, coming down the hallway with Mike, who finally left his fiancé's side. He probably couldn't take the whining either.

Bea rubbed her forehead, a headache pulsing behind her eyes. God, what the hell was wrong with her?

Father Stefano opened his mouth to speak, but then coughed. He looked puzzled and then tried again. Suddenly, he doubled over with wracking coughs, Dad pounding on his back. "Mikey, take him to get some water."

"Sure, Dad. This way, Father." Mike took the priest's arm and led him away. He looked back once, a strange expression on his face as he glanced at Bea.

The coughing, that couldn't be because of her, could it? Bea swallowed, tasting that garlic at the back of her throat. She hadn't meant to do anything, not really, but she couldn't let him go without him knowing that she knew what he'd done, that he'd have to pay for his crimes.

This was why she needed to talk to Daddy. Bea moved in front of him so he couldn't follow Mike down the hall. "Daddy, can we talk?" She hugged her arms around her body, feeling cold all over.

"Sure, sweetheart, what's the problem?" He seemed distracted, not looking at her, but over her shoulder to the lobby beyond.

Daddy would know what to do. He always did. Bea swallowed and tried to find the right words. "Before she died, Nonna told me about being the family Strega."

His attention snapped completely on to her, his eyes wide as if she'd shocked him. Had he not known? "She shouldn't have done that."

"She was going to teach me," the words came out in a rush. "I was supposed to go back to her house. That's why I was there when I found her."

"Come here." Dad held out his arms and pulled her into a hug, stopping the flood of words for the moment.

Bea closed her eyes and sunk into the warmth, breathing deeply to take in the scent of his cologne and...cinnamon? When had Daddy started smelling like cinnamon? Once again, her senses were telling her something. It took a moment to remember what her grandmother had said about that particular spice.

Love. Cinnamon meant love.

She relaxed. Daddy loved her. He'd fix this. "She awakened my powers. She expected me to take her place when she was gone. She was supposed to train me. I think, I think someone killed her."

Daddy went stiff and pulled away from her. He touched her chin to make sure she looked him in the eye. "Sweetheart, you let me worry about that." For a moment, she saw something flash in his gaze. Anger? Did Daddy know who'd hurt Nonna?

"I need someone to help me," Bea explained. "I don't know how to use magic and I might accidentally hurt someone." She'd done something to the priest, she knew it. Bea didn't know what, but her instincts had gone off and Bea hadn't put the brakes on fast enough.

"Baby girl, do you trust me?" Daddy gave her his best smile, the one he reserved only for her.

"Of course."

He nodded. "Then do you think I'd let you get mixed up in this without having a backup plan? Nonna isn't the only witch in the Family."

He must mean one of the three women who'd come to pay respects. Bea nodded to show she understood.

"I've got someone I'd like to introduce you to, but not here. This isn't the time or place. Let me get through the funeral first, okay? His face fell, and he looked so tired.

Bea shouldn't forget that he'd lost his mother. And he had this whole thing to arrange, the viewings, the funeral, the transporting of the body back to Italy. Somehow, while also managing the family business. Damn it, he had much bigger things to worry about. "I'm sorry."

"Hey, don't be sorry." He patted her cheek. "I will always make things right for you. You got it?"

She had to smile at that. "I got it."

"All right. Let's go back. People are gonna notice if I'm gone for too long."

She followed by his side, aware of how people stared at her, especially as her father escorted her back into the room with the coffin. The mourners who had come early had gone, and there was a new crop of strangers to hear condolences from. Her dad maneuvered her next to her mother, standing at the front of the room. Mike and Lucy came over and stood on the other side of Dad, and for the next few moments, she was too busy accepting sympathies to think about anything else.

Eventually, they sat back down, and Father Stefano entered the room to give the blessing. He had a small black book in one hand, which he paged through for a moment. The crowd grew silent, waiting. "Brothers and sisters," he began. Then he coughed. He cleared his throat and tried again. But the words caught in his mouth and nothing came out.

Bea realized with dawning horror that her worst fears had come true. When she snapped at the priest, she'd literally stolen his words. *Oh God.*

Father Stefano doubled over and started coughing again, wracking heaving coughs. Her dad jumped up to help, along with a few others.

"Someone get that man some water!"

"What's going on?"

Bea took advantage of the chaos to slip out of her seat and out of the room. Her body flushed with heat and guilt. This was exactly what her grandmother had warned her about. Don't make any wishes, she'd said. She probably should have added, 'don't accidentally curse priests you suspect of child abuse.'

For a moment Bea wished she'd done more than stolen his voice. *No, stop it, that's what got you into this in the first place!*

She ran down the hall, to the front doors of the funeral home, and right into the waiting arms of Dante.

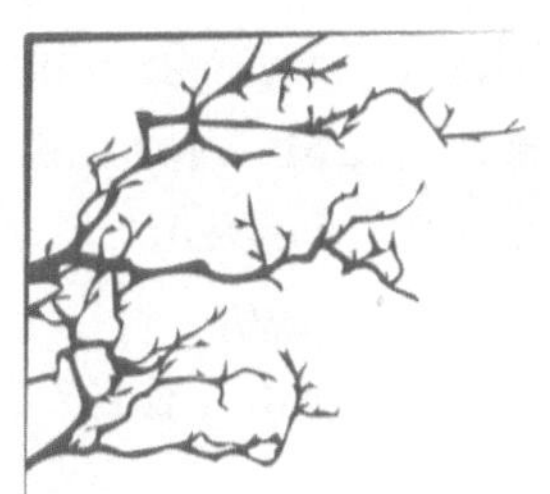

Chapter 14

Dante took a step back as Bea rushed out of the funeral home and tumbled against his chest. He grasped her by her shoulders to steady her. "Hey, are you all right?"

She trembled in his arms and when Bea looked up to meet his gaze, her eyes were wide and her face drained of all color. Something was horribly wrong. It made the hackles on the back of his neck rise. Who had hurt her?

She let out a little laugh and took a step away from him. Bea wrapped her arms around her chest, as if protecting herself. "Why am I always running in to you?"

"I guess I'm a magnet." Dante chuckled at his own joke, but didn't miss the way her smile didn't seem to reach her eyes. He stepped aside, putting his hands in the pockets of his third best suit. It was the only one the FBI deemed fit for his cover. The others were too nice. "I was coming to pay my respects, but I didn't want to show up too early."

She ran a hand through her hair and looked behind her. The door opened to let someone else out, and Dante had a clear view of the packed lobby inside. "Oh. Right." Her lips trembled, and she looked right on the verge of tears.

He really needed to get in there and start making connections with Bea's family. The only event more attended than a wedding would be a funeral. He wasn't sure if he'd be welcome there, since he'd only recently been introduced to the family, but viewings were open to all.

But looking at Bea's crestfallen face? The way she seemed moments away from breaking apart? He couldn't force his way inside and not see what was wrong. "Hey. Do you need a moment away from all of that?" He gestured at the funeral home.

She turned back toward him with shining eyes. "Yeah. I think I need that."

"Let's go for a quick walk around the block? Maybe get a soda or something?" Dante gestured at the convenience store down a few storefronts from where they were standing.

They walked side by side down the city street, the sun still beating down in the early evening. Cars beeped and jostled for position on the road next to them as rush hour got fully underway. Yet there was privacy somehow, being anonymous as they walked by the laundromat, an electronics store, and then finally the convenience store.

"Let me buy you a soda." Dante gestured inside. "Or, um, maybe a sports drink? Times like these, you need to hydrate."

"Soda is fine. I'll take a Coke. Thank you."

Dante darted in to grab them both cans of Coke. This store was tinier than the bodega across the street that carried basic groceries as well. Here people came for cigarettes or newspapers, or to grab some lottery tickets. He paid for the drinks on his FBI card and grabbed two straws on the way out.

Bea waited outside for him. He let out a sigh of relief that she was still there. Some of the color had come back in her face and she didn't look so brittle any more. "Here you go." He handed her the soda and cracked open his own can.

Bea fumbled a bit, getting the straw inside her can. She took a sip and gave him a thumbs up. "Yay for hydration." Dante found himself fascinated by the way her lips closed around the straw.

They walked a bit more, turning the corner to go around the block. The funeral parlor was a long way behind them, far enough to be another world. "Are you all right? Stupid question, I know, but…"

She coughed in response. Cleared her throat, then tried again, but she coughed this time too. Soda probably went down the wrong pipe. Bea clasped her hand over her mouth, her eyes wide.

"Bea?"

She took a large gulp of her soda, swallowing a few times before finally speaking again. "I'm sorry. It's been harder than I expected. Seeing her like that."

"I can imagine."

"And then everyone's staring at me. I know they're whispering 'she's the one who found the body' and I want to scream. And if they're not talking about me, they're talking to my brother's fiancé, who will not shut up about her wedding." Bea took a deep breath. "I'm sorry. You didn't sign up for all of this."

Dante took a risk by reaching over and taking her free hand in his. He squeezed gently, giving what comfort he could. "I guess a viewing makes for a terrible second date."

"Two stars, would not recommend."

He couldn't help but laugh at that. "I'll do better next time." He held his breath, wondering if she would protest another date. However, she didn't let go of his hand.

Bea looked behind them, and then around, as if checking that they were alone. There were other people walking down this street, although it had a quieter, more residential vibe than the road the funeral home was on. "I'm going to tell you something, but you're going to think I'm weird."

"I'd never think that."

She shook her head. "It's just. I don't think my grandmother died of natural causes. I think someone else had been there before I got there."

Dante straightened his shoulders. What she said was entirely logical, since her family had a lot of enemies. He had seen no signs of foul play at the scene, but of course, someone could have smothered the poor woman and only an autopsy would pick that up. But he couldn't act like the FBI agent now. Bea needed a concerned potential boyfriend, one that respected her opinions.

"What makes you think that?"

"There was something she was supposed to give me," Bea said slowly, clearly choosing her words with care. "It's part of the reason I had gone to her place first. But before you came, I checked, and it wasn't in the spot where she'd left it yesterday."

"Something valuable?" Dante asked. She probably meant jewelry or something like that. He didn't know why she didn't just say that, though.

Bea nodded. "I think so."

"Something somebody would kill for?" Newark wasn't a low crime city, but these few blocks, belonging as they did to the DiLorenzo family, tended to be safer than most parts of the city. The odds of someone breaking in and stealing whatever it was Bea was expecting to get from her grandmother weren't low, but they'd probably leave far more evidence behind if this had been a smash and grab.

"Oh, I don't know. I told you it was weird. I have this feeling, this intuition, you know? She wasn't supposed to die that day."

"Who else knew about this thing?" Dante tried to logic it out. Who were their suspects? If it was something meant for Bea, then did her cousins also know about it?

Bea opened her mouth and then closed it. "I don't know."

"Did your grandmother have any enemies?" he asked seriously. Dante may know she did, but Bea didn't know what he knew, so he had to play this smart.

"That's an odd question." Bea stopped walking and gave him a considering look.

Sweat gathered at Dante's temples. It was far too warm to walk in a suit. "I listen to a lot of true crime podcasts while I work."

Bea tilted her head in his direction, as if conceding the point. She took another long sip of her soda before responding. "The thing is... Yeah, I think she did have enemies."

"Have you mentioned this to anyone?" Like the police. But Dante knew Bea's father had dealt with the cops yesterday, men who were part of the local force that were probably on the take. There was a special place in hell for those cops—traitors to law enforcement. If Don DiLorenzo thought his mother had been murdered, the boss of the DiLorenzo family wouldn't take this to the police. He'd handle it himself.

She sighed. "I mentioned it to my dad. I wouldn't say he dismissed me, but I don't think he took it seriously."

"Why not? You have a missing valuable object and you know your grandmother has enemies." Dante counted out the points on one hand.

She hesitated. "It's a bit more complicated than that. Most of my family thinks she was just old, and it was her time, you know? But I can't shake the feeling there was something more involved."

He reached out and touched her shoulder. "Hey, thanks for trusting me with this. Are you going to do anything about it?"

"Right now, I guess I'll leave it up to my dad. I just needed to talk about it, you know?"

"Of course."

They were getting close to the funeral home again, almost finished with their walk. Although Dante knew he needed to get inside and get intel, he wanted this moment to last longer. He enjoyed talking to Bea, especially during this moment of quiet. Once they got inside, that would end. It had been nice to have a simple conversation.

God, when was the last time he'd been on an actual date? Before Quantico, if he wanted to count a proper sit-down movie and dinner type of thing. After going through training, it became very obvious that being in the FBI was hard on the social life. It had never bothered Dante before.

Until he had to start fake-dating for the Bureau.

"You okay?" Bea asked as they passed the parking lot for the funeral home.

He gave her a startled look. "I should be asking you that!"

"You had this sad look on your face." She shrugged. "Thanks, I guess. For being sad on my behalf."

He swallowed hard. Janet would bitch at him for his terrible poker face. Dante scattered about to find a reason and came back to what he'd told Bea on Monday. "Thinking about my grandmother, I guess. Wish I remembered her more."

Bea slowed her step as they got closer to the main entrance. There were several people milling about outside, groups talking in hushed voices. One man stepped out of the group and blocked their path.

"Bean-Bea, who's your friend?"

Dante recognized Bea's older brother, Mike, but he had to pretend he didn't know this man. Mike wore a sharp looking black suit, probably more expensive than anything Dante had in his closet, with a gold watch that glinted as he gestured. It was a far cry from the surveillance photos, which mostly showed him in gym attire. From the way his shoulders filled out that suit jacket, the gym thing clearly paid off.

He's a bully, remember? Dante stepped in front of Bea, knowing he had to show he meant business for their first interaction. "I'm Dante. Who are you?"

She laughed and patted his arm. "It's fine. This is my brother, Mike. Mike, this is Dante. I met him at the feast."

"Right." Mike narrowed his eyes at Dante, looking sleepy and like a shark all at the same time. He had dark hair like Bea, although his was currently slicked back. His features were not only more masculine, they were sharp, threatening where Bea's were soft. "The guy you were with when you found Nonna."

Bea went stiff, her entire demeanor changing. "Mike, come on."

He tilted his chin toward the funeral home. "Go in. Mom is looking for you. I want to have a few words with your friend."

When she hesitated, Dante leaned forward and whispered, "Go ahead, I'll be fine."

I won't be fine. The Don's son, the mafia heir, wanted to have a word with him? Dante was so screwed.

"So, you gotta thing for my sister?" Mike crossed his arms over his chest.

Dante tried to let himself loosen up. He was not supposed to know the man before him was a cold-blooded killer. Did Bea even know? "We just met. I'm still getting to know her."

Mike snorted and laughed as if that were the most ridiculous thing he'd ever heard. "And you show up at her grandmother's wake?"

"I'm here to pay my respects."

"You ever think you have shitty timing? Trying to make time with a girl, and you show up right as she finds her dead grandmother?" Mike had a cold look on his face, like his own words didn't faze him at all. She was his grandmother, too.

"It doesn't mean I should quit." Dante would not back down. That would admit weakness, and one thing that mobsters hated was weakness.

Mike shook his head. "Yeah, you're stubborn as hell. I can respect that." He took a step forward, getting in Dante's face. "Remember, she's my sister. Don't fuck with her. Otherwise, my fist is the least you can look forward to."

Meaning his gun would be next. Dante swallowed hard. "Understood. I have no plans to hurt her."

Liar, liar pants on fire, his brain blared at him. Putting Bea's family in jail would hurt her, and Dante damn well knew it.

Mike didn't seem quite convinced. He held Dante's gaze for a little longer, an epic starting contest with high stakes. Just when Dante was about to blink, Mike grinned and stepped away. "Go on. You're here to pay your respects, right?"

Dante swallowed and tried to regain his composure. He didn't have his sidearm or even any backup right now. Standing toe to toe with a mobster hadn't been on the agenda. Who could blame him for the shaky hands as he walked in to the funeral home?

There were a lot of people in here. Good, that meant he could blend in. He barely remembered his own grandmother's wake, but one memory remained clear. Unable to deal with being in the same room with her body, he'd slipped out and into another room with a closed coffin and a single mourner. That person had no one left to cry for them.

Wasn't this better? A sign of a long life well-lived? He shook his head, pushing down thoughts of who would mourn him if this job went sideways. Dante never thought much about his own mortality, but his boss's insistence on him knowing the stakes of this job had put it in his head.

"There you are." Bea appeared out of nowhere and took his arm. It surprised him as she clutched him tighter. "You look so lost."

He gave her a tight smile. "I don't know anyone else here."

"And I bet my brother gave you the shovel talk." She rolled her eyes. "He's scared away every single one of my boyfriends."

Warmth rushed through him as Dante realized that meant she was putting him in the category of 'boyfriend.' That was good. Good for his assignment. He was better at this than he thought.

"He was a little intimidating," Dante admitted.

She laughed, covering her mouth when they got a few glares. "Come on. I think my dad is going to say a few words, and then they'll close things down for the night."

He nodded and followed her in to the main room. Most of the benches had been taken, and the entire room felt crowded and stuffy. He pulled at his collar. Not even the air conditioner blowing above him could cool the sudden flush that went through his body.

Bea led him to the front where he shook hands with her father, kissed her mother, and mumbled something about being sorry for their loss. He made the sign of the cross while kneeling in front of the coffin and said a quick prayer—he figured he could always use it—before going back to sit with Bea.

Her father moved to stand in front of the coffin and cleared his throat. Immediately, the room went silent. Dante did a quick assessment, picking out the men with guns, especially those who flanked the exits. He recognized the faces he'd memorized; the bodyguards working for DiLorenzo, and some representatives from rival families.

"Thank you all for coming tonight," Bea's father began. "It means a lot to me and my family to see how much my mother meant to so many people."

There were nods and murmurs of agreement from the audience. Bea, sitting to his right, swiped at her eyes. Dante reached out to grab her hand and give it a squeeze. While turning to look at her, he met the eyes of someone he didn't know, a young woman with blond hair swept up into an oddly formal updo for her age. She narrowed her eyes at Dante, and he felt a jolt of ice go through him.

Dante blinked and sat back, trying to shake the cobwebs out of his brain. What the hell was that? And who was she? He'd memorized the faces of everyone in the family.

"...my mother was an incredible woman. It wasn't easy raising three small boys in a new country. But even though we started poor, she really lived out the American dream. Momma always said...she always said..." Don DiLorenzo stopped. He gasped for air and clutched at his chest.

"Michael?" his wife stood from her seat.

He tumbled over and collapsed in front of the coffin.

"Daddy!" Bea screamed.

Dante leaped to his feet, along with everyone else in the room. He darted through the crowd to get to DiLorenzo's side, feeling for a pulse. "Call an ambulance!"

"I'm a doctor." A man kneeled next to Dante and immediately started CPR. Dante sat back and let the man do his thing. His own first aid cert was up to date, but better to let the doctor have at it.

The bodyguards at the door started shooing people out. Dante got to his feet and took a few careful steps away from DiLorenzo and the family that clustered around him. He had no place here.

It seemed Bea thought the same thing. "You should go," she said as she drew up next to him, her hands clasped together in worry.

He wanted to say something like "Call me," or "I'll call you," but before he could even respond to her words, Bea's mother pulled her away. Dante backed away, taking stock of who remained in the room. The rival families had made a break for it—probably not wanting to get caught up in the blame game if Don DiLorenzo died.

Dante frowned as he followed the crowd out of the room. Sirens wailed from outside.

It seemed like the DiLorenzo's were having especially bad luck. Shit happened; he knew that. His own family was the perfect example of that kind of thing. But Bea's father having what looked like a heart attack right after Bea talked to him about her grandmother's death? There was such a thing as too many coincidences.

He had to report this. Something bigger was going on here. While the mob usually had flashy, over the top power plays, he had the feeling someone was playing the long game here. Dante needed to know what the Bureau knew.

Once on the sidewalk, he stopped and looked back. Poor Bea, she didn't deserve any of this.

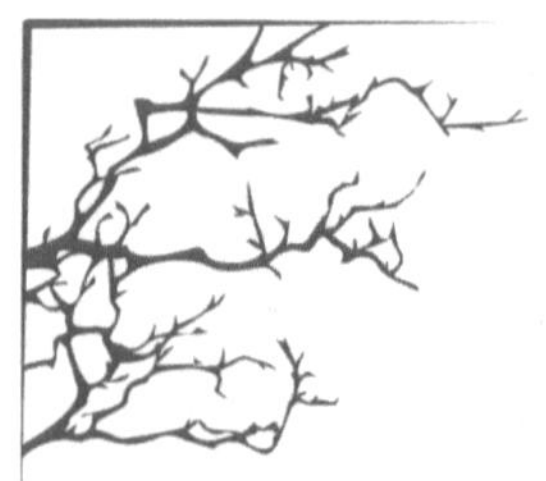

Chapter 15

This is all my fault.

She should have known something bad was going to happen. There should have been some warning. The cloying scent of the flowers clogged her nose, and Bea couldn't tell roses from lilies. Would it have made a difference if she could? From the moment she found that broken charm this morning, she should have been on her guard, prepared for the worst. But nothing could have prepared her for this.

Bea dropped to her knees next to her father, reaching out with one hand. Before she could make contact, Dr. Joe—one of the paisans—kneeled next to Daddy. He started CPR and she knew better than to interrupt. She clutched her hands to her chest instead and willed Daddy to breathe. Please breathe.

Oh, God, he was going to die. He was going to miss the Italy trip. Mike's wedding. He'd never walk Beatrice down the aisle at her own wedding—whenever that would be. She covered her mouth to choke down a sob. No, he couldn't! She wouldn't let him die.

If only she'd been trained in magic. There had to be something she could do, something to stop this from happening, to make Daddy cough and sit up like nothing was wrong. She'd accidentally used her magic only a few hours ago. Why couldn't she use it now when she wanted to?

"Bea," Connie's voice was quiet in her ear, one hand heavy on Bea's shoulder. "Come on. Let the paramedics do their thing."

She'd been concentrating so hard on willing Daddy to be okay that Bea hadn't noticed the EMTs entering the room. God, the room where Nonna's coffin still sat a few feet away. Bea choked back tears, letting her cousin help her up and out of the way as the paramedics got to work.

Bea knew she should get out of the way, to let the people in uniform do what they needed to do. But she couldn't, not when she could still find that spark of magic to help Daddy. She kept her gaze on Daddy, leaning heavily against her cousin for support. She gasped when the paramedics took out the electric paddles. Bea had only ever seen that on TV before.

"Come on, everyone get back." Mike took charge, stepping between the people milling around and their dad.

Bea looked up for a moment, noticing how empty the room had gotten. She spotted two of her cousins leading the stragglers out of the room, leaving only their immediate family—her mom, standing on the other side of Daddy, her hand covering her mouth; Aunt Julia with her youngest cousin next to her; her uncles standing at attention near some chairs that had fallen over in the chaos.

She dismissed all of that. Bea kept her focus on the paramedic with the paddles, chanting in her head *Please work, please work*. Her vision went blurry, and she stumbled back against Connie, dizzy. Her stomach turned over with nausea and for one terrifying moment Bea feared she'd vomit right here in the middle of the room.

"I've got a heartbeat!"

"Let's move."

The nausea faded at those words. Bea blinked away the blurriness from her vision. Hope fluttered in her chest. Had she done something to actually help?

The paramedics moved Daddy to a stretcher, one of them barking orders to the other as they wheeled it out of the room quickly.

"I, I need to go with the ambulance." Mom stumbled forward, her ankle twisting as her heel caught on the carpet. "Damn it." She kicked off her shoes, grabbing them before darting after the paramedics in her stocking feet. "Bea, meet us there!" She turned once more to nod at Bea before heading out of the room.

Bea opened her mouth, and then snapped it closed again. She needed to go. They had to follow the ambulance. She tried to step away from Connie and nearly went down, her head swimming.

"I got you," Connie said, holding on to Bea's arm. Warmth flooded her, as if Connie had infused Bea with her own energy.

Bea blinked at her cousin, wondering if she did that on purpose.

Mike stepped forward. "Uncle Tony, can you and Uncle Guido take the girls to the hospital? Bea doesn't know where they're going."

While that was true, it stung a bit. Bea should know, and she'd be able to follow the ambulance if she could muster up enough energy to run after Mom. "I can drive."

Mike put his hand on her shoulder and squeezed. "You don't have to. That's what family is for, right?"

She swallowed and nodded at him, appreciating the comfort. Look at him, being all big brother and shit. Of course, now with Dad out of the picture, he was the man of the household. The thought made her close her eyes in pain.

"What about...?" Uncle Tony trailed off. He tilted his head toward the lobby. "There are some guests from other families still hanging around."

Bea caught the implication. Other mobsters. Maybe Families they were at war with or had deals with. She didn't know enough to guess what Uncle Tony actually meant.

"We got this, Dad," her cousin Junior said. "Mike and I know what we're doing. We've been ready for years."

Uncle Tony frowned at his son, but after a moment, he nodded. "I'll stay to deal with the funeral home. Guido, take the ladies to the hospital. The boys will take care of business."

"Marco is coming with us," Aunt Julia protested.

"Aw, come on, Mom."

"Listen to your mother," Uncle Tony stepped in, stopping her youngest cousin's whining. Marco was only sixteen. Maybe that meant he was too young for family business.

"Come on, let's go out the back." Uncle Guido led the way out of the room.

When Bea went to follow, she stumbled, grabbing on to one chair for balance. Connie and Lucy flanked her on either side.

"You're in no shape to drive," Lucy said sternly, somehow still sounding like her usual chipper self. "Let me have your keys. We'll follow your uncle's car. Mike can pick me up later."

It sounded so reasonable. Bea couldn't think of any reason to refuse, though it felt wrong to hand Lucy her car keys. She didn't think Lucy was going to come along at all, but where else would she go? Especially with Mike taking care of family business.

"Where did your boyfriend go?" Lucy asked as they stepped out into the evening air.

It helped to clear Bea's head a little, and she could take a few steps without feeling dizzy. "I told him to leave," she replied absently. "And he's not my boyfriend."

Dante probably wanted nothing to do with their crazy family after tonight. How many bodies would the guy have to check for a pulse before he ditched her? Bea resigned herself to never hearing from him again, especially after she basically kicked him out of the viewing.

Lucy didn't comment, only unlocked Bea's car and slid into the driver's seat like she belonged there. Bea buckled in next to her, while Connie took the back. As they took off into the night, Bea prayed for good news when they arrived at the hospital.

"YOU'RE BACK EARLY. I expected you to maybe offer to take her out for a drink afterward." Janet narrowed her eyes.

Dante looked away from her shrewd gaze. He'd come directly to her apartment after watching the ambulance leave the Funeral Home. They'd played the "hi neighbor, can I have a cup of sugar" game once he knocked on the door. Now he was safely inside. Rocky had greeted him with a tennis ball that Dante tossed the length of the living room.

"There's been a development," he said. Rocky had returned with the ball, which he deposited at Dante's feet. He scooped up the ball and hefted it across the room once again. "The Don collapsed in the middle of the viewing. He was still alive when I left. I stayed long enough to watch the EMTs take him away."

Janet's eyes widened and she let out a whistle. "Well, fuck. I got some work to do. You realize what this means?"

"I have an idea. It means the Family is without a head."

"Right, so who's in charge? His brother? The son?" She tapped her chin, looking off in the distance as she thought. "And I bet a bunch of rival families were there tonight to pay their respects, right?"

Dante nodded. "I spotted representatives from the Five Families." He rattled off the names of those he recognized from his crash course in NJ mob families. The Five weren't what they used to be, thanks to the FBI, but they were still active.

"They'll gobble up the DiLorenzos if they're not careful." Janet mused. "I'm going to have to reach out to my contacts and see what the buzz is. The DiLorenzo's were untouchable for decades."

Not so untouchable now, with the matriarch dead and the Don incapacitated. It seemed a bit too coincidental to Dante. Bea was already suspicious of her grandmother's death. Could someone have poisoned her father? There were various drugs that could fake a heart attack, although the ones Dante could think of wouldn't have let Don DiLorenzo speak for as long as he had before going down.

"What's our next step?" He asked as the dog once again nudged him, his entire body pressing against Dante's leg. Dante had missed the tennis ball sitting at his feet and clearly Rocky wanted him to throw it yet again.

"You're going to stay on target." Janet held out her hand for the tennis ball. Dante tossed it to her, and now Rocky scampered over to her feet. "Text the girl. Play the sympathetic boyfriend. She's going to need support, and you're going to offer it."

Something about her words didn't sit well with him. Dante knew it was the job he'd signed up for, but he hadn't expected this—watching a young woman lose two people she really cared about, right in front of her. His empathy wouldn't have to be faked. But at this point what more could he learn from Bea?

"It's not Bea you're after," Janet answered his question, putting the ball away with the other dog toys in one of the kitchen drawers. Rocky let out a little whine in response. "It's the family. You've already gotten great intel. Keep it coming."

Her words should have filled him with pride. Dante was getting the job done. It was hard to get praise from Janet Carter, and here she was handing it out. That did nothing to change the sense of unease growing in his chest. "Got it."

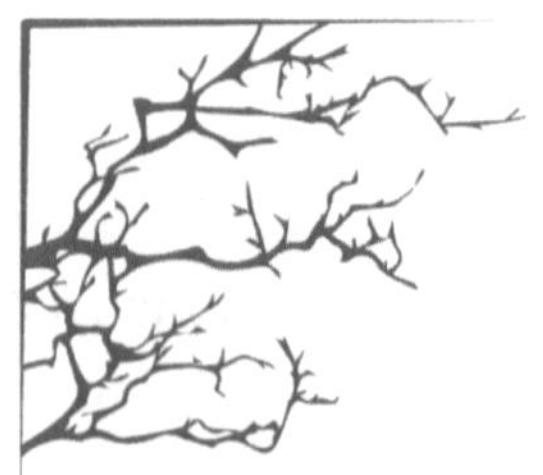

Chapter 16

"*He's in a coma,*" Bea typed into her phone. She sat cross-legged in the middle of her bed, hunched over the tiny screen. "*His surgery went fine. Docs told my mom that sometimes the body needs more time to heal.*"

She'd been texting Dante updates since her dad had been rushed into surgery the night of the viewing. Dante had been the one to reach out first, sending her a message asking if she was okay. Bea had told him, truthfully, that she wasn't, but thanks for asking. Getting that first message had undone a knot in her chest. She hadn't scared him away completely.

He proved an escape from her family, someone she could talk to and be herself with. It gave her something to do while sitting in the waiting room of the hospital, desperate for news.

"*And how's your mom taking it?*" he sent back.

"*She's crying all the time,*" Bea typed. With a sigh, she dropped the phone onto the bed. She'd never seen Mom like this. No matter what had gone wrong, Mom always had a solution. She'd put on a fresh coat of lipstick and tackle whatever they had to deal with, from vendors at the church, to the financial aid officers at college when they lost Bea's application. Mom never seemed to lose it completely. Until now.

"*I'm sorry,*" Dante responded after a few seconds. "*Is there anything I can do? Do you need to get away for a bit?*"

It would be nice to go somewhere with him, to leave the sounds of her mom weeping behind. But Bea couldn't do that, not yet. She had a responsibility to her dad. Her magic had done something the night of the viewing, she knew it. It kept his blood pumping or oxygen in his lungs. Something had kept him from the brink of death from what the doctor called the widow-maker heart attack. Bea knew it had to have been her power.

She'd been weak and tired the whole next day. Of course, that could be from staying up all night waiting for news. But she'd learned by now what using her magic felt like. If only she had a better idea of how to use it. Bea got up and paced her bedroom, easier now that she'd shoved her moving boxes against the wall.

Somehow, she'd cursed Father Stefano at the wake, and she hadn't even been trying. She'd just been so angry once she figured out what the smell surrounding him had meant. Bea stopped in the middle of her pacing. She'd figured it out only because of the memory of her Nonna teaching her about herbs had suddenly surfaced.

"Healing," Bea murmured. "What herbs are for healing?"

She sat back on her bed before closing her eyes and diving deep into the memory. They were back in that kitchen again, Bea stirring the pot of simmering red sauce. She stood on the kitchen chair, wooden spoon clutched tightly in one hand as the fragrant smell of garlic and onion hit her nose. She tried to direct the vision like a movie, fast forwarding to the part where her Nonna taught her the meaning of herbs.

Sage. Rosemary. Chamomile. Peppermint. Depending on the purpose, all of these herbs could be used for healing.

Bea snapped her eyes open. She scooped up her phone and tapped out a quick message to Dante. *"Sorry. Not now. I need to visit my dad. Talk later."* There, now, he wouldn't be worried when she didn't respond to his texts. Bea needed all her concentration and focus to be on magic, not Dante.

She grabbed her messenger bag and trotted down the stairs. They had to have some herbs in the spice cabinet. Bea would grab what she needed and then go see Daddy. Maybe more memories would kick in once she found what she needed. Bea could do this. She had to.

When she opened up the cabinet, Bea's shoulders dropped in disappointment. Unlike her Nonna's carefully curated bottles of spices, her mother had a small selection of supermarket brand herbs. Garlic and oregano they had in abundance, along with pepper grinders and sea salt. Bea grabbed the sea salt and tossed it in her bag. Salt was useful, her memory told her.

Mom didn't stock any dried rosemary, sage or peppermint, but...Bea moved to the tea cabinet. They always had chamomile tea on hand for the occasional stomach ache. She grabbed the box of tea sachets and tucked it away with the salt.

"Bea?" Mom called from the living room. "What are you doing in the kitchen?"

Bea snagged a box of granola bars out of the cabinet. "Grabbing a snack. I'm going to the hospital to visit Dad."

When she turned around, her mother stood in the entranceway to the kitchen. She looked tired and nothing like her usual put-together self. Mom always wore makeup, even at home when no one else was around. But today her eyes were tear-streaked and devoid of eyeliner.

"They would have called me if anything had changed."

"I know that, Mom." Bea tried to keep the frustration out of her voice. Mom looked terrible. "I want to see him." She couldn't tell Mom the real reason—wanting to use her magic to heal him.

Mom nodded. "You go. I can't. See him like that."

This was wrong. This wasn't her mother. Bea put down her messenger bag and pulled out the espresso pot. "You need coffee."

Bea puttered around the kitchen, measuring the coffee grounds into the little metal strainer that went over the bottom half of the pot already filled with cold water from the filtered pitcher in the fridge. She put it on the stove, keeping the flame at medium so as not to scorch the bottom. In a perfect world, she might have some biscotti to offer as well, but Bea didn't see any in the cabinets.

They didn't have Nonna around anymore to bake them. Bea swallowed down the lump in her throat. She knew how to make the dough cut with honey to make softer versions of the hard cookie sold in Starbucks and coffee shops. Maybe later she'd bake some. It would be something to do to work on more memories from her childhood.

"Look." Bea pulled out a small espresso cup from the cabinet and placed it on the kitchen island in front of Mom. The best thing to do was to get her mom back to her normal self. That meant giving her a project. "Don't you have shower planning to work on? Isn't it next week?"

Bea had lost track of time herself—understandable with all of this going on. Luckily, all the gifts had already been purchased and stored in the basement. But there was still plenty to do—seating arrangements, favors, centerpieces. All the things Mom liked to make just so.

Mom said nothing until Bea poured the espresso. Then she took the sugar and put a few spoonfuls in the cup. "You're right. I need to go to the craft store and pick up more yellow tulle." She took a sip of espresso and then patted her hair. "And my hair is a mess."

Bea nodded, sagging a bit in relief. Now this was her mom. "Finish your coffee, okay? The craft store can wait."

She picked up her messenger bag and snagged her keys off the rack hanging on the wall near the garage. "I'll be back later."

Mom nodded, the color already returning to her cheeks. "Don't make any plans for tomorrow. We're going to Nonna's apartment to clear out her things."

Bea stiffened. So soon? Of course, it had to be done. They couldn't leave the empty apartment sitting there. Someone might try to break in. Maybe this would give her the chance to look for anything that could help her. At the very least, she could raid Nonna's spice rack.

The funeral itself had been yesterday and hard enough without her dad there. There had been a hush throughout the church, more so than normal, as if everyone knew the wrongness of this moment. Immediately afterward, her Uncle Tony had left with the coffin to go to the airport. Nonna would be buried in Italy, as she always wanted.

It should have been Dad accompanying her. He was the oldest son.

She blinked back tears. She was done with crying. Time for action. "Okay."

"And Bea? Thank you."

Bea nodded and gave Mom a tight smile before escaping to her car. If only coffee could fix all of her problems so easily.

They'd transferred Daddy to Morristown Medical Center after getting him stabilized at University Hospital in Newark. It was the better hospital, Mom had said. It was also an extra thirty minutes of driving.

Bea used the time to think about how she was going to approach using her powers. She'd spoken the words out loud to curse the priest. Maybe the same thing would work at her father's bedside. She needed to be careful about which words she chose. Otherwise, she might make things worse.

And Bea didn't want to find out how much worse things could get.

She'd already lost her Nonna and came close to losing her dad. She wanted to lock Mom and Connie in one room and tell them not to move.

I'm being ridiculous.

Bea laughed to herself as she found parking in the hospital lot. Now that she knew what she wanted to try, Bea didn't want to wait any longer. She all but ran to the front desk to get permission to see her father. She would need an arm band to get up to ICU. The hospital was very strict about security.

"You're the second visitor," the nurse commented as she stuck the band around Bea's wrist. "The limit is two, so make sure you stop here to check out when you leave. Otherwise, no one else can go up."

"Right." Bea frowned. Who else had come to see Dad? As far as she knew, Mike was still home in bed. He'd normally leave after dinner to take care of business, but these past few days, he'd been leaving earlier. Without Daddy around, he probably had more work to do, although Bea couldn't imagine what that looked like.

Bea kept her messenger bag close as she rode the elevator up to the ICU floor. Nobody stopped her to demand what she had in it, which was good. Although she probably could explain away the box of tea and granola bars as snacks for later.

Once she stepped off the elevator, her skin prickled, like shards of ice crawling up her arms. Something dark and heavy lay over this entire ward. There were too many smells for her to pick one out. She stumbled and had to hold on to the wall to settle herself.

Too much death in this place.

Could she shut this off? The ability to smell death might be useful in some context, but really not helpful in the hospital right now. Nonna had warned her about being open to the universe now that she had awakened. If only she'd given Bea a way to shut these senses off.

Bea curled her fingertips against the wall, focusing on the feel of the hard surface against her skin. She took a deep breath, smelling only disinfectant and seizing on that. This was real. Not the swirling in her head. Focus. She needed to see her daddy. Magic could wait.

Once she felt more settled, she made it down the hall to her father's room. The door was ajar. She slowed her steps and peeked inside, curious to solve the mystery of who the second visitor was. A woman sat in the chair next to Daddy's bed.

Daddy looked horrible, hooked up to machines that let out a steady rhythm of sound. His face had a sunken appearance, his skin was pale, and sweat slicked back his hair. At least his chest rose and fell, reassuring her with its reliability. The woman had her head bowed, with one hand on Daddy's bed. She had dark hair in loose curls down her back and wore a bright teal blouse. Bea had never seen her before.

Who the hell was she? How had she gotten in here? Bea didn't think they let just anyone in, especially considering who her father was. "Excuse me." Bea stepped into the room fully. "Who are you? What are you doing with my father?"

The woman jumped out of the chair. Bea got a quick impression of dark eyes surrounded by eyeliner and lips with smudged rep lipstick. She looked older than Bea, but not as old as Mom or Dad. "I'm sorry!" the woman said as she pushed past Bea and out the door.

Bea rushed to her father's side to make sure he was okay, that this stranger had done nothing to harm him. She reached for her father's hand, and that's when she noticed a glint of gold around his wrist. It was a necklace, like the one Nonna had given him, but the charm hung from it was different. Instead of a horn, it was a circle inscribed with symbols that looked like the alphabet but slanted. When Bea touched it, she got an impression of warmth and safety, the same feeling she'd always gotten from touching her own charm and had never recognized until now.

Bea whirled around and ran into the hallway in time to see the woman disappear into the stairwell.

Bea darted after her, throwing the door open and skipping down the stairs. "Wait!"

The woman kept going down the stairs, her high heels making a clattering noise against the concrete.

"I need to talk to you!" Bea tried again. Not only was this woman a witch, she'd left a protective charm for Daddy. She could be the witch Daddy at mentioned at the viewing. If that was the case, Bea desperately needed her help. "I saw the charm! I could tell you were trying to protect him."

The woman stopped a few landings below Bea. Bea didn't move. She didn't want to startle the woman now that she had gotten her to slow the fuck down.

"How did you know? He told me you hadn't awakened yet."

"Yeah, that was true until like this week." Bea took a few steps down. "Let's just say Nonna had pretty bad timing and leave it at that."

The woman muttered something under her breath and shook her head.

Bea kept walking slowly. "How do you know my dad?"

She stiffened and took a few steps toward the door on her landing below. "Your father is...very special to me."

Bea stopped and frowned. "What, you're an ex-girlfriend or something?"

"Not ex," she said with a tight smile. "He never wanted you to find out."

Her words made little sense. How could she not be an ex? *Oh.* "He wouldn't cheat on mom," Bea protested.

The woman took advantage of Bea's sudden bout of uncertainty to open the door and dart out of the stairway.

Damn it. She probably said that bullshit on purpose to distract Bea.

Bea ran down the next flight of stairs and reached the door as it slammed closed. She could see the woman on the other side through the tiny window cut through the door. No matter what Bea did to the handle, the door would not open.

"Wait!" Bea pounded on the door. "I need your help. Dad said you could help!"

The woman shook her head. She pointed her fingers at the door, twisting them together and tracing a pattern in the air before she disappeared from view.

Bea gave up trying to open the door. Clearly the woman had locked it, using her magic. That would be a nice trick to learn. She turned and ran down to the next landing. This door opened easily enough.

She ran for the elevator and took it to the floor above her, but there was no sign of the woman by the time Bea made it there. It was a big hospital; the other witch could be anywhere.

Bea got back into the elevator and sagged against the wall. She considered going back down to the lobby and seeing if the woman popped up down there. Or maybe staking out the parking lot. But there were too many ways in and out.

If only she'd been faster, or had some way to counter the magic on the door. Once again, Bea was playing catch up, ignorant of skills that could help. And had the woman been telling the truth? Was she daddy's mistress? If so...Had he really been intending on introducing her to his side piece as the witch who could train her? Anger boiled in her belly.

Did he think she was just going to be okay with that? Or was he not going to tell her at all? She'd had it with being the last to know everything. Her father had kept too many secrets from her.

Flushed with anger, she approached her dad's bedside once more. Some of the color had returned to his cheeks, and he seemed to breathe easier. The charm appeared to be working. But could Bea help at all?

She grabbed some sachets of tea from her messenger bag and placed them under her dad's pillow. Bea touched Daddy's hand, the one with the charm wrapped around the wrist, and tried to feel what was going on with him. The warmth and good vibes from the charm were so strong, but she couldn't get a thing from him. Was that a consequence of her magic or the other witch's?

"I need you to wake up," Bea said, putting the intention in her words. "You need to wake up so I can yell at you."

She choked back tears. Everything was a mess, and Bea was a fool, floundering around with no idea about what to do next. She needed to get her magic under control. No more accidentally cursing anyone. And then once she figured out how to use her ability, she'd wake Daddy up so he could fix everything. No matter what he had going on, Bea knew her father loved her. He'd find out who hurt Nonna and make them pay.

But Bea had to stop playing catch up. No more sitting around at home crying. Tomorrow she would get to her Nonna's before the rest of her family showed up. If she went tonight, she ran the chance of running into her uncle or someone else in the Family. Better to go when she was supposed to be there.

Maybe the book was gone, but that didn't mean Nonna didn't have anything else important stashed away. And Bea needed information. That woman in Dad's hospital room wasn't the only witch around. There had been those strange women at the viewing, who asked her pointed questions about her taking on her grandmother's role. Bea needed to find out who they were.

She pulled out her phone and texted her cousin. Connie would know, and if she didn't, she'd know who to ask. It put her one step closer to finding out the truth.

Bea nodded, satisfied with her plan.

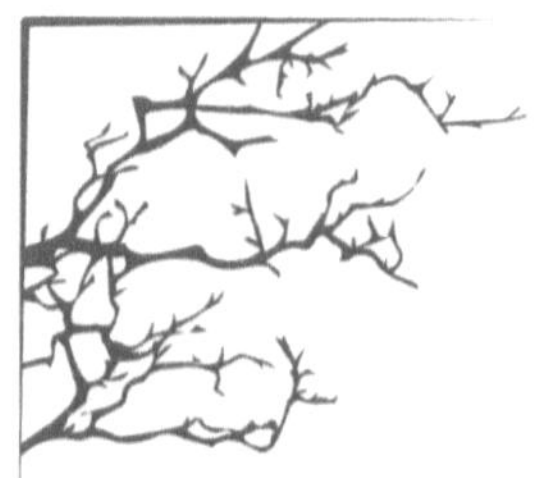

Chapter 17

Bea needed to get to Nonna's apartment before anyone else did. She managed that by setting her alarm for ridiculously early and sneaking out without grabbing breakfast. She hit up Starbucks on the way for some fast fuel for her brain. It almost felt like being back at college again, with her huge latte in one hand and heading out for an adventure. Granted, the adventure usually involved getting lost on some rural roads on her way to her roommate's parents' home to watch some movies and eat ice cream.

Unlike some of her floor mates, Bea had never quite "let loose" at college. She knew better than to call attention to herself as the daughter of a mob boss. More importantly, Bea had never wanted to disappoint her father. That's why she never brought home her long-term boyfriend Bryan despite dating him all junior year. Daddy wouldn't like him. He wasn't even Italian. It probably played a part in their breakup.

None of that mattered now.

Bea parked on the street a few houses down from Nonna's house. She'd never stop thinking of it as Nonna's house, she decided, even when the sharp pain of grief receded. Of course, the building still belonged to the family, split ownership among the three brothers. Using her spare key, she entered the apartment, stepping foot into the kitchen for the first time since that day.

She stopped in her tracks, waiting for something—grief? Anger? Some magic sense? To hit her, but there was nothing. Bea took a sniff and only caught the distinctive smell of rotting food. Nobody had been in here since they came to collect the body.

She had to swallow hard at that thought of her grandmother as nothing but a body. Bea took hold of the doorway and closed her eyes, fighting the wave of sorrow that rolled through her. They'd been sitting at this table not that long ago, her nonna feeding her cookies and coffee. That would never happen again. Bea choked back a sob, pushing down the emotion as best she could.

She couldn't linger here in the doorway. No, Bea had a job to do.

Her intention had been to search the back room where Nonna had awakened her and hidden the spell book. But something pulled her in the other direction, through the living room, to her grandmother's bedroom. She let instinct lead her, trying not to look at the couch. Instead, she gazed at the wall, at the photographs of herself and her cousins as children. It made the living room feel like a little art gallery, the selection of frames arranged haphazardly—a new photo added when a new grandchild was born, and then switched out as the child got older.

They'd spent so much time here as children. Bea and her cousins had grown up as friends, only growing apart when the boys got involved with the family business. It left her and Connie behind, but Bea had never minded. She hadn't wanted to be involved with the family business, anyway. She was going to go to college and study art.

She'd been so naïve. How could she possibly have thought she could just do her own thing? Family was everything, she knew that. But before, Bea didn't know what she could do to contribute, other than helping support her family members and showing up at family events. Now she had magic—useless magic, because she didn't know the first thing about her own abilities. How could she protect her family when she didn't know how? Maybe Nonna had left something else behind that would give her a clue.

What the hell was she doing, standing here and staring at those pictures? It was like two competing forces inside her—the one that wanted her to go into the bedroom, and the one keeping her out of it. Bea pushed forward, stepping into Nonna's bedroom.

It felt empty. Of all places she'd expected to feel her grandmother's presence, this was it. But someone had taken the time to make the bed and cover it with a white crocheted bedspread. Across from the bed was the long dresser with its row of statues of saints and candles. She ran her fingers along the dresser, picking up nothing but dust.

Bea opened up each drawer, finding nothing more interesting than Nonna's clothes and extra linens for her bed. She found a jewelry box tucked in the bottom and pulled it out eagerly, but when Bea opened the lid, she found nothing more than shattered protection charms.

It's all gone.

She touched each gold piece—and how could gold shatter? — but it was only dead metal beneath her fingertips. No traces of magic remained. All of her grandmother's spells had been undone. Was that a consequence of her death or something done on purpose by whoever had stolen her spell book? Bea's heart raced as fear flooded her. None of the family had any protection. Her father was in a coma. Who was next?

"Please, Nonna, give me something." Bea put the box away and stood up. Inside the closet, she found more clothing, including a vintage wedding dress in a zippered bag.

She finally spotted Nonna's purse, peeking out from beneath a sweater draped over the old leather chair in the corner. Bea reached for it and unzipped it, not sure what she expected to find inside. There was a selection of mint candy, which made her smile and the golden lighter, which made her frown. Bea picked up the lighter and flicked it open, the golden flame dazzling.

But there was no warmth, no sign that it had been used for magic at all.

When she opened the purse again, Bea found a small leather notebook. She gasped. Another spell book? She flipped it open to find a list of names and items written in Italian. Bea didn't understand what she was looking at until she found "Vito - Occhi" and a checkmark next to his name.

Bea dropped the notebook and purse and took a staggered step back. This was the list of those who pledged themselves to the Family and what they offered in return should they betray the DiLorenzos. Vito had offered his eyes, and he'd paid dearly for his misdeeds.

That moment in the storeroom came back to her, the smell of burning flesh, the way Vito had screamed.

There were so many more names in that book. Many with checkmarks next to them. Bea didn't want to look and see what her Nonna had done to those people. But she had to. Bea couldn't ignore the fact that magic had been used for horrible things.

It didn't have to be like that. Bea could be a different kind of witch. Nonna's protection charms were extremely powerful, keeping the family safe for years. Maybe she could create charms that kept people like Vito from turning traitor. There had to be another way, and Bea would be the one to find it.

Clutching the purse close to her body, Bea left the bedroom, heading to the back room. There had to be something there. But other than the candle and saint Nonna had used to awaken Bea, she couldn't find anything else that sparked of magic. The hidden compartment in the sewing basket felt slightly warm to the touch, like the spell book had been so strong it left something behind. Bea had to find that book, somehow.

Bea's phone buzzed, snatching her out of her spiraling. She pulled it out to see a text from Connie. Finally. Her cousin had left her on read all night, never replying to her questions about the women at the viewing.

"Where are you?" Connie had texted.

"At Nonna's." Bea tapped out before scooping up the purse and shoving it into her messenger bag. She'd have to take a closer look at it again later, in case there was something she'd missed.

"We're pulling up now."

Shit, she was out of time. Bea did one last scan of the backroom, but nothing pulled her, not the way she'd been pulled when she first entered the apartment. It was cold, empty, without a single scent to guide her. Whatever she had hoped to find—maybe a bit of her grandmother's spirit—it wasn't here. Except for the purse, which exuded warmth through her messenger bag. That had to be it then.

Bea went outside as her aunt's SUV pulled into the driveway. She wasn't surprised when her mom, Aunt Julia, and Connie got out of the car. However, when Lucy followed her cousin, Bea stopped in her tracks. Why the hell was she here? She wasn't family, not yet. The wedding wasn't for another three weeks.

"What are you doing here?" she blurted as Lucy stepped onto the sidewalk.

"Beatrice!" Mom scolded. "Is that any way to talk to your future sister-in-law?"

Her future sister-in-law had no business being here. Nonna wasn't her grandmother. Bea stuffed the irritation down. She'd gotten what she needed. "I mean, I thought she was working."

Lucy came to her side and put her arm around Bea. "I switched shifts with someone." She worked at a fancy dress boutique that Bea had visited exactly once. "I had to be here for all of you. Especially you, Bea. It must be so hard for you to be back here after, you know."

Her voice had a note of sympathy in it that made Bea feel like an ass for doubting her. Bea accepted the hug stiffly before pulling away, untangling her messenger bag from Lucy's arm. "I'm fine." She tried to meet Connie's eyes, but her cousin had gone to the trunk with her mother and pulled out a couple of large cardboard boxes.

"Everybody, grab a box," Mom ordered. "I have labels and markers with me. We'll take care of what we can today and make a plan for the rest. It all goes into storage until the will gets settled."

At least Mom had found something to occupy her, so she wasn't sitting around dwelling about Dad. Bea hadn't told her about the woman at the hospital. It would shatter her to know Daddy had been unfaithful. Bea still couldn't believe it, especially that the woman had the audacity to show up at Daddy's hospital room.

"Give me a second. I want to drop something off in my car." Bea watched the rest of them enter the building before sprinting down to her car and locking her messenger bag in the trunk. She stared at it for a moment, wondering if there was any way to lock the car with magic.

The woman in the hospital had locked that stairwell door with only a touch. Maybe Bea could do the same and ensure that nobody involved with Nonna's death would get the last important thing left inside. Bea put her hand over the lock, closed her eyes and focused really hard on the lock and being the only person being able to open it.

Warmth flooded her, the heat rising in her hand until she had to pull away from the metal and shake out her fingers. "Ouch!"

Maybe that had done it. She stepped away, about to head back toward Aunt Julia's car when a hint of dizziness hit her. Bea grabbed for her car to keep from falling. She took a deep breath, trying to center herself.

Magic apparently had a cost. She needed to remember that.

Aunt Julia had left the back of her SUV open. There were only two empty banker boxes in there, so Bea grabbed them, and then shut the door. When she got back inside Nonna's apartment, she found Lucy sweeping the kitchen with an old wooden broom. Bea didn't even know where she got the ancient thing from. It seemed a little odd to be sweeping now before they even had gone through the fridge.

"Are you sweeping the evil out?" Aunt Julia asked. She took the boxes from Bea.

Lucy looked up with wide eyes. She gripped the broom tightly. "What?"

"It's what my nonna used to say." Julia laughed. "She had a broom just like that, too."

Bea went still. Was this one of those magic things that existed? How would Lucy know that? She wasn't even Italian.

Lucy let out a nervous laugh and went back to her work. "I thought the floor could use a good cleaning. No one has been in here for days. It's all so dusty."

"Bea, help me with the fridge." Connie had a giant black garbage bag opened in front of it. She'd also gotten to work quickly. Bea needed to talk to her, but not here with Lucy, listening to every word.

"I should have brought rubber gloves," Bea muttered. She held her breath as Connie opened the fridge.

It smelled bad, but not terrible. It was a horrible reminder that Nonna had only been gone for a week. That wasn't enough time for her food to rot and go to waste. Bea had to choke back tears when she dumped plastic containers of leftovers in the trash. Nonna had saved food, had every reason to expect she'd be around to eat it.

Wouldn't she have seen her own death coming as a witch? Bea had been given the warning before going to her grandmother's house—that smell of lilies that dogged her until she found her Nonna. Or did their magical alert system only work once the deed had been done?

"It's trash day," Connie said. "If we work fast, we can take this out to the curb before the trucks come."

The worst of it was the fruit left out on the counter. It had gone rotten and moldy, leaving behind messy wet spots when Bea dumped out the basket.

"Toss the basket too. That's not salvageable," Connie said. She opened up the cabinets and pulled out opened boxes of rice and pasta.

"The canned goods we can donate," Bea argued when it seemed like Connie was going to toss cans of tomato sauce into the garbage bag.

Bea found herself stuck with the woven basket in her hand, unable to throw it away, despite its nasty condition.

This basket had been with Nonna for Bea's entire childhood. There was nothing special about it, except maybe for the red braided design along the base. Otherwise, it was a brown wicker basket used to keep fruit. But she couldn't bear the thought of chucking it.

"I can wash this." She went over to the sink and turned on the water.

"Why?" Connie protested.

"We're not throwing out everything she owned!" Bea snapped back.

Lucy stopped sweeping and straightened. "Why don't I sort through the canned stuff while you take the bags outside?"

Great, now Lucy was trying to intervene and make peace. Bea didn't want her involved. Nothing in this house meant anything to her, not the way it did to Bea and Connie. It irked her that Connie could throw things out so casually.

Bea turned off the water, leaving the basket in the sink. "Fine."

She picked up one black garbage bag and tied it shut. Connie took another. Nonna always had so much food ready, prepared to feed the entire family if necessary. Now it was trash, gone bad without having fulfilled its function.

Once they got out of the house, Bea took a deep breath. She hadn't realized how stuffy it had been inside. The air had been so thick and oppressive, like moving through a swamp. Out here she caught a mix of spring air and fresh garbage from the cans placed on the curb all down the street. Ah, Newark, she thought. This was one thing she didn't miss about no longer living in the city.

Connie dragged the trash cans from the yard to the curb. Her motions were stiff and angry, especially when she grabbed the bags from Bea's hands.

"You never responded to my texts," Bea blurted.

Connie slammed the lid on the cans, sealing the bags and the smell inside. "Why did you want that information, Bea? What good is it going to do?"

"I wanted to know who they were," she trailed off, knowing she couldn't tell her cousin the truth: she wanted to know if they were witches, and if so, if they'd help her.

"Really? No other reason?" Connie tilted her head to one side and gave Bea a knowing look.

"You know me. I can never remember anyone's names!"

Connie crossed her arms over her chest and stared at her. "I asked my mom. She got all weird until she finally broke down and told me they were connected."

"Connected?" Bea repeated, stupidly, until she got what Connie meant. "To the mob?"

"Shh!" Connie smacked Bea's arm. "God, could you not? That's not the kind of thing you say out loud."

"Or in a text message," Bea murmured. "I thought you were avoiding me."

"I am avoiding you." Connie sighed. She looked away and then back at Bea. "Because once I found out who, what, they were...I knew they were dangerous."

Bea nodded. "They are. And so was Nonna."

"Not this witchcraft crap again." Connie rolled her eyes.

Bea didn't know if her cousin's anger was better or worse than the gentle condescension from earlier when Bea first tried to confess. "I know you don't believe me."

"Because it's crazy! There's no way you saw Nonna magic someone's eyeballs off!" Connie gestured emphatically with both hands.

"Burn them out." Bea held Connie's gaze.

"You're having some kind of psychotic break because you can't deal with finding her body."

"Wow." Bea took a step back. "We're cousins, Connie. We are also friends. I thought I could trust you."

Connie sighed. "I'm sorry. But you have to drop this. You can't get messed up in Family stuff. That's for the men. You know that. It was drilled into our heads since we were kids. The boys have their own role."

No, that's not what Nonna told me. The "men" couldn't function without Nonna's power behind the Family. Now, without her, everything would start falling apart. Daddy being in the hospital was only part of that. What else would start to fail?

Maybe this, the friendship she shared with her cousin, was yet another casualty.

Bea's phone buzzed, and she took it out of her pocket to see another text from Dante. Instead of ignoring it, she read it and tapped out a quick response. "You know what? You're right. Lucy's right. I obviously shouldn't be here. Finish working on the apartment without me."

"Bea, come on!"

Bea ignored Connie and got into her car, slamming the door behind her. She didn't have to drive off in a huff. Connie had already turned around to go back inside. Bea looked at her phone again.

Hey, I know things are rough right now. I wanted to let you know I'm here for you when you decide you're ready. Dante had sent.

Bea had typed back, *Thanks. You free?*

Because if she couldn't rely on her family, maybe she could rely on this man, the only one who'd listened to her when she talked about the odd circumstances around her grandmother's death. If she was going to figure this out, Bea would need all the help she could get.

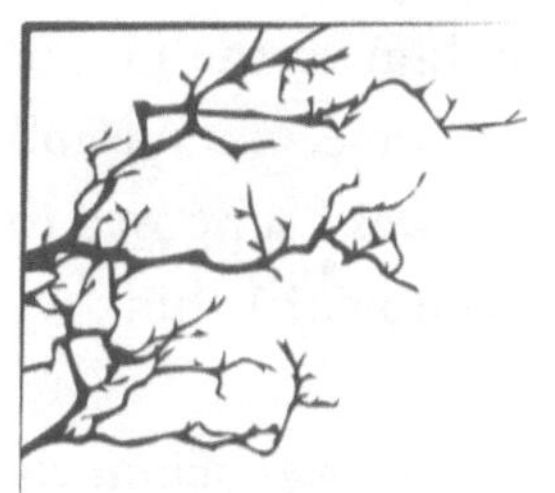

Chapter 18

Dante stood outside the Metropolitan Museum of Art, staring up at its familiar facade, his hands tucked in the pockets of his khaki pants. He'd been here once before, on a school trip he vaguely remembered. Tourists chatting in different languages swarmed the steps along with lines of kids on school trips in matching t-shirts. New York had a very different vibe than Newark—more alive, more colorful. Most of the people surrounding him were visitors, not residents, so everything was new and exciting. Newark, in contrast, seemed older, more run down.

When Bea had texted him asking to meet her here, he'd jumped at the chance. This was what he and Janet had been waiting for—Bea making contact. But part of him wondered if this was a trap, meant to capture him in a lie. Was he really who he said he was? Because if so, he should be booking his "freelance" work in the city, which was his whole reason for moving to Newark, for the proximity to the train station.

His whole web of lies could come crushing down on him today. Dante swallowed and threw his shoulders back. He'd been trained for this.

He trotted up the steps and scanned the large entranceway. Bea waited for him inside and she waved at the sight of him, greeting him with a wide smile.

"Hey!" She dodged the crowds to join him. "You made it!"

"Of course." He grinned at her. "Although I almost got on the wrong bus."

She laughed and grabbed his arm, tugging him to the line of people waiting to pay. "I've done that before. One time, Connie and I got on the subway in the wrong direction. How was I supposed to know the difference between Uptown and Downtown? I think we were sixteen at the time."

"Your parents let you visit the city alone?" Dante was genuinely surprised. He knew Bea's family was notoriously protective.

Bea winked at him. "Well, we were supposed to be visiting Nonna."

"How rebellious of you." He grinned.

She shook her head. "Yeah, my wild and crazy teenage years, sneaking out to visit art museums."

It sounded much better than Dante's teenage years, which had been filled with fear and hiding from his older brother and other bullies. They made it to the counter, and Dante insisted on paying.

"I can cover my half," Bea insisted when he handed over his credit card. "Let me send you the money."

"Later," he told her. Dante had no intention of letting her pay. He wasn't the kind of guy who skimped out on treating a woman, even when it was an actual date instead of pretend. Of course, the museum visit was on the Bureau's dime since they'd set up the credit cards with his undercover identity.

They clipped their badges on and then entered the museum proper. Dante let Bea lead, and she led him through the great hall to the arms and armor exhibit. "I loved this as a kid." She gestured to the platform in the center of the room holding fully plated knights on horse statues wearing matching armor. "It felt like being transported to the past."

He agreed as they lost themselves in the twisting hallways filled with swords and full sets of armor. Mostly though, he watched Bea, at the way she came alive when showing him something she loved.

She moved so fast her hair whipped through the air and he wanted to catch his fingers in it, to see if it was a soft as it looked.

"What's your favorite section?" Bea asked as they waited outside the elevator. "We could go there next."

"I really want to see your favorites," Dante said. "Since you said it was your dream to talk about art. So, talk?"

The smile she gave him in response lit up her face and made his heart pound. It made Dante want, and he had to push that sensation down. Today had to be about doing his job. Any connection between them had to be about getting more intel.

They took the elevator to the second floor. Bea gestured to the art covered walls around them. "The Met has a nice selection of Renaissance Paintings. Nothing like being in Italy, of course, but this is the closest I can get right now."

"You've been to Italy?" Dante knew she had, that the family had another trip planned for this August.

"We go every year." She paused in front of a painting, staring up at the vivid colors.

The label on the wall named it "The Annunciation" but it differed from other paintings Dante had seen with the same theme. In this the Virgin Mary, clothed in dark blue, stood before the door to a church, facing the Angel Gabriel, who kneeled before her dressed in startling scarlet.

"This is interesting. Look at the composition. Mary is the church here, reminding us that without her, the church wouldn't exist. Huh." Bea went quiet.

Dante stared at the painting, trying to see what fascinated Bea so much. He imagined the painter slaving away at it five hundred years ago, without any of the modern conveniences such as paint thinner.

"Can you imagine creating something that still lasts after hundreds of years? Being able to tell a story that your great great great grandchildren can still see and appreciate?"

He watched her lips as she spoke, and the brightness in her eyes. God, she loved this stuff. Anyone could see it. "No," he told her, unable to conceive of leaving a legacy that lasted that long. "Why did you want to come here, today?"

She sighed, some of the light leaving her eyes. "I think better when I'm around great art."

Dante waited for her to continue, but when she didn't, he prodded gently, "And you have something on your mind that's bothering you?"

Bea frowned. She turned and went to sit on the bench in front of the painting. After a heartbeat, Dante joined her. He followed her gaze and stared at the painting. From here he could take in the entire thing, not the tiny details when seen close up, but the entire composition. Huh.

"When I was twelve, I got lost in a museum in Italy." Bea leaned forward and clasped her hands together. "At first, I was thrilled, you know? Actually, I didn't even notice I got separated from my family. I was so into all the art. There's this life to Renaissance art, how they suddenly started experimenting with color and perspective." She held up a hand and laughed. "Don't worry, I'm not going to go on about art."

"I don't mind. I enjoy hearing you talk."

Her cheeks turned pink and Bea gave him a smile. "Anyway, so I found myself alone in a foreign country. I panicked. My Italian is okay, but there's too much slang in it. It's not like I went to school in Italy and learned properly. So, when I tried to talk to one of the museum employees, they had no idea what the hell I was saying."

"That must have been really scary for you." Dante reached out and took her hand, squeezing her fingers lightly.

"Yeah. Nonna found me not too long after. But after it, I had this fear of being left behind. My family is so important to me, but...right now everyone is in Newark cleaning out Nonna's apartment." She hesitated for a moment, then finally got the words out. "I feel like they're leaving me behind again."

"Why? Do you think they're rushing things with the apartment?" Dante tried to sound like nothing more than a curious boyfriend. Yes, having her talk about her family was good. He had to keep the conversation going.

Bea sighed and clasped her hands in her lap, staring at her fingers. "It's like after Nonna's death it's all falling apart, and I don't know what to do."

"Why is it your responsibility to fix things?" he pointed out. Here he was, right in her corner, on her side. "You have family to lean on."

She finally turned her attention from the painting to him. "The problem is, I'm not sure that I do. You're the only one who believes me about Nonna's...things going missing. My cousin thinks I imagined it all."

Dante leaned toward her. "I'm glad I can be here for you."

She leaned closer to him. It seemed natural to bend his head and brush her lips with his. Bea made a soft sound at the back of her throat. He carded his hand through her hair, noting its softness as he cradled her head while the kiss deepened.

What the hell was he doing?

Dante pulled away at the same time as Bea did. She let out a little giggle and her cheeks turned bright red. He swallowed hard at the wave of heat that flushed over him. This couldn't happen. No matter how much he was attracted to Bea, Dante needed to keep this as light as possible. Date and flirt with her, yes, go beyond kissing? No. He wouldn't hurt her like that.

Fuck. When had he started thinking about it in terms of hurting her? Before, it had been a role he was playing. But at some point, his interest had become real. Sure, she was pretty, but when she talked about art, her face lit up and she became beautiful. She didn't deserve any of this crap for the bad luck of being born into a mob family.

He was so screwed.

"I'm sorry," Dante choked out.

She looked over and frowned. "What? Why? That, that was nice."

He forced himself to smile at her. "Not too soon for a third date?"

Bea chuckled. "I don't know. I'm thinking pretty good for a third date. Want to get something to eat in the cafe?"

Dante nodded. When they stood, she slid her hand into his, and he held on as they made their way through the museum. He could let himself feel guilty, or he could enjoy the moment. Sure, he had to pay attention to every line of conversation, to catch whatever Bea might drop about her family, but that was no hardship. He hadn't lied. He enjoyed listening to her.

He really had to avoid mentioning the kiss to Janet. She might be fine with it, since it fit into his cover. But it was like the first rule in the FBI handbook—don't fall for your criminal informant. That it had to be a rule meant it had happened more than once before. Dante didn't want to be a statistic.

After grabbing an overpriced snack in the cafe (Dante paid again, of course), they wandered around the first floor of the museum. Bea seemed like she wanted to soak in the experience, spending long moments standing before the artwork and not speaking.

"I don't want to go back," she said once they'd cleared the Egyptian wing. "They'll want me to help with Nonna's apartment, and I can't be there."

"I'll ride the train back with you. Then you can use me as an excuse to not go."

Bea grinned. "You're brilliant, you know that?"

They got on a train already filled with commuters. Bea half sat on his lap—and they were lucky to have gotten seats at all. Dante curled one arm around her to keep her steady during the jolting movement of the train along the tracks. Every so often they'd stop hard, and she'd smush against him.

That's when he'd take a deep breath, pulling in her scent—a mix of vanilla and lilac, perhaps her shampoo. Dante closed his eyes and forced himself to remember this, how she felt in his arms, so warm and soft, and the aroma of her in his nostrils. She'd never forgive him once she found out the truth.

"You don't talk about your family," Bea said as they emerged from the darkness of the tunnel beneath the Hudson. "I mean, you mentioned your grandmother, but..."

He sighed and pulled her a little closer as the train slowed. "My parents are divorced, but it came too late to make any difference in my childhood."

"Ouch, that sounds terrible."

Nights of fights, screaming and things crashing to the floor or against the wall. Yeah, it was pretty terrible. Most of those fights had been about his brother, how Dad coddled him when he should have been disciplining him. "It was rough. I learned not to count on anyone but myself."

That wasn't quite true. He'd been saved in high school by the security guard who finally put a stop to his brother's bullying. Dante had thought of him when he applied for the FBI. He wanted to make that kind of difference in someone's life. It had kept him from joining Aiden on the wrong path, that was for sure, and he'd always be grateful.

The train shuddered to a stop, and then there was the mad race with the commuters to get off and onto the platform before the next crop of people got on. Dante held tight to Bea's hand and guided her safely off the train.

Oh, who was he kidding? He was enjoying holding her hand.

"I parked in the lot across the street," she said as they emerged from the station.

Dante winced. "That must have cost you a pretty penny."

Her lips pressed together in a thin line. "I put it on my credit card. Daddy always paid for it. I guess I need to think about things like that now, huh?"

"Maybe." Dante didn't want to touch that with a ten-foot pole. If she was having some existential crisis about where her family's money came from, all the better for him.

They crossed Market Street with the rest of the pedestrians with the same careless regard for traffic. The lot where Bea had parked charged a premium for being so close to Penn Station. Dante's apartment was only blocks away—useful if he actually had to commute to the City.

As he followed Bea to her car, he asked "When can I see you again?"

Bea came to a stop in front of him and he nearly bumped into her. Dante wondered what was going on. Then he saw her—a dark-haired woman, leaning against a familiar black Volvo, her hands in her pockets as she stared at Bea.

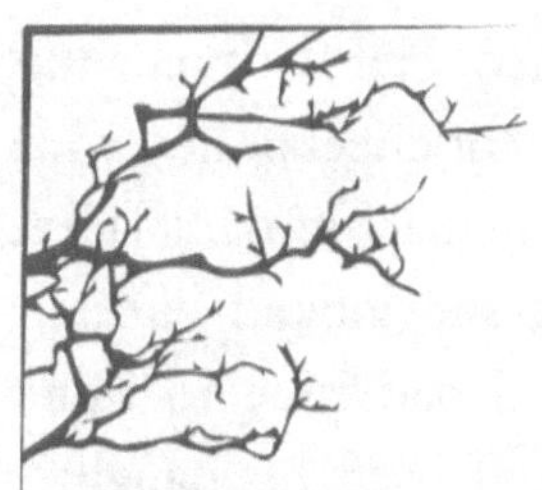

Chapter 19

Bea stopped in her tracks the moment she recognized the woman from the hospital leaning against her car. Her heart raced at both of her worlds colliding. There was a witch in front of her, and Dante was right there, wanting to know about when they'd get together again. It was too much.

The woman looked at Bea, and then moved her eyes to Dante before looking back at Bea. Right. Message received.

Bea faced Dante and squeezed his hand. "It's okay. I know who she is. It's a family thing, you know?" She all but choked on calling this woman family, but it was the easiest way to explain away the situation. "Can I call you later?"

He frowned. For a moment, she was worried he wasn't going to leave. "Yeah. Text me when you get home, okay?"

Bea nodded. "Sure." She watched until he left the parking lot, making his way up Market Street. Once he was out of earshot, she turned toward the witch, still waiting by her car like she had all the time in the world.

"How did you find me?"

The woman snorted. "I'd be a poor witch if I couldn't manage a basic tracking spell. Besides, what you got in the trunk is downright glowing if you know what to look for." She tapped Bea's car. "Nice job on the lock spell, by the way. A little crude with too much power put into it, but it'll hold."

Bea's blood turned to ice. Her grandmother's purse must have been far more valuable than she'd thought. At least she'd done something right by locking it away. "Why are you here?"

"You asked for my help." The woman sighed. Her dark hair was tied back into a bun, accentuating her prominent cheekbones, wide brown eyes, and sharp, pointed chin. She wore a smart-looking jacket over a blue dress and black heels. In short, she looked like any commuter traveling from the train station. "I had time to think about it. Your father would never forgive me if I left his daughter untrained and vulnerable."

Bea searched her face, trying to determine if the woman spoke the truth. Her heart raced again. Here was what she'd been looking for—someone to train her. But could Bea trust her? Only one way to find out—by using her instincts. She held out her hand. "Hi, I'm Beatrice. But you can call me Bea."

The woman smiled. "Carmella." She took Bea's hand and squeezed, the movement intentional, like she knew exactly what Bea was doing.

Bea saw the same glittering purple aura she had around her Nonna. She smelled vanilla and roses, with no sour or burned notes. Warmth flooded her chest, and she knew Carmella spoke the truth. But if Carmella was powerful enough, could she lie through her own aura?

She'd have to keep that in mind, but this was her first lead since Nonna's death. Bea would have to be as careful as she could.

"I have a lot of questions for you."

Carmella nodded. She looked around the parking lot and the commuters coming back for their vehicles. "Not here. I have an apartment at forty-two Bruin Street. Third floor. Meet me there in fifteen minutes?"

Bea nodded. She watched Carmella turn and walk out of the parking lot with far more skill on heels than Bea had ever managed. Only then did she get in her car and lock the doors. Bea rested her head on the steering wheel and shut her eyes. It had been one hell of a day. She couldn't even wallow in the memory of being with Dante, of kissing him in the Met. God, that had been a dream of hers, to have a romantic moment in one of her favorite places in the city.

Bea turned the ignition and threw her car into gear, her hands trembling in excitement. Finally, she had another witch to talk to! For the first time since Nonna had left her with the weight of the truth on her shoulders, Bea felt like she could move forward. She was conscious of running out of time—first Daddy with his heart attack, and then wondering who was next now that their charms had broken. Bea needed answers, and Carmella was the only one who seemed willing to give them.

It took her longer than fifteen minutes to find a parking spot and then walk back down the two blocks to Carmella's building. This area of the Ironbound was a more densely packed than the streets where Bea had grown up. The houses were a little closer together, touching each other, in fact. They were short, squat buildings with brick exteriors but didn't seem to go taller than three or four stories.

Bea walked up the stoop to number forty-two and pressed the bell for the third floor. The door opened without her having to touch it. "Show off," she murmured.

She climbed the narrow stairs that were mostly in shadow. The entire building seemed eerily silent, a little too quiet for such small quarters. The door at the top of the stairs was ajar and Bea knocked on it before entering.

"Come in!" Carmella called. "Have a seat. I'm just finishing up the coffee."

Bea entered to the rich aroma of espresso. She had to stop for a moment to collect herself. That scent brought her back to the feeling of home while visiting her grandmother or any family member, really. It was how you welcomed a guest to your home, and she didn't know how to feel about it now. Granted, it was just coffee, but she had so many complicated feelings about this woman.

Was she betraying her mother by being here? Family was everything, but in order to help her family, Bea had no other choice, not if she wanted to learn how to control her magic. Even if it meant consorting with her father's mistress. If it meant getting Daddy healthy again, Bea would do whatever it took. Even if she'd have words with him afterward.

The front door opened directly into a cluttered living room. There was furniture everywhere, big pieces of heavy dark wood and several small couches arranged in the center. The artwork on the wall drew her attention, and Bea moved closer to get a good look. "This is a lovely Rembrandt reproduction," she complimented. Carmella had good taste.

"What makes you think it's a reproduction?" Carmella approached with a tray holding the espresso and a small plate of cookies—store bought, not homemade. She'd kicked off her heels and lost the jacket, which softened the severe look she had going on at the parking lot.

Bea balked. "That is 'Christ in the Storm on the Sea of Galilee.' It was stolen from the Gardiner Museum in 1990. You can't possibly..." she trailed off, because, apparently, Carmella could.

She did a quick perusal of the other paintings hung on the wall. If these were real, then Carmella had millions of dollars just hanging around.

"Great art is the currency of the underworld." Carmella set the tray down and sat on the couch. "These are my insurance policy."

Bea didn't know what to say. Her mouth opened and closed, and she must look like a giant fish.

"Sit down. Have some coffee." Carmella picked up one of the small cups and sipped at it carefully.

Bea dropped onto the couch across from her, but didn't touch the coffee. She had to reassess everything she thought she knew about this woman. Admittedly, they were uncharitable thoughts about the kind of woman who would sleep with a married man. But she had to separate "dad's mistress" from "conniving witch, who was also apparently an art thief." "How did you get the art?"

"Payment for uncut diamonds, mostly. The Rembrandt was a special case, but you're not here for that story, are you?" Carmella gave her a sly smile, looking much younger than what Bea assumed her age to be, which she guessed was about a decade younger than her parents.

Bea swallowed. She had to remember her purpose here and not get distracted. She needed to learn how to use her magic, to heal her father, and avenge her grandmother's death. Any other misgivings would have to wait. "I have so many questions, I don't know where to start."

"Let's start with the obvious one. You said your Nonna awakened you right before she died? But you have no training?"

"She didn't get the chance." Bea's stomach twisted and she couldn't have had any of the coffee, even if she wanted to. "I think...someone killed her. Nonna. She showed me her spell book before...right before. But when I found her the next day, the book was missing."

Carmella set her cup down with a clatter. She swore in Italian.

"It's weird right?" Bea coughed; her throat suddenly dry. "That she would..." She couldn't get the words out. Bea leaned over, coughing uncontrollably.

Carmella narrowed her eyes. She held out her hand. "May I?"

Bea cleared her throat and sat up. "What?"

"There is some magic residue. I didn't notice it until you started coughing. Did you maybe give someone the evil eye recently?"

Oh. Bea had been having coughing jags on and off ever since... "I may have accidentally cursed a priest."

Carmella closed her eyes and pressed her fingers to her forehead. Then she got to her feet and headed toward the kitchen. From this viewpoint, Bea couldn't see much, but she heard Carmella rummaging around and muttered to herself.

She returned a moment later with something clutched in her hand. "You need to understand magical recoil. Every spell you cast comes at a cost, and there are different ways of paying the bill. But if you don't drain it off, you'll suffer for it later. Take this."

Like the dizzy spells she had every time she used her magic. Bea held out her hand to accept the smooth white stone Carmella placed in her palm. Immediately, she felt something special about it. Huh.

Carmella sat next to her and put her hand on top of Bea's, covering the stone. "Close your eyes. I will draw the feedback into the stone."

"Can you explain what you're doing so I can learn?"

"Later," Carmella promised. "We need to clear your spirit first. Close your eyes and be quiet."

Bea frowned, but did as she was told. It sounded a bit "woo" to her—some rock siphoning off the magical residue? That sounded more like the new age stuff some of her friends from college were into. But when Carmella chanted, warmth spread from her palm, up her arm, through her shoulder and down through her chest. Then it felt like someone took hold of something inside her and pulled.

She opened her eyes with a gasp. Bea blinked and as she looked around the room, she noticed things that shone brighter—that statue near the doorway, or the flowers arranged in a crystal vase on an end table. Magic. She couldn't see them before. Was that because the residue or whatever blocked her sight?

Carmella pulled her hand off, revealing that the white stone had now turned brown and pitted. "Find someplace safe to bury this."

Bea nodded and tucked the used-up stone in her pocket. She couldn't feel anything at all from it now. What had made it special she'd destroyed by filling it with the overflow from her casting the curse.

"Stones will work for small magics. But sometimes there are things you must pay the price for." Carmella had a haunted expression on her face as she stared into the distance. She sounded like she knew what she was talking about.

Carmella stood and paced the length of the room, expertly dodging the large pieces of furniture as she moved. She tapped her chin with one hand, as if thinking.

"You should know that witches are very territorial. It's not common for a witch to be trained by anyone but family." she started what sounded like a long story. Bea settled in to listen, hugging her arms around herself.

"Before your father took over the Thing here," and it was clear she referred to the mob. "There was another don and his witch. Your Nonna had to kill her before he could move forward with taking over."

Bea gasped and covered her mouth. Carmella stopped her pacing and gave Bea a pat on the shoulder.

"What, did you think he was democratically elected? This is a business and a bloody one."

There was a difference in knowing what the mob was and hearing that her Nonna had murdered a woman in cold blood for her power. Then what Carmella was really saying became clear. "You're saying another witch killed her because someone is trying to take the business from my father?"

"That's the way of things." Carmella finally sat, crossing her legs. "Your nonna hated me. Hated that your dad was making time with another witch. She was a mean old bitch. Don't look at me like that." Bea had glared at those words. "You don't know what went down in Italy. There's a reason she left and brought her three young sons here. She needed a new territory."

"What happened in Italy?" Bea asked in a soft voice, not sure she wanted to know the answer. They'd visited Italy dozens of times before. Surely it couldn't be too bad if Nonna didn't have a problem going back there.

Carmella paused in her pacing. "It was before my time. But the gossip says that she destroyed the entire line of Valentini witches."

Bea had never heard the name Valentini before. Why would Nonna do that? Bea dropped her head into her hands, her mind spiraling. She loved her grandmother, and she didn't know what to do with this information. Did it matter what Nonna had done in the past? If she had done this thing, then there would have been a good reason for it. Nonna would have done anything to protect her children and if those other witches threatened her, then Bea could clearly see her going nuclear.

Which was the same position that Bea was in now. Someone had threatened her family. They'd killed Nonna, and put Daddy in the hospital. It was only a matter of time before they went after someone else. Maybe one of her uncles or her brother. Maybe even Mom or Connie.

"I need to protect my family," Bea said finally. "To do that, I need to figure out how to use my magic. On purpose, I mean. I cursed that priest and you see how well that went."

"Look. Magic ain't easy. And if you don't have a coven, it can get pretty lonely." She looked away, staring at that painting on the wall with a frown. "But it's in your blood. You're in danger the way you are. You might do something that you aren't prepared to pay the cost for. Your father might never forgive me, but I'll teach you what I can."

Bea took a deep breath to calm herself. She forced herself to grin at Carmella. "Great. Let's get started."

Carmella crossed her arms over her chest and gave Bea a long gaze. A slow smile slid up her face. "First, I'm going to need you to do a favor for me."

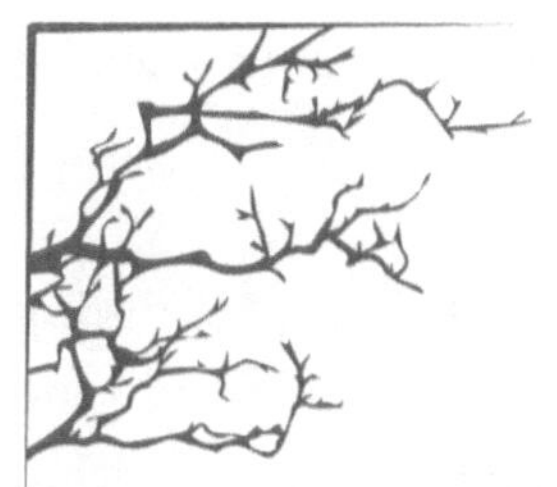

Chapter 20

Something bothered Dante about the encounter the entire time he walked back to his apartment. Originally, he'd planned to double back and try to overhear the conversation between the two women. But he could feel their eyes on him as he left the parking lot, like they wanted to be sure he was gone before they started speaking. He couldn't risk being seen eavesdropping at this point.

He'd always gotten the impression that Bea had nothing to do with the mafia aspect of her family. It was why Janet wanted him to approach her and not any of the male members of the family directly. Of course, the mob was traditionally a boy's club. But the entire encounter outside Bea's car gave him strong secrecy vibes. Whoever this woman was, Bea didn't want Dante to know anything about her.

Which meant she was important, somehow, and Dante should be sure to find out who she was as soon as possible.

If he kept on going as they were going, then maybe she would trust him enough to tell him. Dante touched his fingers to his lips, which tingled in memory of her softness against him. They'd kissed at the museum, and it made Dante want other things, things he shouldn't be thinking of right now, not when Bea was his assignment. Granted, this was the point, right? Make her fall for him, so she'd bring him as her plus one to the DiLorenzo wedding, where he'd have access to many big players in the Mafia scene.

A wedding he wasn't even sure was going to happen now. Janet hadn't told him what the plan was if they canceled the event of the season. He couldn't imagine them killing the mission, not with all the prep work the Bureau had done to get him here. Not when he was so close to Bea already.

And wanted to get closer.

The kiss was a good start. He'd need to report it to Janet during their next debrief. The kiss hadn't been for the mission. He'd be lying to himself if he insisted it was. Dante had wanted to kiss her. That moment had been so magical, Bea sitting so close to him, all aglow from the museum lighting, surrounded by the art she so loved. She'd smelled so good, too.

He licked his lips before making a face at his own love sick actions. There was no room for sentiment in the Bureau. He'd have to quash this growing crush on her, fast. Because that's all it was—a simple crush from playing the role a little too well. Dante needed to remember this was a part he was playing, like when he was up on-stage playing Willy Loman's son in Death of a Salesman.

Oh, but it was so different. Dante had never performed for an audience of one.

Determined to get his head back on straight, Dante charged up the stairs to his third-floor apartment intending to grab his workout clothes. A nice long run would clear his head and would help him keep up his physical fitness requirements. Dante liked rules. He enjoyed meeting expectations, like being able to do the required number of pull ups. Why had Janet thought him suited to undercover work?

He shouldn't have been surprised to run into her while locking his apartment door before heading downstairs. He'd changed into track pants, an old worn t-shirt, and his running sneakers. His body felt itchy with the need to move. But when he turned and saw Janet coming down the hallway, leading Rocky in from one of his walks, Dante knew his workout would have to wait.

"Hey Janet, do you have any bottled water I could borrow?" he said nonchalantly. In reality, Dante had a fridge full of water, and several reusable water bottles in his FBI stocked kitchen. But it was a good excuse to head to her apartment, especially since he had forgotten to grab one on his way out.

"Sure, come on in." Janet flashed him what he called her undercover smile—open and welcoming. She never wore that smile at the Bureau, and in fact, once they were inside her place and the door locked behind him, the smile disappeared completely. Even her posture changed from the woman who walked in the hallway. Her shoulders snapped back with military precision instead of being hunched over. Dante could learn a lot from the way she used body language while undercover.

"I have something for you." She let Rocky off the leash, and the dog ran to greet Dante.

"Oh?" Dante kneeled to get his welcome licks from Rocky. At least the dog had no expectations of him, other than being petted when asked, and that Dante found no hardship in.

"I snagged the coroner's report on Beatrice DiLorenzo. The elder," she added at the panic in his eyes.

Right. Bea was named after her grandmother.

Janet pulled a manila envelope out of one of the kitchen drawers. "Look at it here. I'll destroy it once you've left."

Dante took the folder and flipped through the file. He frowned. "This says she died of natural causes. No marks on the body, so no signs of foul play."

"Hence no autopsy. And since she was elderly the family didn't ask for one. None of the DiLorenzos seem concerned about her death. Except for your Bea." Janet leaned against the counter and tapped her chin.

He blanched at that. "She's not my..." He cleared his throat and flipped through the report in his hands, but his face heated in response. "You think she's seeing something that isn't there?"

"I think she has information the others don't," Janet said carefully, "And I think she told you for a reason. You need to find out what that information is."

"Her family didn't believe her. That's what she told me." Dante frowned. "But you're right, she's definitely hiding something. Today after our date, she met with a woman I've never seen before. Told me it was a family thing."

Janet's eyes sparkled. "Oh, a new fighter enters the ring."

"Your use of boxing references continues to be disturbing."

To his surprise, she laughed. "Finally, you show some gumption, kid. Don't walk on eggshells around me, all right? I've been where you are. I know it's hard."

Dante felt his face heat. He walked to the fridge and opened it, pulling out a bottle of water. "Who do you think she is? That woman?"

Janet accepted the return to the topic at hand gracefully. "You know better than to guess without intel. You have to remember that with the Don out for the count in a coma, there's going to be a lot of people vying for the top spot. We're probably not the only ones with the idea of going for the daughter."

The idea of someone else out there trying to use Bea had Dante squeezing the bottle so hard it let out an annoying crunching sound. He loosened his grip. "Do you have any information on that? Who's going for the boss's role?" Who should he be watching out for?

"Word from the informants from the rival families is that they've been asked to do business with the son." Janet typically kept him up to date with the intel she'd gathered from her other sources. She knew a lot, despite not having any leads within the DiLorenzo organization itself.

No, that was Dante's job. "That's unusual, right?"

She made a face and made the so-so motion with one hand. "It's more usual for there to be some fighting. The word on the street was that DiLorenzo's younger brother Tony was supposed to take over. Of course, he's still in Italy dealing with the body."

Bea's grandmother. He was offended on her behalf to hear the old woman reduced to nothing but an object for the FBI to track. "Is the Bureau delaying his return?"

She snorted. "We don't have to. The Italian government is doing that. Do you know how hard it is to transport a body across the Atlantic?"

"Can't say that I ever tried."

She snorted. "What we need in an inside man with the DiLorenzos. Find out what's really going on. I bet there's more to the story."

Dante nodded. "I guess I'll have to keep trying then."

"And I have every confidence that you will succeed. This is the closest we've ever gotten to this family." Janet wrapped Rocky's leash around her hand. She always did that before putting it away in a drawer. If she didn't keep it out of sight, the dog would think it was time for another walk. Rocky himself had gone to slurp up water from his bowl.

Dante had come a long way from that first meeting, where she'd intimidated the hell out of him. Hearing her faith in him felt good. Maybe Dante didn't suck at his job. "I'll let you know if I find out anything else." He started for the door.

"Oh, how did the date go?"

He stiffened at the question. That was the whole point of reporting to her, wasn't it? Telling him what Bea said. Keeping her appraised on his romantic progress. And Dante had certainly made progress today.

"Good. I'm supposed to call her later. I'm thinking I should give her a gift the next time we meet."

"Piece of advice? Go with something more personal than flowers. Something that shows you know her."

Dante turned back to grin at her. "Look at you, throwing out romantic advice. I must have missed that course at Quantico."

"That comes with on-the-job training," she teased.

He laughed and let himself out of her apartment. By the time he made it around the block, he knew what kind of gift would be more personal than flowers. It wasn't until his second mile that Dante realized he hadn't told Janet about the kiss.

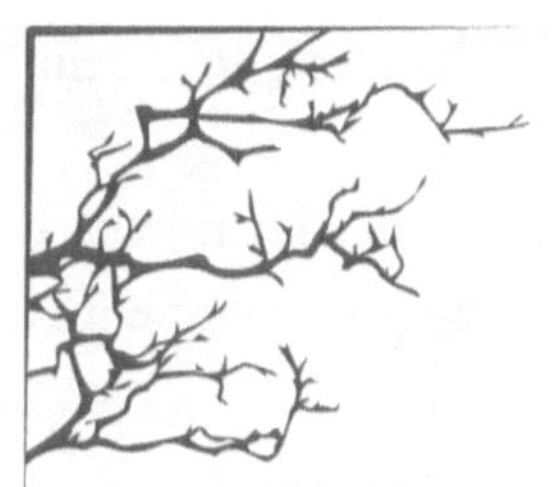

Chapter 21

At Carmella's words, ice ran down the back of Bea's spine. There it was. Of course, Carmella wasn't going to teach Bea out of the goodness of her heart. She'd forgotten her father's most important lesson—don't let anyone do you a favor. "What do you want?"

Better to know now what she was agreeing to, instead of being surprised later with something Bea wasn't willing to do.

Carmella laughed, like she knew what Bea had been thinking. She probably did. Bea bet her open witch aura was broadcasting all kinds of things. If she wanted to learn to control it, she would have to do whatever it was Carmella asked. Maybe there was some room for negotiation here. Bea knew better than to give in without asking questions.

"It's not a big deal, really."

"Who are you trying to convince?" Bea got to her feet, unable to face off Carmella while sitting on the couch.

Carmella crossed her arms. "Really. It's nothing complicated. Your father has a statue of San Michele that I gave him a few years ago. I'd like it back."

That didn't sound so hard, which meant that there had to be a catch. "What's so special about the statue?"

"Come on. You've learned enough to know how important certain objects are in our craft. I'm sure your Nonna showed you that."

And Nonna had used a statue of a saint to unlock Bea's power. It had never occurred to Bea to think that her grandmother had done something to the statue itself. She'd accepted it as a religious relic. "So, what does this one do?"

Carmela made a face. "It is an item of protection. But now that your father is in the hospital, it isn't doing him any good where it is. I need to check if the spell was tampered with."

By the same witch who'd hurt Nonna. Bea swallowed. "Why can't you get it yourself?"

"I'm not entirely sure where he kept it. I think it might be at the social club. But if it is, I can't exactly walk in there and demand it back. You, his golden child, can."

She wasn't wrong. Bea closed her eyes for a moment, trying to remember if she'd seen a statue of St. Michael the Archangel in the club the last time she'd been there—during the day of the feast. God, that seemed like forever ago. Her life had changed so much in a few short weeks.

"How big is the statue? It's not church sized, is it?" Because there was no way she was going to be able to smuggle that out of the club.

"It's about six inches tall. You'll know it because it'll give off a magical spark when you see it. It's a very specific statue I want. No going to the store and picking up any old San Michele." Carmella wagged her finger at Bea.

Bea stepped forward and met Carmella's eyes. "And before I do this, you're going to teach me how to sense that magic spark, right?"

"Of course. And a few more tricks besides. You won't be able to get anything done the way you are now. Do we have an agreement?" Carmella held out her hand. "I teach you magic and you will bring the statue to me?"

Bea hesitated for a moment. She could feel the heaviness of the words. This wasn't just a promise she was making. If she shook Carmella's hand, Bea would be bound to complete the task. "If I can find it," Bea amended. She didn't want to be stuck if her dad had thrown the thing out.

It had to be behind the bar at the social club. Bea vaguely remembered seeing a few statues of saints along the wall, but it wasn't something she'd paid too much attention to. They had saints everywhere.

"Good enough."

Bea took Carmella's hand in hers. A jolt of something ran up her arm, sharper and colder than electricity. It reached her chest and Bea sucked in a great gulp of air, for a moment unable to speak or breathe out. Then, as quickly as it came, the sensation faded, with nothing left except for some pins and needles in her fingers.

Carmella grinned, which changed the shape of her face. She looked almost excited now that the deal had been made. "First lesson is about hiding. You don't want to be shining like that. Any witch hanging around will immediately know you're new and untrained. You gotta suck that aura in."

"Like my stomach?" Bea patted her belly.

"Oh please. Wait until you're my age." Carmella rolled her eyes. "We don't have time for a history lesson, okay? So just do what I do and trust me when I say it works, okay?"

Bea channeled all her good student skills into the lesson, memorizing the shapes of the symbols Carmella drew in the air. She repeated them with her own fingers, again and again until Carmella was satisfied. There didn't seem to be any rhyme or reason to the patterns, but even if there were, Bea knew they didn't have time to go into it. She needed to be protected now.

"Now I want you to trace the shape on your own forehead," Carmella said.

Bea lifted her right hand and, despite how silly she felt, traced the symbols onto her own skin. It reminded her of the priest tracing the ashes on her forehead on Ash Wednesday. When she completed the motion, warmth spread along her forehead, disappearing into her temples with a prickling sensation. Bea gasped.

Carmella nodded. "Good girl. You're a fast learner."

"I'm going to have to be," Bea said grimly. Her off-hand thought about church had her straightening her shoulders. "I know you said you're not going to go into history, but I have a question?"

"Go ahead. I never said not to ask questions."

"Our magic...it doesn't come from the devil, does it?"

Carmella threw back her head and laughed. The laughter went on and on until it was almost insulting. Finally, she wiped tears from her eyes with the backs of her hands.

"The Goddess who chose us is a lot older than the devil. She may wear the face of the virgin Mary now, but that will change someday."

The words struck Bea, like she'd been slapped. She could hear the rightness in them, and something in her soul sang. Finally, finally, she knew the truth, where she came from. Warmth filled her, a sense of welcome, as if the Goddess herself reached out and touched Bea to say, "You are mine."

When she came to herself, Carmella had sobered, giving her a thoughtful look. "Now. Now you are ready to learn."

Bea flexed her fingers. A sense of calm had filled her. Finally, finally magic would make sense, instead of being something unknown and yet part of her.

"Here." Carmella walked into the tiny kitchen off to the left of the living area where she had been brewing coffee earlier. Bea followed.

Unlike the cluttered living area of the apartment, the kitchen was pristine. The counters were old style Formica, but polished clean. There were sets of containers along the backsplash, along with an impressive spice rack. Everything had been put away, except for the container of espresso still open next to the pot on the stove.

"The kitchen is the heart of the home. And it's the witch's hearth," Carmella emphasized the word. "While the men are playing in front of the TV, the real power is here."

Bea refrained from cracking a joke about belonging in the kitchen. She didn't know Carmella well enough to inflict her sense of humor on the woman. Plus, she was supposed to be serious. That was unfortunate, because she really could have used something to lighten the moment.

"My grandmother had spices like this," Bea ventured, running her fingers along the rich wood of the spice rack. "Anything you could think of."

"And she grew much of them in her own garden."

Bea whipped her head around at that. "How did you know that?"

Carmella sighed. "Remember, I know more about your family craft than you do. She had a garden. Of course, she'd use it. Home-grown herbs are much stronger than what you'd get in the supermarket. Magically speaking. We're talking about a different kind of cooking today."

Bea let out a tentative giggle at the apparent joke. Carmella smiled and then went back to her explanations.

"What you use to create spells and potions matter. Wood is good." She gestured to the container next to the stove that held about six or seven wood spoons of different sizes. "It is of the earth, it nurtures. Glass bowls are best."

Before she could continue, Bea raised her hand, feeling a bit like being back in class. "Can I take notes?"

Carmella nodded. "You should be writing this down and creating your own book of shadows."

Bea tugged her phone out of her pocket. "It's going to have to be the notes app of shadows for the moment."

"Get a real notebook." Carmella chastised. "Words are more powerful when written. Not so much on phones."

"I will," Bea promised. And she would once back home. She had a dozen empty sketchbooks waiting for the perfect thing to draw or write in them. One of them would have to do.

Carmella nodded and continued her lecture. To Bea's surprise, not all of it was new to her. Nonna had told her much of this, but in the context of food cooking, not spell crafting. She paused in her typing on the tiny keyboard and closed her eyes for a moment.

It felt like Nonna was over her shoulder, pointing out which herbs she should select in response to the spell Carmella was describing.

"Not basil," Bea interrupted Carmella. "Mint for protection."

Carmella stopped and stared at Bea. What could she see now that Bea had hidden her aura? "You sure your Nonna didn't teach you anything?"

Bea sighed. "I think whatever she taught me, she pretended it was about making gravy."

"You have the knowledge, just not the understanding, to put it in practice." Carmella nodded.

They spent the next few minutes learning how to brew the protection potion. In it, Bea would dip a necklace or other object into in order to infuse it with power. Of course, the potion alone was useless without the words Carmella taught her. Bea stumbled over the Italian, being out of practice and too accustomed to dropping her end vowels.

She ended up typing out the words phonetically on her phone, after turning off auto correct. "What's next?"

Carmella frowned at her. "I'll teach you one more spell tonight, one that will help you with the statue. More after."

Bea supposed that was only fair. She couldn't expect Carmella to give away all her secrets tonight, not when Bea still had to provide payment. Still, having this taste of magic and knowing she'd have to wait for more irked her. "What spell?"

"How to move unseen."

Now that was useful. "Do you mean turn invisible?"

"No, but this will let you move in the shadows. It will keep eyes from noticing you. It's not perfect, of course, and it will depend on how strong of a witch you are."

"Teach me."

Unlike the protection spell, this one didn't involve a potion. Carmella took out a bit of cheesecloth from one of her kitchen drawers. In the center, she put a selection of herbs, then sprinkled olive oil over it.

"Does it matter if it's regular or extra virgin?"

Carmella sighed. "The purer the oil, the better. Much of what you get in supermarkets has been cut with palm oil. Better to go to an Italian specialty store." She pointed at the label of hers, which read "imported from Italy."

"Noted." Bea had only been joking, but who knew how important the quality control on olive oil turned out to be?

"Use un-dyed twine to bind it together. Watch how I tie the knots." Carmella held the string between her fingers, winding it together like tying crochet knots. Once again, it felt familiar, because she had done this kind of weaving at her grandmother's knee.

There were more words to learn then. Bea typed her notes dutifully, nearly dropping her phone when it rang in her hands. Her mother's picture came up on the screen. Damn it.

"One sec," she told Carmella, before taking the phone back into the living room to answer the call. It gave her a small measure of privacy, but there was still an open doorway between her and the kitchen, so Carmella could still hear everything. "Hello?"

"Bea, where are you?"

"Um. Out with Dante." The lie slipped out easily. Better to be out with the guy she'd been seeing than hanging out with her father's mistress. Guilt squeezed her chest. Her mother would never forgive Bea if she knew.

"Tell somebody where you're going before you take off like that," Mom scolded.

Bea rolled her eyes, grateful that this wasn't a video call, so Mom couldn't see. "I am an adult, you know. I can take care of myself."

"I mean you were supposed to be helping us clean out your Nonna's apartment!"

That still hurt. Bea closed her eyes. Had that only been this morning? And her life had already changed in a million ways since then. "Why are you in such a rush to clean it out? There's so much going on." If Mom only knew exactly how much. "And the wedding in a few weeks."

"Because Mike and Lucy want to live there." Mom sighed. Bea could picture the defeated look on her face.

Of course they did. Lucy wanted to be part of their family so badly she'd even take Nonna's apartment. Heat flooded Bea's cheeks. "What? I thought they were moving in to Lucy's apartment until they could buy a house." It was why most of their gifts had been stored at home.

"Your brother wants to be close to the business. And why not when there is a perfectly good empty apartment available?"

Bea didn't know how to articulate that it was still wrong. That place belonged to her nonna. Anyone else trying to live there was taking up space that should still belong to her, because Nonna should still be alive, damn it. And Bea was going to find out exactly what witch had taken Nonna by surprise. The Family business was going to fall otherwise.

"Look," Mom said after a moment of silence. "I know you and Connie are fighting."

Bea sucked in a breath. "She told you?" Connie wouldn't betray her like that, but if her cousin still thought Bea was having some kind of mental break, then she might.

"Oh please. This is just like when you were nine and she destroyed your doll."

"It was an American Girl Doll," Bea protested. Come to think of it, that had been the last doll she'd ever had.

Connie had always hated that doll. Maybe because it had resembled Bea's best friend at the time, Janell. Connie hadn't been too fond of Janell either. When Janell had come to Bea's birthday party, Connie had pushed the other girl off the chair so she could sit next to Bea. Of course, she'd take the first opportunity to take the doll's head off.

She realized suddenly that she hadn't thought about Janell in years. She remembered feeling betrayed when her friend had moved away. Her father had comforted her with the reminder that she still had Connie, and now she should know she could only count on family. It wasn't until after high school she discovered that Janell had died of brain cancer.

Bea swallowed hard at the memory, taking a step toward the couch to hold on to it as dizziness took hold of her. God, what had she done as a little girl? She looked over at the kitchen doorway where Carmella had appeared, a concerned look on her face.

"I'll be home soon," she told Mom and hung up the call before she could protest. Bea whirled at Carmella. "I think I had another memory from my Nonna. I had a doll that I named after a friend of mine."

Bea had spent hours talking to that doll. Pretending it was her best friend, so Janell could be with her even when they were apart. "My nonna called it...a pupazzo? Do you know what it is?"

She could see Nonna shaking her head at Daddy, murmuring words she thought Bea couldn't hear. But Bea had. She hadn't remembered it until now.

Carmella went pale. "Jesu Christo. A pupazzo is a poppet. It can be a doll or something that looks like a person. What you do to the doll happens to the person."

Bea swallowed and lost her footing, sliding to the floor. "I may have done something horrible as a child."

"Oh no. None of that guilt crap in my house." Carmella put her hands on her hips and gave Bea a look that reminded her so much of her grandmother it hurt. "You're not weak. Your father told me you were strong. Is he wrong?"

"No," Bea said quietly, then repeated louder. "No." Her father didn't raise her to sit here and mope over something she'd done in the past. He taught her to take action. There might be nothing she could do to change what she'd done, but Bea could be damn well sure she'd never let her magic get out of control again.

Carmella stepped forward and held out a hand for Bea to grab on to. "The one thing you have to learn is how to deal with consequences. All magic has consequences. The left-hand magic—the dark stuff—comes with more of a cost, but you always pay a price for your magic. You can offset it by doing a little good here and there."

Bea got to her feet. The dizziness had faded and Carmella's words had penetrated. "Yes, that. I want to learn that. How I can do good."

Carmella smirked. "Well, it's not something I do a lot of myself, but I'll teach you what I know. Everyone has a specialty, you know. You could focus on healing, for example. I'm just really good at hiding and getting into places I shouldn't."

Which explained the kinds of spells she had taught Bea. If they had more time, Bea would ask more questions. She had some idea of

Carmella being an international jewel thief or something, but then what the hell was the woman doing here in Newark, New Jersey?

Bea still had a lot to learn. She could keep accidentally fucking up, or she could figure this shit out. Today was the first step on that path. "I'll text you when I have the statue for my next lesson. You do text, don't you?"

"Kids these days. No respect. Of course, I text."

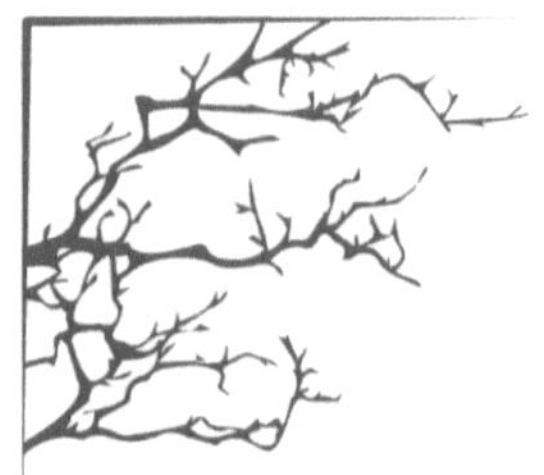

Chapter 22

Bea took her time transcribing her notes into the sketchbook she'd chosen for that purpose. While it was tempting to pick the one with the flashy cover with designs etched in gold, she instead selected one with a simple black cover that could be mistaken for a million sketchbooks in an art store somewhere. It would blend in with the rest of her collection, and no one would think anything weird about her having her nose in the book.

She added to the text with pencil sketches—a corner drawing of wooden spoons, the symbols she'd been taught for protection, even a little picture of Carmella herself. Bea had been drawing her entire life, but there was something different about this. She'd thought Carmella had been merely old-fashioned when she said there was power in writing things down. But when Bea wrote the words of magic, her hand warmed, the sensation traveling up her arm and down the side of her head.

Bea dropped her pencil and stretched, working out the kink that had settled in between her shoulder blades. She sat at the desk in her bedroom, after having to endure twenty minutes of her mother's questioning when she'd made it back home.

Luckily, Mom had believed her about being stuck in rush hour traffic on the train when they were coming back from the city. It had been true, after all. It just hadn't taken as long as Bea made it out to be. Thank God she had Dante as an excuse.

Her face heated again, this time having nothing to do with magic. She felt like a schoolgirl with a crush. He'd kissed her, and he'd been such a good kisser, too. Bea touched her lips, wishing it had lasted longer, that they'd had more time together.

He was a welcome escape from all of this. She got up from her desk and plopped onto her bed, letting her arms fall to the sides as she bounced slightly. A few minutes of daydreaming, that's all she'd allow herself: the moment when Dante tilted his head toward hers, the warmth of his lips against her own. He had tasted so sweet.

Her phone dinged loudly. Bea had to go searching for it and found it next to her messenger bag, which she'd tucked beneath the bed. There was a single text from Dante.

If you're still awake, wanna talk?

She looked at the time—nearly ten PM. Mom would be in bed by now and Mike out doing whatever he did for the Family business. Bea got up to double check that her own door was locked before dialing his number.

He picked up on the second ring. "Hey."

"Hey," she replied, suppressing a giggle. She didn't want to sound like a silly schoolgirl. "Sorry I didn't call earlier."

"You seemed busy. Who was that woman by the car?"

How to explain Carmella? Bea couldn't pass her off as actual family. The last thing she needed was Dante bringing her up around people who didn't know about her dad's cheating. "It's complicated," she said. "That woman is an old friend of my father's, but the family isn't too fond of her. She just wanted to ask me how he was doing."

"An old friend?" Dante repeated.

"More like an ex-girlfriend." That was close enough to the truth to get the picture across. Not like she could tell him the truth. *Oh, I'm hanging out with my father's mistress so she can teach me to use my magic before I do something stupid like curse another priest.* "And she likes to talk, so I got home pretty late."

"Gotcha." He cleared his throat, sounding hesitant. "I wanted to tell you I had a nice time today."

She grinned. He was so damn sweet! God, if she started twirling her hair and sitting on the floor with her feet on the bed, she really would be a twelve-year-old with a crush again. "I did too."

"When can we do it again?"

Bea ached with want suddenly. If she'd been born into any other family, dating could be easy like this. Find a cute guy and do something you like together. Instead, every relationship she had to weigh against the truth of who she was and had the potential for one of her cousins to show up and give the guy a shovel talk that was more than hyperbole. But with her father in the hospital, there hadn't been anyone sent to tell Dante to reconsider his life choices.

She never thought there would be a good side to her father's coma, and a flush of guilt went through her. God, she'd rather Dad be here and fine, of course. But for once, she didn't have to wait for his approval. He'd liked Dante, hadn't he? Dad had shaken his hand, thanking him for helping Bea. Maybe, if things were different, he would have approved of Dante.

This was another reason to get her magic figured out. Bea needed to get her father well and with her. She didn't want to be sitting here guessing what he'd think. She needed her daddy back.

She sat on her bed, tucking the phone under her chin as she got comfortable. "Are you working tomorrow?"

"I freelance," he reminded her. "I make my own hours."

"I don't want to take you away from your work for too long." Deadlines could be sneaky like that. Bea remembered a few that had gotten away from her back at school.

"Trust me, I'd rather spend the time with you."

She flushed at that. Bea touched her warm cheeks; glad no one was around to see her. A compliment would have her turning all blotchy and scarlet. It was not attractive. "That's sweet."

And it made the perfect excuse for having to go back to Newark tomorrow. Bea planned on going to the social club to look for the statue. She couldn't go when the place was closed. While she had every right to be there, Bea would have to explain why to whoever had been assigned to watch the place during the day, and that would draw attention to herself. No, Bea would have to wait until the doors opened tomorrow night.

"How about a late lunch? There's a new rodizio place I want to try."

"Sounds good."

They finalized plans to meet and then said good night. Bea plugged her phone in to the charging stand. She yawned, the day catching up with her. But there was still something she had to do first.

She pulled the messenger bag out from beneath the bed and opened it, revealing Nonna's purse. Now that Carmella had taught her how to see with her second sight, the amount of magic leeching from it seemed obvious. Bea traced the symbols over it—the same ones that dimmed her own witchy glow. The last thing she needed was another witch finding her because this thing acted like a spotlight.

From Carmella's tale it seemed witch rivalries were as common as mob rivalries. Being ignorant of the factions involved, Bea had to tread carefully. It was like knowing she shouldn't go past a certain street in Newark, or else she'd be walking into rival territory. Bea didn't know witch territory. Not yet.

She opened the purse again, pulled out the tiny book, and put it to the side. After her lesson with Carmella, she knew what she was looking at now—the tools of Nonna's trade. There was chalk for sketching out protective circles or symbols on walls. String of various lengths and colors for binding. Her lighter and a small white candle for impromptu spells. There was also her wallet.

Bea flipped through it, but out of everything in the purse, it had no magic residue. It was simply a plain old wallet. Inside, Nonna kept pictures of all her grandchildren, and seeing the ones of herself and Connie made her tear up.

Bea wiped her eyes. God, she wished she could share this with her cousin. If they weren't fighting, she could imagine them working spells together, telling secrets and giggling like they always did. They should be doing this together. Nonna would want them to.

She'd have to figure out a way to convince Connie. Bea would have to learn enough magic to show her the proof. And to do that, she needed more lessons with Carmella. Before that happened, Bea needed to find the statue and bring it to her.

Tomorrow. Bea would figure everything out tomorrow.

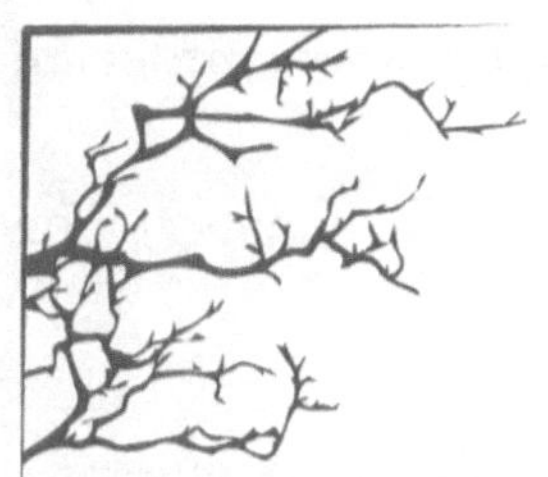

Chapter 23

Dante shouldn't be nervous. This wasn't a real date.

How many times are you going to tell yourself that? Maybe if he kept thinking it, he'd start believing it. When he accepted the mission, he understood the risks, that he'd be leading on an innocent young woman. But he hadn't expected to be attracted to her. He hadn't expected to enjoy kissing her.

Time to refocus. This was the job, nothing more. He was a damned good actor, that's all. Getting lost in a role was what he did. It's why Janet chose him.

Dante shifted his weight as he waited outside the Brazilian restaurant Bea had wanted to try, a long slender cardboard tube in one hand. A few people gave him strange looks as they walked by. He checked his phone again for the time and saw a missed message from Bea that she was on her way. He wasn't being stood up. Good.

And it was far too late to second guess this gift. Part of him wished he'd gone for flowers instead. Flowers were an old standby for a reason—they were reliable. Who didn't like flowers? Unless maybe she was allergic...

"Hey!" Bea waved as she walked down the block toward him. She dressed casually in a dark green button-down shirt and black jeans. The color did amazing things for her complexion, making her skin look creamy and her lips blush pink. "Sorry I'm late. Couldn't find parking."

"That's the advantage of walking everywhere," he teased. As she approached, he leaned down and brushed her cheek with his lips. He hadn't meant for the chaste kiss, but couldn't bring himself to go for her lips as a welcome. "This is for you." He handed her the cardboard tube.

She looked bemused as she took it. "A roll of paper? You shouldn't have."

"It opens at the top..."

"I'll open it inside?" She gestured to the door to the restaurant.

Probably a good idea. He didn't want it to get ruined out here on the street.

They entered, the bright sunlight outside shut out as soon as the door closed behind them to reveal a dimly lit restaurant. The dark wood accents helped give it that dark, intimate feel. A hostess led them to a table in the corner, giving them a bit of privacy. Perhaps she could tell they were on a date.

Once they sat, Bea immediately tried to open the cardboard tube. It took a few moments for the both of them together to figure out how to get the lid off. Dante had opened it that morning, but apparently when he resealed it, he'd put it on too tightly. They nearly bonked heads before Dante finally pulled the plastic lid off.

Bea laughed as she pulled out the contents, but her laughter died as she unrolled the poster paper, revealing a print of "The Annunciation," the painting from the museum where they had their first kiss. She put her hand over her mouth.

"I hope you don't have a print of this already," Dante said quickly, worried at her sudden silence.

Bea shook her head. "No, no. It's...this is the nicest thing anyone has ever done for me."

He ducked his head at her words. Yes, he'd gotten something better than flowers! Janet's advice had been good, although he was the one who picked this out.

"How did you get this done so fast?" Bea stared at the print, one hand on her chest.

"I found it online and had it overnighted." Dante had put the purchase on his personal credit card. The Bureau would have covered it. But that felt like cheating. Dante wanted her to have this gift from him, not as part of the job. Maybe later she'd look back on it fondly once all this was over and he was out of her life forever.

Bea rolled the print up carefully and tucked it away back into the tube. Then she got out of her seat and came around the table to give him a hug. It took Dante a moment to react, but he encircled her with his arms in response.

"Thank you," she said, untangling their limbs and going back to her seat.

"I'm glad you like it. I was worried for a minute."

"It's art, of course I..." she swallowed. "You really get me."

Oh, those words made his cheeks burn. Dante picked up his menu and started flipping through it, unable to look her in the eye.

Bea seemed to mistake his sudden silence. "I hope you're not a vegetarian or anything. I never stopped to ask if you knew what rodizio was."

He looked up in relief at the chance in topic. "I know what rodizio is. And even if I didn't, I googled the restaurant first. Plus, not a vegetarian."

"Sorry." She winced. "I mean, the last times we ate we had grilled cheese at the museum, so I didn't know if I missed something important."

"Don't apologize."

The server approached, and they both ordered the never-ending meat buffet. Bea didn't order any alcohol—granted, it was still afternoon—and Dante followed her lead. Not like he should drink on the job anyway, but he'd do it to fit in if need be.

Their first course came out almost immediately. The server cut strips of tender beef off his skewer. Dante's mouth watered. No, he was definitely not a vegetarian!

They didn't speak at first. Dante took his time and savored his food. "I wondered," he said after a moment. "Why you didn't choose an Italian restaurant?"

"Less chance of running into anyone I know here."

"You don't want to be seen with me?" Dante joked.

She took him seriously. "Oh, no. That's not it at all. You know how old Italian ladies are. They gossip. I really don't want to be the subject of talk, you know?"

She'd given him a nice opening. Dante tried to seize it. "Your family seems nice. I mean, the few minutes I got to speak with them."

"That's really kind of you to say."

"Are you still arguing with them about, you know?" He lowered his voice.

Bea leaned forward. "Not arguing so much as not speaking with them, I guess. My cousin hasn't texted me since we argued, so I don't even know. I guess I could reach out to her, but if she still thinks I'm crazy. Well, I am not going to apologize when I'm right."

She didn't know there wasn't any evidence of foul play in her grandmother's death. That didn't mean someone hadn't taken advantage of her death to steal something of value. Still, Dante had committed to believing Bea, so he needed to continue to support her. "Do you have any suspects?" he asked.

"Suspects?" She raised an eyebrow at him.

Dante cleared his throat. "I got that from the true crime podcasts. You need a suspect and a motive and opportunity."

Bea rested her head on her chin and looked thoughtful. "I think it was someone who wanted to take over my family's business. You know, the pizza supply company?" She added the last bit hastily. Yes, Dante was familiar with the front organization, *DiLorenzo Restaurant Imports,* which appeared to be how the family laundered their ill-gotten money.

Bea continued, "My grandmother was the heart of our family. Now that she's gone, well, we're all fractured."

This was the closest she'd ever gotten to admitting the truth about her family. Dante finished the last bite of his steak. "Like a hostile takeover? Usually when that happens, the person you're looking for is closer than you think."

Bea's eyes went wide. Then they narrowed, and she looked thoughtful. She opened her mouth to speak, but before she could, the server appeared again with another cut of meat, this time savory pork.

"Tell me about your family."

Dante had already gone off script by talking about his actual family. He supposed he should continue. "Nothing to tell, really. My parents are divorced. My entire life, my older brother was the golden child, and they ignored every time he bullied me."

"Yikes," Bea said. "At least my older brother mostly ignores me. That sounds rough."

He nodded, because it was. "I was happy to get out of there. I really found myself at college."

Which was true. They ended up comparing schools, and Dante had her in giggles as he regaled her with tales of behind the scenes in the drama world.

"No, he seriously fell through the set piece?"

"Right in the middle of the performance." Dante laughed along with her. It had been fun, although at the time, he and the others on stage had been mortified.

This time when the server came around with even more meat, Dante had to refuse.

"Oh, we're supposed to put our candle out," Bea explained. "So they know we are done." She leaned over and blew out the little tea light.

Dante found himself entranced by her lips as they pursed. He licked his own, tasting the salty remnants of his food, but what he really wanted was the taste of Bea on his tongue.

He took the check when it came over Bea's protests. "Fourth date, right? You can get the fifth."

"I can't believe you're keeping track." Her cheeks turned a pink so visible he could see the change even in the dim lighting.

Dante couldn't believe he was either. Granted, he'd been putting all of their conversations into reports, but he cherished their moments together. He'd never met a woman quite like her. Once again, he felt a stab of something, this time not guilt, but sorrow. They were building something between them, slowly and tentatively. This was a courtship that was destined to end in failure.

After leaving the restaurant, they walked down Ferry Street, hand in hand. "We have to work off all that meat," Bea said.

There were shops and restaurants all down this street, and it was bustling and full of people. Horns went off constantly as cars tried to navigate the traffic and trucks double parked to make deliveries. It was absolute chaos, but the only thing Dante could focus on was the woman next to him, who walked with her arm linked with his.

"We're having the bridal shower for my brother's fiancé there," Bea pointed out an Italian restaurant down one of the side streets.

Dante perked up at the first mention of her brother's wedding. "Oh?"

"Next week. No wonder my mom is going bonkers about me not being around. She probably needs me to hot glue centerpieces." Bea rubbed her forehead, looking irritated at the prospect.

"I don't mean to be rude, but the wedding is still happening? Even with everything going on?" Dante gestured to show he meant her grandmother's death and her father's hospitalization.

Bea sighed. "You'd think, but apparently Mike and Lucy really want to get married on this date. They'll make the sacrifice, they said." She rolled her eyes. "I mean, it probably helps that everything is already paid for, I guess."

"When is the wedding?" Dante asked, as if he didn't damn well know.

"June 21. I know, I know, usually the shower is much sooner. My mom is freaking out about two sets of invitations and who sits where. At least she's stopped crying about my dad, though."

She went silent, and Dante felt his belly drop. "How is he doing?"

"The same. I should go see him tomorrow. I hate that he's going to miss everything and we're just carrying on without him."

"I'm sorry." Dante gave her hand a squeeze. He stopped walking and touched her cheek with his other hand, wanting to give more comfort with his touch.

Bea leaned into his hand and gave him a smile. "Thanks. He's doing well, though. He just needs to wake up." She tugged Dante's hand to continue walking. "You know, you should come to the shower."

"What?" Dante nearly dropped her hand in shock.

"Not the shower itself. They always have a separate room for the men, and trust me, it's way more fun than what the girls are getting up to. Two words: Paper plate hat."

"That's three words."

She smacked him gently with the cardboard tube. "It will give me an excuse to get out of there as soon as possible."

He nodded. "Maybe text me toward the end so I can show up in time to rescue you."

"That sounds like a plan." She led them down a side street, away from the hustle and bustle of the main drag. Things were quieter this way, with no shoppers or delivery trucks. "I parked down here."

After a few blocks, he spotted her car artfully wedged between two others with only inches to spare on either side. "I am impressed by your parallel parking skills."

"I get a lot of practice." Bea turned to face him.

He couldn't help it. Dante reached for her, tangling his hand in her hair as he tilted her face upward for a kiss. It started sweetly, just as the kiss in the museum had been. That changed the moment Bea made a sound at the back of her throat, something that sounded like a moan.

He pressed her back up against the car, deepening the kiss. She tasted salty, like their lunch, but also there was that taste of her, something like candy and coffee. Bea put her hand on his hips, her fingers sliding underneath his t-shirt, making contact with his skin. He shivered at her touch, feeling warmth flood him all over.

Something vibrated in her pants pocket, and they were so close he could feel it against his leg. He pulled away with a laugh, nuzzling at her chin and neck. Dante didn't want to let go.

Bea pulled out her phone and looked at the screen with a sigh. "I have to go. More shower stuff. I wasn't kidding about my mom and hot glue."

"Hot glue is never funny," Dante agreed. He desperately needed to adjust himself, but didn't want to be rude.

Bea bent to pick up the cardboard tube. He'd missed her dropping it during their kiss. Well, it had been one hell of a kiss.

"Thank you again for this, and for lunch." Bea unlocked her car. "Text me tomorrow?"

He nodded and watched as she skillfully pulled out of the spot. Before this moment, Dante could deny it, could pretend it was all for the job. But he knew he was in real danger of falling completely head over heels for Bea DiLorenzo.

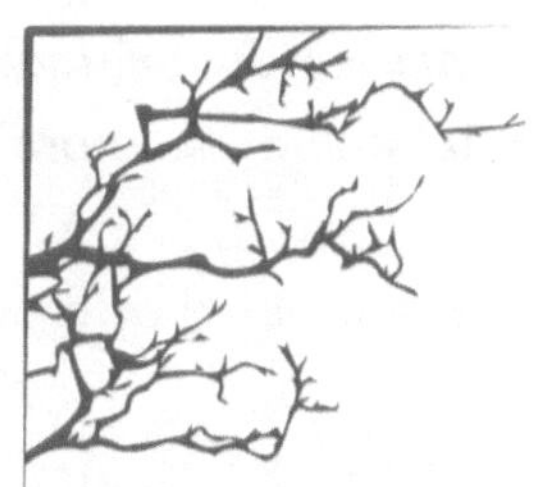

Chapter 24

Bea hated leaving Dante like that. They had been having such a good time. She liked the way he listened, focusing on her like she was the most important thing in the room. Most guys would look at their phones every few minutes or change the subject to talk about themselves. Maybe most of the guys she'd dated before were jerks. Dante was genuinely a good guy.

Which made her feel even more wretched for making up some story about having to meet her mother and ending the night early. Her family was taking her from something she really wanted to do. Or someone she really wanted to do. Bea giggled to herself as she steered her way through the busy streets back toward the social club.

They shouldn't rush things, anyway. She really liked Dante, and what would he think about all of this? Would he tell her magic was made up, and she was having a psychotic break, like Connie had? Or would he smile and pretend to believe her before breaking up with her via text?

Better not to say anything at all.

Bea pulled into the church parking lot and parked in a shaded corner. There weren't any masses tonight, but the priest wouldn't have her car towed. The Family used this parking lot for business pretty frequently. She took a moment, holding on to the steering wheel. Around her neck she had the protection charm she'd made for herself that morning. In her jeans pocket, she had the stealth charm that would only activate when she touched it with bare skin. Bea hoped to avoid using it.

She really wanted to walk in there, grab the statue from behind the bar, and walk out. Something told her it would be more complicated than that.

"Could really use some help here, Nonna," she murmured before getting out of the car.

Inside, the social club was bustling, filled with people. About a dozen tables were set up, the seats filled with men her father's age playing cards. There were people at the bar, laughing as the bartender passed down drinks. The atmosphere differed totally from the church festival, when most of the room had been filled with families eating from the buffet tables and waiting in line for the bathroom.

No, this was a completely different beast. This was Family - made men socializing and planning their next job, whatever that job was. Bea never asked. It had been better for her not to know. That way, if she ever got picked up for questioning, she could honestly say she thought the family business was importing restaurant supplies. Well. It was past time to learn.

"Bea!" a voice called.

She looked over to see her Uncle Guido waving at her from his card table. Uncle Guido was her youngest uncle, the most fun and happy-go-lucky of the three brothers. He looked more like her grandfather than the other two, being thinner and taller.

She crossed the room and bent down to kiss his cheek. "How are you?"

"Good, now that you are here." He patted her arm. "You can be my lucky charm."

"You're going to need more than luck," one of the other men at the table said.

Bea wondered if his name was in Nonna's book. There had been so many names. But now that Nonna had passed and her protection spells failed, would those contracts be void as well? That was something she was going to have to find out from Carmella. All the more reason to get that statue.

They were playing with Italian cards, and Bea recognized the game, Briscola, but she did not know how the betting worked. Bea had learned to play this game with her cousins. Her grandmother always had her own deck, sitting off to the side and playing what Bea thought was solitaire. The memory hit her now, like all of Nonna's secret teachings, with a trace of dizziness.

"What are you doing, Nonna?" Bea remembered asking, though she couldn't recall how old she'd been when this had happened. All she knew was that she wanted Nonna to come play with them.

"I am telling the future, carisima." Nonna dealt out the cards on the table, three rows of four cards. "See this one? It means you are going to marry a very important man someday."

"Ew," Bea had responded in return.

Now the memory inexplicably made her think of Dante. Bea put her hand on the back of her uncle's chair to steady herself. It would be nice if magic didn't make her dizzy. Although to be fair, she didn't know if it was magic itself, or memories of the times Nonna taught her magic without Bea realizing it.

But Nonna couldn't have been talking about Dante in her reading that day. Unless whatever made Dante important hasn't happened yet, and of course, if Bea ended up marrying him. God, just because he was a good kisser and made her laugh didn't mean they'd end up together. It felt right being with him, and part of her wanted that to be because her abilities had given her some kind of sixth sense about him. Nonna had said to listen to her instincts, after all.

Before she could worry about whether Dante and she had a future, Bea needed to concentrate on grabbing that statue. She looked over at the bar, where the statues of saints usually sat next to the cash register, but it wasn't there. Instead, there was one of those stands with napkins and drink stirrers. Okay, so they'd moved it. But where?

Uncle Guido threw down a card and the other men at the table groaned. They played a few more tricks, and it became obvious the game had turned. At the end, her uncle ended up scooping up the pot of money.

"See, you are good luck." He laughed and handed her the twenty he'd scooped up from the table.

Bea pocketed the money, like she was a kid again and her uncle slipped her and Connie cash when their parents weren't looking. "Thanks, Uncle Guido. Hey do you know...?" Before she could finish asking about the missing statue, the vibe in the room changed. The conversation dimmed, became hushed.

She looked around to see what had happened. Her brother Mike had entered the room, flanked by her cousin Tony Junior and his friend Dominick. The sight of it was so reminiscent of how her dad had walked into the back room when Bea had been hiding in the storage room. It gave her a strange tingling sensation at the back of her head.

Mike had a smile on his face, taking time to nod at various people at the bar. Then he saw her and the smile slipped from his face. He said something to Junior and Dom, and they left his side. Then Mike stalked across the room to her side. "Bea, what the hell are you doing here?"

Her heart raced. Bea stalled. "Why can't I be here? I'm here all the time."

"After church on Sundays is different. You know that." He took her arm and looked like he was about to escort her out. Although the men around them continued to play cards, Bea knew they were being watched.

She couldn't make a scene, but she couldn't leave here without the statue either. Putting on her most innocent little sister look, she tried telling a version of the truth. "I was looking for Daddy's St. Michael statue. I thought it would be good to bring it to the hospital. It might help." She sniffed a little. Not for the first time, she wished she could do the whole fake tear thing.

He narrowed his eyes at her. Bea had seen that expression before, when Mike was trying to tell if she was lying or not. It must have been a convincing performance, because he let go of her arm. "I put it in the back in storage. We needed the room on the bar. And I'm sick of all this religious stuff being around all the time."

"What do you mean?" Bea had been so occupied by her mission that she hadn't noticed the removal of the other statues of saints that had been in this room, along with the crucifix that had hung on one wall. It had hung there so long that the paint had discolored, so the shape of the cross was still there. Her skin crawled at the sight—there was something wrong about it.

"Time to modernize this place."

"No, I mean, why are you doing this? Dad's going to get well and when he gets back..."

Mike let out a laugh. "Grow up, little sis. Dad's not making it out of that coma."

The tears she'd wanted moments before pricked behind her eyes. Bea swallowed it down, not wanting to cry in front of everyone. "You don't know that."

He held her gaze, and that tingling sensation returned to the back of her neck. Something was wrong, but Bea couldn't put her finger on what. There was no scent to guide her. It would be hard to make out in this room full of people and cigarette smoke, anyway.

"Mike, can I have a word?" Uncle Guido stood up and got between them. He looked over at Bea and then back at Mike. "In private."

Mike took a step back. "Outside then. Bea, the statue is in the back room. We're going to be back there soon, so grab it and get the hell out."

Bea watched them leave, her heart throbbing so loud she could hear it above the voices in the busy club. How could things just keep rolling on without Daddy being here? And Mike didn't even think Daddy was going to get better. How could he think that?

Well, for one, he didn't know about Bea's magic or the witch who'd stolen Nonna's spell book. He had no idea she was working to figure out her magic to make Daddy well and find the person working behind the scenes to steal the family business from them. All the more reason for her to hurry so she could get more magic lessons from Carmella. Bea slipped into the backroom.

It didn't take her long to find the statue in the corner with the other saints Mike had removed from the club. The wood and stone figures had been piled up like so much garbage. As soon as Bea touched St. Michael, a jolt went up through her arm. Yep, something magical about this statue. Clearly, Mike had no magic of his own, or else he wouldn't have left this here with the others.

Before leaving, Bea hesitated. There was an exit that led to the loading dock behind the club. If this hiding charm worked, she might find out what Uncle Guido wanted to talk to Mike about. She tucked the statue under one arm—it was heavy, but no heavier than her backpack full of textbooks back at school—and put her other hand in her pocket.

Bea murmured the spell to activate the charm, making sure she got each bit of Italian phrases perfect. Then she opened the back door and slipped out, letting the door shut and lock behind her. Loud voices to the right drew her in that direction. She stayed along the wall and the shadows gathered around her feet, keeping her hidden from view.

"...don't know what the hell you think you are doing..." That was Uncle Guido.

"I am doing what my dad would want me to do. Keep the business running."

"You father never messed with drugs. Heroin? Fentanyl? We don't bring that shit in the house." Guido snapped. His words sent a chill down Bea's spine. She had never really thought about where the money came from, but apparently, not the drug trade.

Until now. *Oh, Mike, what are you doing?*

Mike let out a sharp laugh, a nasty sound that make Bea's skin crawl. She moved closer, wanting to see exactly what was going on.

Mike and Guido were staring each other down at the entrance to the alleyway. Mike had his finger pointed at their uncle. "You think I don't know what this is about? You're just mad I've pushed you out."

Guido straightened his shoulders and slapped his chest. "I am your father's consigliere..."

"I am his son. And this is a new day, Uncle Guido. We're not running this thing the old-fashioned way, not anymore."

"You listen here, you have no business squeezing me out."

"Nonna's not here anymore to play favorites," Mike snapped. "I'm not in the dark anymore about what's really going on."

Bea froze at those words. Could it be that he only recently learned about magic, too? Did that mean he might know about Bea? Or was he talking about something else? He hadn't picked up on the statue, still tucked under her arm and warming the side of her torso.

Guido sucked in a breath. "You son of a bitch!" He grabbed Mike by the lapels of his jacket and slammed him against the wall.

Mike responded by head butting him. Guido staggered backward, his nose gushing blood. But Mike wasn't done. He raised his fist and punched the older man in the face.

Bea gasped, but she didn't dare put her hand over her mouth. She needed to keep in skin contact with the charm, and the other hand was currently keeping the statue of saint Michael from tumbling to the ground. No amount of magic would stop them from seeing her if she made that kind of clatter. And she couldn't risk them seeing her suddenly appear out of the shadows.

What she wanted to do was step forward and tell them to stop fighting. They were family! When the doors to the club opened and several people ran out, she thought it was to break up the fight.

She was wrong.

Dominick held uncle Guido by the arms while Mike punched him in the stomach. "I am in charge now," Mike snarled. "You swore loyalty to this family, and I'm the boss now. Got it?"

Guide doubled over in pain, coughing, and vomiting onto the ground. Bea took a step forward, almost losing the grip on the statue. That stopped her. She couldn't be caught. She couldn't risk losing the statue and her chance at learning how to use magic.

Mike grabbed his chin and forced Guido to look at him. "You tell the other old men that it's my way now. They think Nonna was tough? Well, I'm a million times worse."

"The fuck is wrong with you?" Guido choked out. When Mike raised his fist, Guido held up a hand for mercy. "I got the message."

Mike stepped back and shook out his hand. "I think it's a good idea if you take over the shop downtown. It should keep you busy."

Guido wiped the blood off his chin. He didn't speak for a moment, then finally nodded. "I'll head right over."

He staggered away while Mike and Dominick watched him leave. Bea couldn't go anywhere until they left, since they were between her and the street. The door behind her was locked, and that reminded her she to add "unlocking spell" to the list of things she needed to learn.

"You think that's gonna keep him out of trouble?" Dom muttered.

"The shop is old school," Mike said. "Right up his alley. He can handle chopping up a few cars. That's small potatoes, anyway. We got bigger things."

Dom let out a laugh and slapped her brother's arm. "We sure do. Come on. The Mangiapanes will be here any minute now."

"Glad we got the old man out of the way…"

Mike and Dominick went back into the club.

Bea waited a heartbeat to make sure they were gone. It was clear there was a lot of shit going on that she had no clue about. She darted out into the street, the shadows still following her since she hadn't let go of the charm. She kept her fingers on it until she made it safely around the block to the church parking lot.

Once she got into her car, Bea locked the doors and let herself freak out. "What the absolute fuck." Her hands were shaking as she curled them around the steering wheel, gripping it so tightly her knuckles went white.

She was so far out of her depth here. The only thing Bea had going for her was magic. She took a deep breath. Stick with what she knew.

She sent Carmella a quick text. "I got it."

The response was quick. "Excellent. Are you ready for more lessons?"

Bea swallowed as she stared at the phone screen. Carmella said she could learn to do some good with her magic. And with the way things were going, Mike was going to bring the entire family to ruin. She needed Daddy awake and with them to fix things.

If Bea went ahead with this, there was no turning back. She had to be sure that she wanted to be caught up in this business. But she couldn't let Mike go on like this. She couldn't let him bring down the family.

She owed it to Nonna.

"Yes." She texted back. "Can you show me how to use magic to get Daddy out of his coma?"

"Bring the statue over and I'll show you anything you want to know."

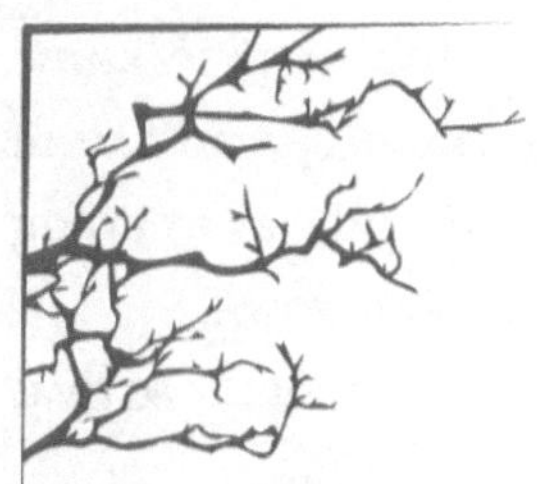

Chapter 25

Dante stumbled upon Janet walking Rocky through River Bank Park on his daily run. It was no accident. Janet knew he ran here at this time—if he didn't have a date planned with Bea, of course.

He slowed down to say hi, and Janet invited him to walk with them.

Dante crouched down to give Rocky the required scratch behind his ears and then moved into step with Janet. Rocky trotted between them, happy to get his daily exercise.

"What's up?" he asked lightly, although he kept looking around them, trying to spot a threat that wasn't there. As far as he could tell, no DiLorenzo family goons had ever followed him here.

"A little update from our man in one of the other families that might affect your job."

Dante stiffened. "That doesn't sound good."

"It's not. Some of the old men don't like that the son took over for his father." Janet let Rocky sniff at the base of a tree. She leaned back and looked around at the busy park. They weren't the only ones on this track. "Guido DiLorenzo has been bitching to some members of the Bonetto family."

"What does that mean, exactly?"

"It means we may be looking at a mob war." She sighed. "Tensions are rising and sometimes that spills out to the streets. Your girl might be in danger if she gets caught in the middle of it."

His girl. The words made him flush with heat. Dante hadn't confessed his crush to Janet. As far as he was concerned, it was just him getting a little too close to the job. She didn't need to know about it, not unless it started affecting his performance. And Dante knew what he was doing. He wouldn't let it get in the way of doing what needed to be done. The mob needed to be taken down.

"Do you think it will spill out at the wedding? Lots of those rival families are invited," he pointed out.

"It's entirely possible. I want you to watch your back, especially if she takes you to any family functions. And see if she knows anything about what her uncle is up to."

"Got it."

BEA CHECKED THE DOOR yet again, glancing out the window as the nurses walked by her father's room, oblivious. She didn't know how long the locking charm she'd set would last, although Carmella had watched as Bea had traced the symbols and called her magic into being. The woman would have said something if Bea had done it incorrectly.

Nearly a week had passed since Bea had brought Carmella the statue. Carmella had grinned in delight at receiving it, before placing it on one of the end tables beneath the largest painting on her apartment wall. Bea couldn't help herself. She'd had to ask. "What's so special about it? I can sense the magic in it."

Carmella had hesitated before responding. "Like I said. It's protection. You can sense that about it, right?"

That had led to their next lesson. Since then, Bea took any opportunity she could to learn more.

Carmella wasn't exactly frequent with the praise, but would definitely point it out if Bea made a mistake. It made sense. This wasn't a class with a grade attached. This was magic, and if Bea fucked up, there could be consequences, bad ones. She didn't even want to imagine what she might call up by accident.

Bea fidgeted as Carmella laid out her items on the tray table they'd swiped from another room. Daddy's room was filled with the equipment keeping him alive, and the two chairs for visitors. He looked terrible, still pale, so unmoving, unlike the father she knew, a man full of life.

Stop it, she told herself. That's what they were here for. To fix him.

"Stop pacing. You need to focus." Carmella straightened and pointed to the items in front of her.

Bea darted forward, eager for the lesson. Since that night she'd brought Carmella the statue, she'd been true to her word, teaching Bea the basics of magic. Today, they'd put all of that work to the test, using their combined abilities to pull Daddy out of his coma.

On the table Carmella had put a tiny tea light candle, a small Tupperware container of white powder, a feather, and what looked like one of the bottles of holy water the church gave out sometimes. Next to it were two pieces of chalk and a dry erase marker.

"It would be better if we could have moved the bed away from the wall." She shook her head. "It can't be helped."

"Not unless we want to kill him first." Bea balked. Moving the bed would require unhooking machinery and despite her faith in magic, her faith in the science keeping him alive was a lot greater.

Carmella made a face at her. "I said it would be better. Not that I wanted to try it. Tradition says to make a circle around the person three times."

Bea bit her lip and committed her words to memory. She'd have to write this all down later, but now she had to focus. "Right. What are we going to do instead?"

"You stand over there." She gestured to the bed. "I will do one side, and you the other."

Bea made her way carefully to the other side of her father's bedside, the machines continuing to whirr and pump, the soft beeps coming from the heart monitor a reassuring sound. No matter what, her dad was a fighter. That steady heartbeat confirmed it. All they had to do was wake him up, then he could fix this mess, stop whatever the hell it was that Mike was doing to the family.

Carmella pointed to the items on the table. "Now, what do you think these are?"

Bea bit her lip. The thing about a crash course in witchcraft was that there was so damn much to learn. Every so often, Carmella would quiz her. None of her actual college professors were so relentless with the pop quizzes. "It looks like ... the elements? The candle for fire and there's water and the feather for air. But what is that white powder?"

She let out a little chuckle. "Baby powder. It's mostly talc. That represents earth nicely. Much easier to carry around than graveyard dirt."

Half the time Bea didn't know if Carmella was kidding or not. She had a sense of humor that showed up every so often, however, sometimes magic was just weird enough that the things Bea thought were jokes were deadly serious.

"Okay. Why the elements and not, like, herbs or something?" Bea remembered the "healing" she'd tried to work here, using the herbs from her mother's herbal tea collection. God, she'd known absolutely nothing.

Well, not nothing. Just enough to be a danger to herself if she'd continued without training.

"Because we're not going to work a healing. Not yet." She held up her hand in reaction to Bea's opening her mouth. "We need information first. This spell will tell us what we are dealing with. Then we can figure out how to fix him."

Bea nodded, swallowing down her worry. This had to work.

Carmella picked up the dry erase marker and sketched out symbols on the wall over Daddy's bed. By this point Bea recognized them: the curved sigil for protection, the hourglass for knowledge, the scales for balance.

"I'm going to give you the element at the foot of the bed," Carmella directed. "You repeat what I did and give it back to me over his head, got it?"

"Got it." Bea moved into place. She took a few deep breaths to settle herself, reaching for the core of her magic that burned in her chest. It was so easy to reach for it now, the warmth inside her, and call it to life.

Carmella started with the water, sprinkling it down the side of Daddy's bed, murmuring words in Italian. Bea strained to hear them. She caught something like "Reveal us the truth, where is water in this working..." but couldn't be sure. Later, she'd have to ask for the exact wording to write it all down.

She took the bottle from Carmella and repeated the motion all up the other side of the bed, handing it over when she reached Daddy's head. They repeated the action with each of the elements, sprinkling the powder, carefully moving the lit candle, and then stroking with the feather to simulate air.

When she handed over the last item, Bea held her breath. She felt pressure swell in her forehead as the magic crashed to a crescendo. A blast of cold air rushed through the room, knocking her against Daddy's bed.

Carmella cursed in Italian.

"What is it?" Bea straightened, not sure what she should pay attention to. Her nose caught the scent a moment after she spoke, the metallic tang of blood.

"Look at his aura," Carmella commanded.

I don't want to. Because Bea already knew, somehow, that this was not good. She reached out with a trembling hand and put it on Daddy's shoulder.

As soon as her skin made contact, his aura sprang to life. It was a dull yellow, intersected with threads of red that looked like pulsing veins, wrapped all around him. If this was a piece of thread, she wouldn't be able to pull it out without ripping up the fabric it bisected.

Bea snatched her hand away as if burned. It didn't just look horrible, it felt horrible too. Her belly twisted and her head pounded. If she had kept contact any longer, she'd be retching in response. "What the hell is that? What does it mean?"

Carmella blew out the candle, tucking it and the rest of her supplies back into her large black leather purse. She wouldn't meet Bea's eyes as she used a microfiber cloth to remove the symbols from the wall. "It means that the witch who cursed him tied the spell into her life force. This is blood magic." She all but spat out the words.

Bea frowned. "Blood magic?"

"Evil stuff. You don't want any part of it."

No, she was done with not knowing stuff. "You told me all magic has a price. That it wasn't necessarily anything evil about it." Despite the things she knew her grandmother had done. Was this worse than even that? Then again, her grandmother had made deals with those she cursed. That implied some sort of consent. Daddy didn't agree to be cursed into a coma!

"That is mostly true," Carmella agreed, rubbing her forehead as if she had a headache. "Because I never intended to teach you any of the darker arts. What we are dealing with here... this is a witch who isn't afraid to use sacrifice to get her way."

"All right. Then how do we stop her? How do we get this curse off Daddy?" Bea gestured to her father.

"We don't," Carmella said quietly. "The only way to end this curse is to kill the witch to cast it."

The words made Bea stumble backward. Kill the other witch? She shouldn't have been surprised at those words. Carmella had told her from the beginning that was how it was done. That Nonna herself had killed the witch in power before. Bea had balked at the idea of putting someone's eyes out. How could she kill someone?

Bea raised her hand. "I vote for another option, please."

Carmella let out a shaky laugh. "I wish that were possible. Of course, we have to find her first."

Maybe by then, Bea would come up with a different option. Or maybe she'd be able to deal with the possibility of having to kill another human being. Another human being who'd killed her grandmother and put her father in the hospital. She might be able to call on the anger that burned in her belly to get the job done.

One thing at a time.

"That's not impossible, though, right?" They'd already gone over basic scrying. How hard could it be to find a person?

Could it be one of those women who had come to Nonna's funeral? Bea tried to picture herself stabbing one of those old ladies and her mind went blank.

Bea realized she was spiraling, her mind shattered as she tried to come up with a solution.

"I've been trying to find her," Carmella admitted. "But she's powerful enough to cloak herself. I can't even pick up anything from her spell work." She gestured to Daddy. "Most of the time, witches leave something behind. Your magic, for example, is very distinctive."

"Does it smell?"

"I wouldn't describe it like that." Carmella didn't seem to perceive magic the same way Bea did. Normally, Bea would find that fascinating. Like art, it seemed there were different ways of achieving a similar result. But they didn't have time to compare magical theories. Daddy didn't have that kind of time.

How long could someone be in a coma for, anyway? Before they started talking about removing life support?

"There is something else we could do." Carmella reached out to take Daddy's hand. She pulled the golden charm out of his palm and stroked her fingers over it, renewing the magic before tucking it back in place. Somehow, no one had noticed its presence there, and Bea knew it had something to do with Carmella's spell. It couldn't bring him out of his coma, but somehow it seemed to keep Daddy from getting any worse.

"What's that?" Bea asked, when Carmella didn't finish her thought.

Carmella looked directly at Bea, leveling a hard gaze at her. "Draw her out. Force her hand. Make her reveal herself."

"You're saying I have to be bait."

Before Carmella could respond, Bea's phone went off with a loud ring, the ring she only used for her mother. She ran for her messenger bag propped against the wall near the door where she'd stashed her phone before they started. "That's my mom. We're supposed to meet up later for a dress fitting."

The damn wedding. Bea hated it was still going on while Dad was like this.

Carmella wiped the last of the wards off the wall, erasing all the evidence that they'd been there. "Contact me when you're ready for our next lesson."

"Right." Bea was halfway to the parking lot when she realized Carmella never said what they would do if they succeeded in drawing the other witch out.

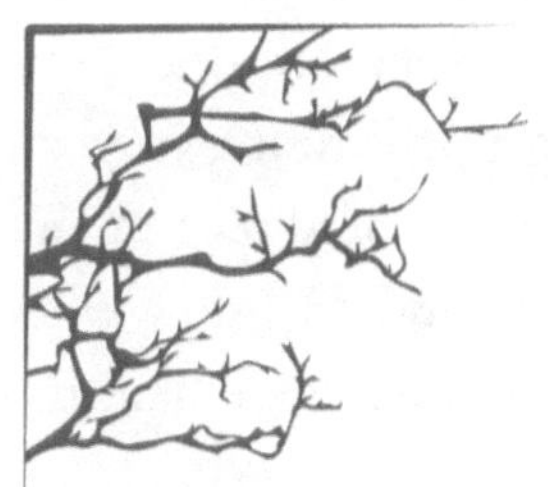

Chapter 26

Someone at the craft store should be fired for stocking such a bright shade of yellow feathers. Bea grimaced as she attempted attaching yet another feather to the mirrored glass circle on the table in front of her. Her glue gun jammed—again—and she ended up adding another stick of glue to the end to hopefully push the rest of the gunk down the nozzle.

Mom had finally roped her into doing the actual thing Bea had been using as an excuse to meet with Carmella. They were running out of time, since the shower was only a few days away. And the glue needed time to dry. Hence, here she was in the basement rec room, surrounded by craft supplies that made her sneeze, instead of either working on her magic or seeing Dante.

After trying to wake up Daddy—and failing—Bea had thrown herself into learning as much as she could. If the witch who cursed him was good at hiding herself, Bea needed to be better with revealing magics. They'd spent the past two weeks practicing. She filled her sketchbook with notes and spells.

But her instincts told her they were running out of time. Much like the feeling she had before Nonna died, Bea knew she had to make a move and soon. Thus, she would have to bait the other witch, and right now she planned on doing that at Lucy's shower.

It made sense. All the female relatives and paisans would be there. If the witch was close, as Dante had suggested, although he'd no idea what he was actually suggesting about, then the odds were she would be in attendance. Bea would have to lay a trap.

These centerpieces were the best way to do that. She'd already sketched out the symbols beneath them, using a pen she'd gotten at the craft store that dried clear. Anyone with magic would pick up on the message Bea was putting in them, one that said: "I know who you are." Now she just needed to make the tops of them look halfway decent, despite Lucy's terrible aesthetic.

As she activated each centerpiece, Bea felt a wave of dizziness. By the time she finished, her head would be throbbing in pain. But she wondered about the consequences of more severe magic. Wouldn't the witch who was using her own life force to keep Daddy in a coma be suffering something? What about those deals Nonna had made, like the one she'd used to punish Vito? She'd asked Carmella about it during one of their lessons.

"I told you your Nonna was ruthless, but she was also smart," Carmella had said. "She made bargains. All the men agreed to those conditions when they were made. So, when she fired off a spell, she didn't get any of the consequences of hurting someone."

It sounded like a loophole to Bea. She didn't know how she felt about it, knowing her Nonna cheated to keep everyone in line. However, it was certainly better than whatever it was Mike was doing. She shuddered, still not over the night she witnessed him beating on their uncle.

Her phone buzzed, and Bea grabbed it, grateful for the excuse to stop thinking about this crap for a while. Her plan would work or it wouldn't, and Bea had to stop dwelling on what she couldn't change.

Dante had texted her: *Deadlines suck.*

He told her he'd had some big advertising campaign he was working on. He'd mentioned that when she bailed on their last date to go do more magic lessons with Carmella. It had alleviated some of her guilt at leaving him after dinner again.

Because Bea wanted to spend more time with him. She loved their make-out sessions against her car—always against her car. He laughed at her bad jokes, and he listened so intently to what she had to say. He was easy to look at, and he smelled so good, like warm driftwood. She made a mental note to ask Carmella if that scent meant anything, although they figured out that Bea was far more attuned to scent than Carmella herself.

At least you're not here for the hot glue gun action. She sent him a picture of the centerpiece she was currently butchering. Any moment now, Mom was going to come down here and yell at her about having an art degree and being unable to do a simple craft.

Art was different than crafts. Bea had tried explaining this to her a million times.

Want to grab lunch tomorrow? I have an hour budgeted.

That would give Bea all afternoon to spend with Carmella. Fantastic. She texted back a *yes* and told him to pick the place.

Warmth filled her as she watched his words appear on the screen. Despite all the crap going on with the family, it was nice to have Dante as a soft place to land. She could spend time with him and forget, for a moment, that she was learning magic to find out who was trying to take over their family.

"Bea?" Mom called from the steps. There she was, right on time to criticize Bea's work.

"Still working, Mom," Bea called back. Maybe her mother would stay upstairs if Bea told her everything was fine.

"Connie is here to help," Mom called, and then footsteps down the stairs signaled the arrival of her cousin.

Bea swallowed and got to her feet, tucking her phone away in her back pocket. This was her mom interfering again. She and Connie hadn't spoken since the fight.

Connie stopped at the bottom of the stairs. She stuck her hands in her pockets and bit her lip. "Hi."

Bea waited for a beat, afraid Connie had only come down here to yell at her again.

When Connie didn't speak, Bea gestured to the half-constructed centerpiece on the table. "Who puts feathers on a table centerpiece? Won't they get into the food?"

Connie let out a half choked out giggle. Oh, good, they were laughing and joking again. Maybe things were going to be okay.

"Aren't we also putting tea lights on them? Won't the feathers catch on fire?"

Bea made a motion like she was checking off a list. "Add fire extinguisher to the shopping list. Got it."

Now Connie did let herself laugh fully as she came over to inspect Bea's work. Admittedly, it did not look good. Bea had dripped glue everywhere, clouding the surface of the mirror and weighing down the feathers. She tsked. "I know you can do better than that."

"If it were up to me, it would have a better design," Bea complained. "Yellow. Feathers. Like the ones we have to wear in our hair."

Connie shuddered. "Don't remind me. I keep looking at that headpiece and consider making a run for it. I hear the Caribbean is nice this time of year."

At least they could always unite to mock Lucy's fashion sense. And the girl worked at a high-end fashion boutique! You'd think she'd have more sense. Then again, Lucy's choices all seemed to look good on Lucy. They were terrible on both Connie and Bea. The maid of honor was one of Lucy's friends from said boutique, and kept gushing over all of Lucy's choices. Bea supposed she should be grateful it was all yellow instead of orange or lime green.

"I'm not going to apologize," Bea said finally. It was Connie who doubted her sanity, who didn't trust Bea to understand the truth.

Connie nodded. "Can we, can we just forget everything and move forward?"

It was better to keep Connie out of it, anyway. The more Bea learned about magic and her family, the more she doubted everything. She couldn't imagine her sweet cousin doing the things that needed to be done. Bea knew she might very well have to kill the witch threatening them, if she wanted her father out of his coma. The thought of that made her sick, so she'd avoided thinking about it. She could make that decision once she found out who the witch was.

Bea got to her feet and wrapped Connie in a hug. She needed her cousin back. "Yeah. I missed you. And I really could use some help with these monstrosities."

Connie laughed as she pulled away. She moved to the table and put her hands on her hips, shaking her head at the project Bea had butchered. "Let's start over." She meant the centerpieces, but Bea could hear the weight in her words.

The work went much faster with her cousin helping. Bea thought of the centerpieces more like art and traded her glue gun for some adhesive medium she had in her art stash. They covered their mistakes with golden glitter, and it actually looked halfway decent by the time they were done. Only twenty-five more to make.

"Are you still seeing him?" Connie asked, preparing the next mirrored plate with the clear glue medium. Could she feel the magic Bea had put into the glass? She didn't seem to react when she touched the plates.

Bea smoothed her next set of feathers, not meeting Connie's eyes. Talking about Dante was sure to make her blush. "The guy from the wake? Yeah."

"Tell me all about it." Connie set down the plate and started working on another. "Let me live vicariously through you."

Honestly, it wasn't hard to talk about Dante, to fall into old habits with her cousin, chatting about guys they liked. She told Connie about their dates, how he met her at the museum.

"He likes the same stuff you do?" Connie asked.

Bea smacked her arm. "Why is that so hard to believe? He's a graphic designer, so he has a passing interest in art. He didn't tune out when I talked about impasto."

He listened to her. Asked her opinion. And he was such a good kisser. Bea leaned on her hand, drifting into a daydream of how his lips felt on hers, how the warmth of his body pressed against hers.

"I invited him to the shower," she confessed, lowering her voice. That had been before her plan to draw the witch out. But now, in retrospect, it seemed like a good idea to have an out, someone to take her away from the shower before the other witch could act. "At least to the guy's part of it. He's going to rescue me from having to stay late."

Connie gasped. "Have you told anyone? They are not going to like a stranger showing up in the back room."

"It's not a Family thing," Bea emphasized. "He's only coming to give me an escape. The last thing I want is to get roped into carting all these gifts to Nonna's apartment."

Connie frowned. "Why are they going there?"

Connie hadn't heard the news, apparently. Bea filled her in. "That's why our moms wanted to clean it out so fast."

Connie slammed down the tea lights. Her face went bright red, and it took Bea a moment to recognize it as anger. "How can they do that?"

"Mike is running the Family business now." Bea didn't elaborate, because then she'd have to confess how she knew. She had to pretend to not know how Uncle Guido got his black eye when they saw him at church on Sunday.

All the more reason to stay on target and get Daddy out of his coma, before Mike destroyed everything. If Uncle Guido was upset with the direction Mike was moving the Family, then it had to be for a good reason. It wasn't like Bea could talk to him about it. As far as he knew, she was only his little sister who knew nothing about the family. Mike didn't seem to know about magic. He hadn't been there when Nonna had done her thing. Maybe Dad was waiting to tell him until the time was right.

Bea rubbed her forehead, the throbbing from using her magic on the centerpieces starting earlier than expected. "I have something for you," she told Connie. "Wait here while I get it, okay?"

"Sure?" Connie gave her a confused look.

Bea had been making more protection charms. It was good practice, and she couldn't stand the idea of having family members out there unprotected. She'd used decorative cord from her art projects to weave together simple necklaces that she charged, using the potion and spell Carmella had taught her. Bea could feel the magic in the objects once she'd finished. They wouldn't last as long as Nonna's gold chains, but it was the best she could do for now, at least until Daddy woke up and they figured out her new role with the family.

She paused at the top of the stairs when she heard voices. Instead of her mom and Aunt Julia, who she expected, she heard Mom and Mike having an argument in loud whispers.

"I'm just saying it's a little early to be putting everything in Lucy's name. You're not even married yet."

Bea murmured the cloaking charm to herself as she stayed pressed against the wall, sliding closer to hear better. Why would he be putting things in Lucy's name? Mom was the executor of Nonna's will, and she was taking care of everything.

"Mom, you know how this works. If I get arrested, do you want to lose everything?"

"Don't get arrested then," Mom snapped.

Bea nearly snorted in response. If only it were that easy.

"Look," Mike lowered his voice, and Bea had to strain to hear him. "...in charge now....have to accept..."

"...you know I don't like..." Mom had dropped her voice as well.

Damn it. Why were they whispering? Bea moved closer, confident her magic would keep her cloaked in shadows. But as she stepped toward the kitchen, she bumped into the shelving unit with her mother's knickknacks—mostly old wedding favors that still had the Jordan almonds attached. One clattered to its side, making a racket as it fell. Bea felt the magic dissipate around her.

Silence from the kitchen. Damn it.

Bea pretended she hadn't been listening and strode in. "Hey Mom, do you have any more tea lights? We're almost done. Oh, hi Mike. Didn't know you were home." She kept her voice light, like she hadn't been eavesdropping and desperate to know what Mike was doing next. She knew Daddy wouldn't approve.

Her mother's shoulders dropped. "Yes, I have some in the garage." She put her hand to her head, as if it pained her, looking out into space like she couldn't focus. Bea didn't like that. It reminded her of how out of it she'd been since Daddy's heart attack. "I'll get them." Mom opened the door to the garage and disappeared, leaving Bea alone with Mike in the kitchen.

She hadn't been alone with him since that night. But he couldn't know that she'd seen him. Bea would have to pretend everything was okay, that she wasn't worried about the direction he was taking the family in. She was only the little sister who knew nothing.

"Working on another one of your art projects?" Mike asked. He wore gym clothes already soaked with sweat and he smelled strongly of BO. At least he'd been working out and not, well, working.

Bea forced herself to smile. "An art project for your wedding. Well, Lucy's shower anyway."

"Glad all I have to do is show up and hand her off." Mike opened the fridge and pulled out a bottle of sports drink. He removed the cap and downed half the bottle of the blue stuff.

"You mean you don't want to watch us play shower games?" Bea honestly wasn't looking forward to it herself. At least she only had to hand out the prizes afterward. The maid of honor had come up with the games.

He chuckled. "No, I prefer hanging out in the back, where I get to eat and drink as much as I want."

That reminded him of what Connie had said earlier. Bea really should ask for permission before throwing Dante to the wolves. "Listen, this guy I'm seeing. Is it okay if he drops by the restaurant afterward?"

Mike's smile widened. "Oh good, I get to interrogate him. I didn't get the chance at the wake..." his voice trailed off. Maybe Nonna's death had affected him more than he had let on. "Tell him to come early for some free food. And that I might have a few questions for him."

This was just her big brother teasing her, not the mafioso who'd so cruelly beaten their own uncle a few nights ago. It loosened some of the tension in her shoulders. "Go easy on him."

"He's already dating my little sister. What more can I do to him?"

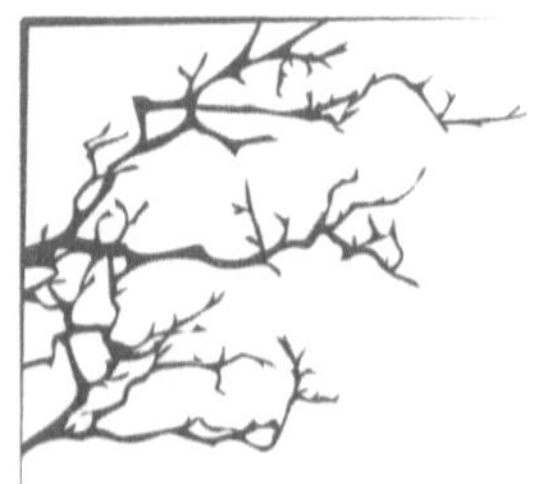

Chapter 27

Janet had been the one to pick out Dante's outfit for the shower. Not because this was an important date, and he didn't know what to wear—which was true, too. But because this was part of the job. He needed to look the part, and he needed to fit in, but not fit in too much. She eventually decided on a pair of black slacks, a cream-colored button-down shirt, and a navy sports jacket.

"Yes, I think that works nicely." Janet rubbed her chin as Dante modeled the outfit she'd chosen. She turned away to go sifting through a drawer, leaving Dante to mull over his new look.

He examined his reflection in the mirror attached to Janet's closet door. Like this entire mission, he'd been Janet's paper doll, dressed up and groomed to get exactly where she wanted him to go. At first, he'd appreciated the help, but now the jacket felt too tight and the pants constricting.

Of course, it had nothing to do with the clothes themselves. The problem was continuing to lie to Bea. He could no longer deny that what he felt for her was real, outside of his job. If she knew the truth, she'd break things off with him immediately. But if he didn't tell her the truth, she'd never know the real him.

Would she even like the real him, anyway?

"Here you go." Janet returned with a shoulder holster and gun. "It's an off-book weapon. Serial numbers have been scrubbed."

Dante took the gun gingerly, checking the safety as a matter of course. "You think I'm going to need this?"

"Think of it as an insurance policy." Janet shrugged. "It might work to give you some street cred with some of these wise guys.

Remember, you're trying to get in with them. Bea opened the door for you. Now use it."

Her words were like a splash of cold water against his skin. It had been easy to woo Bea - because she'd stolen his attention from the beginning. Now he had to work at being this persona he'd created for the job. Bea got all the nice parts—the graphic artist, the guy who laughed at her jokes—and now he had to use some of the darker parts of the background they created to fool the rest of her family into accepting him.

The bitch of it was he was worried Bea wouldn't like him after some of his "background" came out. Never mind that it wasn't real.

"Stop thinking so hard." Janet poked him, breaking Dante out of the spiral. "You've been doing great so far. Keep it up."

He grinned. "Wow. Praise from you? I must be doing halfway decent."

Janet shook her head. "You have been. But you gotta keep on your toes. If you see a situation turning bad, then get out of there." She sounded almost worried.

Dante straightened his shoulders. Janet had picked him to do this job, and he needed to get his head in the game, not stand here mooning over a girl, no matter how he felt about that girl. Seeing justice served was more important than a relationship that would fail. "I will not let you down."

"I know."

Rocky barked at the moment, probably ready for a walk, but Dante took it as an endorsement from the dog as well. He stopped to scratch behind Rocky's ears before leaving.

The weight of the gun felt heavy under his blazer, and it was a solid reminder of the world he was about to enter. Mob life was one of violence, of power plays, of the strongest rule. Dante needed to remember that.

The restaurant hosting the shower wasn't a far walk at all. Dante could learn to appreciate the benefits of living in this city. He certainly loved the food, and the convenience of being able to walk and get what he needed within a couple of blocks. If he had to drive in all this traffic, though, it might be a different story.

He saw Bea waiting for him as he approached. She wore a deep rose-colored dress that clung to her figure. He imagined what it would feel like to get his hands beneath her skirt, to feel the soft skin beneath. Then, when she turned around to grin and wave at him, shame and revulsion rushed through him. How the hell could he be thinking about feeling her up when Dante knew how things really stood between them?

"Hey." Bea greeted him with a huge smile lighting up her face.

His heart melted when he saw it. "Hey."

She tilted her head up for a kiss, and Dante obliged. If he took an extra moment or two to savor how she felt beneath him, no one would know.

Bea took his hand in hers, squeezing it tightly. "Are you ready for this?"

He cleared his throat as if uncertain. "I figure it can't be as bad as the wake."

She winced and a stab of guilt went through him. Probably not a good idea to remind her of the event where her father had his heart attack.

But Bea didn't bring up his faux pas. "The focus is all going to be on Lucy and Mike, anyway. Trust me, she loves being the center of attention."

Dante had picked up on the bad blood between Bea and Lucy. Lucy seemed like a normal Bridezilla to him, but he didn't have to deal with her. "I'm ready to fade into the background."

She led him inside, pushing the heavy wooden door that led to a little lobby with a hostess stand. "It's not technically a surprise, since she knows about it, but we're all going to pretend it is. Mike will bring her in later." Bea looked at her watch. "Um. In about fifteen minutes."

They hurried past the main area of the restaurant to one of the banquet rooms in the back. The room was filled with people that Dante recognized from either his research or the wake. Someone had placed centerpieces decorated with bright yellow feathers and glittering candles on each table. The feathers matched the bright yellow of the tablecloths, the balloons and the streamers attached to the walls.

"Someone likes yellow," he murmured.

"Those are her colors. Yellow and white." Bea had plastered a smile on her face, one that didn't look right and Dante abruptly recognized it as her public facing smile, the one she wore when meeting strangers, or apparently, dealing with a room full of Family. "Come meet my cousins."

Three young men, all dressed in black suits, clustered together in a corner. Like Bea, they had curly dark hair and clefts in their chin. That's where the family resemblance ended. Tony Junior—"call me junior"—had narrow eyes and a cocky grin. Vinnie stood a good hand taller than his brothers. With his broad shoulders, he looked like a bouncer. The youngest, Marco, was still a teenager, all gangly limbs and shy smiles.

"This is Dante," Bea announced. "You're going to take care of him, right?"

Dante swallowed. "Nice to meet you."

"Very important question," Vinnie said. "Yankees or Mets?"

Now this kind of hazing he could deal with. "Neither. Phillies."

All three brothers fell over dramatically, like he'd just insulted their mother.

"Hey, it could have been worse. He could've said Red Sox," Bea teased.

"They're coming!" A young woman appeared in the doorway. The crowd in the room immediately hushed. Someone turned down the lights, and a waiter closed the doors to the entrance.

Dante waited in anticipation, his hand still caught in Bea's. It didn't take long before the doors swung open and everyone yelled "surprise!" at the happy couple. Mike, he recognized right away, but the young woman next to him, his fiancé Lucy, apparently, seemed out of place. Dante couldn't explain it. Staring at her didn't help, it was like his mind couldn't hold on to her features. He caught blonde hair and nothing else.

He rubbed his eyes, unsure what was going on.

"You okay?" Bea whispered.

He didn't know.

"Thank you, thank you!" Mike said as he moved through the crowd, shaking hands and bending to kiss cheeks. When he got to their group, he grinned. "So, you did bring the boyfriend, huh?"

Bea's cheeks turned a delightful shade of pink. What a shame that he wouldn't be spending the next few hours by her side. "Yes. And you're going to be nice to him."

"I never promised nice," Mike said with a laugh. Even though he wore a smile, there was something in his eyes that made Dante think of violence.

Dante had to remember his role here, to earn the respect of these men. "I think I can handle whatever you dish out."

"Is that a challenge?"

Bea nudged him and smacked Mike on the arm. "No challenges. Just sit and eat and watch whatever sport is playing at the bar."

"We got this, sis. Don't you have some shower games to run?" Mike made a little shooing motion with two hands.

Bea rolled her eyes. She turned to Dante and gave his hand a final squeeze. "I'll get out of here as soon as I can. Try to have some fun, okay?" She slipped from his side and moved toward the rest of the women in the room, gently ushering people toward their seats.

Dante looked over at Mike, knowing she'd left him to the wolves.

BEA GLANCED OVER HER shoulder as Dante left the room with the other men. Her stomach twisted into a knot of worry. Maybe she shouldn't have invited him. It was far too early in their relationship for him to meet her family. But if he couldn't accept her family, then he wasn't the right guy for her, no matter what she felt. Bea couldn't separate herself from her family.

And she needed him there with her. His support these past few weeks had meant everything. Knowing he was in the next room over did a lot to quell her anxiety over the possibility of discovering the witch's identity.

"You didn't introduce me." Connie came up to her side. "And I thought he wasn't going to show up until later to pick you up?"

Bea shrugged and tried to play off her cousin's concern. "I asked Mike and he said it was okay. And before you ask, yes, I am regretting that decision."

Connie laughed. "He'll be fine. And you know if he survives that, he's the one."

Warmth flooded her, and Bea could see her skin turning red and blotchy. Just what she needed before pictures. The idea, of Dante being the one—she liked it, but Bea couldn't even think about the possibility. She had too much going on, and she still wasn't any closer to discovering who had stolen Nonna's book and possibly her life. But hopefully her bait should attract some notice today, otherwise this was a wasted event playing bridesmaid for Lucy.

As if her thought had summoned her, Lucy came up to them both, linked her arms in Bea's and Connie's. "Oh, my gosh. Thank you both so much! This is so much more than I was expecting." She giggled and covered her mouth. "Oops, it was supposed to be a surprise, wasn't it?"

Connie patted her shoulder awkwardly. "Don't worry about it. I don't think anyone is actually surprised by their bridal shower."

"Oh, thank you." Lucy beamed. "I'm just so happy to be part of your family, you know? Since I don't have one of my own."

In fact, all of Lucy's side of the guest list were her friends who worked at the boutique. The maid of honor—Bea had to ask Connie what her name was again—had given them the names. Otherwise, the other women in the room were Bea's family, and the wives and sisters of other men in the Family. She didn't think Lucy knew half of them. Hell, Bea didn't recognize a handful herself. She'd been right about this event bringing in a lot of people. The witch had to be here, or at least, have her eyes on this event.

It had been too quiet since Daddy's heart attack. Bea had been expecting the other witch to make her move for weeks, and had desperately given out protection charms to her closest family. That sense of intuition still beat in her belly that something was coming, and soon.

"Come on." Mom brushed past them. "Let's take our seats. The waiters are waiting to serve the antipasto."

After which would be followed by the first game—a quiz that tested the guests on how well they knew the bride and groom. Bea had been up late finishing the gift baskets for the winners. She hoped the prizes would be appreciated.

After the dinner course, they'd start opening the presents. Bea had brought her laptop for recording all the gifts into a spreadsheet, to make it easier to track. Of course, that would be if she had time while running the gifts up to the table and taking care of the torn-up paper. Connie had volunteered to make the hat out of the discarded ribbons, thankfully.

And hopefully by the time she escaped with Dante, Bea would find out if her bait had caught any flies.

Bea settled in next to Connie, but at the same table as Lucy and the Nameless maid of honor. The next few hours would not be fun.

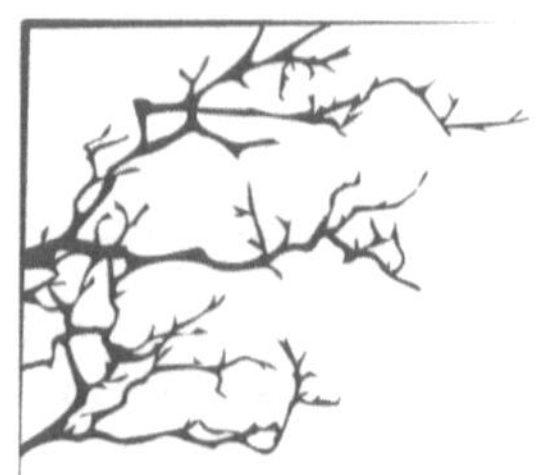

Chapter 28

Dante followed Bea's brother and cousins to the back room that was little more than a bar, several large wide-screen TVs showing different sporting events, and a few pool tables. It had to be for the exclusive use of the Mob. He couldn't imagine the restaurant having real customers back here, so secluded from the rest of the business.

From the moment he walked in the room, all eyes were on him. Dante knew he stuck out. He was the only one not wearing a full suit, for one. More importantly, he was a new face, and he hadn't been introduced to anyone but Bea's cousins. Mob etiquette meant that he couldn't speak to anyone until he had been vetted and properly introduced. Of course, he wasn't supposed to know about the Mob yet.

Although anyone with eyes could see how the older men—those of Don DiLorenzo's generation—kept to themselves, sitting at tables along the wall and in the corner. They murmured in inaudible whispers, giving Dante grim looks before turning to each other and talking again. Mike and those around his age range hung out at the bar and around the televisions. They were noticeably louder and more jubilant, laughing and drinking happily.

"You can sit with us." The youngest DiLorenzo, Marco, gestured to a table near the front of the room.

Dante accepted the invitation gratefully, settling into a seat just as waiters approached the table, carrying trays of food that they set in the middle. The rich scent of Italian cuisine filled the room: garlic and tomato, along with the mouthwatering smell of fried food—it looked to be calamari. Not Dante's favorite, but it all sure smelled good.

Marco got up and went to the bar, returning with a few bottles of beer. He gave one to Dante, another to his brother, and kept the third for himself. If Dante remembered his files correctly, Marco was still a teenager.

"Are you even old enough to get this from the bar?" he blurted instead of saying thanks.

Marco laughed. "All right man, if you think shit like that, then you really don't fit in here."

Dante tried to turn it around. "I just didn't think they gave beer to ten-year-olds."

"Hey, I'm seventeen!"

His older brother, Vinnie, snorted. "He's right, you look like a little kid."

"I do not, shut up."

The two brothers shoved at each other in their seats, but Dante could tell there was no heat in it, unlike every interaction he'd ever had with his own brother. They seemed to enjoy teasing each other, and the shoving eased quickly enough as they made plates for themselves from the platters in the center of the table. Dante passed on the calamari, but grabbed some pasta instead—vodka rigatoni.

He chewed slowly, taking the time to watch the dynamic of the room. Now that the food was out, it seemed everyone was content to stop chatting and eat. Mike remained near the bar with his friends, making comments on the baseball game currently in the second inning. Bea's uncle Tony had returned from Italy and he sat in the corner with his brother Guido, decidedly as far away from Mike as they could get. Interesting. Could that be the trouble Janet had warned him about?

Because he was watching, Dante knew the moment Mike put his drink down and approached Dante's table. So, Dante didn't jump when Mike put his hand on his shoulder.

"We're going to rack up a few balls. You in?"

Any easing of the tension he'd achieved with his meal and making nice with the younger cousins disappeared. Dante forced himself not to tighten up at Mike's touch. He couldn't give himself away. Still, he felt like this game had to be a trap of some kind. "Sure. I don't want to be stuck here at the kid's table."

Marco let out a little "hey!" and Vinnie threw a balled-up napkin at him.

Mike chuckled and led the way over to the tables. Dominick and Junior had racked the balls. They nodded at Dante as he approached. Ok, this was good, this was fine. He was doing manly bonding activities. No need to panic.

Then why did he feel like he had a target painted directly on his back? Dante glanced over his shoulder to see Bea's uncles glaring at him. Oh. By coming over here with Mike, he'd clearly chosen a side. Dante could only hope it was the right side.

"Why don't we make a friendly wager?" Mike pulled out his wallet and laid two hundred-dollar bills on the table.

Dante swallowed at the sight of the money. Yep. Definitely a trap. "I don't have that kind of cash on me."

Mike gave him a smirk and a knowing nod. "Bet you're one of those ATM people. You can't depend on machines, man. Cold hard cash is where it's at. You get me?" He slapped Dante on the shoulder and leaned in. "Don't worry. I know you're good for it. You can pay me later."

"That's if I lose," Dante retorted, making sure to sound more confident than he felt. Sweat iced down his spine, and he was conscious of the gun pressed close against his side. He couldn't take his jacket off to play, which would place him at a disadvantage. The last thing he wanted was to start this day being in debt to the mob. But he had no choice but to play this game.

Mike let out a little laugh. "Right. I see why my sister likes you."

Dante didn't know if that was a compliment or not. He chalked up his cue and surveyed the pool table. The balls were in a neat little triangle in the middle, the white ball placed in the right spot. He had to tune out the crowd of onlookers that circled the table. Not everyone was watching. Some had gone to the bar or surrounded one of the TVs. There were shouts at the sound of the crack of a bat—a home run.

"I'll even let you break," Mike said generously.

Dante pushed down his nervousness and moved into position at the end of the table. Strategically, he didn't know if it was better to lose or win here. It wasn't like he was a pool shark, either. This wasn't something covered at Quantico, but he'd played his fair share of games at various bars in his life.

While losing might ingratiate himself with Mike, winning might earn his respect. Dante resolved to play his best game and see what happened.

After breaking, he chose solids, letting Mike have stripes. They went back and forth a few times, and Dante was damn sure he caught Dominick moving balls to put them in a better position for Mike and worse for Dante. Typical wiseguy. The mob was all about cheating the system, and it was no different here.

Of course, the longer they played, the more sweat collected under his collar. Dante knew he was being sized up, but he couldn't figure out Mike's game other than to cheat him out of some cash.

"Dante Milano," Mike mused as he lined up a shot. "A nice Italian name. Where in Italy does your family live?"

"Somewhere near Milan, I guess." Dante shrugged. Janet had decided it was better for him to have an Italian background, but not too recent. "They immigrated to Jersey in, like, nineteen hundreds."

"Early bloomers." Mike laughed, as he sank two more balls. "It was a different world back then, you know?"

Dante had a feeling he wasn't going for the obvious meaning—of course, the world was very different a hundred and twenty years ago. "Uh, yeah?"

"Because those guys back then? They really worked for it. That's the problem with the world today." Mike stopped for a moment to chalk up his cue. Then he was back at the table and on his rant. "Most people aren't willing to do the work, you know? Sometimes you gotta make the hard choices. Do what nobody else wants to do. You get me?"

He took his shot, skillfully sinking his target.

Dante let out a frustrated breath. He was behind, while Mike had only the eight-ball left. "Are we talking about the Yankees firing their manager at the beginning of the season?"

Mike let out a laugh before taking another swig of his beer. He handed his bottle to Junior between balls and his cousin seemed to have no problem being a beer holder. "You're funny. I'm talking about life, man. If you don't see things my way, you don't belong in this family."

"I just started dating your sister." Dante held up both hands. He didn't want to start a fight, but it was a bit early for a shovel talk.

However, that wasn't the case if Mike meant the Family with a capital F.

"Eight ball, corner pocket," Mike called, lining up to take the shot. But he wasn't done with his talk. "We don't do things casual in this family, Dante. You better figure that out right now."

"Got it." Dante nodded as Mike sunk the eight ball. Well. There went two hundred dollars, even if Mike had been helped by his men to win the game.

"Good game." Mike took the cue from him and handed it to Dominick with a nod. Then he escorted Dante over to the bar, where he ordered a round of shots for them both.

Dante accepted the drink, but he didn't throw it back like Mike did. He took a polite sip, but wanted to keep his wits about him. He couldn't forget the gun in its holster. Alcohol and firearms were a bad combination. As he scanned the room while leaning against the bar casually, he noticed several of the other men hadn't taken their jackets off, either. He wasn't the only one carrying.

Not a good sign in a room filled with tension. The men who'd been at the bar when Mike and Dante approached moved to the other side, giving them both glares. Mike didn't seem to notice. He'd gone all loose with the body language of someone who'd known exactly how much he'd had to drink.

Dante brought the glass to his lips, but didn't drink. He still had to look the part, though.

"Friendly wager on the game?" Mike gestured up at the screen showing the Yankees game. They were up seven to two. "Since you were all knowledgeable about their new manager and all."

He could hear the mocking edge in Mike's voice. "Sure."

"Great. I'll take Yankees to win it. Another two hundred?" Mike's grin was sly, and he stared Dante down, daring him to object.

"I say they lose in extra innings." Dante faked another drink, letting the liquid wet his lips. Well. There went another couple of hundred bucks. Since the Yankees were up in the eighth, it didn't look like he had a chance in hell of winning his bet. Still, it meant that he was fitting in. Another step forward in the mission.

At the top of the ninth—and the Yankees scoring two more runs—Dante's phone buzzed. He pulled it out to see a text from Bea.

She's opened all the presents. I think now would be a great time to come rescue me.

He grinned and texted back. *You're not staying for dessert?*

Half the guests are already leaving. I think it was the last game. I'll tell you about it later.

Dante could only imagine, but he found himself looking forward to Bea's version of events. She had a way with words especially when telling a story. He put the phone away and nodded at Mike. "It looks like they are finishing up."

Mike did another shot, but no matter how much he drank, he didn't seem tipsy at all. The man could hold his liquor. "Going to take my sister out for a night on the town?"

Dante sputtered a bit, the tension that had eased while they watched the game now instantly back. "Well. I mean." Damn it, he'd been doing so well. Consorting with mobsters? No problem, but mention Bea and he was completely thrown off.

Mike patted him on the shoulder. "Take it easy. I'm not threatening you. Yet. You still owe me four hundred bucks."

"The game isn't over yet." Dante pointed to the TV.

"Isn't it?" Mike grinned. "If you want a chance to win it back, we play cards every night at the club near the church. You should come by and try your luck."

Yes. This was exactly the invitation he'd been waiting for. Janet had been spot on with her plans for him to infiltrate the family. Dante forced himself to keep it cool. "Thanks. I just might do that."

He said his goodbyes to the other men and retreated into the restaurant proper. He could hear the giggles and high-pitched squeals coming from the banquet room where the shower apparently was wrapping up. It was a completely different feel from the back room. Dante had been in another world, the mafia world, and now he was heading back out.

Bea waited for him at the entrance to the banquet hall, her messenger bag slung over one shoulder. She'd traded her heels for a pair of canvas sneakers. It didn't matter, she still looked amazing in that dress. Dante grinned at her.

"Ready to get out of here?" She asked, holding out her hand. Dante grabbed it and pulled her away. "Definitely."

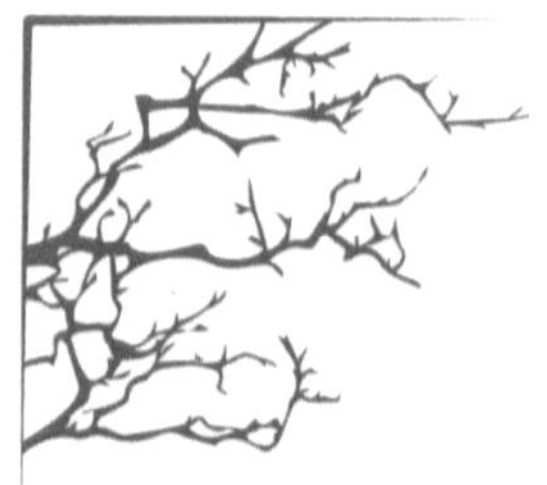

Chapter 29

Bea had spent the entire time at the shower with a smile plastered on her face as she went from table to table. Running the games gave her an excuse to chat with every person and see if her bait had caught anything. She'd kept her senses open, searching for any scents or glimpses of auras that would give her a clue about the identity of the witch. All it got her was a headache.

It wasn't like she expected the woman to stand up and declare: "I am the witch! Fight me!" although that certainly would have made things easier. That was the point of bait after all—cast it out and see what happened. Carmella had warned her that she might not see any results today.

Then when? That instinct pulsed inside her as she surveyed the tables. Most of the women had stood up to make their excuses and say goodbye. Now that Lucy had opened her gifts, it certainly seemed like they'd gotten what they'd come for. Bea had made a list of who gave what so Lucy could send thank you cards later. But she heard whispering as the women moved around the room.

"Did you see what the Gambinos gave? Can you believe they are so cheap?"

"Who gave them the washer and dryer?"

"I heard they are moving into the grandmother's old apartment. Why no house?"

She grit her teeth and desperately texted Dante so she could get the hell out of here. Lucy stood at the back of the room near the gifts, being gracious and shaking everyone's hand as they said goodbye. Mom and Aunt Julia were organizing some boxes on a cart supplied by the restaurant. Connie stood near Lucy and handed out favors to those leaving. Bea met her eyes and gestured with her head to one side.

At Connie's nod, she slipped out of the room. While waiting for Dante, she changed out of her heels and into the sneakers she had stashed in her messenger bag. Mom would have a fit if she saw them, but Bea wasn't going to walk through Newark in heels. Her arches already hurt from the three hours on her fancy shoes.

Seeing Dante come to rescue her helped loosen some of the tension that had settled on her shoulders the entire time. Bea hadn't been able to relax, worried about an attack that never came. She tangled their hands together as they left the restaurant, walking down toward Ferry Street. The late afternoon was busy and soon they were dodging the crowds and carefully crossing the busy roads.

"My brother wasn't too horrible, was he?" She couldn't tell Dante about what she'd witnessed Mike do—no, then she'd have to admit to the whole mob family thing, and she couldn't do that. He'd totally freak out.

Dante chuckled. He swung their arms as they walked. "No, but I lost some money to him. He kicked my ass at pool."

Typical Mike. "Never play a game against my brother. He cheats." As she said the words, something prickled at the back of her head, like her magic was confirming the truth of the words.

"Got it. I figured I should play to get on his good side. I was a last-minute guest, after all." He shrugged and gave her one of his sweet smiles that made Bea want to lean over and kiss him right there in the middle of the sidewalk.

God, she didn't want to think about Mike, or the Family, or the wedding right now. Most of all, she wanted to forget about witchcraft and the fact that she still didn't know the identity of the person who'd cursed her family. She wanted to be with Dante. To do something that made her forget everything going on for a bit.

"You don't live far from here, right?"

He stopped walking and turned to face her, his forehead furrowed in confusion. Damn, but he looked so good in that sports jacket. His shoulders really filled it out, and it made him look taller, somehow. She never got to see him really dressed up like this before, and Bea found she liked it. "Yeah. I'm in one of those artist's apartments near the train station."

"I remember when they started building those. Dad was so pissed about how high they were. Said they ruined the skyline." Bea had been a kid then, and if she understood the timeline correctly, it had been before her dad became boss. Otherwise, she was sure he would have done something about them. "Maybe you could show me your place?"

His eyes went wide at her words, and Bea realized he might have taken them differently than she meant them. Of course, it wasn't that she didn't want to progress further in their relationship. Making out in her car was fine, but she wasn't a teenager anymore. Bea was an adult, and she wanted an adult relationship.

"I mean, I don't want to go to another restaurant. We don't have tickets to a show and there's nothing I want to see at the movies." Bea shrugged and tried to play it off. "Maybe we could sit and talk?"

He smiled and cupped her jaw, sliding his thumb over her lips. "We can take it slow, if that's what you want."

God, this man was too damn perfect. Bea's own experience in bed had been limited to one guy in college, her junior year boyfriend who ghosted her after he graduated. It had been fine. It wasn't a terrible experience, just not earth shattering. She'd thought she'd been in love with him then, but now she realized it had been nothing more than infatuation.

With Dante, she could tumble into love so fast. "I appreciate that."

A flare of heat thrummed through her at his touch, reminding her of why she wanted to go home with him. Bea wanted more, wanted his body against hers, wanted that connection that only sex could bring. And even if they ended up just making out on his couch, well, that would be fine too.

Dante swallowed, his throat working hard. Bea found herself mesmerized by the pulse in his neck, the smoothness of his skin. She stretched up on her toes to kiss him there, her lips against his hot flesh.

"All right," Dante croaked, his voice hoarse. "We can go back to my place."

Excitement and anticipation thrummed beneath her skin. Her instincts told her something momentous was about to happen, and Bea gathered up the magic inside herself and held it close. *Yes,* she told it. *I know.* Bea untangled herself from Dante and gestured to the street before them. "Lead the way."

While she'd grown up in Newark, she wasn't familiar with this side of town, especially the new luxury apartments they'd built outside of the train station. When she was a kid, all of this had still been abandoned factories and condemned buildings, taking up space. Mom used to comment about how it was a shame they were abandoned, that it was a waste of the beautiful architecture of the old factories, those solid red brick buildings with industrial black iron windows.

All of them were gone now, turned into high rises that towered over the train line, giving renters a bird's-eye view of the city below. Bea didn't quite care for that concept. She far preferred the smaller two-story homes near her grandmother's house. It made the city feel more like a small town, less like a, well, city.

"If we cut this way, it's easier to cross the street." Dante gestured to a small side street to their right.

Unlike the bustling main road, this seemed dark, like some streetlights had been blown out. There weren't any businesses down this way, either. As they took their first steps, a smell hit her nose, something acrid and unfamiliar. Bea paused, trying to identify the scent, to listen to her magical senses. But this didn't smell like food, or any of the herbs or spices she'd been taught. It didn't even remind her of flowers...but, wait.

It smelled like decay, like mushrooms decomposing in the compost pile.

Ugh. It was probably someone's trash that had been lying out for too long. Bea made a face and covered her mouth with her free hand.

Dante went still. Bea ran in to his back, confused. She'd been so focused on avoiding the garbage smell that she'd missed whatever had him stopping. "Dante?"

"What the hell is that?"

A prickling sensation started at the back of her head. Bea moved to the side so she could see what Dante was talking about. The entire alleyway dimmed, despite her knowing there was light and music and people a few feet behind them. Pressure swelled in her ears and Bea reached up to grab the sides of her head.

That's when the shadow along the wall moved. At first it was formless, a large gray blob, then it shifted into something vaguely human shaped, if ten feet tall. It detached from the wall, taking a step toward them. The shadows took on physical form, with large horns and dripping fangs from its twisted mouth, its face a mix between a gargoyle and a lion.

"Get back!" Dante stepped forward, pulling something out of the interior of his jacket. Once he took aim at the creature, Bea realized he'd had a gun this whole time.

That shocked her almost as much as the sight of the monster he was shooting at. Why would Dante have a gun? He was a sweet guy, not like her family. But what if she was wrong about him? What if he was involved in the business? That could explain why he seemed to actually get along with her brother.

Dante fired into the shadow, the sound loud at first, then swallowed by the fog rising along the pavement and twirling around their ankles. He fired shot after shot, but the thing didn't seem to care, stooping forward to curl a giant-sized hand around Dante, and tossing him into the pile of garbage along the wall.

Whatever the creature was, it was made of magic. Now that she had stopped ignoring what her senses had been telling her, Bea recognized it for what it was, something not entirely of this world. But had they stumbled upon it by accident or had someone sent it to attack them?

It looked like her bait had caught something after all.

"Shit." Bea reached into her messenger bag, finding the piece of chalk she'd rescued from her grandmother's purse. Carmella had explained why Nonna always carried chalk, and told Bea she should, too. Now she understood.

"Bea, run!" Dante shouted, slowly stumbling to his feet.

Thank God he's alive. Bea couldn't spare another thought for him. She crouched to the ground, her hand trembling as she sketched out a circle of power. First the elements for protection, a necessity when doing any magic that required a circle. Those she could draw in her sleep.

But what Bea needed was a dispelling circle. She'd only done that once, as part of the crash course in protective spells she'd gone over with Carmella. It wasn't like she could pull out her book of shadows for her notes. *Hey, Mr. Monster, can you wait five minutes while I look this up?*

No wonder Carmella had insisted on practicing. However, Bea had only been doing this for a few weeks, not years.

I know this, come on. Bea scratched out the first three symbols easily enough, seeing them behind her mind's eye, the twisted letters that symbolized concepts, given power only by her word. But her piece of chalk snapped on the last symbol. She stared at it, uncertain if she'd even begun it correctly.

She could feel the creature's breath on the back of her neck. There was no time. Bea used the stub of chalk to finish the symbol, even though she wasn't sure it was the right one.

Bea shouted the words in Italian, thankful the language flowed so quickly from her lips. A surge of power swelled inside her and, as Carmella taught her, she grasped on to it, forcing her magic to do her bidding, even if her symbols weren't drawn correctly.

"I banish you," she finished the spell with a gasp.

Time seemed to stop. The breathing on the back of her neck disappeared. The fog slowly receded into the ground. And the light returned to the alley, once again full of sound from the street behind them.

Dante was staring at her with wide, frightened eyes. "What the hell just happened?"

Bea leaned over and vomited, unable to contain the nausea swirling in her belly. Magic always had a cost, and apparently this time it really had to be her throwing up in front of her boyfriend. So much for looking good in this dress. The ridiculous thought made her hiccup laugh as she swiped her mouth with the back of her hand.

"Bea," Dante said, his voice raspy. "Are you all right?"

She straightened, but stumbled, still dizzy from using her magic. He'd seen everything, but did he understand what had happened? From the way he stood several feet away from her, she judged that he'd understood enough to know she was the threat.

"We shouldn't talk here," she said finally. "We need to get to a safe place."

He shook his head, staring at her like he couldn't believe what she was saying. "What?"

Bea limped over to his side and took his hand in hers. "Dante, look at me. I know you're in shock. Hell, I know exactly how you feel. Someone or something tried to hurt us."

"I shot it," he said. "The bullets went right through it."

Right, the gun. Bea cast her gaze around until she found it, lying on the ground a few feet away from them. Probably not a good idea to leave it here. She bent to scoop it up.

"Wait, no." Dante seemed to burst out of his fugue state to bend down and grab the gun. "You shouldn't...you shouldn't..." he trailed off, as if uncertain what to say.

She frowned at him. "You're going to have to explain that, too."

Just as she was going to have to explain the existence of magic and creatures made of shadow. Carmella was going to have to explain this, since nothing in her lessons had prepared Bea for literal monsters.

Dante put the gun away and nodded, but he wouldn't look at her. "Let's go. My place isn't far."

Something sour stirred in her belly. Before, they were going to his place to move to the next stage in their relationship. But now, it meant confessing the truth about her magic, her family, his gun. The excitement and joy from before had dissipated, leaving only fear and concern. How would he take it? Could they still build something together if Dante knew her secrets?

She was going to have to take a chance to find out. Bea followed Dante out of the alley and into the light.

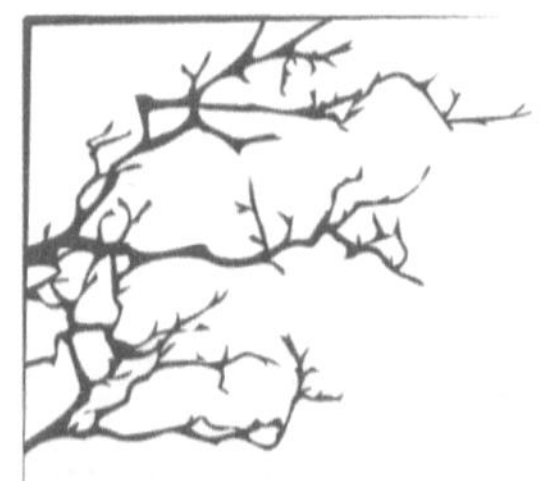

Chapter 30

Dante unlocked his front door with shaking hands. His fingers seemed to belong to someone else as he put the key in the lock, turned it, and pushed the door open. Safe. He gestured Bea in ahead of him, checking the hallway before closing the door and throwing the lock on the other side. He added the chain lock for good measure.

Bea clutched her messenger bag to her chest as she stood in the middle of his living room. Her hair had come out of its updo on one side, her dark locks flowing to her shoulder in a mess of curls and knots. Her makeup had smeared, making it look like she had a stripe of blood along her chin. Or was that actual blood? Dante took a step forward to check.

"Are you all right?" He reached out, but when his hand still trembled, Dante pulled it back, not wanting to show weakness.

What the hell had happened out there? He could almost believe there had been something else in that shot Mike had given him in the bar. Something that made him hallucinate a monster made of shadow. But he didn't know any drug that could make him feel as if the monster had indeed thrown him into a wall.

Dante's entire body ached from the force of that throw. He'd made it here on adrenaline alone. That was the only thing holding him up and preventing him from collapsing into a lump on the couch.

That and Bea in his apartment.

She set down her bag on the floor next to the couch, emerging with a slim piece of chalk. "Am I all right? Are you all right?"

He watched in silence as she trekked to his front door, etching symbols on the gray wall around the door. Bea closed her eyes, pressed her hand to the wall and murmured something under her breath. For a moment the symbols glowed, and then disappeared into the wall, no longer visible.

Dante gasped. "What the hell is going on?"

Bea slumped to the floor in a heap. He ran to her side, putting his arm around her. She felt a little cold and clammy. "Sorry. I must have overdid it."

"Overdid what?" It would be nice if someone could explain what the hell was going on. Dante wanted to tear his hair out in frustration. It couldn't be what it looked like. It just couldn't.

"The spell." She ran her hands over her face, further smearing her makeup. "After banishing the creature in the alley. I needed to make sure we'd be safe in here. That's why I put the protection simboli on the door."

Dante helped her to her feet, leading her over to the couch. She trembled as much as he did, and it was a relief to know he wasn't the only one losing it right now. "Let me get you some water and you can explain."

Because clearly, she knew what was going on, and Dante had a feeling he wasn't going to like it. He took two bottles of water from the fridge and, after handing her one, sat next to her on the couch.

Bea pulled off the cap and downed half the bottle before wiping her mouth. She held onto the bottle, peeling the paper wrapped back as she spoke. "You've always been the one who believed me, Dante. Can you wait until I finish before you ask questions?"

"Of course." He put his hand on her shoulder, squeezing gently. Physical contact between them had always been about comfort. It was no different now, except this time, Dante was taking his own comfort from it. Bea was real, a solid physical presence next to him. He wasn't going insane.

"I'm a witch." She let out a little laugh at the word. "Although, to say it properly, a Strega. I inherited my gifts from my grandmother."

Dante stared at her, not even able to speak if he wanted to. Even if he didn't believe her, he had to pretend to for the sake of the mission. That's how he got this close. Be the sounding board for her when her own family wouldn't listen. But he'd never expected this to be the revelation.

Fuck the mission right now. What did it mean when witchcraft was real? When a freakin' monster—a thing made of darkness and hate—could emerge from the shadows and throw him against the wall. He didn't have to pretend anything. Dante had experienced it—up close and personal.

He didn't know what it all meant.

Bea watched his face with narrow eyes. Was she looking for doubt? Dante couldn't even scrounge up a smile to reassure her.

"That thing that attacked us? Was pure magic." She shuddered.

"Does this kind of thing happen to you often?" Dante asked dryly.

Bea let out another laugh and pressed the water bottle to her forehead. "I didn't even know about magic until right before Nonna died. At the feast, before I met you, she'd awakened my magic. Told me it was my duty to protect my family."

"Protect them from what?" Dante gestured with one hand, letting his very real frustration out. He'd gone into this evening expecting one thing—getting an in with Bea's family—and to find out that something completely different was going on. None of this made any sense.

She sighed and drank more of the water. Bea took her time, draining the entire bottle before speaking again. "This is the part that... Well. Let me start at the beginning. From when I was a little kid, I always knew our family was different. That we were connected." She put the emphasis on the last word.

Even when confessing, Bea couldn't say the word.

Dante got to his feet, pulling away from the warmth of her body. He needed to not be touching Bea right now. He paced the length of the living room, taking comfort in the solid movement of his own legs, despite the pain that arched down his back. It meant he was alive.

He should be thrilled. Bea was about to give him everything he needed. Tell him all about how her family was in the mob. This was the whole point of him being here. But it left a sour taste in his mouth, not only because he'd been lying to her this whole time, although hell, that was a kicker he couldn't forget.

Tonight, the world had changed for him. Monsters were real—and they weren't just the mobsters and their guns. Magic was real.

"I witnessed something I shouldn't have." Bea took up the story again. She sounded far away, even though she was right in the room with him. "My grandmother using magic to punish someone who'd betrayed us."

Dante stopped in his tracks. He turned to face her slowly. "What?"

"I watched her burn a guy's eyes out with nothing more than a magic word." Bea held her hand out and snapped her fingers.

He flinched in response. Vito Morelli. The man who the FBI had tried to turn. Good God. Dante mentally re-evaluated everything he knew about the DiLorenzos—about Bea. Janet had said they never could get any wiretaps or electronic surveillance to stick. Nobody would talk. And hell, if the threat of having their eyes burned out was what it took to keep them in line, then Dante wouldn't talk either.

He tried to imagine sitting Janet down and explaining all of this and couldn't. Nobody would believe him. Finally, he actually understood how Bea felt.

"And you can do that?" he asked, his voice hoarse.

She must have seen something in his face. Bea got to her feet and strode toward him, her arms outspread. "No! Absolutely not."

She took his hands in hers and squeezed before leaning in to press a hesitant kiss on his lips. He remained still, not falling into the kiss, but not pulling away, either. Bea sighed and stepped back

. "She wanted me too. My grandmother, I mean. But she was killed before she could teach me anything. You don't know even know what I went through to find a teacher."

It snapped into place then. "When you told me you thought she had enemies?"

"Yeah. Rival witch. Probably a rival family trying to start a takeover." She pressed her hand to her head as if it pained her. Bea went over to the window and moved aside the blinds to peek outside.

Dante clenched his hands into fists. Part of him wanted to walk over there and take her in his arms, forget about all of this. But that was the part that desperately wanted to deny everything she was saying. It was absolutely ludicrous. Yeah, Family politics often had assassination as part of the takeover attempts, but it was usually limited to the don himself, not his mother. Who was a witch. Who used her magic to keep members in line.

When did he walk into crazy town?

"I need a drink," he said.

"Probably best to keep sober. In case they try again."

His head snapped up. "They?"

Bea turned away from the window and gave him a twisted smile. "More likely 'she' I guess. The witch that killed Nonna and stole her spell book. Carmella—that's the witch teaching me - and I thought we should try to get her to act openly, by baiting her with my magic. It worked, obviously, but I still have no idea who she is."

"What the hell? Putting yourself out there as bait? Are you kidding me? Do you know how dangerous that is?" Dante stalked across the room, pulling her away from the window. He'd come so close to losing her, and to find out that she'd put herself in danger on purpose?

He enveloped her in his arms, and Bea sunk into him, resting her head on his shoulder. Dante ran his fingers through her hair and closed his eyes as he breathed her in. He could smell her perfume—the vanilla—and something else, something that smelled like smoke. Was that the creature? Or her magic?

"You're taking this better than I expected," she said into his shirt.

"I reserve the right to freak out at a later date."

Her laughter soothed the squeezing sensation in his heart. For a moment, Dante contemplated telling her everything. That he was an FBI agent. That he could protect her if she trusted him. They could get her into witness protection. Keep her safe.

But the FBI couldn't protect her from magic. They had no defense against witches who could send monsters in dark alleyways. Dante held his tongue.

Bea wrapped her arms around him and he winced and let out a little groan.

"Dante?"

"Think I hurt my back," he admitted. "When that thing threw me against the wall."

Bea pulled away and tugged at his suit jacket.

Dante held up a hand to stop her before pulling the jacket off himself, revealing the holster beneath where he'd returned his gun. Thankfully, he'd come up with a cover story to explain the gun if Bea asked. When she asked. He removed the holster carefully, checking the safety on the gun before putting it away in a drawer in the end table next to the couch. He'd have to return it to Janet tomorrow.

God, he couldn't imagine giving this report. The thought of laying it out all logically while Janet nodded in response like any other report seemed impossible. She'd think he'd completely lost his mind.

While he was turned around, Bea let out a gasp. "Oh, God. Your shirt is all bloody.""

Now that she mentioned it, he was really feeling it. Pain blazed up and down his back. The shock must have kept him from feeling the pain long enough to get them to safety.

"Do you have a first aid kit? Let me take care of it for you." Bea reached out with one hand, short of touching him.

Dante swallowed as he slowly unbuttoned his shirt. Bea stared at him and licked her lips. He had to fight to keep his composure. "Yeah," he told her, his voice husky. "In the bathroom."

"Let me take care of you."

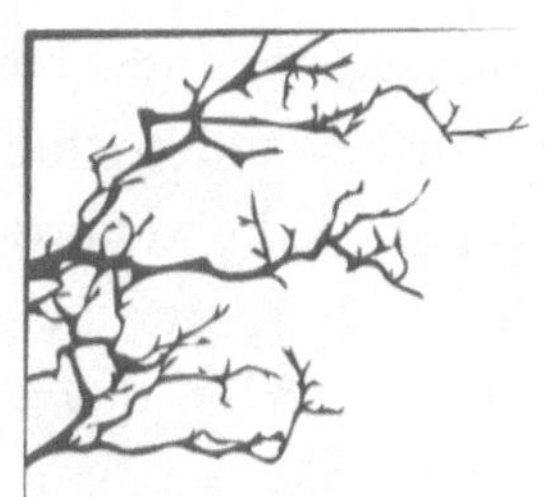

Chapter 31

Bea wished her head wasn't pounding in time with her heart. The pain had started once she cast the spell on Dante's door, and hadn't dissipated even after she'd finished the bottle of water. Added to the nausea and dizziness from banishing the monster and she was a mess of magical consequences. She'd have to search for an ibuprofen later. First, she needed to take care of Dante's back.

Then she could worry about what she needed to do next. Bea pushed down the fear and panic that wanted to rise in her. If she screamed into the void, that wouldn't do anyone any good and might get the cops called on them. One problem at a time. Help Dante. Then figure out how to stop the witch who'd sent a literal monster after them.

She followed Dante to his bathroom, which was the first room down the little hallway after the kitchen area. He lived in an efficiency, she thought it was called, just a step up from a studio. Any other time she'd be stopping to examine his furniture, what art he put on the walls, and if he had an espresso pot. But now it was all she could do to put one foot in front of the other.

The back of Dante's white undershirt was stained with scarlet blood. He'd hit that wall hard. Thank goodness it hadn't been his head. Although he might dispute that when it came time to pull the fabric off of his wounds.

"I should have something," Dante murmured as she waited in the doorway. He opened the cabinet above the sink and pulled out a tiny white first aid kit. "Here."

Bea stepped inside the tiny bathroom and took the kit. She opened it, finding disinfectant and bandages. That would do for now. They might have to consider an urgent care place if the wounds looked bad once she could be sure they were safe.

"Have a seat." She gestured to the toilet, putting the box down on the edge of the sink so she could wash her hands.

When she turned, wiping her hands dry on the hand towel next to the sink, she found Dante still standing between her and the shower stall.

"You don't have to do this." His cheeks had gone pink. How cute. She didn't think she'd ever seen him blush before.

Bea put her hands on her hips. "I don't see anyone else here. Do you really think you can bandage up your own back?" She stared him down, giving him what she hoped was her fiercest glare.

Dante let out a little huff. He turned and sat sideways on the toilet so she could reach his back. His posture was stiff, and she wasn't sure if that was from pain or embarrassment.

Bea lifted the hem of the shirt, frowning as it stuck to the blood when she tried to pull it away. "This is going to hurt."

"I can take it."

She rolled the white cotton up, careful around the wounds. Dante hissed as she pulled the fabric away from his skin, revealing his scratched up back. The scrapes were evenly distributed along his back, probably from where he hit the wall and slid down. She winced in sympathy.

"The good news is that it doesn't look terrible. Just some really bad scrapes." Bea went back to the sink and turned on the water. "Do you have a washcloth I can use? I should clean them before I put on the antibiotic."

"There are a few clean ones in the cabinet under the sink." Dante pulled the shirt the rest of the way off, revealing his naked torso.

Bea took a deep breath as she focused on wringing out the cloth in the sink. This wasn't about ogling him, although, of course, she was going to take a good look. Dante's shoulders were broad and his arms muscular. He kept in shape, although he never mentioned being a gym hound. She frowned as she turned back to him. His skin, where not abraded, was a gorgeous dark cream that begged to be touched.

"Stay still," she warned before touching the worst looking of the wounds. He gasped at her touch, his back arching in response.

Man, if things had gone her way, this night would have gone in an entirely different direction. They'd be cuddling on that couch, the TV playing in the background as he kissed her. She'd have put her hands beneath his shirt, touching that soft skin, until he pulled it off and bared all to her. Bea shook her head to get herself to focus.

There was nothing romantic about cleaning up his injuries—injuries he got in an attempt to protect her. That made her think of being back in the alley, how he'd gotten between her and the monster and pulled out a gun.

"Why do you have a gun?" She asked as she wiped dirt and grime away from the scrapes.

Dante's shoulders stiffened. He lowered his head, giving her a nice view of the curls at the back of his neck. "For protection. This isn't the safest city."

"Do you always have one? I don't remember noticing it before." Not during their make out sessions in the car. Bea would have noticed. All the men in her life carried. Her father had taught her to never touch his gun from when she was very young. Bea had a healthy fear of firearms. They were for others to wield, not for her.

Did Nonna put protection charms on Daddy's guns? The thought struck her suddenly. She'd have to think about the kinds of wards that would need to be there. Something to keep the gun from going off when not wanted. Something to keep the holder of the weapon safe from others shooting at him. Maybe something to make the bullets capable of shooting magical creatures?

"No. I, uh, got it recently. After one of my neighbors got mugged." Dante's voice was hoarse as she worked on cleaning his back.

"Unfortunately, it didn't do a lot of good against that thing in the alley." Bea let out a sigh.

Some of the stiffness left his shoulders as he chuckled. "No. What, what did you do to make it go away?"

"I cast a dispelling charm. There wasn't a lot of time, so I did my best, but..." she trailed off, remembering how she couldn't finish that last symbol. It had worked, but she'd forced the magic through. That's probably why she felt so ill right now.

"But?" he prompted, turning to look at her finally.

Bea gently pushed him back around. She was still working on his injuries. "I'm not entirely sure the thing won't come back. Hence the protection on your door."

"I'm still having a hard time with this," he admitted. He gestured with one hand, making a twirling motion. "The whole witchcraft thing."

She squeezed his shoulder gently, his muscles tight under her touch. "Welcome to the club. Let me bandage these up and you'll be good to go."

Bea slathered on the antibiotic cream from the kit, taking care to get each of the scrapes. There were just enough bandages to cover them all. She took her time, not wanting to leave anything uncovered that would hurt Dante when he went to put a shirt back on.

Not that she minded him sitting around shirtless. In fact, she'd prefer it. She smiled as she pressed the last bandage against his skin. "All done."

"Thanks." He stood and stretched, testing out her work.

Bea didn't look away. She couldn't. Her gaze went to his impressive pecs, the way his abs flexed as he moved.

Dante winced and put both of his arms back down quickly. "I'm just going to go...get dressed."

"Yeah, I'll um wait over there." She pointed back to where they'd come from and took off down the little hallway.

Bea grabbed her messenger bag, pulling out some painkillers, which she swallowed with the dregs of her water. Hopefully that would help her head. Then she took her phone back to the couch, which she sunk into gratefully. Tiredness filled her. She'd used far too much magic tonight.

She had to contact Carmella. Maybe she'd know what that thing was and how Bea could combat it.

Good news is that the witch made her next move, she typed into the phone. *Bad news is that she sent a shadow monster after us.*

Carmella's immediate response was a series of question marks. Then finally *What are you talking about?*

Bea settled against the back of the couch, thinking. How to describe what had attacked them? The funniest thing about the monster was that it reminded her of her father's stories about the Italian bogey-man. He lived in the sewers and would come out of the shadows to steal away wicked children. She'd always thought it was just a story to keep her and Mike in line.

But what if, like everything she'd learned these past few weeks, there was more to it? Daddy knew about magic. Maybe this was something he'd been warned about.

She texted back, describing the thing and how it came out of the shadows. *I used a dispelling circle to get rid of it, but I couldn't finish the circle,* she typed.

Carmella didn't reply for a while.

Bea closed her eyes and rested the back of her head on the couch. Lying down would be better. She was so damn tired. Maybe if she closed her eyes... She shot up as her phone buzzed in her lap.

Someone who can summon the spauracchio is powerful. This is not good.

"You're telling me," Bea said out loud. The drugs must be starting to kick in. The headache had dissipated into a mere buzzing in her head. She shifted on the couch, curling up on her side with her head pressed against the armrest. Maybe if she closed her eyes for a few minutes...

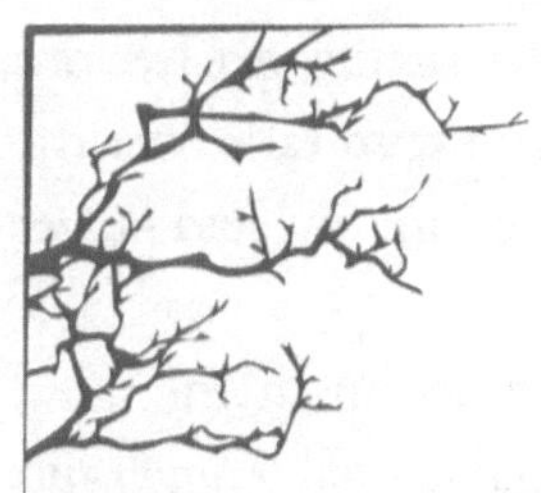

Chapter 32

Dante pulled down the hem of his fresh shirt as he walked back to the living room. Bea had done a good job with the bandages. He barely felt anything as the fabric touched his skin. He opened his mouth to thank her when he spotted her curled up on the couch, sound asleep. Her head rested on the armrest, one hand still clutching her phone to her chest.

He stopped in his tracks and stared. She looked so innocent and vulnerable, her cheeks pink and her lips parted as she breathed in and out. With a sigh, he went back to his bedroom and grabbed a light blanket out of his closet. Bea looked cold.

After draping the blanket over her, he settled on the floor next to her. Dante didn't want to test his back by sitting on the chair to watch over her. He wanted to be close, just in case.

Although if something magical burst through that front door, there wasn't much he could do except wake Bea. Guns were useless.

Dante let his head rest against the side of the couch. *Guns were useless against magic.* Add that to the list of things he'd never thought he'd have to deal with. He'd have to explain all of this to Janet and somehow make her believe it.

It might be time to come clean to Bea. He nearly discarded the thought as it occurred to him. What could the FBI do against magic? He tried to imagine Janet or Garcia reacting to this new information and couldn't. They'd think he was insane, unless he could provide proof. That proof would be Bea. His stomach rebelled at the thought of turning her in as a weapon.

But the Bureau could protect Bea from her family, get her out of the line of fire of whoever it was who was trying to take over the DiLorenzo Family. Would Bea even want protection? She had power of her own.

He marveled at that, the way she'd taken action in the alley, driving the monster away with nothing but a magic spell. *How is this my life?* He sighed, closing his eyes, his body heavy with exhaustion now that the adrenaline had made its way out of his system.

Dante startled awake with a gasp. He'd apparently dozed off at some point, and now the room was dim, lit only by the lamp he always left on when he left. It was dark behind the blinds. He checked his phone. Somehow, they'd slept until nearly midnight. Crap. Someone might be waiting up for Bea.

He got to his feet as she stirred on the couch, letting out a little groan as she stretched. God, she looked so beautiful; he wanted to reach out and touch her. He had one hand out, reaching for her cheek, when Dante snatched it back, placing it on her shoulder instead.

"Hey." She blinked up at him with sleepy eyes and an affectionate smile. "How long did I sleep?"

"I fell asleep too," he admitted. "It's midnight."

Bea sat up and ran her hand through her hair, grimacing when she found resistance. "Ugh. My mom will never let me hear the end of it. But at least my headache is gone."

"And that was from the," Dante waved a hand in the air. "Magic?"

"All magic has a cost." She sounded like she was repeating a quote from somewhere. Bea straightened and looked over at the door. "At least my protections held."

As if on cue, a high-pitched whine came from behind the door. Dante straightened, an icy prickle going up the back of his neck. That sounded like a dog. It couldn't be Rocky, not at this time of night. Janet wouldn't take him for a walk this late, would she? Maybe she'd gotten some intel that she needed to share with him, but she'd knock.

Something was wrong.

The dog let out a howl and scratched against Dante's door. Dante grabbed the gun from the end table, holding it in the ready position before heading to the door. "Stay there," he told Bea before looking through the peephole.

Outside, he saw Rocky jumping up on two legs, banging against Dante's front door with his paws. Nobody else seemed to be in the hallway. Dante unlocked the door, opened it carefully, and then checked both sides of the empty hall.

Rocky didn't come in. Instead, he trotted in a circle before jotting down to Janet's apartment door and back. He clearly wanted Dante to follow him. What made Rocky suddenly turn into Lassie? Dante raised the gun, wanting to be prepared for whatever waited out there.

"I'll be right back."

"What? When there are literal monsters out there?" Bea came right next to him, waving a piece of chalk in his direction. "I believe I have the more reliable weapon right now."

Rocky ran back and forth. He yiped, a high-pitched sound that went straight to Dante's heart. He reached for the dog's collar and held him still. "Easy, boy. This is my neighbor's dog. Something must be wrong."

Bea said something, but Dante didn't hear her words. Once he had Rocky in his grip, he noticed something rust colored and crusted around the fur of his neck. Blood. Blood that didn't belong to the dog. Panic seized his throat. *Janet.* She did not know about the kind of horror that may have followed Dante and Bea back here.

He let go of Rocky and headed for Janet's apartment. The door was ajar—probably how the dog had gotten out. Dante pushed it open carefully, his gun leading the way as he stepped inside. It might not do any good against magic, but they were also dealing with very human threats as well. He entered the apartment, staying close to the wall while he appraised the situation. The living room and kitchen area were both empty and silent.

"Dante?" Bea stood in the doorway.

"Stay outside." Dante couldn't watch Bea and the scene at the same time.

But she ignored him, entering the apartment with that white stick of chalk in one hand, the other clasping the charm dangling from her necklace. Maybe she was right. Maybe her magic was more threatening than his weapon, depending on whatever waited for them inside.

He didn't have time to worry about it right now. Janet needed him. Dante moved through the empty living and kitchen areas. There was no evidence of a forced entry or a fight of any kind. Nothing was disturbed, which made it all creepier. There was even a Tupperware container of cookies on the table.

Then the smell hit him—the acrid iron tang of blood. He followed his nose, Bea on his heels as they moved down the hall. Rocky barked from behind them, seemingly not willing to venture back here. The bedroom door was ajar. With a trembling hand, Dante pushed it open.

He gagged at the sight. What remained of Janet lay on the bed, which was soaked with her blood. Her body had been eviscerated in half, with her legs dropped onto the floor. But her upper body lay propped up on pillows, her eyes still open and wide with fear.

"Oh, my God"

Before Dante could move to comfort Bea—or more importantly, get her the hell out of there, words appeared on the wall above Janet. It looked like someone was handwriting them in large streaks of blood red. More magic.

Dante's belly twisted, and he choked back bile. Magic was death and filth and destruction. And the words on the wall knew far too much. They read:

FBI. Traitors.

Dante's heart raced. Whoever was responsible for Janet's death knew who he was. Knew who Janet was. Their cover had been blown somehow by forces he still didn't understand.

"What?" Bea gasped out as the words faded, leaving no evidence of them ever being there. "What the hell does that mean? FBI? Traitors?"

He grabbed her arm to pull her out of the room, but clearly the wall wasn't done. No, it wasn't enough to spill Janet's cover. More words appeared.

Ask Agent Dante.

Bea shook off his touch as the words faded into nothing once more. She glared at him with fire in her eyes. There it was. The hatred he'd expected from her at the end of this mission. Dante didn't think it would be today, or that it would have ended like this, in blood and death. But now she knew the truth, and he couldn't keep pretending any longer. The pain hurt, but Janet's death added to the anguish.

"Not here. Have some respect for the dead." He gestured toward the door with a meaningful look. She glared at him for a moment longer until finally, to his relief, she turned and left the bedroom.

Dante turned back to Janet's body. He shouldn't contaminate the scene. But no forensic technique was going to pick up magic, so he felt justified in closing her eyes. Dante couldn't stand the look of fear there. What she must have seen before she died... He would find out whoever did this and make them pay.

But first, he had to deal with Bea.

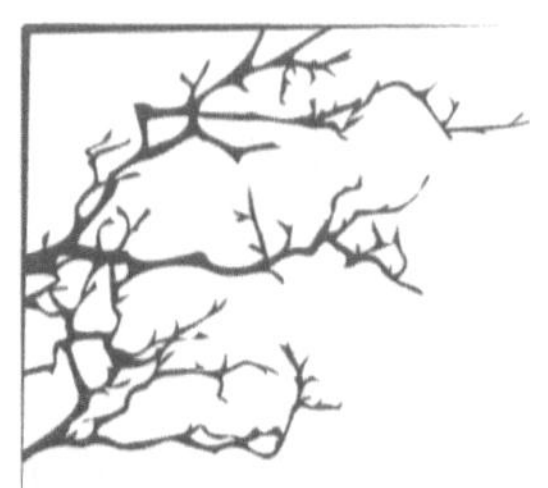

Chapter 33

Bea stumbled out of the bedroom filled with death and magic. She made it back to the living room before dropping to her knees. The darkness of the scene clung to her, and she shuddered, trying to get the taste of it off her body. The dog trotted over to her and started licking her face. Somehow, that helped.

She reached up and tangled her fingers in the dog's golden fur, giving him a good scratch behind each ear. Dog slobber apparently countered dark magic damage. Good to know. If only it had worked on whoever had done that.

With each step she'd taken into this magical world, the more violent it became. Bea had thought witnessing Vito's punishment horrific, but the person she'd been then was still naïve of what was to come. God, if she'd knew it would lead to this, to seeing a woman eviscerated on her bed, Bea would have told Nonna no from the start. She'd never have opened this door she couldn't close.

And even worse than that...Bea had to deal with the words splattered on the wall in magical blood. Dante wasn't who she thought he was. She choked out a sob, tears lapped up by the dog. "Good boy," she told him. Bea couldn't let Dante see her cry.

"He is," Dante said softly from behind her.

Bea got to her feet, not turning around to face him. Not yet. She stared at the television on the wall, how it distorted their reflections on its flat screen. Dante looked elongated and frightening in its mirrored surface. "What did it mean?"

"Bea..."

"What did it mean?" She demanded, clenching her hands into fists at her side. "Agent?"

He didn't speak for a long moment. "I didn't mean for you to find out like this."

Now she had to see him, so she could look him in the eye. Bea turned, still trembling.

Dante looked...sad. Dante's shoulders drooped and his face seemed drawn and pale. And his eyes ... they were glassy. He was probably going into shock himself. That scene in the bedroom wasn't only horrible to her.

Still. She had to steel herself against the flare of emotion inside her that wanted to cross the few steps between them to comfort him. She couldn't turn off caring about him. Hell, she'd been halfway in love with him before this very moment. "Who do you really work for?"

He let out a sigh. "The FBI."

Bea swallowed hard, pushing down the growl of grief and anger that wanted to pour out of her. She took a step back, needing to put space between them. Where had she dropped her messenger bag? Was it back in Dante's apartment? She bet law enforcement was on their way and she needed to be out of here before she got caught.

But not before giving Dante a piece of her mind. "I trusted you."

"I know." He took a step forward, reaching for her with open hands.

Bea retreated, holding her own hands up to ward him off. She'd even ended up dropping her piece of chalk somewhere. She was such a failure at this. "Is your name even Dante?"

He let his hands drop. "My name is Agent David McKenna. They wanted me to get close to your family."

He probably shouldn't have told her that. Did he think admitting everything would get her to forgive him? Bea laughed. "You're not even Italian. I can't believe it."

That made his lips twitch. "That's what you can't believe?"

No, she would not let him do this. The man she thought she knew didn't exist. "You've been lying to me since the day we met. And I've been the idiot who fell for it. Of course, you're too good to be true."

"If anything," he sputtered. "Know my feelings were real."

"Please," she scoffed. "You work for the FBI. I can't believe anything you say."

He gave her an incredulous look. "I'm probably the only person in your life that you can believe right now. If you want to talk facts, someone in your own family probably took out your grandmother and is trying to be the new boss."

It hit her like a slap. There was truth in his words that she could taste in the air with her magic. Dante didn't lie to her.

He wasn't lying now, but his name wasn't even Dante. David. She had to remember that's who he was. And he worked for people who'd like nothing else than to see her entire family in jail.

"Bea, I can help you." He stretched out one arm, but didn't come any closer. "Come with me to headquarters. We can put you in witness protection in exchange for testifying."

"What makes you think I'd testify against my family?"

"Because these past few weeks I've gotten to know you. You're a good person, Bea. I know you wouldn't want to have anything to do with human trafficking or the drug trade. You like beautiful things. You want to be surrounded by art. Not the ugliness of life."

She snorted. "How long have you had that speech prepared?"

His face fell, and part of her wanted to go over there and comfort him. To tell him that of course, he was right, that she'd run right over to the FBI and betray everyone she loved. That part still cared for him. But Bea had to listen to the other part of her—the witch who had a responsibility to her family.

"I only want to help you," David protested, still holding that damn hand out like she was going to take it. "You've seen what you're up against. You really want to go toe to toe with whoever killed Janet?" His voice broke on her name.

Bea narrowed her eyes. "She wasn't just your neighbor, was she?"

David let his hand drop. "She was my handler. She was in charge of the entire operation."

The way he kept dropping information like that. It was like he wanted her to ask him questions, to keep talking. Like he was stalling. Bea's heart raced. Oh no. She had to go, now.

She turned on one heel, not pausing at all once he called her name. Where had she left her messenger bag? She raced to the apartment next door, scooping up her bag where she had dropped it next to the door. The protection symbols she'd etched on the wall were active. Maybe they'd be enough to keep him safe from the witch who was after them. Or maybe she wouldn't care now that Bea knew the truth about who he was.

Fuck this. Bea didn't care what happened to David. She didn't even know the man.

Bea grasped the hiding charm from her bag before darting down the hall. They'd taken the elevator up, but she made for the emergency stairs. That way, she could hide in the shadows.

"Bea, wait!" David chased her down the hall, but she ran, trying to catch her breath. She got to the door moments before he did. Once on the other side, she threw a locking charm on it, repeating the same trick Carmella had got her with at the hospital. It wouldn't hold for long, not with the shoddy way she cast it, but it should give her plenty of time to escape.

Bea pulled the shadow charm out of her messenger bag. She brushed her thumb across it as she activated the charm, sinking into the shadows of the stairwell. It no longer made her dizzy to do this.

Warmth flooded her, the sheer joy of her powers manifesting. Her magic didn't let her down, not like Dante.

David. She had to remember that. Dante didn't exist.

The stairwell spit her out somewhere on the side of the building. This was good. She could stay in the shadows here. David would never find her, not in a million years. Bea kept walking away from the building, not knowing where she was going. She could hear her mother's voice—watch where you are going, that's not a good area—but pushed it down. No one would even see her cloaked like this.

Bea needed to walk. She couldn't face her family knowing what she'd nearly done by exposing them to David. She staggered and nearly lost her grip on the charm. Bea caught a hand on the brick wall next to her to steady herself. Oh god. What had she almost done?

Family was everything. Family was the reason she was conspiring with her father's mistress in order to learn how to master her magic. She needed to protect her family. It was the last thing Nonna told her to do.

And the worst part about it was that she still cared about Dante, about the man who didn't exist. There had been more than physical attraction between them—although that was nice, too. She didn't meet guys who pushed her buttons like he had very often. She'd thought they had a connection. He cared about the things she'd cared about—he loved art and theater. They were supposed to be going to a show tomorrow.

Bea dropped into a crouch, her entire body shaking. Even overcome like this, she had better sense than to put her bare knees on the ground in Newark. Tears spilled from her eyes as she sobbed. *Why can't I have something for me?*

Dante had been friend and confidant. God, she'd told him so much about things that mattered. And he'd betrayed her.

Bea wiped at her eyes. There was no time to sit here and cry about it. She needed to do something.

But Bea couldn't do it alone. She'd been relying on Dante as her sounding board, but all of his advice had been based on lies. David just told her what she wanted to hear. She'd have to go to Carmela. She grabbed her phone out of her messenger bag, glad she'd remembered to grab it before she left David's, and shot off a quick text to Carmella.

Carmella's place wasn't far from here. Yeah, it was late, but this was pretty fucking important. Bea needed her help and, more importantly, she needed to make sure the other woman was safe. If the witch had gone for Bea and Dante, she might have gone after Carmella, too.

Bea got to her feet, taking a moment to adjust her dress and settle her messenger bag over her shoulder. The charm she kept carefully clutched in one hand. Not only would it keep her safe on the streets of Newark, it should hide her from anything magical that might be out to get her.

And to think she'd had such different hopes for tonight. Bea pushed that thought back down. She and Dante weren't a thing anymore. Anything she'd felt for him was merely a lie.

That didn't stop her from taking one last longing look behind her to see if he somehow followed her. Instead, she saw flashing blue and red lights. Police. Bea turned on one heel and started for Carmela's apartment. It should only take her ten or fifteen minutes to get there. Too bad she didn't know any magic to make her move faster.

With each step, her back straightened. The tears dried up. Fuck him. Bea knew who she was now. She was a DiLorenzo. And she didn't need Dante or David, or any other man at her side, to do what she needed to do. She was a witch. She had her own power, and once she figured out how to use it, that witch would find out that you don't mess with the DiLorenzos.

Bea climbed the steps in front of Carmella's building. A gust of wind captured her hair and tossed it over her shoulder. She paused at the entrance to the building. Even though she was still holding on to her concealment charm, the door was open. She dropped the charm back into her bag, her heart racing. Something was wrong. Had the witch gotten to Carmella, too?

Once inside, she paused and took a breath, fearful of what her senses were about to tell her. But she smelled nothing more than dust. Bea sneezed. She rubbed her nose as she climbed the interior steps that led to Carmela's apartment. This door, too, was ajar, but it didn't swing open for her like it usually did when she visited.

Bea pushed the door open, expecting to see the over furnished living room, perhaps smell whatever Carmela had cooked up this evening for dinner. The apartment had become familiar to her these past few weeks. She knew what to expect.

It took her eyes a moment to adjust to the dim lighting—only the street lamps outside illuminated the room. None of the paintings remained on the wall. All the furniture was still there, but the valuables? Those had been removed.

Except for one thing. In the center of the couch sat her father's statue of Saint Michael.

"What the hell?"

Bea lifted the statue. A rush of magic flew through her, a warmth that filled her body. Bea closed her eyes and, like watching a grainy old TV, saw a vision play behind them.

Hands that were not hers touched the base of the statue, revealing a drawer that opened at her touch. The same hands pulled out a velvet pouch, revealing glittering diamonds.

Bea's eyes flew open. That's why Carmella had wanted the statue. She'd hidden diamonds in there. Bea pulled the base open now, finding only a slip of paper.

"I'm sorry, Bea. It's gotten too hot for me here. You're gonna have to deal with her yourself."

Bea dropped the statue. It clattered to the ground and broke into several pieces, the saint's head bouncing across the floor.

What the hell was she going to do now?

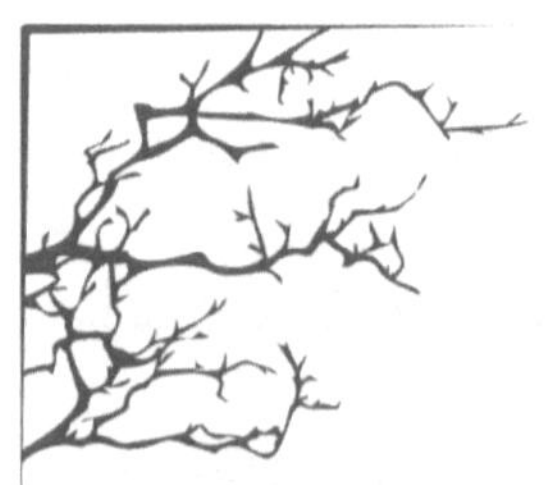

Chapter 34

This can't be happening.

David ran down the stairs on the opposite side of the building, his hands shaking as he pushed the fire door open. But by the time he ran down the block to the exit Bea had to have taken, there was no sight of her. Had she used magic to disappear? She'd closed that door behind her with a wave of her hand.

This can't be real.

His hands weren't the only thing shaking as he took the elevator back up to his floor. David pulled out his phone and hit the panic button hidden in an innocuous app on the home screen. His throat locked up when he added a text note that read *agent down*.

The elevator dinged, and he stepped onto the landing. He should...he should secure the scene. He'd left the dog up here, somewhere...

David felt his grip on reality unravelling. He'd accepted this job was dangerous. He'd known from the beginning that his life was on the line. But he'd thought the threat the muscle head mafiosos who'd sooner shoot him than talk to him.

David hadn't expected magic. There was no way he could have prepared for the supernatural, not when, as far as the bureau was concerned, it didn't exist. They would have had a class on it, if they'd known. He would have been trained. He should have been prepared.

And now Janet was dead, and it was his damn fault. He'd left them both exposed to a threat he couldn't comprehend. A threat he still didn't quite believe.

David leaned his head back against the wall as he sat on the floor in front of Janet's apartment. He wanted to bang against the drywall, to feel something physical that was real. As if catching the direction of his thoughts, Rocky came out of Janet's apartment and licked him on the chin. Then the dog sat and whined, a soft cry like he was mourning his owner.

"They didn't hurt you." David put his hands into soft dog fur, focusing only on the feel of that.

He should have been faster and stopped Bea from leaving. He had questions, damn it, and only she could answer them. How the hell was he going to explain this to his boss? To the rest of the FBI? *I got Janet killed by magic?*

Mostly, he missed having her next to him. If they were together, truly together, a real couple, then nothing could get past them. They'd be able to fight this...whoever this was, this witch, Bea had called them, who was trying to take over the Family. Of course, that depended on Bea trusting him once she knew the real him.

He'd violated that trust. David knew that. But he really wanted to explain to her that he wasn't the bad guy here. He was trying to do the right thing. She had only been a means to an end.

And yeah, that really made him sound like an asshole. David banged his head against the wall again. She had no reason to trust him. He'd fucked her over like the rest of her family, treating her like a child who didn't understand how the world worked. It turned out Bea had a much better idea about what was really going on here. He should have listened to her more in the beginning.

David shook his head. There had been no way to know back then what Bea had been hiding. She'd been suspicious of her grandmother's death, but couldn't explain why. She held back critical intel. Not to say that he could have helped her figure out the murderer's identity if David had known then, but, well, he'd have a better picture of how the world worked.

"Agent McKenna!"

The door to the stairwell burst open. Ah, that magic lock crap hadn't lasted very long then. David got to his feet, swaying a bit as the hallway spun. Rocky barked next to him, and he quickly reached for the leash he'd clipped on shortly after Bea disappeared. The last thing he needed was to get Janet's dog killed by gun happy agents.

The hallway was filling with them now, securing the perimeter before they'd let the paramedics up. Not like the paramedics could do much. How the hell did you piece back together a body ripped in half?

"Agent McKenna," someone was repeating.

He blinked, belatedly recognized Agent Lucas. He'd been pretending to be Dante for so long that he'd momentarily forgotten the other agents on the team spearheading things back at the office. Ariel Lucas was a tiny blond woman who had a right hook like a motherfucker. She was apparently ridiculously good at undercover work and had helped Janet with the briefings back at the beginning.

A lifetime ago now, really.

"Agent Lucas." His voice caught on the name.

She gave him one look, then grabbed his arm and dragged him into his apartment, still holding on to Rocky's leash. There were agents swarming around here, too. She pushed him down toward the couch. "Sit down before you fall over. I'm going to need a medic in here!"

"I'm fine," he protested. The scratches on his back didn't even hurt anymore.

"You're in shock," she countered, crouching in front of him. "Can you tell me what happened?"

David bent over and let his face drop into his hands. How could he explain? "You wouldn't believe any of it."

"Okay," she said. "I'm going to get the dog taken care of. I need you to sit here for me and breathe a bit, okay? Someone's going to look you over in a second."

He let her untangle the leash from his hand, only belatedly realizing there was blood on his palm. Janet's blood. David wiped his hands on his pants—God, his good slacks that Janet had helped him pick out that morning. He couldn't believe she was gone.

The paramedic approached him with a bottle of water. David drank slowly while the man took his pulse and checked his pupils.

"I'm fine. I wasn't there when it happened," he protested. Bea had taken care of the only injuries he'd sustained. The water felt good, though. Helped him back into the land of the living.

The guy made soothing noises before retreating. Probably going to report back to Lucas. Good. Let her handle things for now. David was over it. Damn, but he missed having the dog next to him. How could he ground himself now?

Lucas returned a few moments later. "Feeling better?"

David swallowed another mouthful of water. The shaking had stopped, at least. "I'm fine."

Lucas gave him a look, but she didn't question him. Good, because he didn't think he could say it again. David was very much not fine. He didn't know if he'd ever be fine again.

"Good. Pack up your stuff. We're heading back to the field office. Garcia wants to talk to you. And forensics needs to sweep this place."

"Got it." He needed to get out of here. Maybe once out of his apartment, away from the memory of blood and horrible violence, he could think again. Right now, he could only follow Lucas's lead.

Time seemed to move very fast after that. They left the forensics team to do their thing and David was ushered back to the field office in the back of Lucas's SUV. He could feel the glances she kept giving him in the rear-view mirror. She had to be burning up with questions. But if Garcia wanted to see him, then he must be the one taking David's statement.

Who else had gotten his handler killed? It was usually the other way around and while he really was glad to be alive at the moment, David couldn't help the sense of crushing guilt that weighed down his shoulders. What could he have done differently to have protected Janet? It wasn't like he even knew magic existed until today.

That didn't mean he wasn't a failure. David should have known. They'd told him at Quantico that things could change in an instant. A properly secured prisoner could slip his cuffs and become a threat. The receiver of a warrant could snap and pull out a weapon. That's why agents needed to be prepared for absolutely anything. He should have expected Bea running from him.

It still hurt that she'd chosen her family over him. He'd felt they had a connection, something real between them. Of course, he'd been lying to her about his name and job, but not about anything important, anything real.

Don't be an idiot. He could almost hear Janet's voice in his head telling him that. This had been a job, his first and most likely after this only undercover assignment. They didn't let you back in the field after getting someone killed.

Those thoughts swirled around his head as they made the short trip back to the field office. David barely paid attention as Lucas lead them both upstairs to the bullpen. It felt like years since he'd been back here, instead of months. Months he'd been living an entirely different life. At this point, he couldn't say where David ended and Dante began. He was both men, and right now, that thought was really confusing.

Maybe he should have gone with the paramedic for monitoring. David rubbed his forehead, feeling a headache brewing.

Lucas knocked on Garcia's door, opening it when Garcia called "enter." She ushered him inside and disappeared.

So strange to see darkness outside the windows instead of sunlight streaming in. Garcia himself looked like he had hastily put on his clothes—his shirt was buttoned up wrong, and he didn't wear a tie. He had thrown his suit jacket over the back of one of the chairs across from his desk.

"David," he said, his voice raw and wrecked. "What the hell happened?"

Garcia never used his first name. David dropped into the chair without waiting for an invitation. He ran his hands through his hair. "They killed her. They fucking killed her."

Then there were tears to wipe away. Great, he looked like a probie again. Janet had been his one connection to the Bureau during the op, and he relied on her. He never considered they'd become friends during the process.

Garcia didn't mention the tears. Instead, he pulled a bottle of whiskey from his desk and poured a generous splash into a coffee to-go cup, the kind they kept in the staff room. "Drink." He pushed the cup across the desk.

David took a long swallow, taking a moment to let the alcohol burn its way down his stomach.

"Lucas described the scene," Garcia said delicately. "That was no mob assassination. That was a hatchet job."

"It's so much worse than you think." He swallowed another mouthful before putting the cup back down. "My cover is totally blown." Even if it meant the end of his career, David had to tell the truth, every horrible moment of it. In halting words, he explained everything that happened, starting with the attack after the shower, and Bea using magic in front of him. David couldn't look at Garcia, so he kept his eyes on the empty cup as he described the words written in blood that disappeared once read.

Garcia probably thought he was nuts. David didn't blame him. He crushed the to-go cup in his hands, needing to do something.

He finally looked up, ready to face Garcia blasting him for being so foolish. Maybe even firing him on the spot. Or hell, calling in the paramedics to take him to psych observation.

"You're saying what, that a shadow monster killed Agent Janet Carter?" Garcia rubbed his chin thoughtfully.

David blinked at him. "You're taking this awfully well." It almost sounded like Garcia had expected some kind of supernatural element. Well, to be fair, no one could see the scene in Janet's bedroom and think there was anything natural about it. Still, something was off about Garcia's question.

Garcia let out a shaky laugh. The bottle of whiskey made another appearance, but this time he poured only himself a cup. "There are a couple of things you need to know. First, you know we had guys following you, right? You're not the only one who saw the thing in the alley. Meyers is pretty shaken up. Thinks he's nuts."

"I know how he feels," David muttered.

"Second..." Garcia down his whiskey and then wiped his lips. He looked like he was stalling. Finally, with a sigh, he said, "Carter had a feeling something more was up with the DiLorenzos. There were stories about women with power that kept the men in line. Most of the time we discounted them, but Carter? She kept track of every scrap of intel, no matter how crazy it sounded."

Because Janet would. She never discounted anything that might be important. Why hadn't she said anything to David? Maybe because she knew he wouldn't believe, not unless he saw magic for himself. Well, call him a believer now. If only she was here to tell her that.

David's shoulders dropped. He didn't realize how much relief he'd feel at being believed. But that still didn't solve any of the problems. "How the hell can we fight something like this? You can't get a warrant for witchcraft."

"What do we do any time we need more intel? We find an expert." Garcia drained his cup. He got to his feet and stared out his windows, mesmerized by the lights in the city beyond.

By the time he spoke again, David had already figured it out, a sick feeling in the bottom of his stomach.

"Do you think Beatrice would help us catch this witch?"

"She wouldn't go against her family."

Garcia held a finger up as he turned around. "Ah, but the witch is threatening her family, isn't she? What if we promised to protect them in exchange?"

"You'd give up the DiLorenzos for the witch?"

"For Janet's murderer."

It was a terrible idea. "I'm not sure I should show my face around DiLorenzo territory again."

"Right, right. We need to consider how to approach her."

Janet would know. She'd have some insight after doing undercover work for so long. David wiped at his mouth, wincing at the suddenly foul taste on his tongue. "I could try texting her. After I give her some space, I mean."

Garcia nodded. "Hold on to your cover phone. She might reach out. We'll discuss this again in the morning with the team."

"Yes, sir."

"Go home, get some sleep."

"My statement…"

"Can wait for the morning. Lucas will drive you to your place."

Right. Because his apartment in the city was burned. It was never his to begin with. David didn't know how to go back to his old life, to be Agent McKenna again. He also doubted the rest of the team would believe witches existed. Except for maybe Meyers, who'd seen the shadows attack.

Fuck. This was a mess. And all he could think of was Bea, going back to her family, to face alone a murderer who was more powerful than David could even imagine. She needed help. He wasn't sure he could be the one to do it.

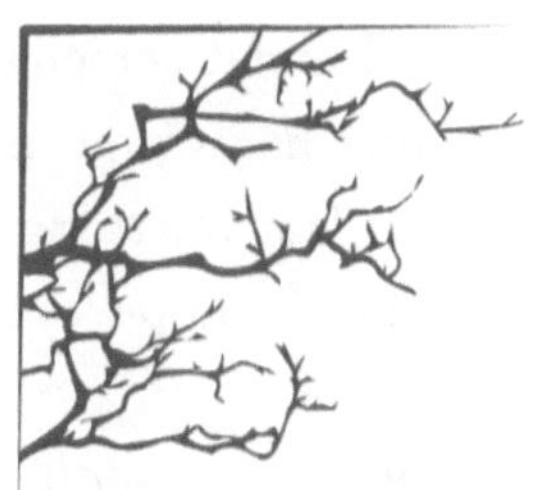

Chapter 35

Bea pulled into the driveway, noting that her mom's car was there, parked next to her father's SUV that hadn't been moved since his heart attack, but Mike's car was missing. Maybe he stayed with Lucy for the night. Or he could still be working at, Bea checked her dash, two AM. She'd heard him stumble in later many nights before.

None of the lights were on inside the house. Good. She didn't want anyone to see her like this. Her knees were stained with who knew what she had kneeled in while in that alley. She didn't have to look in a mirror to know her makeup had streaked and smeared, while her hair had completely fallen out of its updo. She looked, as Mom would say, a sight.

To be fair, she'd survived a monster attack, found another dead body, lost the man she'd been falling for, and been ditched by her witchy mentor. Bea figured if there was any time to look like a wreck, this was it.

She fled upstairs to her bedroom, stripping out of the cranberry-colored dress she'd fallen in love with. Bea stuffed it in the trash in the bathroom, knowing she could never wear it again without thinking of tonight and...Dante. David.

Would she ever remember that?

Her hands shook as she tried to wash the grime off in the shower. If anyplace, she should be safe in her own home. She'd spent the past few weeks etching protection sigils and stashing charms all over her bedroom and the entrances to the house. But Nonna had those as well, and it hadn't helped her.

This witch was too powerful. So powerful she'd sent Carmella packing, and from the short time Bea knew her, that had to mean something. Carmella didn't seem to be the type to fear anything. And here she was, leaving town before Bea's dad had woken up from his coma. Did she really even care about dad?

This isn't about Carmella. No, because Carmella wasn't family. She'd helped Bea out for a favor, and now Bea was on her own.

The entire drive home, she'd been contemplating what to do. Bea needed, desperately, urgently, to speak to her Nonna. She'd know what to do. She'd know who her own killer was.

Why not try a good old-fashioned seance? Carmella hadn't taught her anything like this, but now that Bea knew the basics, she felt confident in her ability to put some sort of spell work together herself. That was the whole point of her book of shadows—experimenting and pushing the limits of what the craft could do.

After her shower—cleansing her body was the first step in any ritual—Bea gathered her materials and locked the door to her bedroom. She rolled back the throw rug in front of her bed and drew a circle with white chalk. Inside the circle, she placed four candles at the cardinal points, with a single white candle in the center. Bea sat crisscross in front of the candle, where she placed Nonna's purse. In her hands, she held the Italian playing cards Nonna had given her years ago.

Bea set them down only long enough to light the last candle. Then she picked up the cards again, shuffling them absently. The flame flickered before her eyes, dancing to the non-existent wind.

"Nonna," she whispered. "If you can hear me, I could really use your help. I don't know who to trust." She'd trusted Dante, and he'd betrayed her. She trusted Carmella, and she left. Bea had to stop the witch before things got any worse.

The cards grew warm in her hands. Startled, Bea stopped shuffling. She turned over the top card and hissed. She knew the meaning behind this one. Betrayal.

"Yes, exactly. They betrayed me." Bea's eyes teared, and she wiped at them. No, she couldn't waste time crying. She had to figure out a god damn solution. "What do I do? Help me. Please."

She put all the effort she could into the spell, tugging at the core of magic inside her. Carmella had taught her how to reach for it, the warmth in her belly that signified the source of her power. But it had always been Bea performing the spells, Bea's magic, Bea's power. "Don't fail me now."

A gust of wind rushed through the room, extinguishing all the candles at once. Bea gasped.

Her eyes adjusted to the darkness after a moment. Her room seemed dimmer than it should be. Then Bea saw her, Nonna, standing at the door to her room. Nonna put her fingers over her lips, commanding silence. She gestured with one hand, and Bea was following her, with no conscious choice to stand or move.

Nonna led Bea down the hall, two doors to her brother Mike's room. They moved through the door without opening it. Bea never came in here, but she wasn't surprised to see the car posters still on one wall, and the mess of dirty laundry piled up at the foot of the bed. None of that mattered, though. Not when Nonna was pointing at Mike's bed.

No, not the bed, what was underneath it.

Nonna nodded slowly when that revelation dawned on Bea. Something was hidden there. Something Bea needed to find.

She snapped back to herself, like waking from a deep sleep, still in her own bedroom. The candles were still lit. In fact, the white one was leaving a waxy mess on her hardwood floor. Mom would have a fit if she saw. Bea leaned over quickly and blew out the flame. She blinked back a wave of dizziness at the motion.

It hadn't been real. It had been a vision. There was something her grandmother wanted her to see underneath Mike's bed. A sinking feeling started in the pit of Bea's belly, a swirl of nausea that warned her of what she was about to discover. She quickly blew out the other candles—not wanting to burn down the house—before venturing out of her room, running down the hallway to Mike's door.

He hadn't locked his room. Why would he? Bea would never violate his privacy and come in here. Except now she was. She turned the knob and pushed the door open. Bea flicked on the light. She dropped to her knees in front of his bed, pulling up the covers to reveal what lie beneath, which was a pile of dirty socks.

Gross. She pushed the socks away, making a mental note to wash her hands after. Beyond the socks, she found it. Her grandmother's spell book.

"What the hell are you doing in here?" Mike's voice sliced through the room.

Bea curled her fingers around the spell book and snatched it up before turning around to confront her brother. She got to her feet, holding the book tight against her chest. Mike stood in the doorway, his face flushed and red. He looked large and menacing, and her heart raced at being caught in his room. She'd seen what he'd done to their own uncle. Bea couldn't assume she was safe.

Why hadn't she sensed him before he entered the room? Bea thought back and realized she'd never picked up any kind of aura or scent from her brother. Fuck, she felt like an idiot. Someone had to be masking him.

Bea faced him, hoping she looked a lot more courageous than she felt. This was her big brother. Sure, he always teased the shit out of her, but she'd never been afraid of him before. Until now.

"Why do you have Nonna's book?" she countered. She couldn't push past him. He took up the entire doorway, and it didn't look like he was moving anytime soon.

If she screamed, that would wake up Mom and she'd come running, wouldn't she? Bea swallowed. Could Mom even stop him? Mike had become someone else without Bea even noticing.

"How about you mind your own business?" He crossed his arms, a nasty smile on his face. The expression sent chills down her spine. He wore the same smile before punching Uncle Guido in the stomach.

She clutched the book closer, feeling the warmth of the magic inside it spread against her chest and arms. Whatever happened here, she knew Nonna had meant for her to have this book. Nonna would protect her, somehow.

"You took it from Nonna's apartment," she said, the revelation coming slowly but surely. It hadn't been there when Bea had discovered the body, and there was no reason for Mike to have snatched it unless he knew the value. "You killed her."

Mike snickered. "You think you're so clever, don't you? With your little stunt at the shower."

The words hit Bea so hard she staggered backward. How could Mike know about her baiting the centerpieces? He didn't have magic. He didn't even know about magic...unless he did. But men couldn't be witches, so that meant...

"It's Lucy, isn't it? It's always been Lucy." The words tumbled out of her, the realization feeling right in her chest. Now that Bea knew the truth, she could see it on her brother, the wards around him that prevented Bea from noticing the spell work that kept his aura and intentions from her.

"You're such an idiot." Mike took a step forward, out of the doorway. "Playing with magic like you know what you're doing. Lucy has been training since she was a kid."

There was a hint of pride in his voice when he said that. Mike had that dopey grin, like he always did whenever he talked about his fiancé. God, he really was in love with her. They had some crazy

Bonnie and Clyde thing going on, and in any other circumstances Bea might think it romantic.

Right now, it devastated her. Mike had taken sides, and it was against Bea and the family.

"How is that possible? She's an orphan…" and not Italian, and and…did Bea really know Lucy at all? She'd always seemed overly clingy and happy, to where Bea hid from her instead of getting to know her. Bea regretted that now.

Mike barked out a laugh. "Exactly. You know shit about her. You're so busy with your head in the clouds you got no idea about the real world or this family."

"I care about this family. I'm the one trying to get Daddy back." Bea bit back, stung. This was like when they were little kids. Mike needling her until she yelled back. Only dad wasn't around to separate them and make Mike apologize. Dad wasn't around because of Mike's actions.

"You don't have the stones to do what needs to be done to keep this family running," Mike spat. "Nonna never got that."

"Nonna always believed in me." Bea reached into the pocket of the cargo pants she'd put on after her shower. She'd gotten into the habit of stuffing magical supplies in her pockets and was relieved when her hand curled around a small warm stone.

Mike rolled his eyes. "Doesn't matter now, does it? Besides, this is how things are done. Dad wanted to stay in the past. I'm the fucking future."

"Humble, too. I'm not going to let you get away with this." Bea traced shapes around the stone in her pocket, saying the words in her mind, hoping that would be enough to get her out of this.

"No, Little Bean." Him using that childhood nickname now was like a punch to the gut. It hurt more than if he'd actually punched her. This was her own brother. He walked toward her, an evil glint in his eyes. "You're going to be a good little girl. I'm the boss now. My word is law. Be careful or you mind find yourself married off. I hear Nick is single and looking."

"Fuck you," she snapped, throwing the stone at his feet. It let off a flare of light that had Mike covering his eyes and cursing at her. It gave her enough time to run past him, back to her own room.

She slammed the door shut, locked it, and then shoved one of her still full packing boxes against it. She dropped to her knees, hugging the book to herself.

God, she had been so damn stupid. Dante had even told her, back in the beginning, to look at someone close to Nonna. Granted, in hindsight, he probably knew that because he was FBI, but he'd been right. Bea had thought the threat was coming from outside, not within her own family.

But Lucy was an outsider, some small voice said inside her. She'd come, seduced Bea's brother and led him on this path.

No, don't give him an out. Bea saw for herself the kind of man Mike was.

He was the same as the people who made up her family—murderers, men of violence, thieves. It was time she came to grips with that. She could either accept that was who they were, and that's what her grandmother wanted to continue, or Bea could decide here and now to make a different future.

She swallowed and sat back, letting the book fall onto the floor in front of her. With a shaking hand, she cracked it open. The amount of magic coming from it generated heat that could be felt before she put a finger on it. When she opened it, the words on the page began to shimmer and blur. It took Bea a moment to realize what she was seeing.

There had been recipes on the page—normal, food related recipes. Now that Bea had her eyes on it, the text changed. The writing was small, and in cursive. It was going to take her some time to go through this.

Hope flared within her. Nonna had fooled Mike and his witch fiancé. This gave Bea a fighting chance. But only if Mike didn't know. She had to play along for now, at least until she was strong enough to face Lucy and...

And what? Kill her? That would make Bea just as bad as Lucy herself. She couldn't decide she didn't want to live her family's lifestyle and commit the same sins. Bea pulled out her phone, but didn't go beyond the lock screen. There was Dante, after all. David, the FBI agent. She could turn traitor, turn them all in.

As if the FBI could do anything against magic. Bea dropped the phone and turned back to the spell book. Ok, step one, read the book. Take notes - that was the lesson she'd learned from Carmella. Write it down and make the magic hers. There was a lifetime of experience in here. There had to be something to guide her. Nonna wanted her to have this.

Bea was a DiLorenzo. She was a fighter. There was no way in hell she was going to let Lucy steal her family.

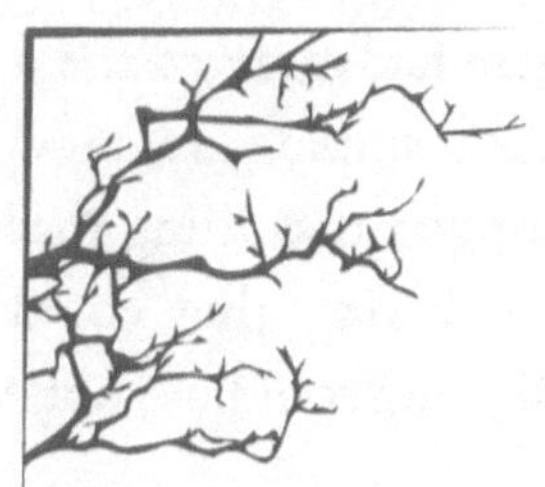

Chapter 36

David watched from a distance as they lowered an empty coffin into the open grave at St. Sebastian's cemetery. He couldn't bring himself to walk down the hill and stand with Janet's family as they mourned. Hell, most of them didn't even realize the body hadn't been released yet. Janet's mother had wanted closure, and so held the memorial despite the FBI still holding on to the remains.

Remains. What a shitty word to describe what used to be a person. But they were the only evidence the FBI had of magic. Janet had been killed by something clearly not human, perhaps not even of this world. They couldn't let her body go without investigating every bit of the evidence left behind. Surely there was something left behind that would help them figure out this new world.

He thought of the creature of shadows and shuddered. That thing had claws, giant talons that had reached for him. It had smelled of smoke and rot. Thinking about it now brought back the sense of panic and fear he'd felt that night as he faced something he could not comprehend. David had been lucky it only tossed him aside. It could have slashed him to bits.

And it hadn't because Bea had been there to save his life.

Even now, he ached with regret. He couldn't help but believe they could have had something special. He wished he'd met her under some other circumstances, that they could have built a genuine relationship. The undercover phone felt heavy and unused in his pocket. It had been four days since that fateful night, and she'd yet to reach out to him.

He hoped she was safe. Something out there had targeted them both. He wanted to protect her, but he wasn't stupid. He knew nothing about magic. How could he have stopped that thing that walked through bullets? Only Bea knew how. If only they could work together. Now that she knew he was FBI, they could use both of their skills to find the witch and stop her.

Stop her and avenge Janet's death. He clenched his hands into fists. David hadn't forgotten that. He would make them pay.

"Shame, isn't it?" A voice said from behind him.

Startled, David turned around to see a young blond woman dressed in a black dress, wearing an old-fashioned hat with a veil covering the front of her face. "Excuse me?"

"She died so young." The woman gave an exaggerated sniff, putting a hand covered in a black lace glove beneath her nose.

A prickling sensation went down the back of his neck. There was something familiar about her, but David couldn't put a finger on it. "Have we met?"

She stepped forward until she was standing beside him. A handful of trees hid from the mourners below them. Janet had been given a full ceremonial funeral, complete with a twenty-one-gun salute. Garcia was down there, getting ready to hand the flag that had covered her casket to her family. All the other agents from the department were there as well. David couldn't bring himself to face the family.

"Are you related to Janet?" he tried again when the woman didn't answer.

She looked down at the memorial service below, at the sobbing family, before turning back to David with her lips stretched into an unnatural smile.

That prickle at the back of his neck turned to ice. Fear spiked in his belly, which was ridiculous. There were fifty FBI agents below and scores of military personnel. He was perfectly safe.

But no one knew he was back here, hiding from the ceremony.

"Allow me to introduce myself. Lucia Valentini, soon to be DiLorenzo. We've met several times, but I always wore a cloaking spell, so I couldn't be recognized by members of law enforcement. It's how I knew exactly what you were from the first moment we met at Nonna's wake."

Shit, shit, shit. David took a step back, his hand fumbling for his side arm beneath his suit jacket. It was her—the witch! The one who'd killed Bea's grandmother and Janet. He opened his mouth to call out to the agents below.

She raised her hand into a fist, and no sound came out of his mouth. David stood there gaping like a fish. "You really think that gun is going to do anything to me?"

Her fist rotated, and the gun dropped from his nerveless fingers, bouncing on to the grass below. Luckily, the safety was on or he could have gotten himself shot with that move.

Laughter caught in his throat, hysterical giggles that couldn't get out, because that's what he was worried about? The gun going off? When this witch had paralyzed his voice and his hands with nothing more than a gesture? David tried to step away, but found now that he couldn't move his legs, either.

"It's not personal, you know." She carefully peeled the lace gloves off her hands. "We just need to borrow you for a little bit to make sure naughty Bea behaves herself at the wedding."

David stared at her fingers, dainty, pale, and pink. He couldn't look away as she curled one hand in front of her lips and blew across her palm. Smoke or dust rose from her skin and he had no choice but to breathe it in. The world faded to black, and he swayed backward, only to be caught by brawny arms.

His rescuers were two tall men in suits. David belatedly recognized them as working for the DiLorenzo family. God, she'd come with backup. He guessed magic couldn't be used to cart him back to wherever they were taking him.

David couldn't fight the darkness any longer. His body no longer belonged to himself. The last thing he saw was Lucia bending down to pick up his gun. She faced him and grinned. "Now this, this we'll make use of. Thank you so much for making it so very easy for me."

The darkness claimed him.

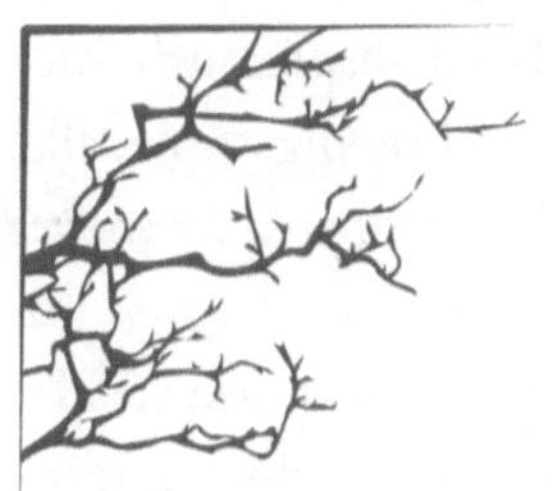

Chapter 37

The wedding was tomorrow, and Bea was no closer to figuring out what to do than when she started. She'd spent the past few days working through Nonna's spell book, making notes in her own, and trying out various spells. The more she practiced, the better she would get at it. Still, there were things in that book Bea never wanted to try. Nonna had outlined her process for ensuring loyalty in intricate detail.

Bea should have listened to her instincts the first time she witnessed that. She knew she wasn't the type of person who would burn someone's eyes out. But she let Nonna convince her by reminding her of her loyalty to the family.

That was the past. She couldn't worry about what she hadn't done. Bea had to think about acting now. Unfortunately, she couldn't figure out what to do. The book had a spell for binding a witch's magic, and at first Bea had rejoiced. This would save her from having to kill Lucy and might break the curse on Daddy. But it wasn't an easy spell and required destroying all of a witch's protections first. Bea didn't think Lucy would stand there and let Bea do that.

Her phone buzzed from where it was charging on her desk. Bea sat curled up in bed with the spell book, and for a moment she wanted to ignore it. She was too comfortable, and she had too much to worry about. Soon enough, her mother would be banging on her door, telling her to help with some more pre-wedding plans, like the rehearsal dinner later tonight.

God, the thought of having to sit next to Lucy and Mike and pretend everything was fine made her want to vomit. Neither of them had said anything—in fact, Mike had been suspiciously nice to her around Mom. But he always had that knowing smile, like reminding Bea that Lucy could call up a shadow monster whenever she felt like it. Bea had doubled up her protection charms, but constantly looked over her shoulder, expecting the next attack. Her dreams were filled with shadows and blood, and as the wedding approached, a creeping, crawling sensation grew at the back of her neck. Something was coming, and it was centered on the wedding itself.

The phone buzzed again, two more times, as if someone was texting multiple times. "Fine, fine, I'm getting up."

Bea tucked the book beneath her pillow before trucking across the room and pulling her phone off the charging cord. What she saw nearly made her drop it.

The text had come from David's phone. She hadn't had the heart to block the number. The first text was a picture—a close-up shot of David tied up with a bandanna around his eyes and duct tape around his mouth. It was filtered to hell and impossible to tell where exactly he was.

"Oh, God."

The next few texts read:

If you want to see him alive again, you'll behave. I'll give him to you after the reception ends in the kitchens of the Manor.

The Manor was where Mike and Lucy's wedding reception would be held. Bea felt her legs go weak, and she dropped to the floor, still holding on to her phone. Fuck them both. She'd broken things off with David. He had nothing to do with this.

Damn it. She still cared about him. Bea had deliberately kept him out of her thoughts. It was easy not to think about him when she focused on her grandmother's spell book. It was like cramming for an exam again. She shut out the rest of the world, took notes, and focused on one thing.

She didn't have to think about her broken heart, about how she'd lost someone who didn't really exist. She could ignore the fact that he wanted her to betray her family, a family whose business she didn't want to protect anymore.

Somehow, Lucy and Mike knew he was still her weak spot. She dropped her head into her hands, at first overwhelmed with anger and fear.

And then it occurred to her. If they went to the trouble of kidnapping an FBI agent to keep her in line, then they thought she was still a threat. More of a threat than the FBI.

Bea got to her feet and paced. She didn't have a lot of time. Her evening would be taken up by the rehearsal dinner and pretending to be a good girl for the family. Whatever she was going to do, she had to figure it out fast. David's life depended on it.

She didn't have to do it alone. Bea stopped her pacing when it hit her like a brick. Mike and Lucy had each other to scheme. Bea had been relying on David because Connie hadn't believed her, but that was when Bea couldn't prove magic existed. She'd come a long way since then.

Something inside her told her that this was right. Warmth filled her chest and Bea recognized it for the flare of intuition it was. Connie would awaken to her powers on her twenty-first birthday in August, and it would be better for her to be prepared. And she trusted her cousin, out of everyone else in this family, to do the right thing.

Bea scooped up her car keys and slipped into a pair of flats. She had to take the chance.

"BEA? WHAT ARE YOU DOING here?" Connie answered the door to her home, wearing a pair of yoga pants and a sports bra. She looked like she'd been in the middle of working out.

Bea hadn't called or texted first. Now she felt sheepish about that. Well, Connie's workout could wait. "I need to talk to you."

Connie frowned. "You haven't texted me for days. You disappeared after the shower and I didn't know what to think." Her expression changed. "Oh god, Bea are you okay? You left with that guy and..."

"Funny story..." Bea pushed past her, not wanting to have this conversation on the front porch of her aunt and uncle's house. "Are your parents home?"

She shook her head. "My mom is out getting her manicure."

Right, lots of prep for the wedding. Still, Bea didn't want to risk anyone walking in and she especially didn't want to damage anything in her aunt's immaculately curated living room. The furniture and rugs were all in tones of cream and white. As kids, they hadn't been allowed to sit on that couch. "Let's go up to your room."

This was it. She had one chance to convince Connie that magic was real, that her brother was threatening her with the power of his own witch. God, even thinking the words sounded crazy. The only thing Bea could do was prove it with actions.

She jogged up the steps ahead of Connie with the ease of familiarity, having done this hundreds of times before. This wasn't usual, the time spent away from each other. If only Connie had believed her from the beginning. But really, Bea understood how fantastical it could all sound if you didn't see with your own eyes. Which was why she needed to show Connie.

The door to Connie's room was ajar. Bea ducked inside and slid up against the wall, where the shadows were darkest. Then, with a motion long practiced, she slid her hand into her pocket and touched the concealment charm. Luckily, Connie's room was only illuminated by the fairy lights strung through the canopy over her bed. Her curtains were still drawn, letting only a bit of daylight in from the edges.

Connie stepped into the room. She got to the center, stopped, and whirled around. "Bea?" She even went to the other side of the bed, ducking her head as if to check if Bea had hidden beneath.

It was almost funny. For a moment Bea regretting having to tell her anything. Connie was always so sweet. She didn't have to be dragged into all of this.

Except she was family and destined to be a witch herself. Bea would do her no favors by denying her the truth. With a sigh, Bea let go of the charm and stepped out of the shadows just as Connie turned in her direction.

Connie screamed.

Bea winced and held her hands out. "Hey, it's okay."

"How the hell did you do that?" Connie's eyes were wide. She took a step back, like she was afraid of Bea.

Bea let out a sigh. "Magic."

Connie let out a shaky laugh. "No, seriously."

"Do you have a logical explanation for it?" Bea snapped back. "I love you, but we really don't have time for you not to believe me right now. What else do you want me to do? Set something on fire? Oh, or how about this?" Bea put down her messenger bag, opened the top and then straightened up again. She held her hand over the open bag, and Nonna's spell book floated in the air to meet her palm.

Connie sat down hard on the floor, her face going pale.

Bea set the book down and rushed to her cousin's side. "Hey, it's okay. Just breathe. In and out."

Connie breathed along with her, like that time when they were kids and she fell down the stairs at Nonna's and got the wind knocked out of her. Bea had been there to help her find her breath then.

After a moment of silence except for their joined breaths, she spoke. "So. Magic."

"Yeah. I tried to tell you. Only then I couldn't show you because I didn't know what I was doing."

"And now you do?" Connie looked over.

Oh, man. Where to start? Well, some place more comfortable for starters. Bea got to her feet and held out a hand to help Connie up. She settled on the bed while Bea took the pink sparkly bean bag chair.

"It's a long story, and I'm going to need you to save the freaking out until later, okay? Because I need your help." Bea curled her hands around her knees, trying to make herself smaller. It seemed she'd outgrown the bean bag.

"My help?" Connie folded her legs under her. Now that the initial freak out was out of the way, she stared at Bea with an intense gaze, looking like she was ready to absorb everything Bea had to tell her.

"It's best if I start from the beginning." Bea retold the story of Nonna's death and why she believed someone had murdered her. When she got to Carmella teaching her magic, both of Connie's eyebrows went up, but she didn't interrupt. Then the story got harder to tell.

"What? Dante was FBI?" Connie got to her feet, gesturing wildly with both hands. "Are you kidding me?"

"I wish that was the worst part." Bea ran a shaky hand through her hair. Relieving the events of that night made her heart race and blood thrum in her ears. Sometimes she could even feel the fetid breath of that thing on the back of her neck. She shivered.

"How can it get worse than you discovering your boyfriend is a cop and finding yet another dead body!" Connie flailed now, gesturing with both arms to emphasize her point.

"Finding out who is responsible for it all," Bea said quietly, all amusement at her cousin's actions now gone.

Connie went still. She crossed the room and kneeled in front of Bea. "Who is responsible?"

To her horror, Bea burst into tears. She hadn't been able to cry or mourn for the brother she loved since the confrontation with Mike. It had all been bundled up with the ball of rage and anger in her belly.

"Bea, it's okay." Connie reached out and hugged her, holding her close.

God, it felt good to share this, to not hold this burden alone. Finally, someone else could comfort her and, most importantly, help. Bea held on to her cousin, taking the moment to let it all out. There wouldn't be time for tears after this.

Connie let her go long enough to grab the box of tissues off her nightstand. She held them out and Bea took a bunch. She blew her nose and wiped at her eyes, doing her best to look presentable. When she finished, her throat was scratchy and sore, but Bea felt more settled.

"Sit down before I tell you." She didn't want Connie collapsing in shock again.

Connie parked herself on the floor in front of Bea, still within hugging range if needed. Bea appreciated the consideration.

Then she told her about finding the spell book beneath Mike's bed, and the confrontation that followed. Connie's jaw dropped as Bea continued, pulling out of her phone to show the picture of Dante tied up and gagged. "All this so I don't interfere with their wedding and family takeover."

Connie took the phone and stared at the picture. She frowned. "You know, I never liked Lucy."

Bea barked out a laugh, unable to help herself. "Me either."

"And now we know why. She was giving off bad vibes this whole time. We just didn't know what we were sensing." Connie bit her lip, looking thoughtful.

Bea swallowed. "Are you okay with knowing you'll be a witch when you turn twenty-one?"

Connie made a face. "Well, you said Nonna had to unlock your magic. As long as I don't do that, I wouldn't be a witch, right?"

"I'm honestly not sure. Not an expert here. They don't exactly offer online classes in this shit."

To her relief, Connie giggled at that. Then she grew serious. She curled her arms around her knees. "What are we going to do? We can't let Lucy get away with murdering Nonna."

"That's gonna make for some awkward Christmas Eve dinners," Bea tried to joke, but the words fell flat. "According to Mike, it's how things are done. I don't know about you, but I will not be a part of this world anymore."

Connie hesitated. Bea must have pushed her too far. It was one thing for her to have come to that conclusion after witnessing the things she had over the past few weeks. She'd never forget the sight of Mike punching their uncle in the name of business. David's words circled in her mind, too, how she was better than her family. Bea wasn't sure she believed that, but maybe she wanted the chance to find out.

Bea went on, letting Connie chew on that for as long as she needed to. "I think I found a spell in Nonna's spell book that we can modify and bind Lucy's magic for good. That means she won't be able to hurt anyone else in our family."

Connie went pale. "You think she's going to kill someone else?"

"We're both witches, Connie. Think about it. We're threats." Bea reached out and squeezed her cousin's hand. She was too sweet to think about things like this. "But if we're going to bind her magic, we need to set a trap. I'm thinking the wedding reception, at the meetup to free Dante." It was the only place where they could guarantee when and where Lucy would be, both essential in this kind of powerful magic. "Will you help me?"

Connie nodded, her eyes sparking with fire. "When? After the rehearsal dinner?"

Bea grinned. "I think we can both be fashionably late to the dinner. We got lost after leaving the church. That should keep both Lucy and Mike busy while we set our trap."

Connie took a deep breath and let it out. "Tell me what I need to do."

For the first time since finding the spell book in her brother's bedroom, Bea felt hope flare within her.

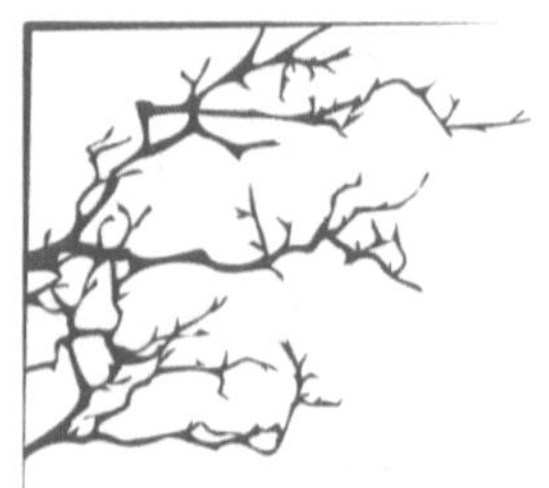

Chapter 38

Consciousness returned slowly. David dozed, caught between sleep and awareness. His eyes twitched, but no light seeped in. He couldn't feel his body at first, and he floated in the darkness like in a pool of liquid. At first it was peaceful, like soaking in a full tub of warm water, or having laughing gas at the dentist's office: floaty and free. As the fuzziness faded, his mind snapped awake, and the horror of his situation hit him all at once.

She'd drugged him, that witch. She'd told him her name was Lucia, but she had to be Lucy, Mike's fiancée. David had never been able to pick her out of a crowd, and now he knew why. *Magic.* It seemed to explain everything, and it would make him laugh if he could move his lips.

If he could move anything at all. Feeling in his body returned much slower, coming back with pins and needles in all of his extremities. It took a while to realize he was bound with his hands behind his back, his eyes and mouth covered. But no matter how hard he tried to wiggle his fingers, David couldn't manage it. The drug or spell, whatever it was, had paralyzed him. Not completely. He could still breathe and swallow. But anything more than that was beyond his ability at the moment.

How long had he been unconscious? David couldn't tell the state of his body, disconnected as it was from his own mind. Was he hungry? Thirsty? Did he have to pee? Or maybe the magic had preserved him in stasis, trapped forever in that moment in time. If he could shudder in horror, he would, because this was fucking terrifying. That tiny woman had caught him unaware and imprisoned him like this, with nothing more than a snap of her fingers.

The sound of voices broke into his perpetual silence. David held his breath and tried to listen. Wherever they'd stashed him, he was no longer alone. He had to find a way to break free, to get a message to Garcia, anything. They took him for a reason, and it couldn't be a good one. Whatever the reason, he knew his time alive had to be short. The Mob didn't keep FBI agents around for fun.

"You take the feet." The voice was much closer now. "I'll grab his arms."

David recognized the owner—Dominick, Mike's friend. From the way Dom had acted at the Bridal Shower, he probably acted at Mike's consigliere, a mob boss's closest advisor. But why wasn't Mike here himself? Too fancy to do the dirty work now that he was in charge?

"Gotta secure the gun first," a second voice chimed in. It could belong to Junior. David hadn't spent as much time around him to be completely sure. "She was real particular on that point."

"Hurry up, why don't you? We gotta get him moved fast. Can't be late to the church."

"Like Mike would get married without his best man." Junior snorted.

David strained to hear, to make use of the most important sense left to him. He could only smell sweat and dirt, probably his own BO after being kept like this for...when had been the wedding date? Bea had told him the 21st and Janet had been buried on the 19th, so...God, had they kept him tied up for two days?

He could make out the telltale noises of a clip being checked, the way the metal slid together as the parts of the gun moved. They were playing with his official sidearm, the one he'd gone back to carrying after leaving his undercover role. What did they want with that? The Mob had tons of firearms at their disposal.

"What does she want this for, anyway? We can't use it. Hasn't been scrubbed."

No, the serial number on the weapon would lead law enforcement right back to the FBI and David himself. No one in the mob wanted to get caught with that kind of thing on their person. But hell, these guys in particular never seemed to get caught. Another side effect of that magical protection.

What else could witches do? David had seen the monster Lucia had summoned. He'd seen the aftermath of what she'd done to Janet. His body went cold. What kind of nightmare was he in store for?

He shouldn't have thought himself in the clear once Bea had left him. David had been so stupid. He'd tried to betray the mob. There was still a target on his back. He should have expected the mob to tie up any loose ends. That meant himself...and Bea. Shit.

"Explain to me why we shouldn't just dump him in the Passaic River?" Junior grunted as he lifted David's feet.

For a moment, David's world was lopsided until Dominick picked up the slack and grabbed David beneath the armpits. At least he could feel the hands on him, no longer completely cut off from sensation. Did the spell have a time limit? Would he suddenly come into his body, tired and aching and really needing to pee?

"No, no, we want the cops to find his body," Dominick said with a snicker. "Teach 'em all a lesson."

Junior joined in the laughter as David swayed from side to side.

They wanted his gun for a reason. They wanted the cops to find his body. David tried to fight the clouds in his mind as they carried him. There could only be one reason for that. They were going to frame him for murder, and then make it look like he turned the gun on himself. But who? Mike was already Don and...

Oh god. Bea. It had to be Bea. Why would Lucia let a rival witch live? Not when she could kill her explosively as a warning to others?

David's heart raced. Adrenaline coursed through him, letting him feel the pulse of his blood behind his ears. He struggled, putting everything he had into fighting the paralysis in his limbs. At first, there was nothing, no response.

But then, with one final push, he could move his head, slamming it back and hoping like hell he hit something. Dominick let out a cry. Good. David hoped he smacked him right in the nose. He continued to struggle, now able to feel his hands and feet. He kicked out, flailing as both men dropped him.

"Mother fucker," Junior swore. "She said the spell would last until after the wedding."

David now had a timeline, at least. He knew exactly how long he had left to live. Both men were about to be late for church and needed to drop him somewhere. The wedding was today. The stupid wedding which had been the entire goal of his entire undercover mission. It seemed so pointless now. There was no way the FBI could ever take the DiLorenzo family down, not when they had magic on their side.

David tried to roll to his feet. He couldn't let them use him against Bea. He had to fight. How he was going to do that while bound and gagged he didn't know. But David would not go down without a struggle. They thought him soft? They had another thing coming.

"Christ, grab him!"

"He's like a fucking fish."

Maybe he was, flopping on the ground and trying to slip their grasp. If he worked hard enough, maybe he could get his legs free. A heavy weight sat on his chest, trapping him.

"Going to have to do this the old-fashioned way."

What the hell did that mean? David tried to growl through his gag. "Let me go!"

In response, something slammed against the side of his head, hard. And then he knew darkness once more.

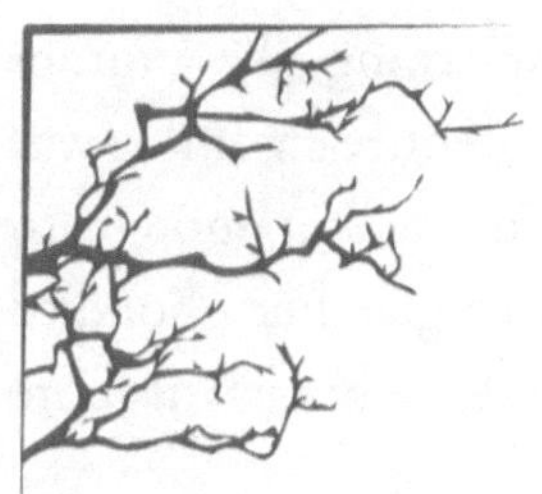

Chapter 39

Flowers flooded the church. Every other pew leading up to the altar had bouquets of yellow roses attached to them. Bright floral arrangements in all shades of yellow, from buttery cream to bold sunflower decorated the altar itself. There were even clear vases with fresh-cut flowers stationed in front of the saints.

Bea wrinkled her nose as she poked her head in to check out the decor. She and Connie were waiting in the vestibule for Lucy to arrive, along with the maid of honor. They'd come to the church with the groomsmen, while Lucy had her own damn limo. Mike already stood up at the altar with Father Roberto. Father Stefano hadn't been in church since the funeral.

The problem with the floral scent invading her nostrils was that Bea couldn't distinguish it from any more magical scents that might alert her to danger. *Who the hell am I kidding?* This entire wedding was dangerous. There were mobsters in every pew in there, even keeping magic out of consideration.

She and Connie wore matching yellow gowns that had off-the-shoulder ruffles tracing their necklines and around their arms. The maid of honor—Bea had forgotten her name again—had a completely strapless top instead. The dress didn't look terrible on her. Bea kept eyeing her, wondering if Lucy's best friend was also a witch. She tried getting a look at her aura, but it was blank, no signs of magic. That meant nothing if Lucy was good at shielding, which she seemed to be.

Bea wore a pair of white leggings beneath the dress, just in case she needed to pull an action hero move and rip off her skirts to chase after someone. Or, more likely, run from something like another shadow monster. The only good thing about the entire ensemble was the matching yellow purses they all carried. It was big enough to hold Nonna's spell book perfectly. She'd had to give her phone to Connie, since Bea couldn't hold on to both and the book was more important.

"Are you ready?" Connie asked as Bea made her way back to her side. She raised her eyebrows so Bea knew what she was really asking.

Was she ready to face down Lucy and implement their plan? So much depended on Lucy springing their trap. Bea rubbed sweaty hands on her satin skirts. They'd done everything last night, using that bubble of time between the rehearsal and the dinner to sneak into the reception venue and leave behind sketched symbols and herbs. Bea could only hope that it would work.

Bea put a bright smile on her face. "Of course! Can't wait to get to the reception."

"There's going to be so much food." The maid of honor laughed.

Connie's smile wasn't nearly so bright. "Yeah."

"What about you?" Bea reached for Connie's hand and squeezed it. Even though she didn't have magic, Connie had an important role to play tonight.

Connie sighed. "Just a little nervous, I guess."

"Don't worry. Everyone will be looking at the bride." Maid of honor reassured her.

Those weren't entirely comforting words. Bea didn't know how she was going to stand being next to Lucy for so long without strangling her. David. She had to remember David's life was at stake.

Because now she knew for sure that the family business was a thing of evil. Bea had rationalized it to herself for too long. Nonna had made her believe her gifts protected her family, but what she'd meant was the entire bullshit system. It wasn't about binding Lucy's magic to get revenge for Nonna's death anymore.

David had tried to get her to do the right thing. Bea regretted walking away from him that night. Maybe if she'd stayed to listen, they could have worked together somehow. She could have helped bring down the entire organization. Instead, she stood here in a bridesmaid dress celebrating the marriage of the two people who'd murdered their way to power.

Bea had been so stupid. She should have known from the beginning that Mike was the only one to have benefited from everything that had happened since Nonna's death. Even if she couldn't see through Lucy's shielding spells, she should have been suspicious that she saw nothing at all. But Mike was family, and everything inside Bea had told her he wouldn't do that.

It had taken her long enough, but Bea knew it didn't matter if you were related by blood or not. People could still be shitty to each other.

"Hey," Connie said in a low voice as the front doors of the church opened. "It's going to be okay. We got this."

Lucy strode in through the doors in her icy white mermaid style gown. Lucy had slicked her blond hair with some kind of glitter gel, making it sparkle beneath the tiara and lace veil she wore. She saw Bea and Connie and gave them both her usual smile. *God, what a bitch.* That she could still pretend, even now. But there was no pretending. Lucy was getting everything she wanted. Why shouldn't she smile with happiness?

Connie's father, Uncle Tony, stepped forward. He was going to walk Lucy down the aisle since she was an orphan. Or was she? Bea was pretty sure everything Lucy told them about herself and her family had been total bullshit.

"Places, everyone!" The wedding planner called out, shuffling forward to organize the line. The church organ above them started up the entrance theme for the bridal party.

Bea swallowed. There was no going back now. She smiled at her cousin Junior and held out her arm for him to take as he escorted her down the aisle. She'd keep that damn smile on her face all day. Nobody would be able to tell from looking at her the anger and hate she felt in her heart for the married couple, for all they'd done to her and her family, and all the evil things they planned on doing. But once the reception was over, all bets were off. Bea would take back Dante—David. Lucy wouldn't have her magic to rely on anymore. Then Bea could take the curse off her father and put the family back into his reliable hands. And Nonna would finally be avenged.

Tonight.

HER FATHER'S ABSENCE didn't hit her until the band played the Tarantella. Bea had grown up dancing the whirling frenetic moves with her father at various weddings and events. She'd spin around so fast she'd get dizzy, then laugh and clap along with the beat, moving her feet faster and faster as she leaped into the air. No one could leap as high as her daddy, with his hands in the air as he spun in time to the familiar music.

Bea watched the dancers converge in the middle of the dance floor. Lucy and Mike were in the center of it all, clearly enjoying their wedding reception. Bea herself didn't even have an appetite to partake of the ridiculous amount of food. She kept pushing her dinner around on her plate, and that was after passing on the tables and tables of appetizers at the cocktail hour. They'd even had a suckling pig. *Seriously?*

They had paid for and planned all of this before Daddy's coma. A mob wedding was always a show of money and power. Bea had never noticed it so clearly before. Her eyes had been opened now and she couldn't ignore what was right in front of her. The tables had been arranged to keep rival families apart. She sat with the bridal party near the head table, squarely on the DiLorenzo side of the room. Lucy's guests—her friends from the boutique—had a single table they used to separate two rival mob families.

"You're not dancing." Mom stopped at the table where Bea sat alone, still stabbing at her steak. Connie had escaped to the restroom, while the groomsmen and the maid of honor had gone out to the dance floor with the others. It seemed like most of the guests had taken part in the show, either by dancing or by forming a circle around the dancing couples.

"Dad's not here," Bea pointed out, although it should have been obvious. She wouldn't do this dance without her dad.

Mom's lips pressed together, turning them white even beneath her lipstick. "Your father wouldn't want you to not have a good time."

Bea couldn't help it. She snorted in response. "You cried for a week after his heart attack. And now you're suddenly fine?"

"I am not fine." Mom took Connie's abandoned seat. "But sometimes you have to accept things as they are. You can't change them."

Bea studied her mother for a moment. Mom didn't have to wear yellow like the bridal party, and had chosen a gown of navy with a crystal embroidered bodice. She didn't look as washed out. However, there were shadows under her eyes. When Bea pushed forward with a tendril of magic, she got a sense of sorrow emanating from her mother's aura.

"You know." Bea kept the words quiet, although no one could hear over the pulsing beat of the Tarantella.

Mom blinked. "Excuse me?"

"You know about Mike and Lucy taking over the Family business." Bea pressed on. "Mom, how are you okay with this?"

"What the hell am I supposed to do?" she snapped. She narrowed her eyes at Bea. "And what do you know about it anyway?"

Mom didn't know about Bea's magical awakening, which meant she probably didn't know about David being held for leverage, or that Lucy considered Bea a threat. At least Mom wasn't that blasé about everything.

"Mom," Bea said gently. "Before Nonna died, she told me I was a witch."

Mom went pale. She reached for a discarded glass of water on the table and gulped it down. This wasn't the actions of someone who faced down Nonna and said under no circumstances to teach her daughter magic. She was afraid.

Once again Bea felt like she'd been told only part of the story. She couldn't even be mad. Bea had her own role in playing that "everything was fine, nothing to see here, what mafia?" game.

"I never wanted this for you," Mom said. "I honestly didn't expect you to come home after college."

"You wanted me out of it?" Bea snapped. "But you were perfectly happy living off of Dad's money when you damn well knew where he got it."

"Don't take that tone with me, young lady. That money paid for your college education. I don't see you returning your diploma in protest."

"I didn't know," Bea rasped. "Not really. Not until Nonna died, and I saw..." she trailed off, not wanting to admit to witnessing Mike beating up Uncle Guido when she wasn't even supposed to have been near the club that night.

And didn't that make her suck as a person? She only cared when she saw her family being hurt. What about the other people being hurt by what her family did? Hell, if she didn't do something about it, she'd be just as bad as the rest of them.

Mom patted her on the hand. "Don't think too hard about it. Come on. It's your brother's wedding! Have a good time. Eat." She pointed to the food still sitting on Bea's plate. "I have never known you to turn down a meal."

"Hey!" Bea protested. Well, it wouldn't be a conversation with her mother without Mom getting in a dig of some kind.

By this point, Connie made her way back to the table, and the dancing had wound down. "Hi, Aunt Sophy."

"Am I in your seat?" Mom stood up. "Why don't you girls go dance? I have to go around and thank everyone." She waved and set off absently, not getting very far before someone grabbed her and started chatting.

"I can hardly stand it," Connie muttered. "I keep feeling like I'm going to throw up."

Connie had gone to the bathroom several times already. Bea felt a stab of guilt—only a stab? By this point, she should feel a cannonball sized hole of guilt. She'd pulled Connie into this, and now they had to see it to the end.

"Hey. If it goes wrong, I want you to run, okay?" Bea leaned forward to whisper. "They really only want me."

"And you think that makes things better? You're my best friend. Do you think I'm just going to run away and let you face this alone?"

Bea swallowed down a lump in her throat. Maybe most of her family sucked, but not Connie. Maybe somehow, the two of them will find a way to the other side of this intact.

"Thank you."

Connie grinned. "We're going to kick their fucking asses."

Her words surprised Bea into laughter. Maybe it would be all right, with Connie by her side. They still had the rest of the reception to get through - the bouquet throwing and garter, the cake cutting, the room of desserts on the other side of the hall divider. And all the while she had to sit her with a smile while Lucy and Mike thought they had won.

Bea would show them both how wrong they were.

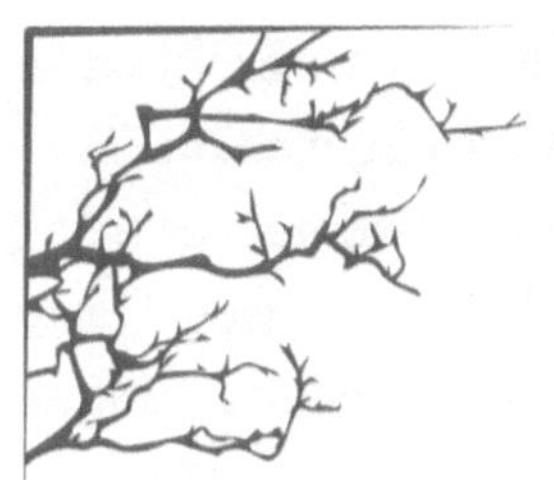

Chapter 40

David's head throbbed in time with a rhythmic, pulsing beat. Dance music, his mind supplied, even as he fought once more for consciousness. The vibrations of it reverberated through his feet and body. Slowly, he came to realize he'd been tied to a chair, his arms now behind him and his ankles bound to its legs.

He blinked, realizing he could see, albeit not much, because the room was dimly lit. He was in a storage room of some kind. There were shelves along one wall, and stacks of things like chairs and boxes. *Where the hell am I?*

The heavy bass faded out, and David could just about make out words, like someone talking on a microphone. It all came back to him with a flash—the wedding. From the sound of it, things were winding down at the reception. He'd been unconscious the entire day, and David didn't know if that was due to magic or the hit he took on his noggin.

Ow. His forehead pulsed, even as the music cut out. Probably the hit on the head then. Magic had made him feel fuzzy, like having too much to drink. This was different and familiar. David knew what a concussion felt like.

In the sudden quiet, he couldn't tell how much time passed before the door to the storage room opened, letting in a blast of light that burned his eyes. David squinted, but couldn't make out the two shadows that entered the room. Both male, tall and broad.

"Sure hope you can walk, fucker," one of them said. He cut the tape around David's legs, freeing him from the chair.

The other cut the ones around his hands, which throbbed in response. Too bad he was too weak and in pain to fight them. They took him by each arm, one on each side of him, like he was being escorted—which he probably was. Once pulled to his feet, David stumbled, unable to get his balance while pins and needles went all up and down his legs.

"Just drag him," the other said, and David recognized that voice immediately. Mike. Bea's brother.

Eyes watering, he blinked, trying to take stock of his surroundings as they dragged him out of the room and tossed him to the ground. David winced at the pain, unable to cry out from the tape still over his mouth. He tried to pull it off, but found he didn't have enough strength in his shaking hands to manage it.

"Now, boys, we don't want to be too hard on him. After all, these are his last few minutes of life." A woman's voice pierced the room.

David sat up. He turned, looking for the source of that icy female voice. There she was—the woman who'd introduced herself as Lucia at the cemetery. She still wore a wedding dress. The reception must have just ended. He looked around to find them in the industrial kitchen of a restaurant—most likely the reception hall. There were long workstations and fancy stoves, all in various shades of stainless steel and polished to a bright sheen. None of the employees seemed to be around, so either it was very late, or Lucia and Mike had ordered them away.

He wished his head would stop throbbing. David couldn't think. He had to find a way out of this, but knew there was no way he could gather enough strength to get his legs under him and run. His entire body felt thick and sluggish, like he was moving through syrup instead of air.

"Let him go." Bea's voice echoed through the room. She stood on the opposite end of the kitchen by a pair of doors, probably where the food was brought in and out for guests.

No. She couldn't be here. They were going to kill him, and there was no way they'd leave her alive if she were a witness. David moaned behind his gag.

Bea stood with her arms crossed over her chest, wearing a yellow bridesmaid dress that had the skirt shredded to reveal the legging she was wearing beneath. She looked like she's escaped a horror movie. David knew she hated that dress. She'd complained about it endlessly. At least she had the opportunity to destroy the ugly thing.

"Bea, we're so glad you could make it," Lucia said in a high-pitched voice. Then she cleared her throat and the lower timbre he remembered from the cemetery emerged. "You've been such a good girl."

Bea scowled. She had something clutched in one hand she kept close to her chest. "Yeah, and now you're going to let him go like you promised."

She didn't believe that, did she? The Bea he knew was far too smart for that, although, to be fair, she had always been a bit naïve about her family, believing the best of them to be true. From the fire in her eyes, that might have changed.

"I'm sorry, Bea, but that was never in the plan." Lucy held out her hand. In response, Mike reached into his suit jacket and pulled out a very familiar-looking gun. "It's going to be so tragic for the staff when they walk in tomorrow. Imagine the headlines, disgraced FBI agent shoots his mob girlfriend and then himself."

"No," David said against the gag. He tried to get to his feet again, but his legs crumbled beneath him.

The other guy in the room—now in the light, David recognized him as Dominick, Mike's right-hand man—grabbed him by the shoulders to keep him from moving any more. Mike kneeled in front of him and put the gun in David's nerveless fingers.

He expected the gun to clatter to the floor. David didn't have any better control of his hands than his legs. But something happened the moment his skin made contact with the cold handle of his Glock. He gripped the weapon, finger on the trigger, safety off. David tried to fire it, to shoot Mike point blank in the chest. But it seemed all he could do was hold the thing as Mike scooted out of the way.

"Shoot her," Lucia said absently. "We have a honeymoon to get to."

To his horror, David found himself raising the gun and pointing it at Bea across the room. She hadn't moved. Why hadn't she run? He wanted to scream at her to get out of there. She had to run. He couldn't. He couldn't let himself kill her. David fought against the compulsion, his hand shaking from trying to bring his arm down.

"Dante," Bea said. She nodded slowly, acknowledging her use of the wrong name for him. "It's going to be okay."

Lucia snorted. "Enough. End this." She snapped her fingers.

David closed his eyes.

Bea said a single word. "*Vieni.*"

The gun went flying from his hand and clattered somewhere across the room. David pulled his hand back and stared at Bea, who held up one hand. The lethargy that had filled his body faded away, and he found himself in control of his limbs.

"Get over here," Bea told him, and Dante scrambled to get across the room, stumbling and tripping to make it to her side, as Bea raised both of her hands.

A wall of flame sprang up from the floor, surrounding Lucy and separating her from the men. David looked at Bea in shock. She had a slight smile on her face and her eyes were glittering with power. That was his girl, standing there and taking no shit.

STEP ONE—GET DANTE out of immediate danger—complete. The knot in Bea's stomach eased a bit. Unfortunately, that was the easy bit. There was nothing but her fire stopping Mike or Dominick from getting across the room, grabbing the gun, and finishing things the old-fashioned way. And from the smile on Lucy's face, Bea knew that bitch was already figuring out how to turn this on Bea.

"Nice trick," Lucy said.

"Thanks. Learned it from my Nonna." Bea had gotten the idea from her. She'd placed the components of the spells all throughout the kitchen, putting the power into casting them last night during the rehearsal dinner. All Bea needed to do was say the trigger word to set them off. This way, she shouldn't be dizzy or incapacitated during this fight. Hopefully. "But that didn't help her when you showed up at her apartment."

"The old woman had gone soft. I can't believe that's the witch who cursed my grandmother so badly she left Italy with nothing but the clothes on her back. She couldn't even see through my glamour. Opened the door for me with a fucking smile." Lucy raised both of her hands, fingers twitching.

"Is that why you killed her?" Bea kept her eye on Mike and Dom, both of whom seemed unphased by the fire. Mike even had that shit-eating grin on his face, like he knew something Bea didn't. She didn't like that. That's what got her into this situation in the first place—him keeping secrets.

"I killed her because there's room for only one witch in this Family." Lucy's eyes were glittering. "She was so surprised when I revealed myself to her. She didn't even have time to defend herself."

Bea took a step forward before she stopped herself. Lucy was just trying to piss her off, so she'd make a mistake. "And that's why you want to kill me. Why make it look like a murder suicide?"

She was aware of Dante beside her as she spoke, but Bea couldn't even give him a look of reassurance. She needed to keep Lucy focused on her and her alone. Because if Lucy tried to attack Dante to get to Bea, well, Bea didn't know what she'd do.

Mike barked out a laugh. "What? Did you forget the first rule of this Thing is secrecy?"

"You didn't care about secrecy when you killed that FBI agent," Bea reminded them. Come on. Keep talking. Give me everything.

Lucy winked at her. "That was a warning for you, dear Bea. Too bad you didn't take it. Don't worry, his death will neatly close the FBI's case on our family. Your sacrifice on the summer solstice will provide enough power to make sure of that. Now, Bea, let's stop playing." Lucy pushed forward with her palms and the fire on the floor diminished, fading back until almost none of it remained.

Behind Lucy and Mike, a door slammed open, ricocheting against the wall with a clatter. "No! No, leave me alone, damn it."

Connie. Junior, her own damn brother, dragged her into the kitchens, despite Connie hitting and slapping the arms around her waist.

Oh fuck. Lucy had just said it. There could be only one witch in this family. Bea swallowed down her fear. She couldn't let it paralyze her and keep her from doing what needed to be done. If this worked, Connie would be fine.

There was no more time for fucking around. Bea held up Nonna's spell book, taking comfort in the warmth of the magic pulsing from it.

"Sorry, baby sis," Junior muttered, throwing Connie down in front of Mike and Dom.

"I think the plans have just changed. A tragic fire in the kitchens after the wedding killed two members of the bridal party. That would make beautiful headlines." Lucy snapped her fingers, and the fire was back, but this time under her control. The flames crept along the floor, warping the linoleum as they got closer to Bea and Dante.

Bea didn't meet Connie's eyes. She had to focus on her spell, the biggest one yet. They'd placed the components for this last night, taking the ingredients right out of Nonna's spell book. Herbs had been hidden, symbols scratched on the wall, and Bea had poured herself and her magic into the floor beneath, laying a foundation for what she was about to do.

She chanted, focusing on the pronunciation of the Italian words. One wrong syllable could ruin the entire spell and destroy hours of work. Warmth swelled in her belly, magic rising within her. Bea used the book as a focus, adding its power to hers as she continued to speak.

Despite all of her precautions, she felt lightheaded. This wasn't a spell one did lightly, and certainly not while being threatened by the heat of the fire slowly surrounding her and Dante.

Lucy cackled. "You think you can bind me? Little witch, did no one tell you this spell required a blood sacrifice?"

Bea didn't stop, but her heart skipped a beat. Lucy couldn't be right. There was no mention of that in Nonna's book. But maybe Nonna didn't write everything down, not when a life was at stake. And Carmella had never said what was needed to truly bind a witch's power. Doubt crept in, despite Bea trying to desperately hold on to the spell before it collapsed.

Sweat poured from her forehead, dripping into her eyes. The flames rose, looking like tiny bodies made of flame. Was Lucy conjuring a monster of fire like she had of shadows?

"I think it's time I take what's mine." Lucy raised her hand and snapped her fingers.

Nonna's spell book went flying out of Bea's grasp and soared across the room, into Lucy's waiting hands.

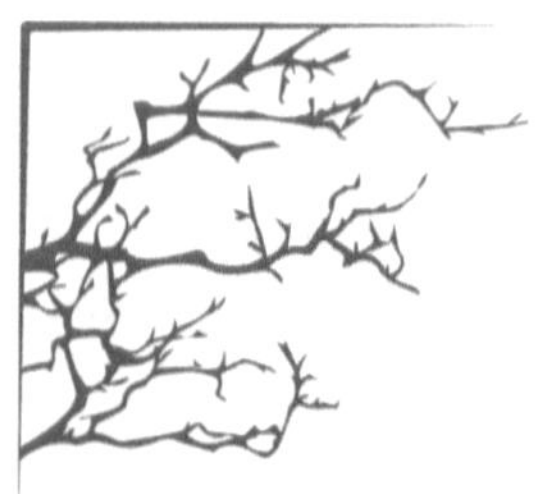

Chapter 41

Connie screamed. Her brother was pushing her toward the flames, and she fought, clawing at his face.

Bea looked at her empty hand in shock, the words of the spell dying on her lips. She'd put all of her magic into that book, and Lucy had snatched it without so much as a word.

"You unlocked this thing. I thought the old bitch had spelled it so only family could see the spells." Lucy flipped through the book nonchalantly, like she was looking at a magazine at the supermarket. "I told Mikey if we dangled it in front of you, you'd take the bait."

Mike stepped to her side and put his arm around her, nuzzling her bare shoulder. "End this, babe. We have our wedding night to look forward to."

Rage burned in Bea's belly. How dare she? How dare he? Mike betrayed their entire family—for what? Power? To become the boss? A position he would have inherited, anyway? He'd kill his own sister and cousin for Lucy?

Bea didn't care why. Tears prickled her eyes, full of anger and frustration. All of her hard work had been bound up in that book, in that spell. If she didn't bind Lucy's magic now, then it was all for nothing. Lucy would take control of the family and Bea would die. Connie would die. Dante would die.

No. This would not end like this. Bea wouldn't let it.

Beatrice. A voice in her head that sounded suspiciously like her grandmother rang out. Bea snapped her head up, even as the flames circling her started to rise. That fire had belonged to her. That book belonged to her Nonna. It was time to take it all back.

You're stronger than her.

Bea didn't know if the words came from her grandmother's spirit, or from within. It didn't matter. She reached out with one hand and flung her will out into the room. She didn't need a spell. Bea was still connected to the book, even though it was in Lucy's hands.

Now that she thought of it, it seemed so simple. Bea closed her eyes and reached out with everything inside her. She gathered all of her magic, the power pooling in her belly, the spells she'd cast all over this room the other night, and then she followed the tether that connected her to that book—to her grandmother. Twenty-one years of being loved by Nonna left an impact, a physical impression, a connection that Bea sunk into.

For a moment she was the book, full of power, of the magic her Nonna had worked her entire life. And she was being held by an interloper, a murderer, the person who had taken Nonna from her. The binding spell was still there, hovering intact around the spell book. All Bea needed to do was command it. And since Lucy held on to the book, it took no effort at all to summon the spell.

Bea snapped her fingers.

Lucy went still. "What..." she didn't have time to complete the thoughts before the book in her hands burst into flame. She screamed and tried to shake it out of her hands, but it was bound to her. Bea could feel it working, sucking out all the magic that belonged to Lucy.

Mike, Dominick, and Junior ran over to beat out the flames that had caught Lucy's dress. The sound Lucy let out was earsplitting and full of pain. Bea used the distraction to douse the fire surrounding her and Dante. The flame disappeared from the floor as if it had never been, leaving not even smoke behind.

Now free, Connie ran across the room. She reached out for Bea as she ran, eyes wide.

Mike noticed, whirling around and ignoring his sobbing wife to pull a gun out of his waistband. "You bitch!"

Bea had no spells left to stop the bullet. She'd used all of her magic, all the spells she'd planted the night before, on binding Lucy. There was nothing left to draw upon, even if she wanted to. Her magic, usually a warm core inside her, had gone cold and empty with overuse.

She rushed forward, meaning to use her own body to protect Connie and Dante. Mike had his hand on the trigger, and raised the barrel, pointing it directly at her. There would be no stopping the bullet. Would her death still act as a sacrifice? Would all of her magic be undone, like Nonna's?

Bea lifted her hands in one last attempt to stop the gun from going off. But she didn't have to do anything.

The doors snapped open, and people in blue uniforms and guns drawn poured into the room.

"Hands up! FBI! Everyone freeze!"

Mike dropped the gun and lifted his hands slowly, his gaze still on Bea. Even he wouldn't shoot his own sister in front of law enforcement.

Bea lifted her hands as commanded, despite feeling like she wanted to drop onto the floor in a puddle of goo. She turned to Connie. "You did it!"

Connie nodded, her own hands in the air. "I placed the call before Junior grabbed me. Bea, he was going to kill me." Her eyes were wide and her face went pale. Bea understood the shock. It was going to take her some time to come to terms with this, but Connie would, eventually.

Then there was no more time to speak as the FBI swarmed them.

DAVID COULDN'T HELP but compare this night with the night Janet died. He'd had time to come to terms with magic, so he didn't have denial about the events happening in front of him to contend with. Still, he couldn't say he was up to snuff and let the medic check him out while Agent Lucas gave him the rundown.

He only half paid attention to her debrief. David couldn't keep his eyes off of Bea. She was sitting on a chair someone had brought in, answering questions from an agent he didn't recognize. Someone had brought her a jacket that was thrown over her bare shoulders and he was annoyed it wasn't his jacket. He wanted to be the one speaking with her, taking her statement, reassuring her that everything was going to be okay.

They'd arrested the bad guys, after all. In the aftermath, he realized how clever Bea had been. She'd gotten Lucy to admit to murder, in front of an FBI agent. He'd be able to testify against her in court. And Mike had his weapon drawn when the FBI burst in. Both of them were in for some serious jail time. That didn't mean Bea was safe. David knew the arms of the mob could reach out of the bars of prison. He'd heard it happen dozens of times.

He needed to protect her. Somehow. Even though she'd shown clearly that she'd been able to protect them both. Maybe it was time to think about things differently. They could protect each other. If she still wanted to have anything to do with him.

"All right. Your head is someplace else right now." Lucas tapped him on the shoulder. "I guess I can forgive you since you've survived a mob abduction."

He made a face at her. "Thanks."

"Seriously, McKenna. You're lucky to be alive." Lucas gave him a stern look that went right to his toes.

David nodded, unable to speak. She was right. If it hadn't been for Bea, he'd be dead.

"Now go talk to your girl." She gave him a gentle smack on the back.

He stuck his hands in his pocket—hard to believe he was still wearing the same suit from Janet's funeral. God, he must stink. But no one could tell with the scent of burning flesh clung to the room, and God, the fact that was a good thing hurt his brain.

Bea looked up at his approach, as if she sensed him before he arrived. She gave him a tight smile.

"Hey, can I talk to her for a moment?" he asked the agent interviewing her.

The guy nodded and took off. David would have to remember to thank him later.

Bea gasped at him. She got to her feet and threw her arms around him, to his surprise. "Thank God you're alive."

He patted her back gently. "Thanks to you."

She pulled away and her cheeks went pink. David didn't know if that was in response to his words or embarrassment at hugging him. "I honestly wasn't sure it was going to work."

"Can you tell me what the hell I just witnessed?" he asked, a bit sheepishly. There was one thing to knowing magic existed, and yet another to understand it.

"Lucy was the witch the whole time. She and my brother were going to take over the family business, but she needed my grandmother out of the way. You were so right. It was someone close."

"I'm glad I was right about something," David muttered. He'd been wrong about so many other things.

"My brilliant plan was to bind her magic so she can't hurt anyone else. It almost failed." Bea swallowed. "The spell required a sacrifice, and I think there was enough of my grandmother in her spell book to count. I'm not one hundred percent sure it worked."

He thought of Lucy's screams and her blistering burned hands. Even if Bea was wrong, odds were good Lucy wasn't going to be doing anything with magic for a while. "Is that why you had Connie call the FBI for backup?"

Bea grinned at him, that bright blinding smile that lit up her entire face. "Oh no. We called them last night. Connie needed to make contact to give them the signal that the meeting was happening. I wasn't entirely sure Lucy was going to actually go through with it. I hoped you weren't already dead…"

She trailed off and looked away, her eyes shining.

It had been an emotional night. David reached for her hand and squeezed it. He didn't stop to think about what he was doing. During these past few weeks, he'd often touched her like this, and it seemed natural now to comfort. "I'm right here. Remember? Thanks to you."

"Stop complimenting me. I almost fucked it all up." Bea didn't let go of his hand, though.

"I won't ever stop complimenting you." He squeezed her fingers again. "Bea, I'm sorry for everything." He never should have accepted the assignment, not when David knew it meant possibly hurting an innocent girl.

Yet, if he hadn't, who knew what would have happened? Maybe Bea would have gone blissfully on with her life, unaware of the threat within her own family. Maybe Lucy would have killed both Bea and Connie, the family take over complete. David couldn't go back over every decision and second guess himself. He could apologize for hurting her, though, because he regretted that with every fiber of his being.

"You were right about my family," she whispered. "They've done horrible things. They are okay with doing horrible things." She lifted her hand and gestured to the scorched floor of the kitchen. Luckily, the fire had been magical, or else the entire place would have gone up.

David rubbed his forehead, wondering when he'd just accepted magic was normal. Possibly at some point in the last five minutes. "But you're not like them."

"I could be," she insisted. "I have this power inside me."

"But you don't have to succumb to the dark side," he insisted, which made her laugh.

"How did I not know you're a giant nerd?" Bea let go of his hand and crossed her arms over her chest.

Because it was obvious why. She didn't know him, only the persona he'd put on for the past few months. "Bea, when I said I was sorry, I meant it. I want the chance to get to know you. And I want you to get to know me. The real me. Without any of the lies."

She took a deep breath. "I'm not sure I can learn to trust you."

He gave her his most winning smile. "I bet you have a truth spell or something that can tell if I'm lying."

"Don't even joke about that. We were just talking about me not going dark side." She smacked his arm with probably more force that was necessary.

She had a point. But David didn't know what he could say to convince her. So instead, he held out his hand for a handshake. "Hi there. My name is David McKenna. I'm a special agent for the FBI. My college major was accounting. I like acting, dogs, and sci-fi movies."

She hesitated for a moment, a long moment, which made David question all of his life choices until now. Was she going to walk away from him forever? He couldn't let that happen. David had seen death, and he knew he didn't want to go on without Bea in his life. He needed more than his work. He needed to live.

She'd shown him there was so much more to the world. Hell, she was magic, only not in the way she thought.

His heart fluttered when she reached out and took his hand. "Hi, David. My name is Bea. I love renaissance art, long walks on the beach, and dogs. And I come from a shitty family. Except maybe for my cousin over there," she motioned with her head at Connie, who was being questioned by another agent. "Oh, and I'm a witch. Do you think you can handle that?"

"I'd love the opportunity to find out."

For a moment, they were the only two people in the room. David started into her liquid dark eyes, unable to look away. Maybe he hadn't fucked this up completely. Maybe they could have a second chance.

Garcia broke the spell, crossing the room to talk to them. "McKenna. Glad to see you among the living."

"Glad to still be here, sir." David let go of Bea's hand and stepped back to face his boss.

"And this young lady is Beatrice DiLorenzo?" Garcia turned to Bea.

Beatrice looked a little flustered. She took a step back and tugged at her hair, which had come out of the updo on one side of her head and fell to her shoulder in a mess of waves. "We spoke on the phone. Please, call me Bea."

Garcia nodded. "Well, Bea. It seems like you know a lot more about what's going on that we do."

"I guess." She seemed confused about where he was going with this. David was too. Clearly, Garcia had a plan.

He grinned at them both. "Bea DiLorenzo. I'm about to make you an offer I hope you don't refuse."

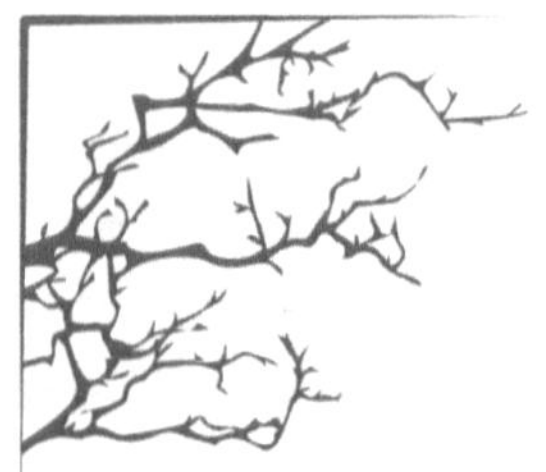

Chapter 42

Bea pushed the lid of her suitcase down and snapped the latch in place. She straightened and looked around her nearly empty bedroom, making sure she hadn't forgotten anything. Unlike packing for college, she wouldn't be able to come back and retrieve something she left behind.

"Are you sure about this?" Connie sat on the still made bed in the center of the room. Bea would figure out bedding later once she learned about the situation in her assigned housing. Her mother could keep the sheets and comforter. Bea didn't have any attachment to them.

The things she did, she lovingly packed away and put into storage until she got her own place and could retrieve them. Except for the print David had given her. Bea hadn't had the heart to throw it away, even when she was mad at him, but she'd stuffed it back in its tube. She had given it back to him and asked him to keep it safe for her until she moved out.

Bea dropped onto the bed next to her cousin. "I am sure. You can come with me, you know?"

It wasn't the first time Bea had made the offer. After the wedding, when Agent Garcia made his proposal to her, she thought he'd been joking. But he'd been deadly serious about starting up a magic department in the FBI. She'd have to go through training like any FBI agent, but once finished, she and David would work together to head up the new section.

She'd told him no, because as a half-trained witch, she was hardly an expert on magic. Garcia had given her a wry grin and said, "that's more than we got now." David had been next to him, looking at Bea, his eyes so full with emotion. Bea knew if she took the job, she'd be able to work with him, maybe patch things up and find out exactly what kind of guy he really was. With a sigh, she had agreed to Garcia's proposition.

Connie made a face. "You know I have a year left at school."

Bea couldn't tell her not to finish. That would be hypocritical of her, since she used the same funds to get her own degree. But Bea had to walk away from the family now, while she had this opportunity, and she really wanted to take her cousin with her.

"I know. But aren't things awkward at home?" She left the rest unsaid, but she meant Junior getting arrested after the wedding and sitting in jail awaiting trial, along with Mike, Dominick, and Lucy. All of them had been denied bail.

Connie sighed. She leaned forward, grasping her knees as she pulled her legs up on the bed. "Nothing I can't handle. And in two months, I'll be back at school and away from it all."

"Have you thought about my other offer?" Bea asked softly. She'd offered to unlock Connie's magic next month, when she turned twenty-one.

"I don't have to decide right now, right?" Connie licked her lips, a sure sign the topic made her nervous. She wouldn't meet Bea's eyes, and instead stared at the now empty walls of Bea's room.

Bea didn't blame her. Connie had only seen the destruction force of magic—up close and personal. She hadn't spent weeks learning the basics, understanding that magic could heal and protect. That was the direction Bea had hoped to move in, anyway.

"No, you don't. You can always decide later. I was unlocked months after, you know? I just... I want to know you're protected." Bea knew Lucy wasn't the only witch out there. And here was Connie, young and untrained and ripe for the attack.

"I have the necklace you gave me." Connie's hand went to her throat to touch the strand around her neck.

"I'm not sure that's enough. Not if you're still around Family." Bea couldn't help fretting. There were those three old women from Nonna's funeral. She had no idea whose side they were on. And Lucy might have family out there. Since she'd lied about so much, she probably wasn't an orphan either. If someone came sniffing after the DiLorenzos looking for revenge, they'd find Connie. Bea left her with the strongest protection spells she could come up with.

"I'll be fine." Connie leaned over and knocked their shoulders together. She grinned, although the smile didn't quite reach her eyes. "I'm more worried about you. Going to work for the FBI? Are you nuts?"

Bea laughed. That was certainly something she didn't consider using her art degree for. "I think it's the right thing to do."

"You know you don't have to do penance for all of us," Connie said softly.

Bea hadn't considered it in that light. Perhaps she should have. If only it were that easy - go to Confession and say five Hail Marys and be absolved. She couldn't carry the sins of all the DiLorenzos, but Bea could make up for some of them.

"I want to do this," she told her cousin. "For the first time, I see a future where my skills are important. I have something no one else does, and I can do some good with it." Bea flexed her hands, considering the power that lies dormant beneath her skin.

"I'm sure it helps that your partner is easy on the eyes," Connie teased.

They were going to be fine, especially if Connie was teasing her about Dante. David. Bea still slipped up now and then. Speaking of, he should be here soon. She pulled out her phone to check her texts, in time to hear the door downstairs slam.

Bea could feel the blood drain from her face. "We were supposed to be gone before they got back."

"It'll be fine. Come on. I'll help you take your bags downstairs." Connie got to her feet and squared her shoulders, as if getting ready for battle. Could Bea do any less?

She gathered her messenger bag with her wallet and other necessities, including her spell book. Bea found she couldn't be apart from her new book for long. It didn't have the same weight of magic as her Nonna's, but she could tell that each time she paged through it, she was imbuing it with a bit of her own magic. Maybe someday it would be strong enough to save one of her descendants.

Connie hefted the two suitcases while Bea opened the door for her. They carried their burdens down the stairs, unable to be completely quiet as they did so. Bea couldn't hide from this meeting as much as she wanted to. She really hoped to be gone before they got back.

Standing at the bottom of the stairs, as if waiting for them, stood her mother and Daddy.

Daddy had come out of his coma the night of the wedding as soon as she'd bound Lucy's magic. It had ended the spell on him, but he'd needed weeks of rehab before he could leave the hospital.

He'd looked bad, the time she'd visited him while in the coma. But now, he hardly resembled the father she remembered. He used to be broad and tall, slightly round in the middle, but he always gave the overall impression of being incredibly strong. Now he'd lost a lot of weight and looked sunken in on himself. But those soft brown eyes looking at her were all her daddy.

It took everything Bea had not to run across the room and throw her arms around him. Despite everything, she still loved her father. But she couldn't be a part of this thing any longer.

"Beatrice," he said, voice raspy.

Her mother didn't speak. She held on to Dad's arm, keeping him upright as she glared at Bea and Connie.

"Daddy." Her voice broke as she said the word. Bea would not cry. But she would not give in either. She'd made her decision, and she was going to stick to it, even if it broke her father's heart. "I'm sorry."

Bea walked past him to the front door, Connie by her side. They made it out to the front porch before her mother ran out; her face flushed and angry.

"That's it? You're just going to leave like this?" Mom snapped.

"Yes." Bea set down her bag and turned to face her, ignoring Connie, trying to tug her away. "You wanted me out of the Family Business, so I'm going."

"Not like this. That's all you have to say to your father?"

Bea swallowed down a lump in her throat. "Maybe someday we can have a real conversation. But right now, I can't."

She grabbed her bag and marched down the driveway. Her phone buzzed in her pocket, but she didn't need to look at it since David's car was visible as it drove down the street. He pulled in to the driveway.

Connie helped her load the luggage into the trunk. "I'll take care of Aunt Sophy," she whispered, giving Bea one last hug.

Bea nodded and squeezed her tight before getting in to the car. Who knew when she'd be able to see her cousin again? "Stay safe. You call me if you need anything. Even if it's just something weird happening and you need advice, okay?"

"Of course. Trust me, I'll be texting you every five minutes, like aways." Connie pulled away with watery eyes.

Bea sniffed back a few tears of her own. This wasn't goodbye. She'd see her cousin again. Warmth flared in her chest and she knew it to be true. That gave her the strength to turn her back on Connie and get into David's car.

David watched her with knowing eyes as she buckled her seat belt. "You okay?"

"My dad is home." Bea would not cry. She wouldn't. But she hadn't expected it to hurt this much. She didn't even know what she could say to Dad. He hadn't been there, hadn't seen the terrible things Bea had to do.

"That's great news." David reached out and tugged on her hand. He always seemed to need to touch her for reassurance, and while they hadn't completely sorted everything out between them, she let him keep doing it. To be honest, Bea needed the physical contact as well, to ground her.

She was grateful he was happy that Dad was okay. She didn't think David was the guy to wish bad things on criminals, to think they were less than people, and so far, he'd proved her right. There was still so much she didn't know about him. But now she was going to have the opportunity to learn, to find out who David McKenna really was.

This was a new start, for both of them. Bea would make a new life for herself, based on what she wanted, not what everyone around her told her she should want. And David would be right by her side as they drove toward the future.

END

About the Author

Caterina Gregori writes from the wilds of the New Jersey Pine Barrens. Her books are semi-autobiographical, except for all the stuff about magic. And the mafia. You can reach her at caterina.gregori.author@gmail.com

www.ingramcontent.com/pod-product-compliance
Lightning Source LLC
Chambersburg PA
CBHW031527150726
47990CB00001B/77